Ann A. Goering

Up From The
Ash Heap

THE MOUNTAIN
REDEMPTION SERIES

Copyright © 2025 by Ann A. Goering. All rights reserved.

Cover design copyright © 2025 by Ann Goering. All rights reserved.
Cover design by: Angela Weldin
Cover Photos: Bigstock.com
Edited by: Rachel Garber
Narrated by: Amberly Stark

ISBN: 978-1-965499-00-9 - Ebook
ISBN: 978-1-965499-01-6 - Paperback
ISBN: 978-1-965499-04-7 - Audiobook

Library of Congress Control Number: 2024922441

www.coveredporchpublishing.com
www.anngoering.com

Requests for information should be addressed to:
Covered Porch Publishing, Ann Goering, PO Box 464, Branson MO 65615

Scripture quotations are taken from the King James Version Bible. Public domain of United States of America.

All rights reserved. No part of this publication may be reproduced, stored in a retrieval system, or transmitted in any form or by any means—recording, photocopy, electronic, mechanical, or any other—except for brief quotations in printed reviews, without the prior permission of the publisher.

This book is a work of fiction. Names, characters, places, and incidents are fictitious and a product of the author's imagination. Any resemblances to actual people or events are coincidental.

Printed in the United States of America

29 28 27 26 25 A 8 7 6 5 4 3 2

*This book is dedicated to my Redeemer,
who has lifted me up from the pit;*

*My husband, who has demonstrated the
tenacity of love so beautifully;*

*And to my mother-in-law, Lois, who has become not only family,
but also my very dear friend.*

FREE BONUS SHORT STORY

We know Mother Emaline from her role as Raya, Chenoa, and Nizhoni's beloved mother-in-law. But while we've seen her unwavering faith and the impact she's had on her daughters-in-law, where did her faith come from and what were her years like before tragedy struck?

There was a time when Emaline's own life was filled with the rosy hues of love and coming of age – yet even then, storm clouds were brewing on the horizon. A family secret, a desperate situation, and a stranger at a ball collide in a perfect storm that promises to solidify her faith and her future – or break her in the process.

To get Emaline's short story absolutely FREE and start reading today visit:
https://anngoering.com/mountain-redemption-series

One

One day. One hour. One accident. One fire. Everything had been lost in an instant.

Colorado Territory, Aug. 1873

"Ms. Applewood, please. You need to move indoors." The man of God standing over her was insistent.

Raya Applewood lifted her face to the sky, letting the pelting raindrops fall on her unchecked. With heavy storm clouds overhead and her heart like a wrenching seesaw of total shock and unbearable grief, she gave no thought to her carefully constructed hair-do, her dress that now had six inches of mud up the hem, or the fact that a head cold was, without a doubt, in her immediate future.

"Why?" her heart screamed up at the sky. "Why?" She could get lost in the question—had, in fact, several times in the past few days. The questions had been piling up, and now her heart was pounding with the echoing, unyielding collection of them. Thinking rationally was beyond her current ability. She felt incapable of caring about anything. The one thing that filled her mind was the painful constricting of her heart. Her husband was dead.

But the preacher was right.

Raya looked around for her mother-in-law and saw the dear woman on her hands and knees in the mud, silently shaking with sobs. The grieving woman had lost all three of her sons in a single day. Raya could not imagine how her heart must be hurting.

Her sisters-in-law were between them, Nizhoni clutching the wooden cross that marked her husband's grave; Chenoa, the youngest of them all at the tender age of seventeen, standing in the mud, her thin arms wrapped around her midsection, her head down, her beautiful dark curls hanging wet and lifeless.

Raya turned back to the wooden cross she knelt before. The future felt daunting and too painful to face. Leaving this place of death would mean leaving her husband—and her heart—behind. She didn't know if her broken spirit could bear the pain of it. Yet Raya turned her eyes to the pastor and nodded, pushing herself to her feet. She clenched her teeth as her soiled skirt shifted, feeling like ice against her bare legs beneath. The day was unusually cold for late summer—even for the high mountain town—and the cold rain that had long since soaked through her clothing only made it feel more so. She kept her teeth clenched to keep them from chattering. Whether they chattered from cold or fear, she didn't know.

The pastor, with his wide-brimmed hat diverting water from his face, walked with her as she crossed the few feet to stand between the two closest crosses.

"Shideezhi," Raya started, using the native word of Nizhoni's people, meaning 'younger sisters' to tenderly draw her sisters-in-laws' attention. "We must get Mother Emaline out of this rain. Why don't we make our way into the church?"

Niz didn't respond, but Chenoa turned pain-filled eyes up to her. "I can't leave him."

Raya stepped close to the girl, taking her face in her hands. Her own lip trembled as she began to speak. "He's not here, Sweetheart. He is dancing on streets of gold and basking in eternal sunshine. You know that. He's not here that you should stay." Raya steadied her voice and smiled through fresh tears. "Shideezhi, your lips are blue, you're wet clear through, and you're shaking from cold. You must go in out of the rain, or you'll take ill."

Chenoa looked at the wooden cross for a moment longer, then nodded, clinging to her when Raya reached for her hand.

"What does it matter if she does? What does it matter if we all do?" Niz wailed, her hands curling into the rocky mud.

Raya stayed quiet. She had no answer, no words of comfort or hope to offer the woman. Instead, she took Nizhoni's arm gently and helped her to her feet. Thankfully, Niz let her. Together, the three of them approached the older woman who knelt between them and the gate of the cemetery.

After a brief hesitation, Raya stepped forward cautiously. She was walking on sacred ground. "Mother, it's time for us to go."

For a long moment, Emaline Applewood stayed crumpled over her knees, her face covered by her hands. But then, stronger of mind and spirit than she was of body, she looked up at Raya and nodded slowly, allowing the younger woman to help her to her feet.

The preacher followed the four widows into the small church building where he said a prayer over them before going out into the rain again to bring their horse and buggy to the bottom of the church steps. They crowded in, huddled together in hopes of sharing their warmth, but there were no men to drive the team. They realized their mistake belatedly, and fumbling out an apology, Raya rose to her feet and let the pastor assist her back down out of the buggy and up into the driver's seat. He kept hold of her hand until she looked down into his kind face.

"I'll send my boy out to check on you in a couple of days. See to the stock . . . anything you need. Can't spare him more than a day with the harvest coming ready, but I want you to know I would send him out every day if I could."

"Thank you, Pastor. We appreciate your kindness," Raya told him sincerely. He nodded before releasing her hand and stepping back out of the way of the wheels. Out of pure necessity, Raya took up the reins, the cold leather feeling foreign in her small hands. Tucking her chin and pressing her lips together, she slapped them over the horse's wet back after venturing one last glance back at the cemetery where three new wooden crosses were only barely visible through the dreary dusk. To her relief, the large horse started moving, and she guided him away from the church and onto the road home.

The reins felt heavy and awkward in her hands and the horse large and formidable, but she had watched Luke drive often enough. Surely, she was capable of getting them home.

The mountain skies had opened just after the ceremony concluded and had been dropping their torrents of rain ever since. Raya's hair and dress had long since been soaked, and now streams of water were running over her face, mixing with her tears as she kept the horse moving down the worn path to their valley. Lightning cracked ahead on the top of a nearby mountain, and thunder boomed all around them so loud that she felt it inside her chest. Behind her in the buggy, Chenoa gave an innocent yelp of fright in response, ever frightened by the thunderstorms that rolled through the mountains frequently on summer afternoons. Raya gritted her teeth as she slapped the reins over the horse's back again, convincing the sodden animal to pick up his pace. They went the rest of the way home at a fast trot, Raya's heart pounding at a similar speed.

Pulling up in their own yard, Raya considered the darkening sky, the stubborn rain, and the shelter of Emaline's house before looking back at their wet and tired horse. Never before had she been the one to see to the livestock instead of going in to warm herself by the fire. Luke never would have allowed it. Now, he wasn't around to take care of her. Neither were the rest of the men.

"Go on in and start some water for tea. I'll tend to the stock and be in shortly," she told the others, as reluctant to take charge as she was to tend the stock. She had always been quiet and meek, happily following along under Mother Emaline's able direction or Niz's commanding personality. Now, with neither woman seemingly able to take charge of their small group, she had no choice but to do so.

Starting into motion at Raya's gentle command, the others exited the buggy one by one and picked their way through the mud into the house. Taking a deep breath, Raya urged the tired horse on to the barn, then climbed down to open the large, heavy doors.

Once inside the structure, sheltered from the rain, she pushed her wet hair out of her face and wiped her eyes with the backs of her hands before approaching the horse. She fumbled with the straps and buckles that hitched him to the buggy. The cold leather was stiff and hard, and Raya had never performed the task before—with three men in the family, it had never been required of her. Until now.

Blowing on her cold fingers to warm them until they moved more nimbly, she finally succeeded in unhitching the horse. She left the buggy where it was and reluctantly approached the massive animal. Raya was terrified of the beast, but he had to be taken to his stall, and she was the only one there to do it. Swallowing hard, she reached up and took the side of his bridle, pulling gently until he took a step, followed by another. Thankfully, he didn't take much encouragement, as eager to get to his stall as she was to get him there. After she successfully led him through the barn to his quarters, she went in search of an old rag and a brush, knowing she needed to rub him down. She had seen Luke perform the task dozens of times. Surely, she could do it as well.

She entered the stall, keeping her chin up, and managed to retain her composure regardless of how the beast stomped, snorted, and flinched. Once she got him rubbed down and brushed, she filled his trough with grain and hay. With their financial situation dismal, she would have to ration his feed in the coming days, but it had been a long day for all of them—animals and humans alike—and he deserved a good meal. She grabbed a pitchfork and began to lift the soiled straw out of his stall and replace it with fresh. Again, a chore she had seen Luke do many times, yet the pitchfork felt heavy and awkward in her hands.

Outside, the lightning storm continued. Thunder shook the wood barn what seemed like every few seconds, agitating the animals. She could hear the rain beating down against the roof and was thankful the men had done a good job with their hand-cut shingles. Though the storm was loud, at least the feed and the animals were dry.

When she was done with the driving horse, she moved on to the work horses, then to the two milk cows who stood waiting impatiently. They swished their tails and snorted as she entered their stall with her pail and stool. She couldn't blame them. The time for milking had come and gone, and their bags were full and likely painful. Sitting down cautiously, she began to rhythmically coax the warm milk out of the first cow's swollen udder.

As the large animal began to feel relief and the risk of being kicked subsided, Raya laid her cheek against the cow's side, letting the warmth and quiet soak into her. This she had done before, and she let the normalcy of her task calm her tumultuous emotions.

For just a moment, the rhythmic action distracted her from her grief. The barn, the animals, the chores, they all reminded her of Luke. This had been his domain, and the fact that she now had to do the tasks he had done only served to remind her of his absence. But here, with the cows, doing the milking, there was relief for her heart. This was something she had done for the past several years, and for just a few moments, she didn't feel his absence quite so keenly.

When both cows were milked, she put away her stool, covered her pail to keep the milk clean, and set it aside. Wielding the pitchfork again, she fed the cows and set about making them a clean place to bed down.

By the time she was done with the chores, her arms burned and her back ached. Tired and in both physical and emotional pain, Raya leaned against the sturdy wall of the barn and blew out a deep breath, pushing wayward pieces of dark hair back carelessly. Looking around the large, quiet space, her eyes burned with tears, and her throat ached until she put her hand to her neck. Never before had this place felt so empty. Usually, Alex was pitching hay out of the hay mow, Luke was cleaning sawdust out of the horses' hooves, and Will was oiling the harnesses. Now it was empty. Tears as big as the raindrops outside began to run down her cheeks.

She had been so happy for five years. Five wonderful, peaceful years.

When Luke Applewood took her as his wife, just a day after their meeting, she had felt nervous and afraid. The pale-skinned man she was given to in marriage was tall, broad, and so very different from those she knew. Still, her father had arranged the marriage, and afraid or not, she had no choice but to become Luke's wife.

Her white husband and his family—his widowed mother and two younger brothers—were frightening to her at first, but it wasn't long before their loving ways won her over. There was peace in their home; peace like she had never before experienced. And hope. She had never known that hope existed. At the Applewoods', it was all around her, surrounding her, engulfing her. She felt safe in their home and in their family—a safety she had never experienced in her fifteen years under her father's roof.

In three years' time, she had left behind her superstitious ways and the metal gods she had grown up serving to follow after the One true God, the God the Applewoods served. She knew very little about Him, but she knew the kind of people the Applewoods were, and she was told their God was the reason for the differences between them and many of the others in the valley. Additionally, she desired to please both Luke and Mother Emaline, and serving their God pleased them greatly.

In the years since coming to the family, she had relaxed in their home and thrived under their love and care. She welcomed her sisters-in-law with open arms as first Alex, then William took wives. Although her heritage was very different from that of the native women Alex and William married, she found both sisters and friends in the girls who looked shockingly similar to her. No one in the Applewood family held her ancestry against her, nor did they with Nizhoni or Chenoa. In the West, one must do their best with what was available, including people . . . and women.

In the Applewood family, everyone was valued as a human being and mention of race was not made. There was no condemnation, no racial slurs, no utter avoidance as Raya remembered there being when her family passed through the eastern part of the country seeking their destination in the West. She had been very young then, but no amount of time could erase the humiliation she had felt.

Back in the old country, before Raya was born, her uncle wrote her parents about a place he called the land of opportunity. Having stowed away in the hull of a ship bound for America, her uncle had braved the seas—and being caught—in hopes of a better life. And his risk had paid off. He wrote that in America's Southwest, it didn't matter who someone was born to—everyone was free to carve out a life for himself and his family. He sent money to prove it, beseeching them to come join him. More than willing to escape their hopeless future in the tea fields of India, her mother and father worked seven years to earn the money needed to pay their passage to America. Their meager earnings were heavily supplemented by provision from Raya's uncle, which covered the lion's share of their fare.

Raya and her three brothers came into the world during those seven years. While traveling west, first by boat and then by wagon, Raya's sister, Sugundarani, was born. After arriving at her uncle's in Colorado Territory, where her father worked tirelessly alongside him to build a better life for the family, two more little ones arrived. However, despite the fact that the family store was well-frequented, and food was in adequate supply, by the time Raya was fifteen, only herself, Sugundarani, and her brother Amhil were left. The others had caught the pox that swept through the valley. There was nothing anyone could do. Raya still remembered how her mother chanted and prayed, burned incense, and called upon her many gods to save her sick children, yet child after child died until only the three of them remained.

When Raya's father gave her away in marriage to the pale man with the unknown faith, he did it for the good of the family.

Unmarried women—and pretty ones at that—were few and far between in the developing territory. The bride price Luke paid was enough to expand the family store and order in goods the town had never seen the likes of before. Additionally, it elevated the family's social standing. Their skin might be darker than the white skin that was held in such esteem throughout the country, but their wealth was accumulating, buying them prominence in the community. Marrying a daughter off to a prominent white man only increased their standing.

Raya doubted her father gave any thought to what kind of a man he was giving her to or the ways of her new family, but fortune had smiled on her the day Luke Applewood experienced what he called 'love at first sight' and took her as his bride. He was hardworking and committed. He was a good man, honest and gentle. And he loved her.

He had told her over and over that her hefty brideprice was a small price to pay for a woman such as her. He would have paid twice what her father had asked in order to make her his wife. And he had had the means to do so. The Applewoods had been well-endowed financially.

In the quiet solitude of the barn, Raya held her trembling hands out in front of her, observing their color. She looked like a white person who had been stained by mud, or who had perhaps been out in the sun too long. Though her bronzed skin was only slightly browner than that of many of the white women in town, she knew her dark hair and eyes gave away her foreign decent, though many people mistook her for one of the natives. While Luke found her beautiful, and she was relatively accepted in the community, she remembered the names she had been called while traveling through the Eastern United States. She remembered how decent folks refused to look at or speak to her parents, and how they were forced to use what others discarded.

Her mind rushed back to the present and the tragedy that had occurred, along with the choices she would soon have to make. She was no longer the wife of the prominent and wealthy

Luke Applewood. Instead, she was his widow—a widow with dark skin and an ancestry shrouded in mystery—an ancestry held in contempt throughout the country in which she now lived. Raya shook within.

Her eyes ran over the good-sized barn: the old driving horse, the team of workhorses, the worn-looking buggy, the half-empty feed sack, the hens in the corner. It had all felt like plentiful bounty only days before. There had been a sawmill full of orders that simply needed to be delivered, a full cashbox, three able-bodied, hardworking men, and a secret stash that held the family savings. Now, this was all that remained. Again, her watery eyes wandered over the barn and its contents.

The hens. She had forgotten to tend the hens. Raya scooped grain up in her hands and walked briskly to the corner of the barn where the hens roosted. She scattered the grain on the floor and hurried to collect the eggs while the chickens scurried to get the food. There were a dozen eggs, and Raya was glad—that would help feed them for another day.

She wrapped the eggs securely in her damp skirt, grabbed the full milk pail, and left the barn, trudging fifty yards through the rocky mud on her short walk to the house. Her hair and dress, which had started to dry, quickly became drenched again, and she shivered violently from the cold. Above her, lightning cracked and thunder boomed, yet her weary muscles refused to carry her to the main cabin any faster than at a slow walk.

As she walked, she surveyed the wet, dismal land through the falling darkness, and her eyes fell again on the blackened, charred remains of what had been the family's source of income. Little streams were now making their way through the singed rubbish as the rain continued to fall, and Raya felt new tears sting her eyes.

If only the mill hadn't caught fire. If only the doors had not jammed. If only the men—Luke—wouldn't have been inside, busy at work. If only the cash would have been in the house as it normally was, instead of in the mill, as Alex was busy balancing the books. If only the men had hidden their savings somewhere other than under a loose board in the mill office.

One fire, one jammed door—her husband and his two brothers were dead, the family's source of income gone, and their life savings nothing but ashes. The despair of their situation settled over her once again, and her shoulders drooped just a little more.

She considered responding like Niz and sitting down in the cold rain and mud, daring sickness to come and take her. She wasn't sure she could go on anyway. Instead, she pushed through the heavy front door and into the light and warmth of Emaline's large cabin.

For one brief moment, everything looked as it should. Niz was standing at the stove, stirring a pot of bubbling stew, the aroma of which made Raya's mouth water. Chenoa was setting the table, and Mother Emaline was darning a stocking. The big room was bright and warm and cheery.

For just one moment, Raya entertained the hope that maybe the last three days had been a horrible dream; surely, the men would come stomping in the door at any moment. As always, they would take off their muddy boots and hang their wet coats by the door, creating the need for her to mop up the floor after their outerwear had shed its rainwater. They would all eat together and enjoy a cozy evening. Then Luke would give her that look that he did every night, and they would shrug into their coats and pull on their shoes. After they said their farewells, they would begin the walk back to their own cabin together. He would wrap his arm snugly around her, and she would stay close to his side, using him as a harbor from the cold.

They would go to their own house—the house they had shared for five years—and go to bed, lying close to ward off the chill, sharing with each other happenings from their days. He would take her in his arms, and she would sleep warm and safe, tucked in against him.

But Chenoa had set only four plates on the table. Four, when there should be seven.

A strange cry threatened to erupt from between Raya's lips, but she put a staying hand to her throat, took a deep breath, and moved forward. She helped Mother Emaline to her seat at the table, then poured four glasses of fresh milk.

Everyone was quiet as they took their seats. Swallowing the pain, Raya took up the ladle and dished the stew, as Luke always had.

"I'll say grace," Mother Emaline offered, her voice unsteady. Joining hands, the widows bowed their heads. "Our Father who art in heaven," Mother Emaline paused, and when Raya glanced up, she realized the woman couldn't go on. The lady had dissolved into tears, speechless before the LORD in the midst of her grief.

"Amen," Raya finished, not knowing what else to say, nor trusting herself to continue the prayer. Her own tears weren't far below the surface.

Mother Emaline wiped at her eyes, and the younger women began to eat, trying to swallow as much of their dinner as they could. Raya was sure the stew was delicious, as Niz had always been an excellent cook, but it tasted like ashes in her mouth. Still, the hunger in her belly won out over her grieving heart, and she emptied her bowl. Growing up, she was taught that when there was food on the table, you ate it, regardless of how you felt or how it tasted. She fell back on that teaching now.

Not one word was spoken that night at the dinner table that was usually so full of laughter and joy. After they were finished, Raya and Chenoa cleaned up the dishes, while Niz took care of skimming the milk. Once their chores were done, they all sat down and took up their mending, not knowing what else to do except what they had always done.

Chenoa was the first to break the silence when she threw down the sock she was darning. "I can't get it! I can't get the hole fixed, and Will's feet are going to be cold!"

Niz gasped sharply. "Don't speak of him, Chenoa! You musn't speak of the dead! You'll offend the spirits."

UP FROM THE ASH HEAP

Realizing her mistake, realizing her husband's feet would never be cold again—or rather, would always be—the dark-haired young woman dissolved into tears. Within seconds, all four of them had tears running down their cheeks again. Overcome with grief for her sons, Mother Emaline wailed into the night air.

As the heartbreaking sound left Mother Emaline's lips, Raya went to her quickly, her heart swelling painfully with compassion. She knelt down in front of her mother-in-law, putting her head in her lap and holding the lady's hand tightly. Raya's tears wet Mother Emaline's skirt, and Mother Emaline bent over her, hugging her close. Chenoa and Niz came too, and they wept together, huddled around each other, holding on for dear life.

That night, just as they had since the fire, Mother Emaline and Chenoa shared Mother Emaline's bed, while Niz and Raya bedded down together on the floor, none of the girls brave enough to trudge through the cold rain to go to their empty cabins alone; none of them wishing to spend the night of their husband's funeral in solitude. The tears lasted long into the night, and finally Raya drifted off to sleep to the sound of sniffling. In her dreams, she saw it again—the whole scene played out before her in painful clarity, as she once again lived out the tragic day.

For nearly ten minutes, the smell of smoke had been curling around the inside of the main cabin. Leaving her afternoon knitting, Raya hunted everywhere for its source. Thunder rattled the house as Raya looked, another dry thunderstorm sweeping through the Rockies. Chenoa and Niz joined in the search, but they couldn't find anything that was burning. Yet the smell of smoke continued to grow thicker in the air. When Raya swept her eyes over the house one last time to try to catch sight of anything at all that might be too close to a source of heat, she saw the black smoke drifting by the window.

She flung open the front door, ran out onto the porch, and down the stairs to where she had a direct line of sight to the mill. By that time, it was too late. The mill was fully engulfed in flames—flames that licked at the sky and sent black smoke billowing upward. Their livelihood was literally going up in smoke. The men would have to rebuild. It would set them back weeks, if not months. She felt her heart sinking, but looked around expectantly for them, knowing they would be running back and forth with buckets of water from the creek. She was puzzled as to why one of them hadn't come to fetch their wives to help and was even more puzzled when they were nowhere in sight. It was then that she saw that the stack of heavy logs, waiting to be milled, had tumbled down and were blocking the mill's large sliding doors. Usually, the men worked with the large doors (that served to let in fresh air and light) open, but today, they had closed them against the unusually high gusts of wind, and now, the doors—the only way in or out of the mill—were jammed.

Screaming for help, screaming for Luke, she ran to the mill, attempting to pull back the smoldering fallen logs with her bare hands. She succeeded in burning the palm and fingertips of her left hand, but nothing else. She had failed to move them even an inch—they were too big and too heavy. Chenoa, Niz, and Mother Emaline tried desperately to help and together they got one to roll a few inches, but they could not clear the door. By that point, there was no hope for anyone inside anyway, regardless of whether or not they could have freed the door. The roof had collapsed even before she had reached the fiery building.

Within minutes, concerned neighbors armed with buckets and gunnysacks started arriving. For the next hour, she worked frantically alongside them and her remaining family members against the high winds to put out the fire before it caught in the trees and burned the entire homestead and valley. By the time the fire was contained, then burnt out, and the ruins cooled enough for them to sift through, the only things left of their menfolk were the buckles of their shoes and a soot covered pocket watch Will carried.

It was at that moment of stark tragedy that terrible pain ripped through Niz, and the young woman sunk to the ground, clutching her abdomen, crying out in pain and fear. She delivered her and Alex's son less than an hour later. Born months too early, the tiny baby boy lived only a few minutes.

Two

Emaline woke early. The house was still dark. Driven by sweet memories of the past, no doubt brought by the warmth of having someone lying beside her once again, she rolled over to put her arm around her husband, Julius. She found her youngest daughter-in-law, Chenoa, lying beside her instead. The recollection of the last ten years and the last week came flooding back. She stifled a groan with her pillow as tears stung her eyes.

Just over thirteen years ago, she and Julius packed everything they owned into two covered wagons, took their three half-grown sons, and started west. In those days, war was in the air, and violence and tension hung like smoke. The states were bickering, and the conflict was escalating. Ways of life, fortunes, and industries were being threatened, and those with the most at risk were not backing down. The political fire was laid. All that was needed was a spark of ignition, and the country would be gripped by war.

Wanting to protect their small fortune and their boys, who were only a few years away from fighting age, she and Julius chose not to heed the advice of all those around them and even the quiet voice that echoed somewhere deep within. They set off for the great unknown, leaving friends, family, and society behind in Cincinnati.

It was on the far edge of the mountains of Colorado Territory—a wild, rugged, and uncivilized land—that Julius finally felt satisfied they had gone far enough to escape the fighting that would surely come in the East. After living under the fear of

Indian attacks while traveling, Emaline was thankful to settle near a fort. Additionally, Julius assured her that the tribes in the area were known to be peaceful and had been living quietly alongside trappers and the growing population of whites for years.

With the town and nearby fort growing rapidly, there were plenty of prospects for a businessman, and Julius quickly identified the developing local economy as a golden opportunity to advance his own financial achievements. Settling in for the long haul, he built a sawmill in a beautiful valley along the banks of a sparkling, cold mountain stream. With the wood from his mill, he built a lavishly large cabin for his family in the same scenic setting. Julius worked the mill with their boys for only two short years before he passed away suddenly and unexpectedly. Emaline mourned him deeply.

On her own, in a strange land full of curious ways and unfamiliar people, she clung tightly to her sons, thankful she had them and that they were old enough to continue on the path Julius had set before them.

Five years after Julius' death, Luke delivered a shipment of wood downriver and brought back a bride—the beautiful and laughing Raya. Initially, Emaline was both shocked and dismayed when her son brought home the dark-skinned foreigner, but pressed down her shame and welcomed her warmly, not wanting to offend her eldest son. Raya was just beyond childhood then, but there was maturity in her eyes that somehow calmed Emaline's fears for her love-stricken son. Raya, as young as she was, had already seen her fair share of death and suffering, yet she was always smiling. She lit up the house with her musical laughter and cheerful exuberance. She was good help and, grateful for female companionship, Emaline soon formed a deep affection for Luke's sweet, dark-haired wife, despite any initial misgivings.

Luke. The name of her son brought a wave of sadness. He had always been the gentlest of her boys. Slow to anger and quick to offer a helping hand and a smile, he had warmed her heart from the moment he was born.

He was her firstborn, born nearly four years after she and Julius were wed. He was twenty-two when he married Raya, and had been completely captivated by her exotic beauty, joyful laughter, and melodious voice. He had enjoyed every minute of being married to the dark-skinned ray of sunshine, Emaline noted, grateful that her son had thoroughly enjoyed his final five years on the earth.

What would Raya do now? She was only twenty, childless, and a widow. Surely the girl would one day want to remarry. Emaline wished she had another son to offer her to keep her in the family, but alas, they were all gone, and before they were gone, they had all been spoken for.

Emaline's eyes moved to the young woman lying beside Raya on the quilt spread over the wooden floorboards. Nizhoni, who they affectionately referred to as "Niz," was a spitfire through and through. Emaline was still convinced it was Niz's ancestry and wild beauty that first attracted Alex. He didn't love anything as much as he loved a good adventure. Something about her was as wild and daring as her people; she seemed as free as the wind. While it may have been the adventure Niz represented that drew Alex initially, it was her spunk and personality that kept him intrigued long enough to realize he desired a wife more than he desired to remain the carefree and fun-loving kid that he was. Despite Emaline's best efforts to quietly point out to Alex the challenges of marrying outside one's faith and culture, Niz was the only wife he wanted. So, the boys raised another cabin in their valley, and after a traditional Native American wedding, Niz was brought into the family.

Emaline nearly chuckled again, remembering how Alex loved to get his wife stirred up. Always the fun-loving one (no matter what kind of mischief it got him into), he would tease Niz mercilessly, always taking it just far enough to light her fuse. Then he would sit back and listen to her fume. She had kept him entertained for the entirety of their three years of marriage. Now, she was also only twenty and had suffered the loss of not only her husband, but her unborn child as well. She would need to make a fresh beginning, or else Emaline feared she would go mad from her losses.

Emaline turned again to the girl in the bed beside her. Chenoa was the baby of the family at only seventeen. William, Emaline's youngest, had only been given six months of marriage with his meek, dark-skinned beauty. Her black ringlets laid in a heap on the pillow beside Emaline, and her delicate face was as pretty as a flower. She had her Blackfoot mother's high cheekbones and fine features and her negro father's warm brown eyes. Her mixed genes had resulted in smooth, perfect ringlets of inky black hair and a skin color just a few shades darker than the other girls'.

Emaline hadn't even bothered to caution William against marrying outside his own race and religion. He seemed as determined to follow in his brothers' footsteps when picking a bride as he was in everything else. Additionally, Emaline could understand his attraction and knew there would be no dissuading him. While Chenoa was beautiful without a doubt, there was also a frail femininity she possessed that compelled a man to want to take care of her. William was smitten from the moment he first saw her in town.

Emaline smiled as she remembered how pleased William was when Chenoa's father agreed to a marriage. On the day of their wedding, when he finally had the opportunity to meet his bride for the first time, he was so proud that Emaline was afraid the buttons on his shirt would burst. In the six months they were married, he made over his petite young wife, always worrying she was doing too much, always asking if she was feeling alright. Chenoa used to laugh and tell him she was made of flesh and blood, not porcelain. He never believed her.

Now Emaline hoped she was right. Otherwise, she wasn't sure the girl would survive William's tragic passing. She had loved him as much as he loved her. Emaline looked at Chenoa's peaceful face, thankful the girl was finally able to sleep. She was barely more than a child with the rest of her life in front of her, as were Raya and

Niz. All the girls would need to move on with their lives, find new husbands, have babies, raise their families.

As scary as it was, as much as it hurt her already shattered heart, the only kind thing to do was to release them. Truthfully, she wanted to cling to them, hold onto them, as they were the only thing she had left in her life. Despite her early misgivings, they had become her pride and joy over the past several years—her best friends, her coworkers, the ones who made her sons happy. She had assumed they would be with her until the day she died, and still she wished it were so. Yet, she could not ask such a selfish thing. As much as her sons had loved them, as much as she herself loved them, she had to think of the girls' happiness.

She had no more sons to offer them, nor did she have the means to sustain them any longer. It was too soon to expect them to remarry, and their group of four women too great a burden to ask any one man to take on, even if one of the girls could bring herself to marry again so soon. There was not enough work to be had for single women in their small, remote town, and there was no longer savings to fall back on. Their food would not last long, and when it was gone, there was no money to buy more.

But all three girls were young, and their families didn't live too far away. She knew they would be welcomed back to their fathers' homes to grieve, and when the time was right, to remarry and continue on with their lives. Emaline knew that as much as it would hurt and as scary and lonely as it would feel, if she truly loved them as she professed, there was only one right thing to do.

She had to let them go.

Three

Startling the small, sorrowful group with her abrupt actions, Mother Emaline pushed aside her plate and put her palms on the table, looking solemnly at each of her daughters-in-law. She swallowed down the pain, drew herself up, cleared her throat, and began to speak.

"You know how much I love each one of you. The five years since our family began to grow," she looked pointedly at Raya, and reached across the table to squeeze her hand, "have been wonderful. It has brought joy to this mother's heart to see each of my sons happily married and to gain the daughters I never had." Her eyes filled with tears. "But our men are gone now." She paused to steady her voice. "As is our livelihood and our money. I'm too old and too sickly to remarry, which is my only hope of securing a sustainable home for you. I have nothing good to offer you. I'm afraid that in a short time, we will run through our food supply and have no money to buy more."

Raya blinked back tears at the beloved lady's very accurate portrayal of their situation. It was dismal and desperate to say the least. Raya had known this conversation was coming, knew they would have to look at what came next, and she had been dreading it as she had never dreaded anything else in her entire life. She had no ideas, no suggestions, no direction in which to point her dear family members. Sorrow and hopelessness were all that was left.

Mother Emaline continued with measured and sad words. "You girls have been the best daughters a woman could ask for, but I have nothing left to offer you, no future to give you. It would be best for you if you returned to your families. Niz, Chenoa, your families live within a day's walk, and Raya, you must take the horse and return to your own family. If we dress you in the boys' clothing and do your hair up under a hat, I don't believe you'll be bothered on the road; or perhaps one of our kind neighbors would accompany you to ensure your safe arrival."

Mother Emaline's words struck the young women like a blunt blow. "No! We won't leave you," Raya cried, standing up. Chenoa and Niz did likewise, voicing their own protests, but Mother Emaline held up a trembling hand to ward off further argument.

"You girls are all young and beautiful. You were good wives and are very knowledgeable about keeping a house. You should return home and find other husbands when you're ready."

"We don't want other husbands," Raya choked. "We want to stay with you."

Mother Emaline shook her head weakly, and Raya could see how difficult the conversation was for her. She began to worry about the woman's health, remembering how she'd been coughing since the fire. The nagging cough reminded her of the bouts of illness the woman had battled in the past, and Raya prayed the fevers would not return as well. Studying her more closely, Raya noticed the dark shadows under her kind eyes. Mother Emaline seemed older, frailer than she had just the week before.

"We will stay with you, Mother," Niz told the woman firmly, coming around the table to cling to her hand.

Mother Emaline was quiet for several moments. When she spoke, her expression and voice were very gentle. "If you stay with me, we will remain four widows."

Chenoa shook her head, joining the first two. "Be that as it may, we will stay with you."

Mother Emaline considered each girl's face for a long moment. Finally, she gave a short nod, smoothing their hair back and embracing them as the mother that she was. She instructed them all to finish their breakfast. She pulled her own plate back in front of her and dutifully began to eat her fried egg and potatoes that were now cold.

She was quiet the rest of the day, and Raya knew she was thinking about their situation. When Raya awakened once in the middle of the night, she saw Mother Emaline sitting in a chair before the fire, rocking as she stared at the flames, lost in thought. Raya's heart hurt for her mother-in-law. She herself was just as confused about what to do and full of dread knowing they would soon have to face the difficult circumstances they had been dealt—and yet she knew Mother Emaline felt not only the despair but also the weight of responsibility as she was now the head of the small family.

The next morning at breakfast, Mother Emaline brought it up again, but this time she seemed more determined. "You have to return to your families, girls," she started, her voice firm. "I know that you are loyal to me and that you love me, truly I do, but I love you, too. I cannot and will not let you suffer as you will if you remain here with me. We have no money, we are running out of food, we have no men to protect us, and you no longer have husbands to have children by. No, if you stay with me, you will suffer greatly, and I cannot bear that. If you love me, please listen to my request. I am releasing you from this place and sending you home."

"And what of you? What will become of you if we return to our families?" Raya demanded, frustrated that Mother Emaline would dismiss her own needs so easily for the sake of their comfort.

Mother Emaline lifted her chin bravely. "Colorado Territory is not a kind place for an old widow without means or family. I will sell the property and with the money it brings, I will take the train back east. I've heard things are better in Cincinnati than they were when Julius and I decided to come west. I will return home and see what can be done."

Raya dropped her eyes to the table, shocked and in despair. Mother Emaline was returning to the East? Surely, Raya knew that life in Colorado Territory would be difficult for them as widows, and she had blocked her mind to what may come down the road, but returning to the East . . . it was somewhere she could never follow Mother Emaline.

"We will go with you, then," Chenoa promised innocently. "Surely, we can manage together in Cincinnati. Perhaps work would be easier to come by."

Raya watched Mother Emaline's expression cloud over.

"Chenoa, darling, things in the East are not as they are here. Here, it is not uncommon for a white man and an Indian to be neighbors or to trade as equals. Here, a white man can marry an Indian girl, and a negro can tie his horse beside the white man's. But in the East, none of these things would be allowed. Things are very different there . . . people think differently."

Raya had never heard Mother Emaline speak so openly about race, and her words stung.

"I don't mean to be harsh," the older woman continued, "but you have to understand what life is like there. You would be persecuted both for the color of your skin and your beliefs. We would be going back poor, and beyond that, you would not be accepted socially. Without a man to protect you, I fear you could be mistreated or taken advantage of." Mother Emaline wiped at tears on her cheeks. "I don't want to hurt you, girls, but you must know, returning to the East with me is not an option. In the East, no respectable man would marry you. Traveling to Cincinnati with me would mean accepting your lot in life as a widow."

Raya swiped at her own tears and folded her hands tightly in her lap, trying to steel herself against the pain Mother Emaline's words inflicted. "Then you should stay here. We will stay with you and care for you," Raya said, trying to cover the hurt she felt. Though Mother Emaline's words had felt sharp and cutting, Raya knew they were true and spoken only in an attempt to keep them from misery.

"And what would we do?" Mother Emaline asked, her eyes gentle.

"We would work," Raya answered bravely.

"Where?" Mother Emaline questioned.

"We could surely find work somewhere. We're able-bodied and hard workers. As you said, we're very skilled in keeping a house," Raya told her, the other girls nodding their agreement.

"Wives are needed in this country, not housekeepers," Mother Emaline answered. "I predict you will have a dozen offers of marriage within a fortnight should we stay, but will you be ready to accept them? And when you are ready, will you feel free to leave? I will not be a weight that holds you back. I couldn't bear it."

"We won't accept them," Raya argued. "We don't want to remarry. We want to stay with you. We will find work. We will make enough to sustain us, and we will get along just fine. You'll see."

Mother Emaline considered her for several long moments, then sighed. "If you refuse to marry and instead remain with me, you'll never again be held by your husband or give birth to a child. You'll never hold your own babe or watch them grow or play." She shook her head. "I love you too much to let that happen. No, you must return to your families and take new husbands when you're ready. It's what my sons would want. They would want to see you, each of you, happy. I want that for you too. And despite your present grief, the day will come when you will want that as well." Raya began to protest, but Mother Emaline held up her hand. "No, I need to go home and so do each of you. No more arguing now, please. Consider everything I've said."

All three young women quietly fell back to eating their breakfast, obediently thinking over their mother-in-law's words, feeling the pain it brought. Raya wanted to argue further, wanted to assure Mother Emaline she would not leave her, but respected the woman too much to do so. Nothing else was said on the topic, and they all solemnly finished their breakfast.

The rest of the day, Raya worked quietly, uncertain about what she should do. Later, as she made her way to the barn to start evening chores, she again contemplated her dilemma.

Over the past five years, she had grown to love her mother-in-law deeply. The woman had welcomed Raya into her home, into her family, and had been a mother to her. The knowledge that returning home meant leaving Mother Emaline utterly alone, without a husband, sons, or daughters, weighed heavily on Raya's heart. The woman would be left at the mercy of strangers without any kin and too old and sickly to work or remarry. Raya could only imagine what would become of her, and who would even be left to care? As a woman who had a full house filled with love and joy only a few days earlier, Raya could not bear to picture Mother Emaline living alone without a single soul who cared for her.

Raya shuddered. She could not imagine, nor would she want to, being so alone in the world.

And yet, in so many ways, she would be facing the same reality if she went home. She had rarely heard from her family in the five years since leaving her father's home. Her father was a hard man, committed to his business and his son. Her mother, too, was a hard woman, bent on survival and hardened by suffering and loss. Raya knew her mother cared for her, but she had never said so, nor was she one to show it. Her sister, Sugundarani, was the only one in the family Raya had developed a strong connection with, and she had been married off years ago. It was something that was bound to happen to Raya again in the coming days should she return home, as she was certain her father would be of the mindset the sooner the better. She would likely be given to a different man and sent off to his home within three months of her return.

Glancing up at the towering peaks that surrounded their little valley as she crossed the short distance between the house and barn, Raya knew that wasn't the only thing that troubled her. Another matter that weighed heavily on her heart was that Mother Emaline, along with Luke, had taught her about the one true God, who was so very different from the gods Raya's own family worshiped. Her own family worshipped gods made of metals, who were as varied as the things they prayed to them for. The gods of her family were fickle and angry, and she had never seen them deal lovingly with their servants.

Yet, this God that Luke and Emaline served was unseen, comprised of nothing man-made. He was constant, steadfast, merciful, and His loving-kindness endured forever. What was more, He was powerful. She had seen Him rescue them from tragedy, restore Mother Emaline to health time and time again when she fell gravely ill, bless their business, give them hope, encourage their hearts, and cause them great joy. She had seen Him move on behalf of the family more than once, and He dealt with them kindly.

Until the fire. She would never understand the fire, or why their God had allowed it to happen as He had. Yet, beyond all doubt, all grief, one truth remained—He was real. More real than she had ever known a god to be. She could see His fingerprints on the majestic creation all around her. She could nearly feel Him when she read the pages of His Word. She could hear Him in the rumblings of thunder across the mountains. She longed to know more, and Mother Emaline was her one tie to this mysterious, real God.

Faced with her present dilemma, Raya considered the reality of returning to the house of her father. She would once again be living under a roof in which many gods were worshipped, and the spirit within her cringed. Her father and brother would not understand this new God that she served and would demand she return her faith and her loyalty to the gods of her ancestors. She would not wish to comply, but she was a timid girl who shied away from conflict. The very thought of contradicting her father or brother made her knees weak from fear. Downright refusal was utterly beyond her.

Still, Mother Emaline would be returning to the East. Raya knew that, in all honesty, it was the right thing for the woman to do. There was no hope for her here where a man was needed for everything, and her own strength was sparse. But it was a place where Raya couldn't go. She bit her lip as she pulled open the heavy barn door and stepped inside, ready to tend the stock for the evening.

"Is it really as she says? The East, I mean."

Raya looked up at Chenoa's words, surprised to find the girl in the barn.

Her surprise must have shown on her face, because Chenoa shrugged one shoulder and said, "It smells like him in here . . . like Will." Suddenly the girl laughed, putting her hand to her mouth. "I didn't mean it like that . . . to say my husband smelled like a barn . . . but you know what I mean."

Raya laughed too, reaching out to hold both of Chenoa's hands. "You're right. Will would be so proud to know he smelled like a barn full of animals." They laughed together, finding blessed relief in bleeding out their emotions that way, rather than through tears again.

When the laughter passed, Raya hugged Chenoa firmly, seeing fresh tears in the girl's dark eyes. Taking her hand, Raya pulled her along to the horse stalls. Leaving Chenoa outside the gate, she grabbed the pitchfork and went inside to work as she talked.

"To answer your question, yes, it is as she says. I was young when we passed through, but I remember how people treated us . . . the things they said," Raya paused, then continued. "They called us names. They thought we were natives. It wasn't until someone noticed the bindi on my mother's forehead that they realized we were foreigners. The names they called us changed, then. I remember being afraid and embarrassed and hurt. They said things that weren't kind. They made inappropriate remarks to my mother. We weren't allowed to eat in dining rooms for the white folks or sleep in the white inns. We could only have what the white people didn't want. I remember going through one city where a group of young boys threw rotten vegetables at us."

The look on Chenoa's face was one of shock and horror. "Why? Why is it like that there?"

"They call it the civilized world, but it's not civilized in many ways," Raya answered quietly. "Luke told me once that it is like that because of fear. We're different from them—we look different, we talk different, we dress different, we cook different. Sometimes people are afraid of differences." Raya blew at a piece of loose hair that was hanging in her face.

Answering Chenoa's questions was causing her great turmoil as painful memories were being brought to the surface, all while her dilemma about what to do stayed at the forefront of her mind. Raya knew all too well that what she said was true. Understanding why she and her family were treated like they were didn't mean she was brave enough to go to a place where she would live with the consequences of such fear day in and day out.

It had been over a decade since she had been in the East, but she was confident such things hadn't changed. She knew without a doubt that if she returned, she would be ridiculed, scorned, feared, and rejected.

Mother Emaline was right. If Raya remained with her, if she returned with her to the East, she would never again marry, never have a child. She would no longer be seen as an acceptable wife. And while she felt now as if she would never want to remarry, and could not bear the thought of being a wife to any man but Luke, she was young. How would she survive without provision? Without any kin to keep her?

She had seen death by starvation, had nearly starved herself in her early years when her parents were saving every rupee they earned to secure passage to America, and it was a slow and painful process. She also knew what happened to women who were alone without protection, and just the thought of it made her tremble with fear. What was more, she had heard it told what some women stooped to when it came down to starving to death or securing another day's food. While she liked to think she never would, again, she had experienced the pain of a stomach that had been empty for days and knew that one's ability to reason was sometimes overruled by need.

If she stayed and returned to her brother, Amhil, and her father, she would have food, safety, and shelter. She would be provided for and protected. She was ensured a home, a fire to cook over, and clothing to wear. In a short time, they would surely marry her off again, but in some ways, that wouldn't be all bad either. She would have a house of her own to keep. She could have children. Her life would be full, and her physical needs met.

Still, what of Mother Emaline? There was no way Raya could leave her all alone and no way she could take her back to her father's house.

"Will you go with Mother?" Chenoa asked, her dark eyes trained on Raya's face.

Raya slumped against the side of the stall and shook her head. "I don't know," she answered honestly. What was she to do? There was no good answer, no easy choice. Should she stay with Mother Emaline and face possible starvation and a lifetime of loneliness, or return home to material security, but face religious bondage, while leaving Mother Emaline all alone in the world?

Pushing a few strands of dark, wayward hair out of her eyes with the back of her gloved hand, she started lifting the soiled straw out of the stall again. No matter what she decided to do next, the horses needed a clean place to bed down.

She wanted to remain with Mother Emaline. It was the right thing to do. And she wanted to be free to learn more about the God she now served. But she was afraid. That was it, pure and simple. And fear was a powerful force.

If she went with Mother Emaline, she knew what she would face, but what she didn't know was what would become of her. What would become of Mother Emaline? Would the woman's own kind be more likely to take her in and provide for her if Raya wasn't with her? Would she simply become a hindrance, a burden to Mother Emaline? But perhaps there would be no one to take her in, regardless of Raya's presence. Could Raya take the chance that Mother Emaline would be left all alone?

What if Emaline's cough progressed into another bout of illness? Who would care for her? Who would nurse her back to health? The last time the illness had seized her, Raya had been the one to care for her. Even with around the clock care, they had come close to losing the dear woman. How would she manage alone?

Could Raya live with herself if she chose to return to material comforts and left Mother Emaline to her fate?

Questions swirled around her mind like the winds that had ripped through the valley the day of the fire. Her head began to ache.

"I'm going home," Chenoa said, pulling Raya away from her disturbing thoughts. Raya looked up, surprised. She saw the tears in Chenoa's eyes. She nodded as she set down her pitchfork and held out her hands to the younger girl.

"Yes, you should. That's good, Shideezhi," Raya said gently, addressing Chenoa in a native tongue. She had learned a handful of words from her sisters-in-law, and that was the one she found herself using most frequently. Inside, Raya's heart was breaking. She couldn't imagine saying goodbye to her youngest sister-in-law, who felt every bit a true sister. Even anticipating the goodbye sent a wave of loneliness over her. Yet, she kept her sadness to herself. She wanted good for Chenoa, and she wanted to support her in her decision.

"Is it? Is it good?" Chenoa asked pleadingly. "Because I don't know. I don't want to leave her, but the East sounds frightening, and I'm afraid. My heart hurts, and I just want my mother." Chenoa started to cry.

Raya's heart moved with compassion for the young woman. She thought of what life would hold for Chenoa if she went with Mother Emaline to Cincinnati, and answered firmly. "It is good. Go. Go home to your mother, your father, your sister, and brothers. It's what Will would want. He would want you taken care of and protected." Raya smiled at her sister-in-law and squeezed her hands. "You know it is."

"That's what I think too. I've been trying to imagine what Will would have me do if he were here and today, I was sitting out on that boulder we used to sit on together, overlooking the river, and I think I know now. Will loved his mother, but I know how much he always worried about me, and I think if he were here, he would tell me to return home."

Raya smiled gently. "I think you're absolutely right. No matter what else was going on, Will always made sure you were comfortable and taken care of. It's a good decision, Chenoa, and I'm glad you have found peace with it."

Chenoa smiled shakily and nodded her head, wiping her tears. "Don't tell Niz that we've spoken of Will. It would upset her."

Raya nodded, understanding. Chenoa did not adhere to the religious ways of her native people as Nizhoni still did. Chenoa felt no fear in speaking the name of the dead, yet she did not want to hurt their sister. Raya appreciated Chenoa's thoughtfulness. "I won't."

As Chenoa left the barn a few minutes later, Raya leaned back against the wall and closed her eyes. What she had said was right. If there was any wavering within Chenoa, she should go home. Life would not be easy nor pleasant should she remain with Mother Emaline, and if Chenoa made her decision for any of the rest of them, she would regret it when difficult times hit.

However, through counseling Chenoa to return home, Raya had found her own answer as well. Unlike Chenoa, she had professed faith in Jesus Christ, the God of the Scriptures. The Scriptures said to love—to love and not fear. Well, love compelled her to take one course, fear another, so she would follow the way of love and come what may, she would make the most of it.

Four

"I never knew I could feel so lonely . . . so alone."

Raya studied Niz's face and wished she had some way to comfort the broken woman. Instead, she took her hand.

"Why, Raya? Why? First my husband, then our baby? I should have had our son left to remember him by! He was so proud that he was going to be a father. He was so proud of our baby."

Raya's heart hurt as it filled with compassion for her sister-in-law. Niz's grief was overpowering even her beliefs as she spoke of her dead husband and baby, though not by name. Raya was thankful; it had been agonizing to see Niz grieving but never hear her utter one word about her loss. Chenoa and Mother Emaline had talked brokenly about the men and the tragedy, but Nizhoni had kept her thoughts and her pain to herself. Raya respected her need to grieve privately and hadn't pushed her, yet she knew the grief and loss of both Alex and their baby must be tearing Niz apart. Raya had prayed that eventually the strong young woman would be able to break her silence and let her grief spill out, allowing them to help her carry the load. Now, after several days of silence, she was finally talking. "I don't know why, Niz, but God's ways are always higher, and they're always purposeful. We have to remember that."

"I don't believe in their God! And neither should you! How can you after what happened?" Niz accused. "Mother Emaline says their God is kind, but surely she can't anymore. First her husband, then her sons and unborn grandson . . . how could she?" Niz demanded, tears coursing down her cheeks.

Raya wanted to implore Niz not to say such things, wanted to remind her that the God she was rejecting was a powerful One who was holy. However, she knew her sister-in-law's words were born of intense grief and such a reminder would not do her any good in her present state. "We musn't let this make us bitter, Niz. We don't know why tragedy happens, but no matter what god a person serves, it does." Raya watched her sister-in-law's head drop, and she placed her hand gently on her shoulder. "Perhaps Mother Emaline doesn't speak of God removing His children from the natural world where bad things happen but of showing them kindness as He helps them through difficulty and causes good to come of it."

Niz's expression was one of great pain. "I don't know how good could come of this."

Raya looked out over the treed mountainside and the stunning peaks that lay beyond. The view from Mother Emaline's front porch had always been breathtaking. She was relieved when the rain stopped and the sun finally came out, warming the late summer air enough that she and Niz could sit out on the covered porch to have a cup of tea. Only in the high mountains of Colorado Territory could rain bring such a chill to the air in August. Now, Raya searched the breathtaking landscape as she searched her mind for an answer. Finally, she shrugged her small shoulders. "Neither do I. But thankfully, we're not the ultimate authority in this world and us not knowing something has little impact on what occurs."

"I should have had his baby to remember him by," Niz continued, as if Raya hadn't spoken. "That son should have upheld the family name, continued their line. Now, there is no one. Three sons, three wives and not one child. How does that happen, Shideezhi? Especially when I was with child! Especially when I was carrying a son!"

Niz's words stung Raya's own heart in a personal way, as she had often longed to carry a child for Luke, to bring forth his children. She spread her hands over her womb, that had remained empty during their five years of marriage, and wondered why, just as Niz was. She had prayed; she had asked for a child, a son or a daughter, but her womb had remained closed, and she appeared to be barren. She felt again the familiar ache to hold a child in her arms—her own child.

With the swiftness of a bolt of lightning in a mountain thunderstorm, Raya was instantly back in bed beside Luke, trying to cover her unwelcome tears. But like he always did when something was wrong, Luke knew. He leaned over her until he could see her face, then pulled her hair back tenderly. "When it's the right time, we'll have our own children," he had said.

Alex and Niz had announced that night at supper that Niz was with child, and Raya screeched and clapped in excitement as she congratulated her dear brother and sister. Her joy was entirely sincere. She was happy for them, delighted, in fact, that there would be a young Applewood. But when sleep was evasive that night, she found herself spreading her hands over her empty womb and hoping, praying, longing to be carrying a child herself. Her child. Luke's child. They had been married the longest. Luke should have been the first among his brothers to be a father.

"Father and Mother were married four years before they had me," Luke had told her, kissing her cheek.

"That's what Mother said," Raya agreed, her voice trembling. "But that was four and we've been married five."

"Four—five. What's the difference? There's still hope. Perhaps we'll be welcoming our own little one when we celebrate six years," he told her.

She hid her face. Her barrenness was letting him down. She was failing him as a wife. She felt useless and guilty, frustrated and sad. He had so kindly rebuffed every one of her self-accusations, assuring her of his affections, and reminding her that there was hope until her peace was restored. But even as she slept that night, her heart was still longing, and she was achingly aware of her empty womb.

Now, she focused again on Niz and squeezed the woman's hand as a fresh set of sorrow came. "I just . . . I feel so alone, Raya! For five months I carried life and now . . . now I'm empty! I'm all by myself in my skin and . . . I just think, why? What could I have done? If I hadn't worked so hard to put out the fire, would my baby have lived? If I had stayed in the house rather than going out to see the sight myself, would my baby have lived? What could I have done to save my baby? *His baby!* I should have been able to save it somehow, to keep it alive! He was gone. It was my sole responsibility to care for the one person that could allow him to live on, and I couldn't. I *couldn't*! I failed him," Niz cried, sobs catching at her throat.

Raya gently stroked the woman's dark hair back from her wet cheeks.

"He was so little, Raya! So little!" Niz cried, her voice breaking. "Did you see him? Did you see how little he was?"

Raya nodded, unable to hold back her own tears. "I saw," she assured her. She would never forget the sight of her tiny nephew, perfectly formed and yet so very heartbreakingly small—too small to live.

"His hand . . . his little fingers . . . his face . . . Why, Raya? Why?" The woman began to sob so deeply that her back shuddered violently, and she crumpled over her knees. The squirrels in the trees stopped their chatter, and for once, the birds were all quiet. Even the animals seemed to sense the sorrow of the moment, the intense grief.

Raya thought of the tiny baby, buried in a shallow grave under the shadow of the cross that stood in his father's memory, and hot tears rolled down her cheeks.

Knowing nothing could be said or done to ease Niz's pain, Raya wrapped her arms around her sister and held her. If nothing else, Niz needed to know she wasn't alone.

***

"Raya, you have to leave as the other girls are. Go home to your family." Mother Emaline's lip trembled.

"I will not. I will stay with you," Raya answered calmly, not even pausing in her sweeping.

Mother Emaline shook her head. "No. Return to your family. I cannot let you come with me. It won't be kind to you. Luke wouldn't have wanted it."

Raya's face gentled. "Nor would he have wanted you left alone in this world without any kin or loved ones," she countered, continuing to sweep.

"You've been to the East, you know what it's like. I cannot in good conscience take you there. And you know my situation. I cannot promise you anything—not food, nor safety, nor shelter, nor provision. All I can guarantee you is difficulty and discomfort. Go home, Raya. Go back to your family."

Raya stopped sweeping and looked up to meet the older woman's eyes. "You *are* my family. You have become my mother and my friend, Emaline, and my desire is to remain with you. I cannot leave you. I will not. Where you are is my home, and my place is with you. Please, don't ask me again. We will go to Cincinnati together and see what we can do. The LORD will make a way. 'Tis what you always say, and I think it must apply again here."

Raya watched the inner struggle play across Mother Emaline's face as she came to stand before her. Finally, the older woman's eyes filled with tears, and she framed Raya's face with her hands. "Thank you, child. Bless you. May the LORD God bless you for your kindness, and provide for you out of His own hand for the good thing you are doing for me," Emaline said, her hands trembling, tears slipping out of the corners of her blue eyes.

Embarrassed, Raya looked down. "It's right that I should stay with you."

The front door opened, and Raya turned in time to see Niz walk in, moving very slowly. She had a packed satchel under her arm, as did Chenoa, who followed her. The neighbor who was kind enough to offer to drive the women home would be by for them shortly, and it was time for farewells.

Niz came to Raya and shrugged her shoulders. "I feel so alone. I see their faces every time I close my eyes. I need my mother and my sisters around me now . . . I need the old ways of my people . . . I need to be where my spirit is free . . . I need to mourn for my husband and baby in the ways of my ancestors. I can't do that here. I can't do that in the East."

Raya shook her head, then pressed her face against Niz's cheek. "You don't have to explain anything to me, Niz. I'm glad you're going home. It's what you should do," she paused and then reached out a hand to the young and sad-eyed Chenoa. "You too, Chenoa. You are so young. Go home and grieve your husband in the safety of your family. I hope and pray each of you will grieve and then recover and that someday you will find new husbands that you will be very, very happy with and have lots of beautiful babies. I wish we could all remain together, but I know this is what is best for you, so that makes my heart glad."

Chenoa wrapped her arms around Raya's waist and held on for a long time. Raya held the young woman and smoothed her hair. "Write me, okay, Raya?" Chenoa finally asked, stepping back, her brown eyes teary.

"That's right. You can read and write now," Raya said with a gentle smile. She had taught the younger girl herself.

Chenoa smiled proudly as she nodded, and Raya laid her hand against her lovely, dark cheek.

"I will. As soon as we get settled, I'll send word to you at your parents. I'll include our address once I know it. Let me know how you are as soon as you can. I'll think of you every day."

Chenoa nodded.

"May you find peace and happiness, my dear Shideezhi," Raya finished tenderly, kissing Chenoa's cheek affectionately. She had found a younger sister in Chenoa, and she loved her greatly.

Her bottom lip trembling just a little, Chenoa gave Raya one last hug and moved on to hug her mother-in-law. Niz came back to

Raya after bidding Mother Emaline goodbye and gave her a long hug as well.

"You have become my sister in the last three years," Niz told her.

Raya smiled, her eyes watery, as she put her hands on the woman's shoulders. "As you have become mine."

"I'm going to miss you very much," Niz continued, her dark eyes moist. "And your special dishes and spices."

Raya laughed, the sound almost foreign in the grief-filled house, as she pulled her sister-in-law into another hug. "And I will miss cooking for you." Tears filled Raya's eyes as the sound of the neighbor's horses pulling up in the yard filled the air. "Give yourself grace to heal. You have lost much," Raya said, squeezing Niz one last time before kissing her cheek and releasing her.

"We all have," Niz replied as she stepped back, her words thick with emotion.

Chenoa and Niz took up their satchels and walked out the door together without looking back. Raya and Mother Emaline went out onto the porch to wave goodbye and watched as the wagon disappeared around the bend in the lane. Just like that, Nizhoni and Chenoa were gone. Raya felt their loss greatly. Her sisters and friends were gone, just as Luke was gone, just as her brothers-in-law and nephew were gone, never to be seen again. She wiped her eyes with the hem of her apron and turned to Mother Emaline.

The lady's eyes were full of tears. Raya went to her and hugged her, resting the side of her head against Mother Emaline's. "I have not only lost my sons and grandson this week, but two of my daughters," Mother Emaline whispered.

"We will get through this," Raya told her, hugging her tightly around the waist.

Mother Emaline was quiet for a long time, her tears flowing freely. Finally, she responded. "He may have taken so many that I hold dear, but I thank the LORD He compelled you to stay with me."

UP FROM THE ASH HEAP

"From this day forward, I'll go wherever you go, I'll love those you love, and I'll make my home where you make yours. You're stuck with me now," Raya told her, mustering up a brave, bright smile.

Mother Emaline smiled too, and patted Raya's head. "Praise God for that."

Five

Raya looked up from her thread and needle, startled, when a loud knock sounded at the door. She was mending a tear in her dress that happened just that morning when she was tending the stock and caught it on a nail. Mother Emaline was mending a piece of Alex's clothing, which they would sell in town to buy another small bag of flour. Now, they looked toward the door together. "Why, I wonder who that might be?" Mother Emaline thought aloud.

Raya hurried to her feet before Mother Emaline could. The woman hadn't been well since the day of the fire—too much smoke in her lungs, the doctor had said, which had aggravated a preexisting condition of weak lungs. The woman had already been frail before the fire from recurring bouts of sickness over the past three years, and now a cough had settled in her chest, and she seemed a little less steady on her feet each week. Raya was set on making her rest as much as possible before they embarked on their journey east. Swinging open the heavy front door, her heart leapt into her throat. "Amhil?"

"Choti behen," Amhil answered, greeting her tersely as his younger sister in the language of their homeland.

Shocked into a state of numbness, Raya stepped silently out onto the front porch, pulling the door shut behind her, her eyes never leaving Amhil's face. "What are you doing here?" she asked, using her native tongue. She hadn't spoken a word of it in five years, yet it came back to her instinctively.

"I've heard the news of your husband's passing. Why do you not wear white? Have I heard wrong? From what I heard, he has not yet been gone thirteen days."

She stood still and quiet for several long moments, too stunned to speak. She had not seen her brother in five years, and now, he stood before her on this beautiful late summer afternoon as intimidating and commanding as ever. Finally, she began to recover from her shock and found her voice. "No, you have heard right. My husband has passed away." She paused. "How did you know?"

"One of your neighbors traveled down river. He stopped in at the store and was telling us the news from out this way. Uncle recognized the name right away and got father."

Raya nodded her understanding. Although she hadn't considered the possibility of her family hearing about the tragedy, she understood that news spread. "Amhil, would you like to sit down?" She motioned to one of the chairs situated at the far end of the porch. Watching her brother cross the floor to the wooden rocking chairs and sit down stiffly, she followed slowly behind trying to compose herself and collect her thoughts. Raya hadn't seen him in five years. To be talking to him now felt surreal.

"How long has it been since the passing of your husband?" Amhil demanded.

"Eleven days," Raya said softly, sitting down as well.

Amhil's full lips flattened into a hard line. "Where is your white dress? What is this black that you wear? Are you not in mourning, sister? Have you forgotten the ways of your people?"

Raya stared at the porch floor, intimidated and frightened. "I do not. . ." She paused to collect herself and clear her throat. "It is the way of my new family that those in mourning wear black," she told him, not daring to look up.

"And what of *your* family? What of your ancestors? What of the gods?"

She had a choice to make all over again. She could easily forsake her new life and go back to her old ways. She was confident he had come to take her home. By doing so, she was certain she would not meet with any opposition from Mother Emaline, whom she knew still only wanted the best for her, and she would not have to anger her brother. The option was so very appealing, especially sitting here beside him, the sound of his authoritative voice ringing in her ears.

Still, she knew there was but one choice to make—a choice she had already made. Now, she only had to summon the courage to tell Amhil—a task she had not thought she would have to endure. "I do not follow the ways of our ancestors any longer, Amhil. I serve the God of my husband." She could feel his displeasure without having to look at him.

"And what God is that?" Amhil asked, his voice hard, his eyes narrowed.

"The God of Abraham, Isaac, and Jacob."

Amhil stared at her so long that she felt faint under his disapproving assessment. Finally, he spoke. "Do you expect Father to let you serve this new god while under his roof? No, you will renounce it and return to our gods." Amhil stood. "Get your things. We will not stay here in this place of death any longer. We will both have to wash before entering our father's house as it is."

Raya could feel her breath quickening, and her heart was drumming. To make the decision to stay with Mother Emaline had been difficult enough. To tell her brother she no longer served his gods had been terrifying. Now, to refuse to return to her father's house with him . . . she did not know if she had the strength.

Amhil stood and crossed the porch impatiently. Looking back, he realized she was not behind him but still sitting in her chair instead. Showing his first bit of emotion, his face gentled just a little, and he held out a hand. "Little sister, come. It's time to go. Mother has sent me to fetch you. She's expecting our return. You don't belong here anymore."

Raya's breath caught at the mention of her mother. She wanted her to come home? Should she? She knew her parents would expect it now that they knew about her widowhood.

She knew they would accept the responsibility of her keep until they could arrange another advantageous marriage. Perhaps her mother missed her, even if she hadn't reached out these past five years. Did Raya's responsibility lie with her parents or with her mother-in-law? Raya closed her eyes against all the questions. She took a deep breath, and when she opened her eyes again, one truth stood out from the questions Amhil's comments stirred up in her. Her mother was home in a place where she had grown comfortable with her uncle, father, and Amhil around her. If Raya didn't return, very little would change for her mother, but if she did go with Amhil, Mother Emaline would face everything changing, alone.

"Amhil, I'm not going back with you. This is my home. I will stay with my mother-in-law. I am her only family now. I cannot leave her," Raya told him weakly, her voice unsteady. Though she kept her eyes downcast, she knew his face would be darkening. She was raised to be obedient in all things. Well, she could not be obedient in this. Not this time.

"I'm taking you home as I was instructed. Get your belongings!" he ordered.

She shook her head, still keeping her eyes on the porch floor.

Amhil spat on the porch at her feet. "Who are you? You do not look like the little sister I knew five years ago. You shame your family. Here you are in a dress! Your sari nowhere in sight. Mourning your husband in black. Saying you no longer follow the gods of our ancestors. Forget it! Leave your things. They're not suitable for you, anyway. We're leaving."

Raya came up out of her chair, raising her eyes to meet his, spurred on by the finality of his words. "I'm not going! I'm staying with Mother Emaline. She is my family now! Her ancestors are my ancestors, her home is my home, her family is my family!" she told him, her eyes flashing. "I will return to the East with her when she leaves in a few weeks, Brother! My place is with her. I have made my decision, so do not come here and try to change my mind."

Her brother took a step back, both shocked and appalled by her behavior and her words. "The East?" he echoed. "Why in the world would you go to the East? Do you know what they will do with a girl like you?"

Raya looked away.

"Do you not remember what it was like before we got to the West, little sister? Do you forget such shame so quickly?" He crossed the porch floor and took her chin in his hand, his fingers digging into her flesh painfully. "They will not be kind to you. They will not respect you. You will endure much persecution. They will not allow you to make your home among them! They will not allow you to claim their ancestors!"

"Be that as it may, I will stay with Mother Emaline," Raya answered, her voice shaky. Everything he said was true. She did remember. She remembered the East all too well. She knew how people would treat her if she went back. She knew how difficult life would be.

"You have turned stupid in the years you've been away, little sister! Come home with me. You will have food and shelter and fine things. You will have every comfort you could ever want. If you go with your dead husband's mother, you will be hungry and cold, dressed in rags and forced to live the life of a slave."

Finding a strength she didn't know she had, she raised her chin and met his eyes. "What is it to be full of stomach and satisfied with material things if my spirit is dying and my conscience unclean?"

"You are a fool," Amhil scoffed. "Shall I return to my mother empty-handed and tell her of your faithless and rebellious ways? Surely not. I think I would rather tell her the reports were wrong. That you died too. Then at least she would not know of your disgrace."

He was testing her, covering her with guilt in an attempt to persuade her, and she knew it. Raya folded her hands demurely, lowering her eyes. "Tell her what you feel you must."

Amhil threw up his hands. "You will starve, little sister! Or worse! But let it be known that I have done my duty. I have tried to take you home."

"Yes, you have. Thank you for coming, Amhil. Truly. I appreciate your kindness," she told him sincerely. He was trying to do right by her.

Amhil studied her for a long moment, then turned on his heel and left without so much as another word. He mounted his horse and rode off at a gallop, never looking back.

Raya watched until he disappeared around the curve in the lane. Then she turned and went back into the house.

Mother Emaline was watching for her, and her face was lined with questions. "What was that all about?"

"That was my brother, Amhil," Raya answered.

Mother Emaline smiled gently. "English, please, Raya."

Raya stopped where she was and sighed, leaning back against the door she had just closed. "I'm sorry, Mother. I didn't even realize... That was my brother, Amhil. He came to take me back to my father's house." Raya saw the look of concern on Mother Emaline's face, followed by an expression of sorrow. "He has left now," she finished.

Mother Emaline's surprise was obvious, as was her relief, but she quickly recovered. "You should have at least invited him in for tea."

Raya smiled, letting out a deep sigh and relaxing for the first time since the moment she saw Amhil standing on the porch. "Why don't I make us some instead?"

***

Amhil came again a week and three days later. Knowing the time and effort he had sacrificed by coming all the way to her valley not once, but twice, Raya agreed to hear him out. He ranted and raved at Raya, induced guilt, and tried to stir up fear in her heart, all in an effort to convince her to return home with him. Touched by his sincere concern for her should she return to the East, she tried to be as gentle as possible while telling him that she would not be going back to her father's house. She explained that she had been given to her husband, and his wish would be for her to remain with his mother.

Amhil went so far as to say that her father would allow her to worship her new God while in his house, as long as she paid proper homage to the gods of their ancestors as well. While it was almost enough to make Raya reconsider her decision, the spirit within her shrunk back from her brother and the offer he extended, and she knew she could not accept. She did not know enough about her faith or the God she now served to be able to hold to the practices apart from the presence of other believers; nor in a place where so many other gods were worshipped. What was more, she could not leave Mother Emaline alone. To leave with Amhil would mean leaving her completely and utterly desolate.

He cautioned her that he would not return, that he would leave and wash his hands of her. What happened to her in the months and years ahead was not of his concern. He had offered her safety and comfort, food, and provision, and she had denied it all, not once, but twice. He warned her it would not be offered again.

Regardless of his threats, Amhil was forced to leave alone for a second time. Setting off for their uncle's store yet again, his expression was like a storm cloud as his chestnut mare thundered down the lane.

She had stood her ground. That one fact alone assured Raya that she was doing the right thing. If there was any wavering within her, Amhil's tactics would have been her undoing. As it was, she was more certain than ever of her decision to accompany Mother Emaline east.

Six

Raya and Mother Emaline ate sparingly, and Raya rationed the food for the animals. Within three weeks of Amhil's last visit, a buyer had been found for their valley. The horses, milk cows, and even the hens were sold, and after they settled their debts in town, they had enough money to pay their passage on first a stage, then a train bound for Cincinnati.

On the morning of their departure, Raya made the walk over to her own cabin and stood for a long time, looking around the home she had shared with Luke. It was the first time since the fire she'd spent any time in the cabin, save grabbing necessities to move up to Mother Emaline's. Now, she felt almost reverent standing in the small home. She ran her hand over the furniture he had built as she looked lovingly around the room.

She had shared such wonderful years with her husband here. Luke was a good man, kind and gentle. He loved and cared for her. He took her as a young, frightened foreigner and made her his bride. She felt her eyes swimming with tears, remembering that she would never again share this home with him, never add on as he had intended, never see their children sitting before the fireplace as she had dreamt. After today, she would never again see this place that held so many memories of him. Walking away from the cabin would mean walking away from her last physical remembrance of him.

She had sold his clothing to the general store in town to secure a few more coins to provide for her and Mother Emaline's future, just as Emaline had sold Father Julius', Alex's, and Will's. She had given the heavy quilt that had covered their bed to a couple who had only recently arrived in town, having lost their wagon and supplies while going over the mountains. Luke had never sat for a photograph. All that was left of him was the cabin and the bed, table, and chairs that he had fashioned with his own hands. All of that was included in the sale.

She glanced around the small room looking for something, anything, that she could take with her as a memento. Then she glanced down at the handkerchief she held in her clutched hand. It was a small item, but it had been his. He had kept it tied around his neck, had used it to breathe through when operating the saws, had used it to dry her tears whenever they talked about the babies they hadn't had. She traced his initials in the corner of the handkerchief, where she herself had stitched them. She'd been carrying it since the day of the fire, using it to dry her frequent tears, so it hadn't been sold with all the rest of the clothing. Now, she realized, she had her memento. It wasn't much, but it was something to remember him by. This one thing she could keep. She tucked it carefully into her apron pocket, feeling comforted that she was taking something of Luke's with her.

Picking up her satchel, which contained her three nicest dresses and the few other garments she could fit inside, she walked slowly out of the house. She glanced around one last time before shutting the door on the home her husband had built for her.

Crossing the yard, she found herself standing before the pile of ashes that marked the site of the family's great loss. The metal blades of half a dozen saws stuck up from the ashes, jagged and singed. The valley was quiet and still. The silence of it rang in her ears; it had always been so loud and full of activity when the men were alive.

Looking down at the pile of black rubbish, Raya dropped to her knees and sifted her hands through the mess. This is where her future, her security, her life as she knew it, had gone up in smoke. This was where her husband died. He had taken his last breath here. Worked his last day here.

UP FROM THE ASH HEAP

She tried not to think of how frightened and desperate he must have been as he tried to get out of the burning building. The thought was too painful, her imaginings too traumatic.

She leaned into the ashes, her palms spread flat on them, hot tears coursing down her cheeks. Luke's ashes were here, in this place, along with the ashes of the men who felt like her brothers.

She cried, allowing herself to experience the tragedy of the event and the grief that still consumed her heart. When she left, she would never again see this place, never again see their blackened final resting ground. In time, the ashes would disperse and the mountain rain would wash any that remained away. Next spring, little blades of grass would shoot up and brave little flowers would uncurl their leaves to the sun, clinging tightly to the rocky mountain soil. Nothing would be left to mark the spot where her husband and brothers had lived and died. Tears ran from her face as she allowed herself an uninterrupted and unhurried moment to say goodbye to her husband, her brothers, her happy life. Then she stood to her feet, went down to the little creek, and washed her face and hands in the cold mountain water. She picked up her satchel and continued on her way to the main cabin.

This time, she crossed the yard quickly, trying not to notice how quiet the valley sounded or how the blackened pile of ashes rose up from the flame-singed ground. As she entered the main house, Mother Emaline was just adding the family Bible to her own satchel.

Turning, she smiled at Raya as she entered. Mother Emaline's eyes were still red and swollen, but her tears had dried. "Are you ready, dear?"

Raya glanced around the house and out the windows at the dense forest and the towering peaks that would soon be covered with snow and wanted to say that she wasn't. She wasn't ready to leave their home. She wasn't ready to accept the fact that her husband and their way of life were gone. She certainly wasn't ready to begin the long journey to the East, knowing that upon their arrival, they would be just as destitute and hopeless. But there, she would be reviled for the color of her skin.

She said none of it, though. What would be the point? Mother Emaline could not rewind the past any more than Raya could, and to share her apprehensions would only result in fresh tears and another heartfelt plea from Emaline to return to her family. Instead, Raya nodded, clutching her satchel in both hands while waiting for Mother Emaline to finish her packing.

When Emaline was ready, they stood arm in arm and looked around one last time. Their house, that had been full of such laughter, family, peace, and merriment, was still and quiet. "I will miss them," Mother Emaline said, her voice wobbling.

Knowing they were saying goodbye to the people and memories more than the physical house, Raya dipped her head. "As will I."

"Thank you for cleaning the house, dear. It looks nice," Emaline told her, dragging her fingertips beneath her eyes.

Raya answered with a humble nod.

"It disturbs me that we had to sell at less than half of our property's worth, but I suppose it's all we can expect. Without a man to take care of us, Raya, I'm afraid we have to face the reality that we're going to be taken advantage of on many occasions."

"It's because we had to sell in such a hurry, Mother, that's all," Raya comforted softly, knowing what she said was only partly true. The man who bought their homes and valley was known for being a shrewd businessman. Knowing their precarious situation, he used their dire need and his ready money to swindle them out of the price they deserved. He would undoubtedly turn around and sell the property to new buyers for nearly double what he paid them for it. Yet, not knowing when another offer might be made to them and seeing how their food supplies were dwindling, they felt they had no other choice but to accept. With his finances secure, the new owner had the luxury of waiting for a good offer for the property. They simply did not.

Mother Emaline pulled the door shut, then walked down the porch stairs and started down the lane without pausing. Raya followed, matching the length of her strides to the older woman's steps.

At the bend in the lane, Mother Emaline turned and looked back. Despite her efforts to stay composed, a small whimper escaped from between her parted lips, and she began to cry. "I came here a full woman, but now I am leaving empty."

Mother Emaline's statement pricked Raya's heart. She had given up so much to make sure the woman was not leaving alone. Yet, she knew what she meant. Mother Emaline had come to this place as a young woman with a husband and three strapping sons, resources, and hope for the future. Now, she was leaving with only her grief and her widowed daughter-in-law.

Out of tears, Raya simply looped her arm through Emaline's and encouraged her to keep moving. The walk to town was long and parts of it steep. They needed to be on their way if they were to catch the stage. It didn't ever stop for long.

Raya wished now that she had pressed Mother Emaline to accept their neighbor's offer of a ride into town, but alas, the woman had wanted to travel the road for the last time privately, and Raya had respected her wishes. It was a walk they had made often enough, but now, with Mother Emaline's health failing since the fire, Raya wished she had insisted on a ride. However, it was too late now, and she had no option but to press Mother Emaline to keep moving forward.

Once they came to the outskirts of town, winded and weary, they made their way to the church and went past it to the cemetery. There, they entered the rudimentary gate that kept the small collection of graves a private place.

Weaving respectfully through the final resting places of the town's past inhabitants, Raya and Mother Emaline stopped in front of the three simple crosses at the back of the cemetery that all bore the same last name. The crosses were close together, as they did not mark graves but simply stood in remembrance. Stepping forward, Raya knelt down and placed fresh flowers they had picked that morning from the hillside of wildflowers north of the house, at the base of each cross. Once each cross had a small bouquet at its base, they went in search of Father Julius' grave and laid a bouquet on it as well.

When they finished their task, Raya reached for Mother Emaline's hand. "We have to go, Mother."

Mother Emaline's blue eyes were closed, and silent tears trickled down her cheeks. "It feels wrong to leave them."

Raya didn't say anything, afraid she would take advantage of Emaline's momentary weakness and try to convince her not to return to the East. To do so because of her own fear would be wrong.

"How does a mother leave her only children and her beloved husband?" Mother Emaline whimpered.

Raya shook her head. "I do not know, except that I do know they're not here to leave. Father Julius has been gone many years, and your sons' bodies are in a burnt down mill, not laid beneath the soil here."

"You're right. I know you're right."

Raya gave the woman another minute, then guided her toward the small gate. "The stage will be here soon. We have to hurry."

Mother Emaline didn't respond but allowed Raya to guide her out of the cemetery and through the dusty streets toward the general store where the stagecoach stopped. They had already settled all their debts around town from the proceeds of the sale of their valley, so they simply sat down on a bench in front of the store to wait.

Mother Emaline's tears had dried, and with a serious expression, she turned to Raya and took her hand. "Raya, are you sure you want to do this?"

Raya glanced away as she felt her hands begin to shake. It was the question she had been asking herself all morning. To say she was going to stay with Mother Emaline and go east was one thing, but to purchase a ticket, board a stagecoach and go . . .

it was altogether different. The fear of the unknown—and the known—was most frightening. Raya shuddered within. Yet, she knew she could not leave Mother Emaline to fend for herself so late in life, nor did she wish to return to her father's house or his superstitious ways. She nodded.

"Darling, I look at you and see a beautiful woman, inside and out, but back east . . . things will be different."

Raya nodded. "I know that."

"The war is over, and Indian attacks not nearly so frequent as in days past, but I'm not certain how people will treat you. Though your features are fine, and your skin not very much darker than mine," Mother Emaline observed slowly. "That will help."

"Dark enough that I am quite certainly not white," Raya added, knowing it was true. She knew she was pretty. Her features were as fine and delicate as the white women in town, her skin very light considering her ancestry, and Luke's constant declarations were ample proof. However, she knew it wouldn't matter in the East where people were judged only by the whiteness of their skin. In the East, her darkened skin would be a fault that overshadowed everything else and marked her as a social outcast.

"People may treat you unkindly," Mother Emaline continued slowly, as if not wanting to speak the words but feeling she must.

Raya took a deep breath. "I know, Mother Emaline. Trust me. I traveled through the East with my family when I was young. I remember how people treated us. And I still choose to go. I will not leave you."

Raya's words seemed to bring Mother Emaline relief, and the woman settled back against the bench. "We're living in a new age now. The slaves have been free for several years, the Indians are not causing as much trouble as they were . . . at least not in the East . . . perhaps things will be better than we assume."

"Either way, I'm coming," Raya said, patting Mother Emaline's cold hand. Tucking the lady's shawl over her hands to keep them warm, Raya looked out over the town.

It was no more than a general store, one inn, a saloon, the church, a livery, and the blacksmith's shop, with a number of small clapboard homes scattered about. Still, it was large for a mountain town, with the majority of the residents being soldiers who lived in the fort, followed by hunters or trappers who were dispersed over the surrounding mountains. There were a few dozen miners who were hoping to strike it big and a few less farmers, who worked hard for a meager profit as they tried to get a decent crop out of the high valley. Despite the sometimes difficult living conditions, the residency continued to grow steadily each year, supplying work for the mill, as did the residents of the surrounding towns.

Raya noticed with a slight smile that the aspen grove on the west side of town was beginning to foretell the arrival of fall and whisper of the coming winter. Its rustling leaves were taking on a golden hue, and it wouldn't be long before the tall trees with the smooth white trunks were completely arrayed in golden splendor. Shortly after, snow would begin to fall. Soon, the small mountain town would be sacked in for the winter and cut off from civilization.

Turning her head, Raya looked to the East, where the wide valley gave way to the high mountains. They would have to go through them to reach the train station in Denver, where they would ride the rails to Cincinnati. They were told by the storekeeper that the trip to Denver would take three to four days, an extensive amount of time for so short a distance; the rugged trails and treacherous terrain they would have to pass over accounted for the delay. Raya hoped they could beat the snow, even in the high mountains, where it had been known to snow as early as the first week of September. They were already past that on the calendar, and crossing the mountains in the snow could take an already dangerous journey and turn it fatal. Soon, the stage lines would close for the winter to protect both property and life.

Drawing in a deep breath of clean mountain air, Raya calmed the nerves within and focused her mind on enjoying the beautiful scenery that surrounded her. Once they left the mountains, they would never see them again. The thought brought her sorrow. The towering peaks were another item on the long list of things she would undoubtedly miss in the days ahead.

    She was young when her family finally found her uncle and settled down to help run his store, but she was not too young to recognize the splendor of her new surroundings. She saw many sights as she traveled as a child, but never had she seen a land so unpolluted, so untamed, or so majestic as the mountains of Colorado Territory. With its towering heights, clear blue skies, icy mountain streams, plentiful and varied wild game, and views that seemed to go on forever, her new home had won her over instantly. The breathtaking beauty and crisp, clean quality of the air had been enough to make her overlook the weeks she spent terrorized by the pitching ship and tumultuous seas, large cities full of pale people who were cruel to her family, long days of walking with little food or water, and even longer nights of being afraid of savage Indian attacks, which she heard of nearly constantly while traveling west. Upon reaching their new home in Colorado Territory, she had known the perils of the trip had been worth it. And now, she was leaving this beautiful place that had become her home.

    A cloud of dust outside of town drew her attention, and Raya watched as the stage approached from the west, the hooves of the horses causing a haze of thick dust to fill the street.

    Holding her handkerchief over her nose and mouth to keep from choking, Raya stood and helped Mother Emaline to her feet. Taking both of their satchels in hand, she stepped off the boardwalk bravely. Approaching the stagecoach driver, Raya paid their fare, lamenting the coins even as she surrendered them. The driver took their satchels, opened the door, and held out his hand to assist them. The coach swayed as Raya stepped up into it, and she quickly took her seat, grasping the window ledge as she did to steady herself. Reaching back to assist Mother Emaline, Raya helped the woman settle safely onto the seat beside her.

They politely greeted the other passengers, then waited quietly until the driver had their satchels lashed to the top amongst the others. They felt when he climbed aboard onto his seat, and shortly after, the horses took off at a fast trot. Mother Emaline and Raya both watched out the window as they traveled down the dusty main street, then watched as the buildings grew smaller as the horses took them farther away. At a sharp bend in the road, they got their last look at the town where they had both gained and lost much.

Seven

Their ride in the stagecoach felt unending and tedious. The coach traveled nearly twenty-four hours a day, stopping only to switch teams every ten to fifteen miles and to allow the passengers to eat. Raya and Mother Emaline did their best to sleep in the bumpy coach, but nights were long and uncomfortable. By the second day, Raya's nerves were wound so tight she felt like screaming. The horses moved slowly as they tried to find sure footing, and the inside of the coach was stuffy and stale.

While there were windows covered by black oiled flaps that, when pulled back, allowed passengers to see out and enjoy much-needed fresh air, Raya chose to keep the one next to her down. The last time she had lifted it, she had been unable to see any road, simply a horrifying drop-off that went down several hundred feet. With the coach lurching and swaying as usual, seeing how close they were to the cliff had nearly cost Raya the contents of her stomach. Dizzy and unwell, she sunk back weakly, letting the flap fall, opting to shut out the sunshine and fresh air for the comforting ignorance of not seeing where they were. The flap had not been lifted since.

In addition to Raya and Mother Emaline, the coach was occupied by four men. Though they acted as gentlemen, Raya was quite certain their presence aggravated them. By having women on board, the men had to limit their conversation as well as their drinking and smoking—a fact they did not seem happy about. No more eager to be trapped in the small space with the loud men,

Raya did her best simply to direct her attention elsewhere, though in such small quarters, it proved to be most difficult.

One of the men wore furs and smelled like a trapper, while the others wore top hats and tailored frock coats; all of them were loud and partial to conversation. During their journey, she learned that the three well-dressed men were traveling from Utah Territory where they had been on a business expedition of some kind. They were returning to their homes in Denver. The fourth was a trapper who had spent years wandering the American frontier. He found success in Colorado's Rockies and was going back to Denver to buy supplies before heading up into the mountains for the winter. He watched Raya with open curiosity, but the others kept their eyes averted and did not speak to her other than when politeness called for it. Each of them made small talk with Mother Emaline on several occasions.

By the time the stagecoach finally arrived in Denver, Raya was certain they needed to part with the money necessary to spend a night in an inn before boarding a train and continuing their journey. She had been bounced, jarred, bumped, and jostled to the point her entire body ached, and she felt as if she might be permanently ill. Her legs were stiff, and the sum of her body protested when she was finally able to climb out of the coach and stand on the street in Denver. Feeling as she was, she could only imagine Mother Emaline's discomfort, and quickly turned to give her support as she exited the coach.

While they waited for the driver to retrieve their satchels for them, Mother Emaline and Raya spent a few moments taking in their new surroundings. Although Denver was still a small and rugged city compared to those in the East, it was the biggest town either of them had been in for over a decade, and it was growing rapidly. With the completion of the railroad going north to Cheyenne and east to Kansas just a few years earlier, visitors, freight, and new residents were flooding the city.

The collection of sounds, smells, and sights was overwhelming. Seeing that Mother Emaline's face was pale and her hands shaky, Raya hurried to guide her to a nearby inn and out of the chilly fall air. The recent influx of visitors had driven up the cost of a room, but Raya didn't question the rate. Mother Emaline had to rest, of that she was certain.

Exhausted from their long journey and the restless nights on the coach, they went straight up to their room, and Raya insisted Mother Emaline lie down to sleep. When Mother Emaline implored Raya to lie down and rest herself, Raya complied, and they both quickly fell asleep and slept deeply.

When Raya woke slightly to turn over, she realized darkness was settling over the room. Afraid they would miss the evening meal, she forced herself to wake up fully, pushing herself to a seated position while rubbing her eyes, still gritty from the dusty coach. She quickly woke Mother Emaline, and, after washing, they went down to eat. Thankful to have hot food once again, they ate slowly, enjoying their supper. Once they were finished, they returned to their room and slept soundly through the night.

The next morning, they made the long walk to the train station, their satchels in hand, opting to save the fare of a carriage. They were only two blocks away from the train station when Raya heard Mother Emaline let out a startled yelp of pain. Turning, she barely caught the older woman as she reeled toward her. Helping her right herself, Raya's eyebrows drew together in confused concern. "Are you alright? What happened?"

"Someone pushed me," Mother Emaline accused, looking around. Suddenly, she let out a gasp. "My reticule!"

As Raya's eyes jumped to Mother Emaline's empty hand, a sense of dread filled her. The reticule that carried the majority of their cash stores was missing.

In desperation, she spun, scanning the crowd for any sign of the beaded, pale green clutch. "There it is! That man! He has it!" Raya cried, spotting the green item for just a moment, the culprit looking back over his shoulder nervously. A look of panic showed on his face as he realized she saw him, and he took off running, turned a corner, and disappeared from sight.

"Help! Someone stop that man!" Raya cried, forgetting propriety and running after him, pushing her way through the crowded street. Those around her watched curiously but continued on their way. By the time she made it to the corner he had turned at, the man—and the reticule—were nowhere in sight. Her heart sinking, Raya stared down the street, searching for even a glimpse of the man so she would know which way he went. But he was gone. And with him, most of the money they had gotten from the sale of their valley, the livestock, and the clothing and household items they had tearfully parted with. A shudder of despair shook her. What had been a difficult situation now felt impossible. Behind her, Raya heard Mother Emaline calling for her. After one last look down the street, she turned, hopelessness overtaking her as she made her way back to the older woman, her feet dragging.

"Raya, what are we going to do?" Mother Emaline was wringing her hands. The woman's eyes were full of tears. "That was nearly all our money. I shouldn't have had it out. I shouldn't have been holding it in my hand. I planned to put the reticule away in my satchel once we purchased the train tickets. I don't know what I was thinking. I had it looped . . . it was looped around my wrist. I had no idea someone could pull it off and take it so easily. I was just keeping it out until we paid for the tickets. Oh, what have I done?"

Mother Emaline's wail fit their dire situation. Tears stung Raya's eyes, and she took a deep, shuddering breath, pulling herself up to her full height, and reaching out to put her hands on Mother Emaline's shoulders. "This is not your fault. We are going to be okay. We will make do. You'll see." She sounded more confident than she felt.

"Did you get a good look at the thief? We could go to the authorities."

"I saw him," Raya answered. "He had a gray cap . . . a white shirt . . ."

"Anything else? That could be anyone, dear." Mother Emaline's voice dripped with despair.

Raya racked her mind, and her brief memory of the thief's face and finally shook her head dismally. "No, that's all I remember. I barely got a glance at him before he was gone."

Mother Emaline put her hand to her mouth. "Oh," she moaned, tears spilling out of her kind, blue eyes. "First the fire, then the baby, now this . . . Raya, I don't know what we're going to do. I'm so sorry."

Raya wrapped her arms around her mother-in-law and held her for a long moment, her thoughts swirling as she did. People streamed around them, hurrying on their way. Fear and anguish vied for her attention, and she pressed a hand to her forehead. Trying to make a plan, she stated what she knew. "We split the money in case something like this happened. Thank goodness for that."

"It wasn't even half."

"But it's something. We have to hold onto that. We'll continue on to the train station and see if we have enough," Raya continued. "Once we get to Cincinnati, I'll find work."

"Shouldn't we go talk to the authorities? Perhaps they could find the thief."

"You were right, though. How would they find a man with a white shirt and gray cap in a city so large? And we would undoubtedly miss our train and have to stay another several nights in Denver while they investigate . . . all while we both know it's probable he will never be found, and even if he is, the money will likely be gone by then." Raya paused, the truth of her words sending waves of anguish over her. "I don't know, Mother. What do you think we should do?"

Mother Emaline looked one way and then the other. The crowd continued to split and go around them, the sidewalks full of people hurrying in all directions. Raya looked, too. There were just so many people. Too many people ever to find one man who had stolen a small, pale green reticule from a frail, heartsick woman.

When Mother Emaline met her eyes again, Raya recognized a look of defeat on her face.

"They would never find him," Mother Emaline admitted softly.

Raya pressed her lips together and shook her head.

"I suppose we have no choice but to make do with what we have."

Raya had to agree. It was a difficult pill to swallow, and yet what else could be done? Pressing on was all she knew to do. Looping her arm through Mother Emaline's, she blinked back her tears, moving forward with a strength she didn't feel. They continued on their way, their situation even more desperate than it had been.

Once they arrived at the train station, they found with relief that they still had enough money to get them to Cincinnati. Raya stood in line to purchase tickets, sending the distraught Mother Emaline to rest on a nearby bench. With thoughts tumbling through her mind, her heart was drumming as person after person in front of her purchased their ticket and exited the line.

They had lost nearly three-fourths of their money. What had been a difficult situation was now dismal. But what were their options? They could secure passage back to their high mountain town on the stage, but then what? They had no home, no work, no family. The situation was no brighter in Denver. The only thing she could think to do was to continue on as planned and see what could be done once they arrived in Cincinnati. Or Raya could purchase a train ticket for Mother Emaline and send her on her way, hoping someone would take pity on the ailing lady, while purchasing a stage ticket for herself and going home to her father's house.

Raya watched with growing apprehension as the last person in front of her paid for his ticket. It was nearly her turn. And with their money stolen, their future even more bleak than it had been, Raya was only too aware that this was her last chance to turn back before making the dreaded trip east. This was when she had to know without a shadow of a doubt that staying with

Emaline was the right thing for her to do . . . even in light of their present circumstances. After she stepped on the train, she couldn't go home.

When it was her turn at the window, her tongue felt thick and forming the words to request their tickets was difficult. Finally, she spoke the words, and with shaking hands, she paid the fare.

Purchasing their tickets felt so final—there was no going back, no changing her mind. While they were already days away from her father's house, the train ticket was a stronger commitment—a greater hindrance in returning home to safety and provision.

But she had already paid the money, and the ticket master handed her two tickets to Cincinnati. Her moment of decision over, Raya took a shaky breath. She had been so sure about what she should do before they left home, and she knew it was still the right choice, but she was frightened. Especially now when most of what little they had was gone. How were two women supposed to live on a sum so meager, especially when work was not guaranteed, and they had no prospects in sight?

Despite the circumstances, with her ticket in hand, she resigned herself to the fact that she was truly traveling to the East—a frightening and hostile land. She took a deep breath and folded her hands tightly as she made her way back to where Mother Emaline sat on the bench looking weepy.

"I just can't believe it," Mother Emaline murmured. "I can't believe that man stole the reticule right out of my hand."

"It's dreadful," Raya agreed sympathetically. Then she squeezed her mother-in-law's arm gently in a comforting gesture. It was tragic, but they couldn't go back and change the past hour. They had to move on. "Come, let's see what we have left."

She set about carefully counting the money they had remaining, using the folds of her skirt to keep anyone around them from seeing their slight stash. "Paying off the accounts at home was more than we had hoped, the stagecoach and train tickets were expensive, and of course we hadn't planned on what happened today, but we should still have enough for food on the trip, and if we're wise, we'll have a very small reserve for when we arrive in Cincinnati," Raya said slowly.

Mother Emaline nodded, still teary. "That's good, dear. At least we had thought to split it. I don't know what we would have done if..."

"Let's think of happier things," Raya suggested, slipping their money back into her satchel. "Like how large this train station is, for instance."

Sitting together in silence, they watched people mulling through the station. Many of the patrons were businessmen dressed in top hats and frock coats, much like the men in the stagecoach, but there were occasional women and children, soldiers, trappers, and miners. They watched them all in wonder.

"I've never ridden on a train," Raya finally said, falling back on the easy chatter she was accustomed to.

"Nor have I," Mother Emaline answered. "It will be a new adventure for us both."

"Yes, it will. We must think of that," Raya agreed, setting her mind to do so.

The train showed up right on schedule an hour later, and Raya carried her own satchel along with Mother Emaline's, leaving the older woman's hands free to safely board the train. Raya followed her across the platform and onto the train car after handing their tickets to the conductor. She followed Mother Emaline down the narrow center corridor and stowed their bags as Mother Emaline slipped into an empty seat.

As she sat down, Raya looked around in awe. The train car was beautifully finished and luxuriant—nothing at all like the stage they took to Denver. They had their own section of the car with a narrow door that could be closed to shield them from the curious eyes of others. The woodwork was a beautiful black walnut, and the fixtures were polished brass. The seats were plush and comfortable, and there were framed mirrors on either side of the window. The faint smell of smoke hung in the air as oil lamps burned in the narrow center corridor even in the light of day.

UP FROM THE ASH HEAP

As they boarded the train, Raya had overheard a porter explain to another passenger that a bed would fold down from the ceiling in the evening to allow them to rest, and now she looked up to see if it was so. After identifying the bottom side of the bed, she rested back against her seat, her eyes as wide as a child's.

Although she had never been on a train, this was never how it was in her imaginings. She had expected the comfort and conditions of the stage or perhaps a covered wagon like the one her family had traveled west in. This opulence was something she had never seen the likes of. While still in the depot, she had overheard a group of travelers complaining that the train they were to travel on was not one of the newest, nicest models. Now aboard, she could not fathom anyone complaining about accommodations such as these.

For just a moment, her heart began to race. Seeing the luxurious car, seeing how other passengers were going about as if it were nothing special, she got a small glimpse of how different city life was going to be from life on the frontier, to which she had become so accustomed. Perhaps even all of her imagining and memories from the past had not begun to prepare her for the civilization she was about to enter.

The conductor gave the last call, drawing her back from her troubling thoughts. The train groaned and scraped, then lurched forward into motion. Watching everything that was taking place, Raya folded her hands in her lap and tried to keep them from trembling. Despite the grief that threatened to overwhelm her as they began their departure from Colorado Territory, her despair over the theft, and her fear about the future, she was determined to take in this new experience. Whatever awaited them in Cincinnati was tomorrow's problem. Today, she was full, warm, sheltered, and safe. She would do her best not to continue letting yesterday's tragedy or tomorrow's unknown overshadow her gratefulness for her present day. After all they'd been through in the last month and a half, she had never been so aware that tomorrow was not guaranteed, nor what a gift simply being alive really was. For now, that had to be enough.

Eight

At the train station in Denver, Raya had overheard a group of gentlemen talking about the dining cars the trains in the East had recently acquired. They had said they were as comfortable as a fine restaurant with the food to go right along with it. They spoke of feasting on veal, buffalo, oysters, and champagne, all while riding the rails. Raya was disappointed to hear that trains traveling through the West did not yet have dining cars, as the threat of Indian and bandit attacks were still high and the innovative new cars were expensive. Instead, the porter told them the train would stop at depots where a meal could be purchased.

As promised, the train stopped for the noon meal at a town several hours up the tracks. Raya and Mother Emaline tended to their needs and washed their faces before sitting back down in their seats, thankful for the brief chance to stretch their legs without having to worry about losing their balance. Watching the rest of the passengers making their way into an inn just to the west of the depot for lunch, Raya pulled a bundle out of her satchel and untied the towel to lay out the bread and cheese it contained.

They had finished the bread and strips of dried venison she had brought from home while on the stage. She had purchased the fresh loaf of bread and block of cheese just that morning at the train station in Denver, knowing their meager budget would not allow them to eat at inns for every meal. She broke some of the bread off for herself and Mother Emaline, then cut slices of the cheese with a knife she had brought along. It was a simple lunch, but it was sufficient.

Mother Emaline gave thanks for the food, and they ate slowly, making it last. "It feels odd not to milk the cows in the mornings," Raya commented, eating her cheese.

"I'm sure it does. Our lives have changed greatly, Raya."

"Yes, they have," Raya agreed.

"Like this meal, for instance," Mother Emaline continued slowly. "Never in my life have I had to ration food before. At home, we had plenty . . . certainly we didn't have all the same delicacies we enjoyed in Cincinnati once we were on the frontier, but there was never a lack of tasty things on our dinner table. Now, we have cheese and bread . . . likely one of the simplest meals I've ever eaten. And yet, this is our new reality, Raya. Yesterday has come and gone, and what we're left with is how things are."

Raya looked up quickly, concerned by the hopeless sorrow she heard in Mother Emaline's voice. "It's a fine meal. We don't need as much as what we are accustomed to. There are only two of us to eat it," she pointed out, hoping her cheerful reply would encourage the older woman.

"I'm thankful we have food to eat at all. When you're being disciplined by the LORD, nothing should be taken for granted."

"Mother, you're not being disciplined," Raya quickly replied, soothing her mother-in-law.

"Don't say that, Raya," Mother Emaline answered forcefully, surprising the younger girl. "I *am* being disciplined by a Heavenly Father who loves me enough to do so."

Raya shook her head, not understanding.

"How could I not be? I left Cincinnati with a full house, a full purse, a full heart; I am returning empty. Empty in every way."

"That's not discipline. It can't be. You said your God was kind," Raya objected, hoping to make Mother Emaline see reason.

"Raya, when we left Cincinnati, it wasn't under the direction of God. We didn't feel He was calling us west. Julius feared for his money, I feared for my sons. In the Old Testament, it says not to put any other gods before God Almighty, but we both did. Julius was serving his money. I was serving my children. We didn't seek the LORD diligently in prayer, or ask if it was His will for us to go west. We simply did what we thought would protect that which we were serving." Mother Emaline paused. "The LORD is kind and merciful, Raya, but He's also just. When we make decisions that aren't in line with His will—and because of freewill we can—there are consequences for our decisions. Likewise, when we make righteous decisions, there are also consequences. We call them blessings."

"Luke's death was a consequence?" Raya asked, her heart falling.

Mother Emaline sat still and quiet, her eyes closed for several moments. "Not every hardship is a consequence, Raya; neither is every blessing. Sometimes things just happen. And the consequences, they're not doled out by God, they're natural results of walking certain paths—good or bad. God doesn't put trials on us to teach us or punish us. Trials . . . tragedies . . . happen because we live in a fallen world full of imperfection. It's because of His kindness that He works in the midst of our fallen circumstances to bring about good, even when it doesn't seem possible . . . as it does now. I don't know how to explain what happened to our men or why it happened. All I know is I feel the discipline of the LORD, and deep in my heart, I know it's good."

"Good?" Raya questioned incredulously.

"Discipline is not meant to harm us, Raya, but to encourage us to amend our ways. Better to be disciplined and begin to live in righteousness than to be left to our sinful nature and face the harsh consequences that come with sin. Discipline corrects in love to bring good; sin destroys."

Still thoroughly confused, Raya didn't understand. Yet Mother Emaline had gone back to eating her bread and cheese, and Raya was hesitant to continue the conversation. She saw how much sorrow it brought the woman. So, she kept her mouth shut and nibbled at her bread, making her small piece last as long as possible.

When they finished their meal, Raya carefully tied up the rest of the loaf of bread and wedge of cheese and put it back in her satchel. They waited in silence for the passengers to return and board the train. The train whistle blew, and then the train groaned, scraped, and lurched ahead again. This time, Raya was prepared for the jostling start, and braced herself.

During the afternoon, they talked on and off and watched the passing landscape out the window. Raya insisted that Mother Emaline rest, and she was able to take a short nap by resting her head on Raya's shoulder. When the train stopped for the evening break, Raya stood and stretched the kinks out of her back, trying to ignore the soreness the jarring train ride had inflicted.

Again, they tended their needs and washed, then ate a cold supper of bread and cheese in their booth. The porter came by and lowered their bed, and the two women marveled at the ingenious of it. Darkness had fallen by the time the passengers boarded the train again and kerosene lamps were lit in every cabin. Feeling weary from their long nigh-on week of travel, Raya suggested they retire to their bed, and Mother Emaline readily agreed. Shutting the narrow door on their small space, Raya turned down their lamp, and they soon slept, too weary to care about the jostling train or the small, hard bed.

The next day was much like the first. With so much time to think, Raya knew both their minds wandered to their husbands and their loss. Raya saw the tears Mother Emaline tried to hide behind the black mourning veil she wore, but she smoothed her hand over her own black skirt and pretended as if she didn't. If she had a veil, perhaps she, too, would give way to the tears she blinked back.

After the train stopped for the noon lunching and started on its way again, Raya watched a servant girl tending to her mistress and turned to Mother Emaline. "Slavery is ironic, don't you think, Mother Emaline? It's so hated, so accepted, and so widespread, all at the same time."

"The war is over, Raya."

"And yet slavery remains," Raya answered softly.

"Was there slavery where your parents were from?" Mother Emaline asked, her interest piqued, clearly thankful for the distraction.

"Yes. Of course, the slaves in my father's country were foreigners or those deemed to be less."

"And who deemed them less?"

"Society, I suppose. The upper caste, maybe. They just were. It was not something to be questioned. They were born into their station. Nevertheless, there was slavery. And here, the war is over, and yet slavery remains."

"Perhaps that girl is merely a servant. She's likely paid a wage."

Raya weighed Mother Emaline's words against previous experience. "Perhaps, but what is her wage? I'd like to know. Enough to live on? To be free on? Or does it tie her to her master as much as slavery would? Is her wage room and board? If so, how could she be free? She would end up on the streets, penniless and hungry." *As we soon may know*, Raya thought sadly, but she brushed the troublesome thought away.

"It makes me thankful for my freedom," Mother Emaline admitted.

Raya looked at her incredulously. "Why, we are no more free than she."

Mother Emaline shook her head, not understanding.

"My parents were servants before they came to America. They worked in another's house to add to another's wealth. Their pay was so little that they had no hope of anything else. They were stuck. They only escaped that life because my uncle was able to send them money to buy their freedom. Within my family, my mother was a slave to my father. She cooked his meals, cleaned his house, and raised his children, as was her duty. They were his, and she worked for his benefit. She was not free to leave, nor did anything belong to her. They both made their sacrifices, said their prayers, and burned their incense, in duty to their many gods, just as we pray and confess our sins and live obediently. Mother Emaline, we are all slaves to something, whether willing or not."

Mother Emaline again gave a small shake of her head. "I am no slave."

"Did you not serve your husband? Do you not serve God? I know you do. I have watched you. You are a faithful and good servant."

"It's willingly, Raya. I have been set free. My price from slavery has been paid. I serve out of love, not as a slave serves a master but willing, as a woman truly desiring to please my Beloved."

Now it was Raya's turn not to understand. She angled herself toward her mother-in-law; the conversation taking a serious turn. "You speak of love when obedience is what is required. I know this to be true. I have seen it my whole life. I have read the Scriptures, thus I know it to be true with your God as well. Luke read to me the commandments your God has. We keep those or face the consequences. He looks for our obedience. You yourself said so yesterday."

"But the first commandment is to love Him, Raya, with all your heart, soul, mind, and strength."

"And we love through obedience. I am his servant, He is my Master. We are saying the same thing, Mother."

***

Emaline looked at her sweet daughter-in-law, and wondered how to help Raya understand the truth. She was right. What they were saying sounded so similar, but Emaline knew that Raya was wrong, although she couldn't exactly put into words why. Without completely knowing how to articulate the difference, she wasn't sure how to help Raya see her mistake.

"I serve Him out of love, Raya."

"As do I. I fear and respect your Holy God. My Holy God."

Emaline could see the sincerity in Raya's brown eyes, and wished she could explain things in a way the girl would comprehend. It was a mindset she had known the girl had, a misconception she had been aware of for years, yet she had never figured out how successfully to address it.

She had watched Raya serve Luke out of duty for five years. Over time, she came to care about him deeply, even to the point of love, but even then, she would cast her eyes down and do his bidding, always the submissive servant. Luke was good to Raya, had treated her well, but there was something lacking in their marriage, something that stemmed from this view Raya had of all relationships being that of master and servant.

However, Emaline rationalized sadly, they had truly been reduced to the station of servant now, completely at the mercy of another's goodwill. With no money, no men, and no prospects, Raya would have to search out work. Due to the color of her skin, Emaline was certain admirable work would not be easy to find. Perhaps the girl's concept that she was already a servant, as was everyone around her in some way, would make the coming days easier for her.

Emaline thought again of the handsome inheritance in Cincinnati her husband or sons should have had when Julius' father eventually passed, and frustration grew within her; as women, she and Raya were not able to claim it. Though they were technically rich, they would live as if poor. They had no means by which to claim their rightful inheritance.

Focusing back on the issue at hand as a slight movement from Raya caught her attention, she sought some way to correct the girl's thinking. However, before she could find the right words, Raya changed the direction of the conversation, obviously satisfied they were saying the same thing, and thus seeing no need to discuss the issue further. Carefree once again, the girl chattered guilelessly about the scenery they were passing.

"Yes, dear, the landscape has changed quite drastically," Emaline responded, following Raya's conversation.

Nine

"Mother Emaline, what was it like in Cincinnati?" Raya asked, dragging her eyes from the landscape passing rapidly outside her window. They had left the wide, open plains, and were back amongst the rolling countryside where farms were stretched out between patches of trees. Her body sore from sitting on the bench for so long without much activity, she repositioned gingerly to face the woman beside her.

"Let's see. How would you describe it? Well, it was bustling and busy, with much freight coming through town. Pork packing plants are quite a lucrative industry, and herds of pigs frequently get herded through the streets. I was nearly caught in the middle of one once, and was so terrified, I nearly burst into tears every time I saw a pig for the next month."

Raya smiled broadly at Mother Emaline's admission. She had noticed that her mother-in-law was not fond of animals. She never went in the barn, and it was quite understood that she did not do any of the milking or collecting of eggs, no matter the occasion.

"There's a large German population that immigrated from the Old Country and found a home in Cincinnati. Much of the culture has been influenced by them . . . or I should say us. Both Julius and I hail from German descent, though Julius had some Scottish ancestors as well. The land around town has rolling hills and many trees. Not like the evergreen trees we're used to in the mountains, but trees that lose their leaves every winter and gain new ones every spring . . . trees like the ones we're passing . . . they're like the aspens, in sorts. The mighty Ohio River runs through town, which has opened much trade up to the city as goods are transported by water, though I suppose with the railroads popping up as they have, perhaps much of the freight goes by rail now rather than by boat." Mother Emaline paused and smiled faintly. "Life was good in Cincinnati, and society was varied and sophisticated. When I was young, I attended a ball nearly twice a month."

"Your family was rich?" Raya asked, curious. Mother Emaline's family was not a topic that had been discussed frequently over the past five years. Now, sitting on the train, having seen a glimpse of the culture, and yet knowing she had so much more to see, Raya wondered if Mother Emaline's years in Cincinnati had simply felt like a different lifetime after being in the West for so long.

"Hm. Yes, I suppose you could say that. We were in the high circles of Cincinnati society. So was Julius. We actually met at a ball. He was the son of a wealthy banker, and he asked me to dance three numbers with him in one evening. He came a'courting that next week, and we were married two months later."

Raya smiled. Despite the fact that Father Julius had been gone several years, Mother Emaline's voice still held great fondness when she spoke of him.

"Of course, things were very different in Cincinnati when we left. Tension was high as a result of the coming war. My mother and father had both passed away, and my brother had taken the family fortune and moved to New York City. Julius and I had been married for nigh on twenty years, and we had our three sons, so we didn't often attend the balls, though we did still frequent dinner parties on several occasions throughout the year. Every time we dined with our friends or family members, the discussion was always about the conflict between the states and the upcoming war.

"There were many who shared different viewpoints then, among our close friends, even among those in the same family. Some believed the South had the right to secede, others believed in a unified United States of America. Some agreed wholeheartedly with the abolitionists, others were as bent on slavery as their brothers who lived across the river. Tensions were high as neighbors disagreed with neighbors, reflecting a larger conflict taking place in the country. Though the true start of the war proved to still be a couple of years away, a preordained boding seemed to hang in the air. And the strangest part to me was that people seemed excited about it." Mother Emaline paused. "Everyone but us, that is. We did not see the coming conflict as something to embrace, but instead, to resist."

"That's why you left?" Raya asked. She had heard more about the Applewood family's departure from Cincinnati in the past twenty-four hours than in her previous five years in the family, yet she had more questions. None of it had seemed relevant when their life was full and busy in Colorado Territory with a mill and household to run. Now, it felt very important.

"The boys were getting to the age where they would be looked at to enlist within a few years, and despite what everyone said, we had our doubts that the war would be over within a month. Julius had quarreled with his brother—they never did see eye to eye—and he was concerned about the effect the war would have on our economic standings. He said it was risky to stay when we had so much to lose. He was referring to his money, but looking at my sons, I agreed. We decided we wanted a fresh start, away from the coming fight."

Raya nodded. She could understand such reasoning. To anticipate a coming war, knowing you had three sons within fighting age, would truly be a dreadful thing. She could only imagine the fear it must have caused Mother Emaline. "Did the boys want to join the fighting?"

Mother Emaline gave a dry chuckle. "You know Alex did. He was always looking for an adventure—some kind of entertainment."

Raya nodded, unable to hold back a smile. She could have predicted Alex would have wanted in on the action.

"Luke was the one we were most worried about, though. He was nearly old enough to join, and we knew when the need was desperate enough, recruiters wouldn't be rigid on the enlisting age. We could already see him being persuaded by his friends who were ready to lead the charge. He reasoned that it made more sense for him, a single young man, to go fight, than a father and husband who had others depending on him. He was ready to go off, win the war, and come back a hero," Mother Emaline finished softly, her expression sad.

Raya nodded, her heart swelling with pride for her husband. He was a good man. "It makes sense."

Mother Emaline shot her a look. "It might make sense, but he was my son. We left within a week of him declaring his intentions."

Raya smiled. Mother Emaline was always the mother, making sure her little nest of chicks were safe and on the straight and narrow. *Until the fire.* Raya blinked back the tears that suddenly stung her eyes.

Mother Emaline gazed out the window. "Those who weren't excited about the war were afraid. Afraid that if war came, we would lose our loved ones, and life as we knew it would be forever changed. We were afraid soldiers would invade our towns, pitching their tents and raiding for whatever they wanted or needed. We knew Kentucky would undoubtedly be under Confederate control, and the river would only stop them for so long should the war happen to swing in their favor. 'Twas a frightening thought to think of a hostile enemy encamped among us." Mother Emaline let out a long sigh.

"On the way west, there was more fear. Indians were raiding, and whites were being killed, just for the scalps on their heads. Added to that, we took our team of oxen, all we had in the world, and our sons over the treacherous mountain passes, which you know can easily claim a life or livelihood, even without factoring in the threat of Indian attacks. I'll never forget the day when we arrived safely on the far side of the high mountains. When we found our little valley, filed the claim, and stood on our own property in Colorado Territory for the first time, I remember just standing there with Julius, on that hill at the turnoff, you know," Mother Emaline waited for Raya to nod in understanding. "We watched the boys unloading the wagons, and there were no noises save their usual teasing, the birds singing, and the horses stomping. There was no one else in sight, the Indians in the area were peaceful, and there was a fort nearby. For the first time in a long time, I felt safe. All was quiet and peaceful, and I remember taking a deep breath and looking at Julius and being so thankful finally to be there that I couldn't even begin to put it into words. He looked back at me and smiled. I could tell he knew exactly what I couldn't express."

"That sounds like a beautiful moment," Raya commented, picturing the scene Mother Emaline described.

"Yes, well, it turns out tragedy can strike anywhere, even in the most peaceful of places," Mother Emaline finished sadly.

"It's true that the valley turned out to be no safer than Cincinnati, I suppose," Raya agreed.

The Applewood men met a fate in the valley that was every bit as tragic as what they might have met on the battlefield. Though Emaline left Cincinnati in hopes of keeping her children safe and well, she ended up losing them just the same.

***

In the following hours before reaching their destination, Raya kept up a lively chatter, distracting Emaline from any dismal thoughts. As they approached the city, the young woman finally fell quiet, watching out her window with rapt attention. In the momentary silence, Emaline reflected on her thankfulness for Raya's company on the journey. She wasn't certain she could have made it without her.

The young woman had been helpful at every turn, always making sure Emaline was comfortable and secure, and taking her mind off her loss with her precious conversation. She was grateful beyond words that Raya had chosen to stay with her.

Still, coming back to this city felt empty. It made the wounds of her heart raw. This was the city where she had met and married Julius, given birth to her three sons, and was known and respected in all the right circles. She had left rich and admired, with a loving family she could be proud of. Now, she was returning poor and empty. Her heart ached for all she had lost.

Her mind moved ahead to what would happen once they arrived. While still in her valley, she could not think of anything beyond simply returning to Cincinnati. It was time to go back to the place they never should have left. It was time to face the correction of the LORD. Additionally, the prospect of life in Cincinnati seemed easier—the war was over, the city familiar, and she would at least be among her own people. Now, as they were close to finishing the final leg of their long journey, she wondered what the best course of action was.

She had no close family still alive and in the area. Julius' brother had fallen in the war, and his father lived with a cousin. Her mind reeled. Only distant cousins and long-ago acquaintances remained—no one she could expect to take her and her daughter-in-law in and provide for them.

They had been careful with what remained of their money, eating only bread and cheese, making what they had stretch. With what they had left, they would simply have to find some sort of accommodations, then see what could be done.

Perhaps Raya could get a job and secure a wage. Emaline knew the girl would have no objection to the possibility and indeed was fully planning on it, though she herself disliked it. To see her son's wife, who had been a happy homemaker working hard in his home just weeks before, have to work for a meager wage just to keep food on their table and a roof over their heads, would be a hard pill to swallow.

She would prefer to take a job with Raya, but knew she was not at an age people would gladly employ, and even if she could find a job, her health would not allow it. She had fallen ill with a high fever several years back, shortly after Alex and Niz wed, and had never fully recovered. Now, her joints ached, and her movements were slow. If she overdid things, she wound up with a terrible cough and a fever that sometimes kept her bedridden for weeks. She could perhaps take in mending or darning, something she could do from her chair, but it wouldn't be enough to provide for her own needs, much less her daughter-in-law's.

Still, Raya's presence was the one thing that gave her hope. In that one kindness, she found peace that although she was being disciplined; she had not been deserted. If she had been left on her own with all of her daughters returning to their families, she would have fared no better. In fact, her situation would be far more destitute. She would be all alone in the world, without anyone to care for her or help meet her needs. More importantly, she knew loneliness would have set in immediately following Raya's departure, and her spirit would have been all but broken. She likely wouldn't have had the motivation or strength to go on. The LORD had shown kindness to her by compelling Raya to remain with her, and she would be grateful for the rest of her days.

Now, she prayed fervently that Raya would be able to secure a job upon reaching the city. With all the slaves being free, Emaline wasn't sure how the proportion of work to workers was faring. Even if there was work, she wasn't persuaded anyone would hire Raya. She was a hard worker and a quick learner, but Emaline feared no one would see beyond the brown of her skin to find her admirable qualities. In a time when the end of slavery and the rise of the negro were on the forefront of societal change, she wasn't sure what people would make of her foreign daughter-in-law who looked like a native. While mindsets toward blacks were changing, she wondered about the perception of Indians.

"Look, Mother, look how big the city is!" Raya was saying beside her. Emaline gave a half-hearted nod, her mind already on what would come next. All too soon, the train depot came into sight, and the giant machine was slowing down. Raya stood and began making preparations to disembark, keeping her hand on the seat for balance amidst the jerking and swaying of the stopping train. Fifteen minutes later, the train pulled away with its normal groans, scrapes and lurches, leaving Emaline and Raya, with their satchels, on the wooden platform in Cincinnati.

Ten

It was nearly five in the afternoon when the train pulled away from the station, leaving Raya and Mother Emaline behind, and darkness was quickly descending. The mid-September air was chilly, and the leaves were just beginning to show signs of changing. Heavy clouds were piled up in the western sky, casting shadows that were longer than normal, considering the hour.

A crowd of people bustled around them, some of them calling out gaily, spotting those they came to meet, joyous reunions ensuing. Others were all business as they collected their belongings and hurried off the platform to waiting carriages. Raya wished they had someone waiting there to meet them, but alas, there was no one waiting for them, no one who had come to carry their satchels, order a good dinner, then send them to bed, knowing how exhausted they were after their long journey. Tears of weary loneliness stung Raya's eyes.

The hum of the city was loud, and there were noises and people everywhere. The clatter of buggies and other traffic on the road outside seemed like a cacophony. Hundreds of people were shouting, conversing, laughing, children were wailing. Trains were lurching and scraping as they came into the station, whistles were blowing, conductors were calling, and axles were grinding as others pulled out. Someone outside was blowing a whistle, and a girl ran by Raya, laughing. The roar of the crowd was so different from the peaceful, quiet valley they had left behind that both women stood dazed for several moments. Raya had known it would be different than what they were used to, but this felt like a different world.

She looked around, thoroughly overwhelmed, trying to take it all in, while attempting to formulate some kind of plan. She had spent so much time dreading their arrival to Cincinnati that she had never once truly considered this moment—or what they would do once they arrived. After a quick glance at Mother Emaline, Raya knew the older woman was experiencing the same dilemma. She looked overwhelmed and stunned.

Raya's heart constricted with compassion. Mother Emaline had been in the West for as many years as Raya, and Raya was certain things were very different from what they had been when she left Cincinnati. It likely felt little like returning home. Raya hoped the woman was not experiencing a sense of disappointment.

"Let's find a room for the night, Mother, and look for more permanent arrangements tomorrow," Raya suggested, forcing her voice to remain cheerful.

Emaline nodded. "That's a splendid idea. I think we also need a warm meal for supper tonight."

It would be only their second hot meal since leaving their valley, and while Raya felt reluctant to part with the money, they had little choice as they had finished their bread and cheese at noon. Additionally, she knew a good meal and a full night of sleep would do wonders for making their overwhelming situation easier to grasp. Her mouth began to water at Mother Emaline's suggestion, and her empty stomach growled. Something hot and flavorful sounded good. "I agree."

Looping her arm through Mother Emaline's, they made their way off the train platform, their satchels in hand, then through the city streets until they found an inn that looked to be a respectable, though not too fancy, establishment. Raya paid the price for a room, then carried both their satchels while keeping a steadying hand on Mother Emaline's back as they climbed the steep flight of stairs leading to the guest rooms.

On their way upstairs, Raya tried not to dwell on how the innkeeper avoided looking at her, or how he addressed Mother

Emaline, even when Raya was the one who had spoken. She knew that was how it would be, and yet it startled her. On the stage, in Denver, even on the train, she had not encountered such obvious discrimination, and though she had done her best to prepare herself, it still took her by surprise. Yet, if she was going to live in the East, she would have to learn to endure it. She had to learn to release the stinging embarrassment, or else she would grow angry and bitter—something she certainly didn't want to allow to happen.

Their room was simple, yet adequate, and they freshened up for supper, which was already being served down in the dining room. While Mother Emaline finished, Raya stood and peered out the second-story window.

She was very young when her family left the East, no more than five. Her memories of it were vague and frightening. Now, the noises and smells were all strange to her, and she longed for their quiet valley, their roughly built houses, the warm barn, the noisy mill, the clean air, and the freshness of the trees. Still, she knew this was where she needed to be—with Mother Emaline. And Mother Emaline wanted to return here, to the land of her people, where she was born and raised, where she had lived with Julius and her sons.

Raya had gathered on the train ride that Mother Emaline did not have any close relatives remaining in the area and intended simply to return to her homeland, rather than to anyone in particular. Raya understood her need to do so and was glad to make their new home in Cincinnati if it would bring Mother Emaline comfort.

Her only concern was being able to provide for their needs. The duty rested solely on her shoulders, and she was unsure she would be capable of fulfilling it adequately. What if no one would hire her? What if she could find work, but her wages were insufficient? What if she was unable to provide? What if she failed Mother Emaline? She glanced back to where the lady stood, brushing out her long, graying brown hair. Mother Emaline was depending on her, needed her, yet Raya was unsure she could deliver. She would do everything she could to ensure Mother Emaline's comforts and needs were met, yet what she feared most was that she would not be given the chance.

Like a shimmer of hope in the midst of dreary uncertainty, a story she had read out of the thick family Bible came to mind, and Raya's heart quieted. Though she could not remember the entirety of the story, she knew it referenced the birds of the air and the lilies of the field as examples of the care and provision of the Applewoods' God. He knew what they needed, the verses had said. Man was encouraged to stop worrying and to put first the Kingdom, knowing his every need would be met by the same God who cared for the birds and the flowers. The remembrance brought peace, and Raya let out a deep sigh, pressing a hand against her stomach. It was not much, but it was enough, and Raya would cling to it.

When Mother Emaline had neatly parted and braided her hair and wound it into her customary bun once again, they made their way back down the stairs to the dining room with Mother Emaline leaning heavily against Raya's arm. A cough seized the older woman's body, and Raya tasted fear as she realized how taxing the journey had been on her mother-in-law. Raya fussed over her as they settled at an empty table near the back of the dining room, making sure the woman was comfortable and warm.

Finally, taking her own seat, Raya turned her attention to their surroundings. It was a small inn, and she was certain it would not be considered a fine establishment by many in their new city, but she had never seen anything so beautiful.

The railing coming down from the upstairs was wood, polished so smooth that it shone. Glass lamps hung in collections on every wall, the bases ornate and the chimneys clear and tall. There was a shiny wood bar top on one side of the room, where several gentlemen sat, all in top hats and short frock coats. There were pairs or groups of people scattered about the rest of the tables, and Raya snuck quick glances, curious and in awe, though not wanting to appear rude. It quickly became obvious to her that the latest fashions had failed to reach their small mountain town.

Instead of being bell-shaped like her own, the fullness in the women's skirts had moved to the back, where cascades of lacy ruffles tumbled over large bustles and down into beautiful short trains. Lace billowed up softly from v-shaped necklines, and their sleeves clung tightly to their arms. Raya's eyes moved to the hairstyles of the genteel city women, and found that the sides were pulled back and curls cascaded down the backs of their heads, complementing well their full bustles.

Without meaning to, she found her hands smoothing the black fabric of her very full skirt and noticing the wideness of her sleeves. What had seemed like a perfectly adequate mourning dress just a week earlier in Colorado Territory now made her appear dreadfully outdated and plain. She thought of her hair, braided, and twisted into a bun at the nape of her neck, and wished she could curl it as the women around her had, wondering what it would feel like to be arrayed so fashionably. Suddenly coming to her senses, she chided herself for having such thoughts at such a time. There were far more important matters that took precedence. She turned her attention back to the fine room and its lovely occupants, careful this time to guard against the temptation to compare.

Thoroughly distracted, Raya did not notice the serving lady until Mother Emaline said her name softly. Apologizing, Raya lifted her teacup for the woman who held a teapot. When her cup was full, the lady spoke briefly to Mother Emaline, and then left.

Pushing down her reaction, Raya propped up a bright smile for Mother Emaline, refusing to acknowledge or take offense at how the lady had neither spoken to, nor looked at her while at their table. Nor did anyone else in the room. Their careful efforts to ignore her became more obvious, and Raya clasped her hands tightly in her lap. She was allowed to sit in the dining room, likely for Mother Emaline's benefit only, but it was clear she was neither accepted nor wanted. Her heart twisted. She had forgotten what it was like. She looked around and saw others just like her, but they looked at her and saw an outsider, an individual worth far less.

She smiled at Mother Emaline to cover her hurt and discussed the grand room with her. When a large bowl full of chicken and noodles was placed before her, she smiled up at the serving lady brightly and sincerely thanked her, hoping to put at bay any unease the woman might feel about serving her.

Mother Emaline was quiet during the meal, and Raya wondered if she was ashamed to be sitting with a person of color now that they were back in the civilized world. The color of Raya's skin had never been an issue in Colorado Territory, but then again, there, it was mostly acceptable to socialize with people of another race. It was the West, after all, and things were untamed. Civilized society had yet to reach their small mountain town, and all people worked and ate together.

Here in the East, it was clearly different. It was hard to miss how the dining room was packed with guests, save the tables directly around them. While diners were making an attempt to avoid Raya, Mother Emaline was inadvertently avoided as well. That wouldn't do. The woman needed community in her present grief, not isolation from polite society.

Despite the fact that her heart hurt and her embarrassment was stinging, Raya enjoyed the hearty chunks of chicken, cooked carrots and wide egg noodles that filled her dish. The warm meal tasted good, and Raya ate until she could hold no more. She drank the hot tea and ruefully wondered when they might eat a hot meal again. They certainly did not have enough money to afford one every day. Their funds would be depleted in no time if they took up such lavish living. She made room for one last chunk of chicken and egg noodle in her very full belly, then carefully laid her silverware aside.

"Are you ready to retire for the evening?" Mother Emaline asked, watching Raya lay down her spoon.

Raya glanced up and saw that Mother Emaline's eyes were warm, yet full of sadness. Raya nodded, and Mother Emaline laid down the coins necessary to cover the cost of their supper. Raya stood and helped Mother Emaline out of her chair, then steadied her as they climbed the stairs up to their room. After so many days on a stage and then a train, it was clear the older woman's body was protesting so much movement. She shuffled slowly and, if one could assume by the expression of pure concentration on Mother Emaline's face, with much pain. As soon as Raya used the key to unlock the door to their guest room, the woman made her way to the bed and sat down carefully, letting out a deep sigh.

When the door shut behind them, Mother Emaline looked up at Raya, her face full of sorrow. "Raya, I apologize for how those in the dining room acted tonight. My heart hurts for you, dear, seeing how you will be treated, knowing I brought you here. I had no right. No sense."

Raya knew then, it had been shame and sadness, not embarrassment that kept Mother Emaline from speaking much during their meal. Raya took her hand, leveled her gaze at her, and smiled warmly, drawing strength and determination from somewhere deep within. "I knew it would be like this, and still I chose to come."

Mother Emaline shook her head. "I should not have brought you here. I should not have allowed it. We should have stayed where we were."

Though nothing sounded sweeter at the moment than the possibility of going home, Raya shook her head and squeezed Mother Emaline's hand. "We are in your homeland, as we should be. You need to be here right now. It's okay. I'm glad you were able to come home, and that I could accompany you." Raya bent down and kissed Mother Emaline's cheek, moved by the regret and sorrow she saw on the older woman's tired face. "I don't wish things were different," she began, "at least, not in coming here. Some things, I know, we both wish were different."

Mother Emaline's eyes filled with tears that were forever near the surface these days. "Yes. Yes, there are some things we both certainly wish were different, but wishing never accomplished anything, I suppose." She reached out and grabbed Raya's hand, pulling her close, hugging her tightly. "Thank you for being here with me. For staying with me. I have lost much, but not everything."

Raya hugged her back. "This is where I belong," she told her, her voice clear and sincere.

Raya stepped back and convinced Mother Emaline to turn in for the night. She helped her get ready for bed, then helped her lay down and settled the blankets over her. Breathing a sigh of relief when the woman was tucked into bed, Raya thought back to the few times Mother Emaline had coughed during the evening, each cough shaking her frail frame. Bed was exactly where she needed to be. Rest and sleep would do her good and hopefully put to rest the tickling cough. Surely, Raya reasoned, she would be better in the morning.

Turning, Raya sat down at the small desk tucked into the corner and turned the oil lamp up to give herself better lighting. Taking up the provided quill and dipping it in ink, she penned a letter to Chenoa, letting her know they had arrived in Cincinnati safely. She knew the letter may not make it across the pass until spring, but she wanted the letter to be waiting for Chenoa whenever the post did make it through. Then, her sister-in-law would know she had thought of her.

She wrote her of their journey, the long days on the coach and the grandness of the train. She told her about what little she had seen of the city thus far and described the inn where they were staying. When she ran out of words to write, she promised to write again soon, then signed her name and laid aside her quill. After allowing the ink time to dry, she folded the letter carefully and set it aside. She would post it first thing in the morning.

Covering a yawn with the back of her hand as she laid down on the feather tick next to Mother Emaline, Raya shut her mind and heart to the worry that tried to find its way in. She forced herself to stop thinking about their meal in the dining room and the behavior of the patrons. To do so, she sang a song Mother Emaline sometimes sang, over and over in her mind until sleep finally came. Whatever happened on the morrow, there was nothing she could do about it tonight.

Both women rested well, grateful to be off the noisy, lurching train. After several weeks of restless sleep caused by both tragedy and travel, they found blessed relief in a soft bed, a quiet inn, and the deep sleep brought by absolute exhaustion.

Eleven

When Raya woke up, she didn't have the slightest inkling as to where she was. She looked around confused, alarm tapping a fast beat through her chest, until the fog cleared and their location registered. Mother Emaline was already awake and sitting in the small chair in the corner.

Raya quickly pushed herself up into a sitting position, sweeping loose strands of hair back from her face. "I've overslept. Why, you're already dressed. Why didn't you wake me?"

"Overslept?" Mother Emaline asked, a wryness in her voice. "For what, Raya? We have no house, no chores, no food to make, no menfolk to feed. Why should I wake you from restful slumber when there's nothing to wake you for?"

The hopelessness of Mother Emaline's words settled over Raya, and she scooted back to rest against the wooden headboard, rubbing her tired eyes.

"Nevertheless, I would like to visit some old friends today that I've kept in some contact with over the years," Mother Emaline continued. "Securing lodging is likely the most important item on our to-do list; however, I would like to contact a few people first. Perhaps they will know of something that is available and point us in the right direction."

Raya nodded. The plan was logical, though she was acutely aware of the scarcity of the money she had sewn into the hem of her dress during their train ride. She expected any accommodations Mother Emaline's past friends might suggest would be sorely beyond their means.

Contemplating the upcoming visits and remembering their welcome in the dining room the night before, Raya weighed her options for the day. She was reluctant to see Mother Emaline go off on her own in the city, especially since her cough had grown progressively worse since their travels began, but she wondered if the woman might be received more warmly if she went calling alone.

"Perhaps I will stay at the inn today. I have a letter I wish to write, and it would be lovely to pen it by daylight," Raya said slowly. It would break her heart if Mother Emaline's old friends were less than friendly to the woman as a result of her presence. After all of her loss, the woman needed support and camaraderie, not to feel torn between past acquaintances and her daughter-in-law.

"Nonsense. We'll go together." Raya opened her mouth to object, but Mother Emaline raised a finger, signaling for her silence. "You, darling, are a devoted, caring, extraordinary daughter-in-law whom I wish to introduce to my friends. Don't refuse me the pleasure."

Raya shut her mouth, backed into a corner by Emaline's request. Standing, she crossed to where she had neatly laid out her mourning gown the night before and dressed dutifully. She brushed out her long, dark, wavy tresses, then braided them before twisting the long braid into a neat bun at the nape of her neck. For just a moment she thought of curling her hair and wearing it swept up on the sides like the women from the night before, but she put the idea out of her mind as quickly as it entered. She was in mourning, in a dire situation, and far from being a genteel lady in Cincinnati society; the hairstyle was beyond her class. After washing her face and making the bed, Raya followed Mother Emaline out of the small room and down the stairs to the dining room.

Breakfast was included in the cost of their room, and Raya was thankful as they sat down at a table in the back. They were served eggs and salt pork, fluffy biscuits, and browned potatoes. It was a hearty meal, and Raya ate her fill. When they were finished, she helped Mother Emaline to her feet, and together they went out the large front door, onto the street.

The air was pleasantly warm, and the sun was out. Raya tucked her hand into the crook of Mother Emaline's arm and considered the woman for a long moment. Mother Emaline had not eaten much of her breakfast, and Raya could tell the woman was not at full strength. "Should I flag down a driver?"

Emaline shook her head. "It isn't far and it's a lovely day. Let's walk."

Raya nodded, trusting that Emaline knew her own limitations. It was a good decision. Walking was free. Additionally, they had been sitting for far too long during their travels, and it would be nice to stretch their legs.

As they passed city block after city block, Raya began to wonder just how far it was. Still, Mother Emaline held her head high and didn't slow her pace, so Raya kept quiet.

She watched with rapt attention as they left the busy downtown area and found themselves in an upper-class residential district. They passed many houses that were larger and grander than any Raya had ever seen before. Finally, Mother Emaline slowed and opened a gate for Raya. The large three-story house looked fine and luxurious even from the outside, and Raya felt unfit to enter it. Yet, Mother Emaline put her hand on Raya's back and gently pushed her forward, so she started up the walk dutifully.

Raya marveled at the older woman's composure as she smoothed the front of her own black mourning dress, then took the large brass knocker in her hand and rapped it sharply three times. The door was opened by a servant girl in a black dress and a white apron, which matched the white cap on her head.

The girl, whose own skin was several shades darker than Raya's, looked at her with open wariness, before directing her attention to Mother Emaline when she spoke. Mother Emaline stated her name and her desire to see Mrs. Post. They were escorted into the parlor. Raya could feel the open contempt in the servant girl's expression as she passed, and her heart plummeted.

She was viewed with disdain even by the servants, even by a girl who was undoubtedly a former slave. And why not? While Blacks had won their freedom, Indians were still both feared and despised. No distinction was made between the American natives and her own people, who seemingly bore such a close resemblance to those who were not educated to know the difference.

Raya waited anxiously for Mrs. Post to appear, biting her lip, and worrying about what the rich woman would say when she saw that Emaline had brought an Indian into her house. When the servant returned with her mistress, the woman greeted Emaline warmly. Raya was as polite and polished as she knew to be when Emaline introduced her, but the woman gave her no more than a cursory glance before she turned a pitying expression back to Emaline. Emaline's introduction of Raya revealed much, and Mrs. Post took the direction of offering her condolences as a response, then turned the conversation to the tragedy.

The minutes passed in agonizing slowness as the family, the man, and the life Raya had loved were discussed in hushed conversation, of which Raya was obviously not a welcome part. Mrs. Post sat with her back to Raya and addressed Emaline alone. She was dreadfully sorry about the accident, had always thought Julius was mad to have taken them to such a wild and untamed land, and to hear that their sons had taken savages as wives... she simply could not imagine. Poor, poor Emaline. Raya was not sure if the pointed words were more painful to hear, or if it was worse to watch the way Mother Emaline shifted in her seat, so very obviously uncomfortable and ashamed of her friend's words.

"The fire will always mark a time of great loss and intense grief in my life, but having Raya remain with me is my bright spot of hope. To be utterly alone, that is what I cannot imagine. Come now, Francine, tell me of your family. How is Theodore? And the children? I'm sure they're all grown by now."

The rich and stately woman shut her mouth and lifted her chin, looking both appalled and offended at Emaline's gentle declaration. She answered her questions stiffly at first, but softened as the conversation moved to her own family, and Raya and the Applewood family's misfortune was forgotten.

Raya's heart was still smarting from the woman's earlier comments, but it soon began to fill with compassion, too, after hearing the woman had lost two of her own sons in the war, and her sister's son had returned missing a leg. Her own doorstep had been touched by tragedy, and Raya's eyes brimmed with tears for her. Even after so many years, the woman could not speak of the war and maintain her composure.

"Your sons died a noble death. They were young men you can be proud of . . . they were heroes to their country," Raya offered, speaking for the first time, her words heartfelt.

Mrs. Post looked startled by the very fact that Raya had spoken. She didn't respond, yet her face grew more peaceful. Raya was glad her words, whether welcome or not, had brought the woman some sort of peace. Mother Emaline shot her a warm look, and the stinging hurt from earlier seeped out of Raya's heart. The people around her were not her enemies. They were people, just like her, who had experienced the trials and blessings of life, and were doing their best to cope along the way.

When Mrs. Post called for tea to be served, though she did not speak to Raya, she instructed the servant girl to serve her tea first.

The rest of their day was spent in much of the same fashion. They visited different long-ago friends of Emaline's, and at each home, the visit was similar. Emaline's friends were glad to see her, sorry for her misfortune, thankful she had been spared. They filled her in on what had happened in the city since her departure, how the war had changed things, and how they were all recovering and moving forward.

Raya listened to conversations about children who had grown up, babies that had been born, husbands and sons lost in the war, marriages that had taken place, and tragedies and scandals that had rocked the town. At each home, she was politely ignored, her presence gracefully overlooked for Emaline's sake. Near the end of each visit, Mother Emaline asked if they'd heard of anywhere that was hiring, or perhaps knew of a place to rent. Only one woman had a friend who was looking for a tenant for a property he owned. All the rest gave the same shake of the head, the same neat folding of the hands as they wished Emaline luck in her search. Raya was acutely relieved when Emaline announced that she had visited all the friends she intended to visit for the day.

Though Mother Emaline's friend had not known the monthly rate of the house, they decided to check on the rental property they had been told about earlier on their way back to the inn. They walked what seemed to be halfway across town before they arrived at the right address. It was a much smaller house than any of the homes they had visited that day, and Raya held on to hope as they were shown through the furnished house. Two bedrooms, a comfortable sitting room, an adequate kitchen, and a nice garden plot out back made up the property. While it was not fancy or elaborate, it was comfortable. Raya found herself holding her breath as she waited to hear the monthly rate, hoping and praying it would be within their means. If she could secure a job as a servant for a family like one of those they had visited earlier in the day, then perhaps, just maybe, they could live in this house, which felt safe and comfortable.

When the landlord's son, who had shown them the property, named the price, all the hope went out of Raya, and she felt as if darkness had fallen. There was no way they could afford such a price, even if she secured a job at the wealthiest home in Cincinnati. She let Mother Emaline politely excuse themselves and bid the boy goodbye. Raya blinked back tears and tried desperately to cling to optimism that was quickly slipping away.

She had allowed herself to hope, to dream, that perhaps they were not as destitute as they feared. Perhaps things were different in Cincinnati than they envisioned. Perhaps rent would be less, wages would be more. Perhaps they could afford a comfortable home, even if it was small and plain. Simply having a roof over their heads and living in a safe part of town was what was important to her.

Yet, it was not to be. Hearing the monthly price of the house was a clear picture of exactly what they could afford in the city . . . and what they could not. Comfort and safety were simply out of their price range. Even should they still have the money that had been stolen in Denver, they would not be able to afford the modest home. They had gravely underestimated the price of lodging in the city. Steeling herself, she forced her voice to remain cheerful as they made the long walk back to the inn where their belongings were, as much for Mother Emaline's sake as her own.

The sun had sunk from view, and the air was rapidly cooling off. Raya was shivering under her shawl and knew that her mother-in-law must be doing the same. Wanting to hurry their pace, but feeling Mother Emaline's weariness in every step, Raya forced her steps to match the older woman's. Looping her arm through Mother Emaline's, she gave the woman support and counted down the blocks until finally their inn was in sight.

As they crossed the last street that separated them from the inn, Mother Emaline began to cough. The coughing fit was so violent that Raya put her arm around Emaline's waist to keep her upright. When it finally passed, she kept it there and hurried Emaline into the inn. She knew the next spell would hit soon, and was well aware that she needed to get the woman lying down before what little remained of her strength was spent by coughing.

Raya chided herself for not insisting they get a carriage. She should have known. She had seen Emaline through too many of her spells of illness to not have seen it coming. She should have taken precautionary measures.

They had to stop on the steep stairs of the inn as another coughing fit hit her, and Raya cringed as she watched her beloved friend double over with every cough, covering her mouth with one hand while clutching the railing for support with the other. Once it passed, Emaline's steps were shaky, and Raya knew her strength was failing. As soon as they reached their room and the door was shut behind them, Raya unbuttoned Mother Emaline's dress as fast as she could and helped her change into her nightgown. Folding back the covers on the bed, she helped Mother Emaline lay down, then quickly gave her a drink of water.

After drinking the water Raya brought her, Mother Emaline collapsed back against the pillows, her relief to be lying in bed, evident. After a few minutes, the coughing began to lessen, and as it did, Emaline closed her eyes and fell asleep. Raya sank down wearily into the chair in the corner and watched her mother-in-law rest.

She was sick again. After nearly three years, her illness had returned. She had barely survived it the last time it came upon her, just after Alex and Niz's wedding; could she survive it again, especially being so grieved in spirit? If something were to happen to Mother Emaline... Raya turned her thoughts away from such a terrible path. Mother Emaline would be fine. Raya would make sure of it. She would nurse her back to health, just as she had last time.

And nursing her back to health started with a warm meal. Raya slipped quietly from the room and went down to the dining room, where she asked if she could have a single meal brought up to their room, letting them know her companion was ill. Obviously thankful that they wouldn't have to deal with her in their dining room for the second night in a row, the server quickly agreed.

Raya climbed the stairs again and waited quietly in the falling darkness until their food was delivered. Once it was, she woke Mother Emaline and helped her sit up in bed to eat as much of the chili over noodles (something Emaline identified as a traditional Cincinnati meal) as she could, her meal interrupted twice by fits of coughing. When Emaline declared she was done and too exhausted to eat any more, Raya finished what was left in the bowl. She prepared to go to bed, hoping things would be better in the morning, when Mother Emaline opened her sleepy eyes and pinned them on Raya.

"Will you read the Scriptures to me?" Mother Emaline asked, her blue eyes shining up at her daughter-in-law.

Raya smiled softly. Mother Emaline may not be physically strong, but inside she had great strength. Even in the wake of her sons' tragic deaths, her eyes could shine, and she could draw delight from the Scriptures. Raya's heart warmed to the woman in front of her once again, and she realized anew just how much she admired her. While Raya was wallowing in their hopeless situation, Mother Emaline was turning to the one place they could find hope and rest, peace and help from their very present trouble.

"The practice would do you good," Mother Emaline teased gently, settling back in her pillows, a smile on her face. Raya used to read to the family every night, but hadn't for several weeks.

It had been important to Raya's father for his whole family to sound like Americans, so they had learned English from a private tutor who taught them the language, as well as the art of cadence and tone. Listening to her read had been one of Luke's favorite things to do. He'd said listening to her voice was like listening to the prettiest song he had ever heard. The memory brought fresh tears to her eyes, but she blinked them away. She had no energy left for tears.

Raya went to Mother Emaline's satchel and carefully removed the heavy family Bible. She smoothed her hand across the leather cover, and opened it just a little, peeking inside at all the names that had been so beautifully written on the first several pages—Applewoods that had lived before her, the line her children would have been a part of. She noted that Mother Emaline had filled in the date of Luke, Alex, and William's deaths.

Raya closed the Bible and carried it back to the bed, pulling the lone chair in the room along with her. She positioned it beside the bed and sat down, turning up the kerosene lamp to give herself better light to read by. Opening the large book on her lap, she leafed through the thin pages until she found the psalms.

She began to read, her first few words stilted until she found herself in familiar territory, and they smoothed out into a harmonious lilt. She read for half an hour, psalm after psalm, before finally stopping.

"Read Isaiah 54, please," Mother Emaline requested softly when silence settled over the room. Raya leafed through the large book, looking for the book of Isaiah. Once she found it, she turned the pages until she found the passage Mother Emaline had requested. Pulling the oil lamp closer, she began to read again.

"Sing, O barren, thou that didst not bear; break forth into singing, and cry aloud, thou that didst not travail with child: for more are the children of the desolate than the children of the married wife, saith the Lord. Enlarge the place of thy tent, and let them stretch forth the curtains of thine habitations: spare not, lengthen thy cords, and strengthen thy stakes;

"For thou shalt break forth on the right hand and on the left; and thy seed shall inherit the Gentiles, and make the desolate cities to be inhabited. Fear not; for thou shalt not be ashamed: neither be thou confounded; for thou shalt not be put to shame: for thou shalt forget the shame of thy youth, and shalt not remember the reproach of thy widowhood any more." Raya glanced up at Mother Emaline, and the lady nodded, tears shining in her eyes. Raya looked back down and continued to read.

"For thy Maker is thine husband; the Lord of hosts is his name; and thy Redeemer the Holy One of Israel; The God of the whole earth shall he be called. For the Lord hath called thee as a woman forsaken and grieved in spirit, and a wife of youth, when thou wast refused, saith thy God.

"For a small moment have I forsaken thee; but with great mercies will I gather thee. In a little wrath I hid my face from thee for a moment; but with everlasting kindness will I have mercy on thee, saith the Lord thy Redeemer.

"For this is as the waters of Noah unto me: for as I have sworn that the waters of Noah should no more go over the earth; so have I sworn that I would not be wroth with thee, nor rebuke thee. For the mountains shall depart, and the hills be removed; but my kindness shall not depart from thee, neither shall the covenant of my peace be removed, saith the Lord that hath mercy on thee."

Mother Emaline whispered the last few words along with Raya, then let out a deep sigh as they finished. "This is our promise, Raya, our promise from the LORD."

Despite the Scriptures she had read, Raya's heart felt heavy and full of sorrow. She wanted to cover her face and weep. She was the barren woman. She was the woman who had never travailed with child. She was the woman forsaken and grieved of spirit. She shook her head, too weary to be anything but honest. "No. He has hidden His face from me. He has forsaken me. Us. We are both like the barren woman now—I have never borne a child and all of yours have died." Her shoulders slumped and her chin dropped to her chest.

Mother Emaline reached out and grabbed her hand, squeezing it firmly. "But He will gather us with great mercy and everlasting kindness."

Tears began to spill from Raya's dark eyes. "I cannot sing, Mother. I cannot forget my widowhood."

Mother Emaline looked as though she wanted to offer encouragement and comfort, but like a heavy cloak, her loss laid siege upon her heart once again. Looking away, her eyes became distant. "I too find it hard to sing, Raya. I had three grown sons, three daughters, and a grandchild on the way. I had a comfortable home and a beautiful valley. I had respect in our community. The mill was starting to turn a good profit. And now . . . now we have been reduced to no more than beggars, hoping we can become hired help. Alone in the world. People used to look at me with respect, now they only look at me with pity."

Raya looked up into Mother Emaline's watery blue eyes. The woman who had seemed so strong just moments before now seemed frail and broken. Her heart filling with compassion, Raya reached out and grasped Mother Emaline's hand. "Perhaps He has forsaken us for a moment, but with great mercy, He will gather us. He may have hidden His face from us, but with everlasting kindness, He will have mercy on us. It says so right here, Mother, and we know this is truth. Every promise in this book is truth. If we believed it in the valley, then we can believe it in the city. He is the God of the whole earth."

Raya's soft words seemed to calm Mother Emaline, and the lady closed her eyes and was quiet for so long that Raya wondered if she hadn't fallen asleep. "For thy Maker is thine husband; the Lord of hosts is his name; and thy Redeemer the Holy One of Israel," Mother Emaline murmured quietly. Raya startled when the woman spoke after such a long silence, and then watched her repeat the words to herself over and over, her face relaxing more each time they came from her lips until she fell asleep.

When Mother Emaline was sleeping peacefully, Raya put the Bible away, changed into her nightdress, and blew out the oil lamp. She settled down in the bed, careful not to disturb the woman beside her.

As she closed her eyes and waited for sleep to claim her, the words of the passage she had read replayed in her mind. *For thy Maker is thine husband; the Lord of hosts is his name; and thy Redeemer the Holy One of Israel; The God of the whole earth shall he be called.*

How did the God of the whole earth identify Himself as a husband of a mere woman? How did He humble Himself to such an extent? And how did He act as a Redeemer? Wasn't He far away and distant, the unseen, intangible, unknowable God? Yet a husband was flesh and blood, a redeemer, someone who offered real freedom from real bondage.

Raya could find no way to reason in her mind such a tangible, intimate relationship with One so mighty, so holy, so sovereign, so distant, so abstract. But, oh, if only it were true. They were in desperate need of a redeemer. They were in desperate need of a husband; someone to make a way for them, someone to provide for them, someone to care for them.

She fell asleep with Mother Emaline's words playing through her mind. *"For thy Maker is thine husband; the Lord of hosts is his name; and thy Redeemer the Holy One of Israel."*

Twelve

"We'll take it," Raya said firmly, not giving herself the opportunity to second-guess her decision.

The small-eyed, round-bellied owner of the small shanty eyed her suspiciously. "What are you plannin' on doing here? I don't rent to riff-raff."

Raya steeled herself at his insinuating question and crossed her arms. "My mother-in-law, Emaline Applewood, is currently staying at an inn across town. We came to Cincinnati, whence she originates, from Colorado Territory after our menfolk were killed in a fire in the family mill," Raya said, relaying the story in careful, measured words. "She's taken ill, or else she would be with me this morning."

The short man scratched his stubby chin. "Emaline Applewood, you say?"

Raya nodded.

"Don't know why an Applewood would be looking to live in a dump like this. Her and her husband used to live up on the other side o' town, up 'round where all them rich folk live. Guess I heard of her bad turn of luck, though must be worse'n the stories made it sound if she's taken to living with a heathen and agreeable to living here." He shrugged and handed her the key. "Rent is due the first day of every month, you hear? Don't appreciate it being late."

Raya swallowed back the hurt and shame that his careless words stirred up, counted out the money to pay their first month's rent, and reached out to take the key. "Thank you."

UP FROM THE ASH HEAP

He held the key a moment too long, causing her to glance up at him. "I'll tell you again, I don't rent to riff-raff or loose women, so don't be thinkin' you can open shop here, you hear? If I hear anything of the likes, I'll come put you out so fast your head will spin, understand?"

Swallowing down her shock and dismay, Raya dropped her eyes to the ground, thoroughly embarrassed by his brazen remarks. "Sir, I in no way have any dishonorable intentions. I simply need a place for my mother-in-law and me to live."

"Well, if it is as you say, you'd best watch yourself. You're not living in the ritzy district, girl."

Raya took the key from his hand with a final tug, feeling a general dislike for the man. "We'll plan to pay our rent the first of every month."

He grunted as he turned and left the house. She shut the door behind him, glad to be rid of the foul little man. Her imagination needed no help when looking at their new neighborhood. She knew the part of town they were moving to and the dangers that lurked there. However, it was better than being homeless, and that was the mentality they had to maintain. Even in this place, they had much to be thankful for.

Shifting the direction of her thoughts, Raya stood alone, looking around their new home. It was only one room and obviously had a rodent problem, but with a much-needed cleaning and perhaps a good mouser, it would do. The most important thing was securing a place of their own and moving out of the inn. Room fees at the inn were too high for them to afford for long, and their shallow coffers were quickly diminishing. Besides, the sooner she got Mother Emaline settled, the sooner she could begin looking for work.

Spotting a dusty broom in the corner, Raya got right to work, hoping to have Mother Emaline moved over to their new home before the inn charged her for another night's stay. Scraping the cobwebs off the broom handle, she began knocking down creepy varmints and their homes that hung in every corner of the small space. She brushed down the walls and the one, lone, dirty window, and when she was satisfied that not a cobweb remained, she swept the dirt floor. She scrubbed the dirty window, bought a straw tick liner from the general store several blocks away, purchased fresh straw to fill it, and washed every mismatched dish that the shanty contained.

It seemed as if no one had lived in the vacant home for months, and as Raya looked around the crude dwelling, she could see why. The one window was small and faced a street that was lined with other small, makeshift dwellings. She could see cracks of daylight through three different places in the roof. The furniture was rudimentary, the floor dirt, the air stale and cold. Additionally, it was in a part of town that Luke never would have allowed her to visit, much less live. But things were different now, and their options were slim. With coverings on the newly filled mattress, curtains on the window, and a fire in the fireplace, it would do just fine.

Satisfied that it was at least clean, Raya carefully locked the door and went back to the inn to fetch Mother Emaline, being cautious and moving quickly as she made the long walk through the unsavory neighborhoods.

The woman was still sleeping when she entered the room; another telltale sign of Emaline's illness. The lady woke as Raya shut the door. She rubbed her eyes and yawned, then held out her hand to Raya, inviting her to join her.

Raya hurried to the bed and sat down on the side of it, unable to hold back a smile as she relayed her news. "I've found us a house. It's not much, but we can afford it."

She knew Mother Emaline would not judge the shanty, even though it was far removed from the cozy houses they were used to having. Mother Emaline was as aware of their situation as she was. Raya knew the older woman would simply be glad to have a roof of their own over their heads again.

As Raya had known it would, Mother Emaline's face lit up as she smiled. "You did? Why, Raya, I didn't even realize you had left." A look of concern filled the older woman's face. "Dear, you have to be careful. It isn't safe for a lady to walk around the city by herself."

"It was early in the morning. All the riff-raff were still in bed," Raya assured her, remembering belatedly how she had been referred to in a similar manner just hours earlier. "Besides, we need a place to live and I found one."

Mother Emaline smiled again. "Yes, you did. Let's go get settled." Mother Emaline stood and dressed, and with Raya holding on to her securely, their satchels in hand, they walked the distance to their new house.

Mother Emaline responded to their new home as Raya had known she would—with humble thankfulness and acceptance. They found places for the few things they had been able to bring with them from home, and Raya spread the two quilts Mother Emaline had stuffed into the bottom of her large satchel over the bed. When the house was in order and Mother Emaline was settled in one of the crude rocking chairs, Raya made the trek back to the general store to purchase flour, salt, and a little tin of tea. She purchased a few potatoes and carrots as well, then purchased a rabbit from a young hunter who was hawking his bit of fresh meat on the street for a meager price. Raya wasn't fond of rabbit, but in a stew it would do nicely, and they would go to bed with their stomachs full.

Hours later, after dinner, Mother Emaline napped in the rocker, her sleep interrupted by fits of coughing, her cheeks flushed by fever. Raya sat in the chair next to her and mended a rip in her dress she had acquired while disembarking the train. As she sewed, a movement in the far corner of the shanty caught her eye, and she looked up to find a furry rodent scampering across the room.

Recovering from her start, she put down her dress and grabbed the broom, opened the front door and shoed the little animal out of the house. As she sat back down to resume her sewing, she decided she would go in search of a good mouser as soon as she secured work. With as little as they had, they didn't need mice getting into their food or chewing up their clothing to make nests.

Raya suddenly felt the familiar prick of tears as she remembered how Luke had surprised her with a kitten several years back. He had heard one of the neighbor's cats had a litter of kittens and picked one out for Raya. Of course, the cat was a barn cat and meant for the purpose of mousing, but still, he brought it to Raya to let her pet and hold. The grin on his face was as precious as the gift he had brought her. Tucking the precious memory away, she wiped at her tears and continued mending her skirt.

Thirteen

The next morning, Mother Emaline announced she wanted to visit Julius' father. Raya objected that the walk was too long for anyone in Emaline's condition, but the older woman assured her she was feeling much better and was set on going. Caving to Mother Emaline's wishes, Raya put on her black mourning dress before helping Mother Emaline into hers.

James, Julius' father, was staying at the house of a cousin, his closest living relative, and Raya knew the walk to his house would be long as they lived on the opposite side of town. Flagging down the first horse cart she saw, Raya parted with the fare. Even knowing their resources were low, having seen Emaline's recent health decline, she felt sure hiring a cab was non-negotiable.

Emaline was adamant that they visit today, before the news of his grandsons' passing reached the old man. She wanted to be the one to tell him, and she wanted to relay the news in person.

Due to how much their landlord, Mr. Henley, seemed to know about them the morning before, Raya felt certain the news had already reached the old man's doorstep, but she didn't share her suspicions. She had not shared with Mother Emaline the details of her conversation with Mr. Henley, nor did she care to. The conversation hadn't been pleasant, and it had worried Raya about the part of town they were living in. She didn't want to pass that worry onto Mother Emaline, who could do nothing to fix the situation, but would undoubtedly feel responsible to do so.

Now, Raya felt self-conscience as she climbed the steps leading to the grand front porch of a house which rose up even larger and grander than any they had stepped foot into thus far. This was where Luke came from. This was what Mother Emaline was accustomed to. Raya smoothed the front of her slightly rumpled black dress, still damp from having been laundered the night before, trying to smooth the butterflies in her stomach as well.

She was nervous for this meeting, nervous to hear what James Applewood might say about his eldest grandson's choice of a bride. While the rejection of strangers hurt, James Applewood was no stranger—he was Luke's grandfather. It meant more, would hurt deeper. She had met nothing but suspicion, scorn, and utter avoidance since arriving in Cincinnati, and now she anticipated there would be more of the same. She blew out a deep breath and then felt her heart soften as she cast a quick glance at Mother Emaline.

The lady was obviously just as nervous, but Raya knew it had much more to do with the news she carried. Mother Emaline had told her the night before of how the man grieved when his firstborn son, Jedidiah, had died in the war, then how his grief had almost been his undoing when Julius followed not even a month later. Mother Emaline was worried how the old man would bear the news of his only grandsons' deaths. The end of his line had come, and they were there to bring him the unwelcome news.

Raya watched as Mother Emaline lifted her chin, squared her shoulders, and knocked on the door with the large brass knocker. The door was opened several moments later by a dark-skinned lady in a black dress, a white apron and hat, just like the half dozen others they had seen while visiting Emaline's friends.

Mother Emaline asked to see James, and the woman met her eyes for just a moment in surprise before quickly averting her gaze. "Just a minute, ma'am. I'll go get the master." The door was shut again, and Emaline sent Raya a concerned look.

Several minutes later, a tall man in a fancy sack suit opened the heavy front door. His face was serious as he held the door open for them. "Hello, Cousin Emaline. I heard you had returned. I'm glad to see you well."

UP FROM THE ASH HEAP

Mother Emaline nodded and smiled, but Raya noticed how it didn't reach the lady's eyes. "I'm glad to see you're well also, Mr. Applewood."

The man smiled. "Please, between family, it's Judson."

"Judson, this is my daughter-in-law, Raya. She is the widow of my eldest, Luke."

Raya saw that Judson's mouth pressed into a tight line as he glanced at her. "How do you do?" he asked stiffly.

She curtsied.

"I was sorry to hear of Julius' passing," Judson said, addressing Emaline. "And then just this week, news reached me that your sons have passed as well. It's quite a tragedy. They were the last remaining first cousins that I had. I'm very sorry for your loss." He stepped back. "Come in."

Raya took Mother Emaline's arm carefully and helped her through the doorway and into the parlor he motioned them into. Raya and Mother Emaline settled together on a couch. "I took ill a few days ago, or else I would have come sooner," Emaline explained. "I wanted to tell James myself, but I see your household has already learned of the tragedy within my home."

The man considered Mother Emaline with an odd look. "You did not receive my letter, then? No, you probably didn't. You were likely already on your way here."

Mother Emaline shook her head. "What letter?"

"James Applewood passed away a fortnight ago. I sent word to you, but now I'm sure the letter missed you."

"James is gone?" Mother Emaline asked, her voice weak.

Judson Applewood nodded. "He stopped breathing in his sleep. He was an old man, Emaline. Even still, we have missed his presence in our home."

Mother Emaline looked down at her lap, and Raya reached over and squeezed her hand, hoping to comfort her somehow. That was it. The last man in Julius' line was gone. The finality of it was sobering. A family that had carried on for generations had come to a close. At least the old man had died without knowing his own line ceased to exist.

"When I told my Wendy you had returned from the West, she was so glad to hear it, though dreadfully sorry to hear the circumstances," Judson continued. "We were hoping you would pay us a visit. Wendy wanted to invite you to tea, but didn't know where to send the invitation."

Mother Emaline quickly glanced up at him, then back down at her lap, as if unable to process this last bit of news he had given her. Raya didn't blame her. Were there really invitations to tea among such sorrow? Such loss? Were they truly wondering if they could eat tomorrow, while others were planning tea parties?

After a long silence, Judson shifted in his seat. Standing, he crossed to a tray where a decanter of liquor sat among a few short glasses. He poured himself a little, then returned to his rigid chair. "There's another matter to discuss," he continued, his voice taking on a serious tone. "James left a sizeable inheritance."

Mother Emaline nodded, hope springing into her eyes. Perhaps all was not lost. Perhaps they would have something to survive on. "I expected that to be the case when . . . whenever James passed," Mother Emaline said, her voice still faint. "He was a good businessman."

"Yes, he was. However, without a man to take control of Julius and your sons' inheritance, nor any of Julius' blood remaining in your family line, I cannot release it to you," Judson continued. "I'm bound by law." His eyes were sympathetic, even as he spoke the harsh words.

Raya had been expecting it, knew it was how things worked, but still it proved difficult to hear the words spoken aloud. She and her mother-in-law could be handsomely endowed, if not rich, yet they would continue to live in a shanty on the other side of town, hoping to get jobs that would allow them to keep enough food on the table to avoid starvation and a roof over their heads. All because they had no man to take control of the inheritance.

UP FROM THE ASH HEAP

Emaline's head dropped, and Raya could feel her acute disappointment along with her dashed hopes. Raya stroked her hand. "We'll be alright, Mother," she said quietly, reassuring the lady.

Taking a deep breath, Emaline lifted her chin to meet Raya's eyes before turning her attention back to Judson. She gave a firm nod. "We expected that. We know that is the way of things. I only wish Julius were here to receive his inheritance."

"As do I. Julius was a good man. As I'm sure your sons were. Now, did I hear correctly? Your sons . . . they didn't have any children to carry on the name? If they did, the inheritance would be theirs."

Mother Emaline looked at Raya, her eyes suddenly brimming with tears. Raya cleared her throat, remembering the perfectly formed baby boy she had held in the palm of her hand. "Mother's son Alex and his wife were going to have a baby in the winter, but Nizhoni miscarried the day of the fire."

Judson's eyes nearly flickered to Raya, then returned to Mother Emaline, addressing her instead. "I'm sorry for your loss. Where are your other daughters-in-law? Have they accompanied you as well?"

"No, they returned to their families. Only Raya has remained with me."

Again, Judson almost glanced at Raya, but didn't. He gave another curt nod. "I'm sure the company is appreciated."

Mother Emaline clung tightly to Raya's hand. "More than I can express." Her composure regained, Emaline stood, her shoulders squared, appearing quite regal. "Well, Judson, it has been lovely to visit with you, but we need to arrive home before darkness falls. It's a long walk back to our new house, and I've developed a bit of an illness during our travels. When we are more settled, perhaps we can call again, when Wendy is home as well. I would enjoy having the chance to visit with her."

Judson nodded, following her lead and standing to his feet. "Please, let me send you home in my carriage."

Raya could see the protest on Mother Emaline's face and knew it was pride that would cause her to object. She answered quickly, before Mother Emaline could turn down Judson's kind offer. "That would be lovely. Thank you. It would be a relief not to see Mother Emaline walking so far so soon after feeling so poorly."

Judson nodded, fully acknowledging Raya for the first time. Turning, he went to summon his driver.

When the driver was ready, Mother Emaline and Raya bid Judson farewell and climbed into the carriage. Settling back with a long sigh as the horses began to carry them swiftly home, Mother Emaline rested her head against the cushioned seatback and closed her eyes. "It is such a relief not to have to make that long walk back, nor have to part with the money for a horse cart. That was pure kindness of him to offer us a ride."

"It's too soon for you to be exerting yourself so, Mother," Raya told her, worried. "We never should have visited today. It's been too much for you."

Mother Emaline opened her eyes and stared bleakly out the window. "I know that, dear, I do. I just wanted James to hear the news from me." Tears began leaking from the woman's eyes and running down her cheeks.

Raya took Mother Emaline's hand and held it gently in both of hers. "If James was a believer, as you have said he was, he is with Julius, Luke, Alex, William, and Alex and Niz's child right now. And his son Jedidiah, as well. I doubt he much minds the fact that he's no longer on earth. As if being reunited with his sons, grandsons, and great-grandchild weren't enough, he's with Almighty God. I'm quite certain he's not shedding any tears," Raya finished with a smile, carefully reaching out to wipe the tears off the older lady's cheek with the corner of her shawl.

"These tears are selfish tears—they're not for him, they're for me," Emaline retorted shortly.

Raya laughed, the musical sound filling the carriage and drawing a smile from Mother Emaline. "Well, then, cry all you want, as long as they're selfish tears."

Once home, after thanking the carriage driver, Raya helped Mother Emaline into the house and helped her lie on the bed to rest while she cooked their daily meal. When she was finished, she set their small bowls of rabbit stew on the table beside plates that held a small chunk of bread. She filled their chipped cups with cold water and then helped Emaline to the table, where they sat together to eat. As simple as their meal was, as much as she wasn't partial to rabbit, Raya gave thanks sincerely and savored every bite of her dinner, knowing they may not often have such a good meal henceforth; at least not until she could secure a job with a decent wage.

"I'm going looking for work tomorrow," she commented as she sopped up the last of her stew with her crust of bread.

Mother Emaline nodded slowly. "Do you know where you'll look?"

Raya knew it was difficult for the woman to see her daughter-in-law forced to seek employment outside the home. She kept her voice cheerful, hoping to reassure her. "I've seen several inns that aren't a far distance away. I'll see if they're looking for any hired help. I can wash bedding or clean or cook or wash dishes—whatever is needed. I thought that might be the most likely place to start. I may also step into a laundry business, or perhaps a seamstress shop, if I come across one."

"Yes, you are a very good seamstress," Mother Emaline agreed. "A general store may be another place to look. Perhaps you could help stock shelves or wait on customers. That one we visited isn't far," Mother Emaline added.

Raya nodded. "I'll check there as well."

Mother Emaline set her chin on her hand and smiled at Raya. "Luke would be proud of you. You are a strong woman, doing what must be done. And with a smile on your face, no less."

Raya smiled sadly. "He would be proud of us both. You are so strong, Mother. I look to you as my example. Any strength I have is only what I've seen you model first. You teach me Who to turn to." She reached across and squeezed Emaline's hand. "Your boys, Julius, they would be proud to see how you're conducting yourself. It was honorable of you to go to tell James in person today. It was the right thing to do. I apologize for chastising you."

Mother Emaline brushed her apology away. "I know it was only out of concern for my health." The woman's face grew thoughtful. "I was thinking about it earlier, while I was resting, and I'm thankful he wasn't there to hear the news. Better he die a peaceful old man who missed his sons, but thought his grandsons would carry on his family name. Better to die thinking he had left a mark on the world, a legacy that would continue."

Raya's eyes dropped to her empty bowl. What legacy would she leave? When she died, would she leave a mark on the world? She looked around their humble home, empty save Mother Emaline. Everything around her said she would not. She would work to provide for them until she no longer could, then she would likely take ill and die, no one any the wiser, no husband, children, or loved ones left to miss her or honor her memory. It was a dismal thought, and she pushed it aside. For today, she had life and Mother Emaline. For today, that was enough.

Fourteen

Early the next morning, Raya rose while it was still dark and donned her plain, full black dress. She looked down at the dark color and simple lines and thought of her Sunday best, which lay packed away in the bottom of her satchel on a high shelf, where she thought mice were least likely to have access to it. The dress was a beautiful shade of peach that made her skin look like bronze.

She considered the possibility that perhaps wearing such a fine dress would communicate to potential employers that she was a respectable lady, not a heathen, as they thought. However, even if it would help her secure work, she would never dream of donning it—not while she was still in mourning. She fetched the black cloak from her satchel, choosing it over her lighter shawl, knowing the morning air would be chilly. Then she brushed her dark hair until it shone and braided it neatly before coiling it into a sensible and conservative bun at the nape of her neck. She washed her face and ate a small chunk of bread, chasing it down with a cup of water. After checking to make sure Mother Emaline was still sleeping, she slipped out the door quietly, being careful not to wake the woman, knowing she needed her rest.

Raya hurried down the street, drawing her cloak close around her to ward off the early morning chill, being mindful of her surroundings. After walking several blocks, she took a deep breath and entered her first establishment. She had chosen to inquire first at the general store they frequented, just as Mother Emaline had suggested.

The proprietor looked up, obviously surprised to hear someone come in so early. "What can I do for you?" he asked, his expression suspicious.

"I came to ask if you need any hired help," she answered, putting great effort into covering her anxiety. "I am a hard worker and stronger than I look."

The store owner nodded his head. "I am, but I need a man. Someone who can lift a great deal." He gave her a pointed look. "And someone who can reach the top shelf."

Staying cheerful, Raya smiled. "Well then, it doesn't sound like I'm a good fit with what you're needing."

His suspicion was replaced with an amused expression. "No, I don't think you are."

"Thank you for your time, sir. Have a good day."

He gave her another smile and turned back to writing in his ledger.

Raya left the store and started down the street again. Next, she came to an inn. The wooden sign hanging in the front was broken, and the place looked rundown, but she didn't have the luxury of being choosy. She went in and smiled at the proprietress. "Good morning, ma'am. I'm looking for work. Are you in need of any extra hands?"

The woman gave her a haughty once-over. "I don't employ heathens."

Taken aback by her abrupt manner, Raya stumbled for words. "Ma'am, I'm not a native. My family originated fro—"

"The answer is no," the woman stated plainly, turning back to the window she was washing.

Raya stood there for another moment, unsure of how to respond or even if she should. Her pride was smarting, her feelings were hurt. Yet, the LORD said to bless those who curse you. "Have a wonderful day. I pray the LORD will bless you," she told the lady simply, then quietly left the establishment.

Taking a deep breath, she continued on, pushing down the pain of rejection. She had known all along she would be rejected by some. She knew she would be looked down upon because of the color of her skin. She knew people would be ignorant of her true heritage and would be afraid of the culture in which they thought she belonged. She reminded herself of that now and filled her lungs with cool air. *Keep your chin up* had been what her mother told her when they were traveling through the East. No matter what someone else said or did, just keep your chin up and don't react. Raya had managed to obey then; she could surely do so again now.

Coming upon the next inn, she swung open the heavy door and went inside. The man who came to greet her had spectacles, and the place looked slightly more respectable than the last. She told him she was inquiring about work, and he shook his head, telling her he had no need for extra workers.

Her plight for a job continued in a similar manner for the rest of the day. Either they weren't hiring, she was too short, too dark-skinned, or too much a woman. If only she had been tall, white or a man, she would have had several jobs over, she thought, almost bitterly, as she made her way home late in the afternoon.

Her feet were aching, her stomach was growling, and she was more than a little discouraged. At their shanty's front door, she paused and leaned back against the outer wall. She took several moments to compose herself, spending most of them praying for peace and joy she could share with her mother-in-law. When she felt her discouragement begin to subside, she put her hand to the latch and went inside.

The room was bright and warm, and Mother Emaline greeted her with a smile and an unexpected hot meal of fried potatoes and scrambled eggs. She assured Raya she would find something the next day, and that it was very uncommon to find work on one's first day of looking. Raya nodded and smiled, encouraged by Mother Emaline's cheerful attitude and optimistic hope.

After finishing their supper, Raya read from the Psalms and then they went to bed early to conserve their candles and their firewood. When Raya woke in the middle of the night, she could see her breath hanging in the air. Though she hadn't lived in

Cincinnati for long, she imagined it must be early in the season to have such cold temperatures, and she hoped it wasn't the foretelling of a hard winter to come. Reluctantly, she slid out from under the bedcovers to add another log to the fire, careful not to let out the warmth. Shaking in her thin nightdress, she added the wood as quickly as she could before running the few steps back across the room to the bed. Getting under the covers, she pulled the top quilt up over their faces, hoping to keep their noses warm and Mother Emaline from coughing.

The next morning, Emaline got up with Raya and took a small container of powder out of her satchel. Using the soft pad, she powdered Raya's face and hands, making her tinted skin appear a little lighter. While Raya appreciated Mother Emaline's help, she could not bring herself to meet her eyes. She felt ashamed of the color of her skin, ashamed that Mother Emaline knew she was not being hired because of it, ashamed that it was something they had to attempt to hide and cover up. She kissed Emaline's cheek in farewell when they were finished and slipped out the front door, ready to be out of her presence, where she didn't feel dirty and unworthy.

As Raya started her walk, she looked down at her hands, considering their unnatural paleness. It was incomprehensible to her how the color of her skin and the geographical origin of her ancestors could determine her worth as a worker, and seal her fate before she even had a chance to prove her skill or aptitude.

Her heart hurting, temptation struck. Like a tantalizing, enticing smell, came the unwanted memory of how much money it had taken to pay her way on the train and the stagecoach. She had just enough money sewn into the hem of her dress to pay her passage back. A long train ride and an even longer coach ride over the mountains, and she could be home. Back among people who saw her as a capable human being.

With building longing, she thought of Amhil's offer to reside under her father's roof once again. She would have a comfortable roof over her head, plenty to eat, a warm fire to sit beside. Her struggle to survive would be over.

Like waking up from a dream, Raya suddenly pushed the traitorous thoughts aside. If she returned to her father's house, though her physical needs would be met, she was certain she wouldn't be able to live with herself, knowing she had abandoned Mother Emaline. She was staying. She had vowed it to the lady, and she would not turn back now. One discouraging day of searching for work was not going to change her mind.

She went farther out this time, hitting businesses and inns she had not ventured to the day before. Each rejection stung a little more, each 'no' made her feel a little more desperate. Her stomach growled, reminding her that she had eaten but one meal a day for the past three days, and nothing since supper the night before, adding to her desperation.

She continued to inquire at establishment after establishment, hoping, praying they would show her kindness and give her a job. She would take any job, even if it meant mopping floors or mucking out stalls.

Her efforts were to no avail. No one was looking for help, especially not her help. She went out day after day, striking out farther into the city, walking further, looking for work in places she had not yet looked. Every evening, she made her way home feeling dejected and discouraged.

The days were growing ever colder as an early winter set in, and with only a thin cloak over her thin mourning dress, Raya's teeth chattered as she hurried through the streets looking for work. At home in the evenings, it was barely better as they were now rationing firewood, and at night, she pulled their bed as close to the fire as was safe in hopes of staying warm. In the morning, the water in their water pail was frozen solid. Mother Emaline said it was unusually cold for Cincinnati for the time of year.

As the weeks wore on, it was harder and harder to remain cheerful, and Raya felt herself teetering on the brink of despair.

"Raya, it would have been better if you had stayed with your family," Mother Emaline told her softly one evening. There was no self-pity, no grasping for affirmation in the woman's words. Mother Emaline was simply stating the obvious.

Raya looked up from the tear on her cloak that she was mending in the dim light of the fire. Their last candle was nearly gone, and they were saving it for emergencies.

Their small shanty was cold, with only one log on the fire. They were each wrapped in a blanket and sitting on chairs that Raya had positioned nearly on the hearth to soak up every ounce of heat the lone log gave off. Raya's belly growled, wanting more than the pinch of dry bread she had given it. As small as it was, that bite of food was more than they would have if she didn't find work soon.

She thought back to the moment last week when she had spent the coin that had emptied her coffers to the point she could no longer return to her father's house. She had held onto it a little too long, drawing a glare from the man behind the store counter as she paid for a small sack of flour. Realizing what she was doing, she released the coin and stepped back, leaving the store quickly with her small purchase. Now, Raya glanced at the drooping bag of flour. Almost empty.

Still, she knew that no matter how bleak things were, she could not return to Amhil and her father. Not now, not ever. Her place was with Mother Emaline. Without pretense, vanity, or false front, Raya said the one thing that stood out most concretely in her heart and mind. "You are my family."

"Raya, it would have been better for you if you had gone home. You're so young and sweet. You don't need to be among hostile people, spending every day out in the cold, suffering every night in hunger," Mother Emaline told her, sounding frustrated.

Raya leveled her dark eyes at Mother Emaline, her expression both serious and gentle. "My home is with you."

Tears sprung to Mother Emaline's eyes, and she shook her head. "You are a very good friend, Raya. Too good of a friend."

"As you have been to me," Raya reminded her.

Mother Emaline sat quietly for several long moments. Finally, Raya reached out and took her hand, facing her as she dared to ask a question that had increasingly been worrying her. "If I wasn't here, Mother, do you think one of your friends would take you in? If I wasn't with you, would things be easier, better for you? Answer me honestly, please."

Mother Emaline looked up, her eyes swimming with tears. She shrugged her thin shoulders. "I honestly don't think so. Maybe for a time I could stay with someone, a few days, perhaps a few weeks. But I don't believe I would have a home with anyone for the remainder of my years, and unfortunately, I don't foresee my situation improving."

"Are you certain? Please don't just say that for my benefit," Raya told her, truly concerned.

"I'm certain," Emaline answered dismally. She gave a dry laugh. "Have you not seen how they scorn me? When we left town, I was one of the most prosperous women in the city. Now I have returned in utter poverty. My old friends pity me, but stop short of compassion. They would not bring me into their home. And Judson . . . oh, I've wondered if he might take me in as he did James . . . but there's a difference between me and James—James was a very rich man. Judson is motivated by money and taking me in would come with no advantage to his purse strings, so no, I think he would not."

Raya gave a firm nod. "Then we shall remain together, and we'll make the best of it."

Quiet settled in the room. Finally, Emaline broke it. "You have been a gift to our family, Raya. You have stood by me when I lost everything. You made Luke a happy man. For five years you have brought joy and sunshine into my house whenever it threatens to rain." Mother Emaline's voice broke.

Raya smiled and covered Mother Emaline's cold hand with her own. "And you have led me to Truth and the source of joy, and have shown me how to live rightly."

Quiet settled until again Mother Emaline broke it. "The LORD will make a way, Raya. You'll see."

Raya nodded, but remained silent. She knew the words were Biblical, yet she could not comprehend them now in relation to their present situation. What way could there be, when they were utterly alone, Mother Emaline was too old to work or remarry, and Raya was not an acceptable worker as business owner after business owner had plainly told her? What way could there be when they were nearly starving and freezing to death?

She believed in the goodness of the LORD, believed in His power in the world and in His creation, but to think that extended into her own life seemed like absolute vanity. With all the people in the world, could she really expect Him to give them—her—His attention and meet their small and insignificant needs? The idea was preposterous.

The conclusion she had come to over the past weeks was that she served a big God. He was powerful and mighty. He was King of all the earth. She knew earthly kings did not have time to look in on every servant in their kingdom. Not because the king was wicked or unkind, but because the king had much to occupy his time, and it was not feasible. If that were true of an earthly king, then how could it not be true of the King of kings?

No, He was good and mighty, and she would lay down her life for Him should He ask it, but she could not expect His attention or intervention in her life. She could not expect that He would have the time or desire to set aside His kingly duties to concern Himself with a mere girl and her aging mother-in-law.

"Raya," Emaline said, waiting until the young woman looked up at her. "He will make a way."

Worried that Mother Emaline thought she had lost her faith, Raya answered quickly. "I do not look at the situation and ask why it is how it is, Mother. My faith is not dependent on what happens. I know He's good and sovereign no matter our present or future situation," Raya responded.

Mother Emaline considered her for several moments. "That's good, truly it is, Raya, but He is Jehovah-Jireh—*our* Jehovah-Jireh."

Raya shook her head. "I am not familiar with these words."

"Our Provider, Raya. He is our Provider. He will provide for us. He raises the poor out of the dust and lifts the needy out of the ash heap."

Raya wanted to argue that the King of all the earth would not have time to lift them out of their humble state, but she did not want to contradict her elder. What was more, she was afraid of disrupting the look of peace that filled Mother Emaline's face. The lady had enough troubles without Raya pointing out that their God was too sovereign to interfere in their daily lives.

"He will make a way," Emaline repeated, almost to herself.

Suddenly curious, Raya couldn't hold back her question. "Mother, you yourself say you're being disciplined by God. Your husband, your sons, your financial provision, your home, your grandchild . . . all of it has been taken away. How can you believe God will make a way for you . . . for us?"

"Why, Raya, to believe that God is rejecting me in the middle of His discipline would be a grave mistake," Emaline replied incredulously. "Who am I that His mercy could be outdone by my sin? Who am I that my mistakes could be greater than His love? No, in His great discipline, He has not turned His back on me, but instead, tucked me in closer still. For He loved me when I was far off. He threw a party and rejoiced at my return. Discipline speaks of instruction and training, not punishment. Discipline is a mark of His love, Raya, not His anger."

The log in the fireplace fell, sending a spray of sparks upwards. Raya watched the dying fire and shivered. She didn't feel loved. She felt cold and hungry and alone. The way Mother Emaline talked about her God as being a God of love, a God of love who loved *her* and personally cared for her, felt foreign. She could not begin to comprehend such a relationship with an unseen deity. Especially not here, especially not in their dire state.

Redirecting her attention back to the fire, Raya noticed that before long, it would be nothing but embers. She quickly finished with her cloak, then laid it aside to don the next morning before heading out to search for work.

Pushing back her blanket, Raya reluctantly emerged from her cozy cocoon, and stood, taking the blanket over, and spreading it on the bed they shared. Adding another log to the fire, the last of the night, she set the two broken bricks she had found down amongst the embers. Helping Mother Emaline to her feet, Raya steadied her as she took the few steps from her chair to the bed. Then Raya helped her lie down before taking the woman's blanket and spreading it over the bed as well. She doubled it over so her own portion was also covering the older woman, in hopes of keeping her warmer. Raya shivered as she worked and cast a cursory glance at the paper-thin walls. They had long since discovered the reason why the little dwelling was empty going into winter.

Bending over at the hearth, she pushed the bricks out of the embers with a metal poker and wrapped them quickly in rags. When they were wrapped, she placed one at Mother Emaline's feet and one near where her own would go. Standing up, she smoothed the blankets over the bed, as they had been mussed when she put the bricks under them. Getting lost in thought, she smoothed her hand over the top quilt again, remembering how it had covered Mother Emaline's bed back in Colorado Territory.

It was the quilt she had pieced with Mother Emaline soon after Luke claimed her as his bride. It had been over that very quilt that she first came to know and love her mother-in-law. All those years ago, as they had worked together on the quilt, Mother Emaline had talked, telling her about their family, their traditions, their God. Raya remembered feeling a tinge of sadness when it was done, thinking her uninterrupted time with Mother Emaline was over. That was until Luke saw it.

Raya smiled. Luke said it was the prettiest quilt he had ever seen. He said he would be proud to sleep under something so fine, and asked if she could make one for their own bed. The next day, she set to work on another quilt with Mother Emaline, pleased to have additional time to continue their discussions.

Now, Luke's quilt was gone. She had given it to a family who had lost everything on their way over the mountains. It hadn't been much, but she'd wanted to do something to help when she heard of their terrible plight and the quilt was all she had to offer. And while she wouldn't take back what she had done, she felt unexpected tears sting her eyes. But she hadn't given in to tears in over a week, and she wasn't ready to now.

Taking the candle from the crate that had been turned upside down to be used as a makeshift table between their two chairs, Raya lit it and went to check that the front door was barred. Cold was seeping in around the door, and she shivered as she ran back to the fireplace. Snuffing the candle, darkness fell over their little shanty once again, and she slipped under the covers, glad that Mother Emaline was already warming the bed. She pulled the blankets all the way up over her head and pressed her toes to the hot, covered brick.

"I'm glad you found these bricks, Raya," Mother Emaline said, her face also under the covers, the chattering of her teeth just beginning to ease.

"Me too. It was a lucky find."

"To think someone would throw them away when they were only a little broken," Mother Emaline said with a decided 'tsk.'

"I know. It's difficult to comprehend that kind of wastefulness at this point, isn't it? However, I'm sure we were just as wasteful not so very long ago."

Mother Emaline was quiet for a moment. "When you have much, you aren't afraid to waste some, I suppose. When you have nothing, you realize just how precious every little thing is." Mother Emaline paused and then continued. "When I thought I had the rest of my years to enjoy my husband, sons, and our little family, I didn't enjoy every moment like I could have. I wasn't concerned by letting a moment, an hour, even a day slip by unnoticed every now and then. Now that they're all gone, I realize just how precious each moment was, and is."

"I threw Chenoa's squash casserole out to the hogs once," Raya confessed bemoaningly. "Now, I would climb into the hog's pen to eat it."

Mother Emaline chuckled. "Chenoa is a dear girl, but she certainly doesn't know how to make an edible squash casserole."

Raya grinned in the dark. "That is certainly true."

There was another pause, one so long Raya wondered if Mother Emaline had fallen asleep. "Once, when Julius and I were newly married, I spilt ink on one of my dresses, just so I would have to get a new one," the woman finally admitted, sheepishly.

"Mother Emaline!" Raya chided, surprised at the confession from a woman who was usually so prudent and wise.

Mother Emaline let out something between a groan and a laugh. "Raya, you have to understand how hideous it was! It had once been a lovely green color, but had faded to a dreadful greenish yellow and had long since lost any sense of fashion. And, once I went riding with Julius in it when it rained and after that, it forever smelt of wet horse.

"Julius knew what I had done as soon as he saw the ink spot. I was so embarrassed, I wished the floor would open up and swallow me right then and there. It seemed like a good idea at the time, but then, when I saw that look on Julius' face, I felt like a silly, vain little child."

"What happened?" Raya asked, her eyes sparkling in the darkness.

"Julius just got that silly ol' grin on his face and asked who I had been writing a letter to. I couldn't fib, so I simply didn't answer. He asked if he got me a new dress, if I thought I could manage to keep the ink in the jar. Then we went out, and he bought me material for not one, but two new dresses. He let me pick whatever I liked. I got the most beautiful dark blue taffeta."

Raya laughed in the darkness, picturing how big, jolly Father Julius must have handled his wife's attempt to take her clothing into her own hands. She had never met the man, but knowing his sons, she could picture him easily enough.

"He got a good laugh out of it," Mother Emaline remembered fondly. "In fact, he never did let me live that down. Just a few months before he passed away, he surprised me with the fabric for that paisley day gown I used to have. When he gave it to me, he said he thought he would conserve ink and simply buy me the makings for a new dress."

Raya laughed again, and Mother Emaline joined in.

Fifteen

Raya pressed her fingertips against her forehead and closed her eyes. She was sitting in her chair by the stove and had just finished ripping the last few coins out of the hem of her skirt. In her hand was everything they had left. It was enough for another small bag of flour, a half ration of meat, and a few potatoes. Or it was enough to send a short telegraph back to Colorado Territory, back to Amhil. Perhaps if she telegraphed him of her hardship, he could send her the money to buy a ticket home.

She turned the coins over and over in her hand. She wanted to remain with Mother Emaline. She knew it was what she should do. And yet the cold had seeped into her bones to the point she could no longer get warm. Hunger gnawed at her insides until her thoughts were consumed by the pain of it. She felt faint and weak, and going out looking for a job day after day was getting increasingly difficult as her energy waned.

If she didn't find a job soon, they were going to run out of food altogether, and rent was due again in a week. Their firewood would only last a week beyond that, even being rationed. Meaning, in less than two weeks, they would be absolutely broke without a roof over their heads, food on their table, or a fire in their fireplace.

If Amhil would provide a ticket, though she would go in shame, she could go back to her father's house. She would eventually be married off again, and as frightening as that felt, at least her father would make certain it was to a man who could provide for her basic needs. Food, water, shelter, warmth. At this point, even having her basic needs met felt less scary than her current reality. Additionally, she would be back in the West, where she was at least seen as a woman, not a heathen.

This was her last chance, her last way to reach out and grab the lifeline Amhil had offered her. If she didn't do it now, there would not be another chance. She would be left to simply endure whatever came next. That thought was terrifying. She was hungry now. What might she stoop to when the hunger became unbearable? She was cold as it was. What would happen if their firewood ran out altogether and they were turned out of their humble home?

If only she had some hope, then perhaps she could stay, but in all her days of looking for work, she had not been given one ounce of hope. Not one person had even considered the possibility of employing her. The rejections were always quick, sometimes accompanied by an explanation, most often not. Inns, stores, seamstresses, cafes, families, butchers, factories, banks, schools, blacksmiths, furniture makers—the resounding answer was always the same: "No."

Surely, if she was not with her, surely one of Mother Emaline's acquaintances would extend hospitality to her. Though Mother Emaline herself had refuted the possibility, Raya doubted anyone could be so heartless. Surely at least one of them would find it in their hearts to take the ailing woman in. Then the dear woman would be living in luxurious accommodations, sleeping on a feather bed, eating her fill of delectable feasts, taking tea in the afternoons, and going visiting. Surely, someone would take pity on an old woman left alone in the world and provide for her.

But what if no one did? Raya bit her lip and looked down at the coins. Glancing back up, her eyes fell to the family Bible on the rudimentary table beside her.

Suddenly, like a gust of wind blew in through the cracks in the walls, peace descended over the room and a sweetness filled it. Where there had been fear in Raya, suddenly she felt calm. The hunger in her stomach lessened, her head stopped pounding and for just a moment, she stopped shaking from cold. Finding blessed relief in the quiet moment, Raya breathed deeply.

Afraid or not, she knew what she would do. She knew how she would spend their last coins.

The next morning, she woke up early and hurried out from under the covers and into her black dress, moving quietly. After kissing Mother Emaline's forehead, Raya collected the coins off the table beside her chair and left the small shack. She had no second thoughts or doubts on her way to the general store, surprising even herself. She had made up her mind about what to do with the money.

Going in the front door, Raya headed straight to the counter where the telegraph machine sat. Motioning for the attention of the clerk, Raya took out her remaining coins and put them on the counter.

"I'll take a bag of flour, a dozen eggs, and as many potatoes as this will buy me." Once the clerk counted her coins and gave her the wrapped packages, she hurried home with them and immediately set about making a hot breakfast.

Hungry and cold, she was cheerful as she went about her work, knowing that no matter what came, she had made the right decision and passed her final moment of temptation. After all, she had just spent her last way home.

***

"What's a purty little thing like you doin' out on this cold day?"

Raya looked up to see a group of young men standing in front of a clapboard house, a checkerboard laid out on the top of a keg. They were all watching her, and she couldn't tell who had spoken. Putting her head down, she continued on. She only had four more blocks to go before she reached the relative safety of the shanty. She picked up her pace.

"Hey! I was talking to you!" one of the men called out, sounding offended by her rebuff. Before she knew it, two of them were beside her, one on either side. "What are you doin' out?" the first demanded.

"I'm looking for work," she told them simply, realizing that ignoring them wasn't going to accomplish anything.

"Oh honey, we got all the work you need! We could keep you busy for the rest of the day!" he crowed. "Fellas, she's lookin' for work!"

"Not that kind of work," she told him past gritted teeth, catching his foul direction.

"Oh yeah? How long's it been since you ate? Yer lookin' mighty slim. Might feel good to have a couple coins to rub together. Maybe even enough to get you somethin' to eat if you do us right," the other man said.

Disgusted and degraded, Raya caught up her skirt and began to run, hoping and praying they wouldn't follow her.

"Fine, we'll come by tonight, then. You open the door, and we'll do you right!" the first called after her, laughing.

She watched as a few bystanders who were on the street or out doing miscellaneous chores in front of their homes looked up, but they simply looked back down again, used to the neighborhood and their neighbors. Raya wasn't used to any of it. She wanted to scream at the young men to keep their filthy thoughts and words to themselves, then go home and cry out all the hurt, all the shame, all the fear. Instead, she ran until her legs and lungs were burning. Looking back to see if she was being followed, she saw that she wasn't, and slowed to a walk. The shanty was within sight, and she quickly collected herself as she traveled the final few feet. It would never do to have Mother Emaline know about such an incident. Taking a deep breath, she went inside, shutting and barring the door behind her.

Emaline was asleep, and she was thankful. She sat down in her chair and drew her knees up to her chest, laying her forehead against them in agony. She felt physically ill, violated, and degraded. Yet the worst part was that somewhere deep within, the young men's reasoning made sense. She was starving. Quite literally. As was Mother Emaline.

Raya's stomach burned with hunger, and she knew she had dropped several pounds, even though she had not started with much to lose. Her mourning dress hung on her, and she felt weak nearly all the time. It was sheer adrenaline that had given her the strength to run. Now, sitting in her chair inside the dim, quiet shanty, that adrenaline began to ebb, leaving her terribly tired in its wake. She fell asleep with her head against her knees.

That night, Raya woke with a start, her heart instantly racing. Someone was pounding on the door. Though it was too dark to see their timepiece, she knew it was the middle of the night. No one should be at their door in the middle of the night.

"Who is it?" Mother Emaline whispered, her voice shaky.

"I don't know," Raya told her, though her mind instantly turned to the men who had bothered her earlier. She wondered if it was them at the door now. If it was, she didn't know how they had found where she lived.

They were both quiet for several long moments, then Raya got slowly out of bed. "Do you think I should answer it?"

Mother Emaline looked at her through the darkness, her eyes wide. "I don't think so."

"Me neither," Raya whispered back. They both knew the walls of their shanty were like paper, and they didn't want whoever was outside hearing them.

Raya stood in the middle of the floor, still and frightened, wishing they owned a gun, wishing they had someone to protect them. She didn't know what she would do if someone broke down their door, but she felt better prepared standing up. Wielding the only weapon they owned, she grabbed the metal poker from the hearth, then stood shivering and scared, waiting.

Finally, the pounding stopped. After five minutes of silence, she went back to bed, but laid awake in the darkness, her heart still racing. Tears ran silently down the sides of her face as she longed for her husband, for her brothers-in-law, even for her brother or father. She longed to belong to someone who would protect her.

Like a small flame in the middle of a dark room, she heard again Mother Emaline's words from the night in the hotel. *For thy Maker is thine husband; the Lord of hosts is his name; and thy Redeemer the Holy One of Israel; The God of the whole earth shall he be called.*

The pounding had stopped. She was safe. She was back in bed and still safely shielded by the front door. Letting out a ragged breath, Raya forced herself to be grateful for all of that. She may not have a physical husband, brother, or father, but lo and behold, she had not been harmed.

The next day, their neighbor came over and apologized for her drunken husband the night before. When he came home from the saloon, she said, he had been confused as to which house was theirs. She heard him pounding on their door and came and fetched him. She apologized for any start it may have given them.

Raya accepted her apology wholeheartedly, thankful it had only been a confused drunk and not the men who played checkers. She kept the hood of her black cloak up over her head that day when she went out looking for work and was careful to avoid the area the men lived in. It was one more street she added to her list of streets to avoid. Sadly, her list was growing long; the incident from the day before was only one of many. While honest work was difficult to find, dishonest work seemed to be around every corner.

***

The sickness had officially set in. Raya had no more than walked in the door, cold down to her bones from her long day of looking for work, than she had known the truth.

Even at this late hour, Mother Emaline was under the covers in bed, her eyes closed, her face aflame. Raya barred the door, threw off her cloak, and hurried to her bedside. Mother Emaline's eyes were glazed when she opened them to look up at Raya. She coughed before she could speak.

Raya warmed her hands by tucking them between her arms and her body, before laying one against Mother Emaline's forehead. "You're burning up," she told her grimly. She headed for the pail of water and a cloth. She would start a cold compress immediately. "How long have you had a fever?"

Another coughing spell. "It came on this morning, just shortly after you left," Mother Emaline rasped, her voice weak.

Raya bit her lip as she dipped the cloth into the icy water, then laid it over Emaline's forehead. The last time the sickness came on her, it had nearly done her in, and Mother Emaline had been otherwise healthy. Now, she was skin and bones, living in a cold shack, on the verge of starvation. They didn't have the money for a doctor, nor a way to improve their circumstances to allow her the comforts needed to give her a fighting chance of getting better. Fear gripped Raya's heart.

Going for a chair and dragging it close to the bed, Raya sat down, grasping Mother Emaline's hand firmly in her own. "Mother, besides your fever, what else is wrong?" she asked, needing to assess the situation and discover just how bad this onset of the sickness was.

She had thought perhaps they were getting off lucky this time as nothing but a cough and weakness had persisted since their travels, accompanied by a low fever once or twice. Raya had hoped the cough would go away as well, but considering Mother Emaline's flushed face and high temperature, it was obvious the sickness had truly taken hold instead.

Mother Emaline lifted the corners of her lips in a weak smile. "I'm fine, dear. Truly. It has only been a bad day for me physically, but tomorrow will surely be better." The woman paused for a brief moment. "How was your day?"

Tears sprung to Raya's eyes unbidden, and she failed to keep the bitterness out of her heart. How was her day? Useless. Wasted. Futile. Pathetic. She had walked and searched for work all day, to no avail. She had met nothing but snobbery, rejection, and scorn. Her legs ached, her head was pounding, and she was freezing everywhere but in her belly, which burned with hunger. It was her fifth day without food, having secretly saved her portion for Mother Emaline for the four days leading up to yesterday. Yesterday, the last of it ran out, and there was nothing left for either of them.

And now, her beloved mother-in-law was sick and looked to be on the brink of death. Her heart was heavy in her chest. She was quite certain she did not have it in her to see Mother Emaline to her grave.

Still, she propped up a smile. "I was able to cross several establishments off my list of places to check, and now I know more about where to go tomorrow."

Mother Emaline looked at her out of her blue, glazed eyes, and Raya knew Emaline understood everything she hadn't said. They were running out of time, and they both knew it.

"I'll find work, Mother, I will. Perhaps tomorrow will be the day, and by tomorrow night we can have a hot meal and an extra log on the fire," Raya assured.

"That's right. Don't get discouraged, Raya. By then, I'm sure I'll be feeling better, and we can enjoy it together," Mother Emaline answered, using what little strength she had to smile and reach out to pat Raya's hand.

Raya bit her lip and nodded, hoping that Mother Emaline was right, hoping she would recover once again and be up and around in a short while. Not wanting the ailing woman to see her watery eyes and guess at her lack of optimism, Raya pushed herself to her feet. "Mother, I'm going to have a cup of hot water to chase away my chill. Would you like some? Or perhaps a drink of cold water? I'll get you either."

"A drink of cold water would be lovely," Mother Emaline answered weakly.

Raya smiled at her as she rinsed out the cloth in cold water and laid it back across the woman's head before turning to the water pail. She dipped water out into the teakettle and set it amongst the embers. Then, she dipped up a cup of icy water for Mother Emaline and, going back to the bed, lifted her gently so she could drink. Mother Emaline took only a small sip, but it was enough to send her into a fit of coughing. Raya negotiated with her weary arm muscles to hold Mother Emaline up until the coughing spell ended, then gave her another small sip to ease her raspy throat.

By the time Mother Emaline was resting back against the pillows again, the water in the kettle was hot. Raya pulled the kettle out of the embers with a rag and poured the steaming liquid into a chipped cup. Taking her seat, she wrapped her cold hands around the scalding teacup, enjoying the heat, even if it was a bit too much.

"I can't believe it's come to this," Mother Emaline suddenly wailed, startling Raya to the extent that she nearly spilt her hot water. "This was not how it was supposed to be! We had menfolk, family, a business that was turning a good profit, livestock, our own valley, food, savings, warm houses! They should have kept this from happening to us! They were supposed to provide for us! They were supposed to take care of us! They should have found a way out of that mill!" Mother Emaline sobbed, the haunting sound interrupted by another fit of coughing.

Raya could barely see through the tears that collected in her own eyes, and she swallowed against the pain that gripped her throat. She was tempted to break down, sob and wail as Emaline was, but she couldn't. Not now. Not when Mother Emaline needed comforting. Raya stood up and perched on the side of the bed, smoothing Emaline's hair back. "You're right. They would have never allowed this. They provided for us well. But they're not here anymore, Mother. We'll have to find our own way. And we will. It will just take a little bit of time."

"Why? Why aren't they here? Where have they gone?" Mother Emaline asked, her voice taking on a strange pitch. "Have they gone out hunting again? When will they be back? They haven't been out hunting too long, have they? You have to be careful in those woods. I hope they haven't run into a grizzly. Send Niz to go see if she can spot them. Then tell Chenoa to add an extra log to the fire, dear, it's a mite chilly in here."

Raya sat back, feeling as if the whole pail of cold water had been thrown in her face. Something cold twisted in the pit of her stomach. It was just the fever talking, she knew it was, but Mother Emaline's delusional questions both unnerved and shocked her. On the coattails of the shock came a great sadness. Was she to relay the heartbreaking news to her mother-in-law that her sons were dead? That they were now living in a shanty in Cincinnati, and it was cold because they were out of money with no hope of getting more? Fresh denial, confusion, and grief would follow. What was worse was that, if it were the same as in years past, the woman would ask the same questions again in ten minutes.

Not feeling strong enough to face the present storm, Raya drank the rest of her hot water and stood. "Scoot over, please, Mother. I think I'll come to bed, too, and we can sleep off all that ails us. Surely things will be better in the morning."

She left Emaline to move over while she went to the fire to pull out the bricks. She wrapped them in cloth and put them at the end of the bed as she did every night. She double-checked that the door was barred, applied a fresh cold compress to Mother Emaline's head and crawled between the blankets.

Under the covers, she squeezed Mother Emaline's hand. "Goodnight, Mother Emaline. Sleep well. I pray you will feel better in the morning."

"I'll feel better once the men are home. Women shouldn't be left alone at night."

"I couldn't agree more," Raya told her honestly.

"Where are Niz and Chenoa? They should sleep in here with us until the men arrive."

Raya felt a tear slip down the side of her face in the darkness as she answered the only way she knew how. "They're safe."

When Raya heard Mother Emaline's breathing even out in sleep, she turned over and buried her face in her pillow. *"God! Do You hear this? Do You hear her?"* she cried out within. Desperation trumping all her beliefs about her distant God, she made a plea she never would have made under normal circumstances. *"Make a way for us for the sake of this dear woman, please! You have taken all she had, won't you give something to ensure her survival? Won't you give us enough to keep her from going mad?"*

Tears wet Raya's pillow late into the night as she wrestled against the burning in her stomach and the pain in her heart.

***

Raya was startled by a sharp knock on the door. Hardly anyone had been to their shanty since they moved in. Who had come now? She wouldn't have considered checking, other than it was light out, and the knock came again, harder this time. With great hesitation, she opened the door, hoping the visitor meant them no harm. Her heart plummeted when she saw their landlord standing in the doorway.

"I told you I didn't appreciate the rent being late," he told her, his voice sharp.

Raya was at a loss for words, yet he was obviously expecting a reply. "I . . . I'm sorry. I've been looking for work. I . . . I'm on my way out to look again."

"I don't take kindly to squatters."

"No, sir. I will pay you . . . I just . . . I need a little more time," Raya answered, her eyes on the ground, ashamed.

"I don't rent on intentions. I need the money by Friday or I'm turning you out," Mr. Henley told her, his voice hard and free of emotion.

She had three days. Three days to find the money for their rent. "Please sir, my mother-in-law is sick," she pleaded, casting a quick glance to where Mother Emaline lay in bed by the fire, her face flushed, her eyes glassy. "I'm looking for work everywhere I can. Please, I promise that I will pay you as soon as I find work. It shouldn't be much longer."

The short man considered her for several long moments. "You know, we could make an arrangement."

Cold air was flooding in the open door, stealing what little warmth they had. "Yes, yes, please," Raya agreed, hope springing up in her heart. "Anything! I can clean other rentals you may have, or I can cook, or . . . or . . . I can do your books if you have need. I'm good at reading and figures. Whatever you need! I just can't have her out in the cold. She's very ill."

"I would take payment of another kind."

As the man's gaze drifted boldly, Raya pressed her hands against her cheeks that suddenly felt like they were on fire. "I'm going to pretend as if you didn't say that," she said, carefully keeping her words even.

He tilted his head at her. "Then I'm going to need your rent money on Friday."

Raya stood straight, drawing herself up to her full height. "Very well."

The landlord took a step back. "Friday, then. And my offer stands."

Raya shut the door, then turned and pressed her back against it, sinking down onto the cold dirt floor. Hugging her knees, she rested her forehead against them and began to sob silently. Is this what it had come to? Would she have to dole out favors to dirty men in order to keep them alive?

She knew, without a doubt, that if they were turned out, Mother Emaline would not survive the week. She was barely hanging on as it was. She herself would not last much longer.

"Raya!" Mother Emaline wailed her name from the bed and Raya pushed herself to her feet weakly, feeling dizzy as she did. After the dizziness passed, she made her way to the side of the bed and took the woman's thin hand.

"What is it, Mother?"

"Can you bring me something from the cupboard, dear? I'm so hungry. Perhaps I was sleeping during breakfast and you didn't want to wake me? Well, I'll take something now, please. Perhaps some of Niz's cornmeal pudding? Is there any of that?"

Oh, how Raya wished there was. A bowlful of the filling mush swimming in milk straight from the cow, with a bit of honey stirred in, sounded heavenly. But there was no milk, no honey, no corn pudding, no cupboard to get anything out of.

She looked down at her mother-in-law's rigid cheekbones that rose gauntly out of her sallow cheeks. She was frail and thin, little more than skin and bones, and Raya realized that if she didn't find food, and soon, she wouldn't have to worry about keeping a roof over Mother Emaline's head.

Her mind made up by pure necessity, she pulled on her cloak. She wasn't looking for work. Not today. She needed to do something that would actually produce. She needed to take action to ensure Mother Emaline's needs were met. If that meant swallowing her pride and stooping to a level she had hoped she would not be forced to stoop to, then so be it.

Sixteen

Raya hurried across the frozen street, stomping her feet as she went, hoping to get some feeling back in her toes. She had been walking most of the day, trying to get up her courage, not knowing where to go or how to begin. Now, the shadows were beginning to gather, and she needed to act fast if she wanted to have something to take back to Mother Emaline. She had walked by several establishments throughout the afternoon but had not yet found the courage to go in. Now, she found herself in a ritzy district down by the great Ohio River. It was said that all sorts of freight came into town by boat on the large waterway, and the finer establishments in the district catered to the businessmen who monopolized it.

Finally, she stopped walking and looked up at the sign of the business in front of which she had stopped. The name was painted in a beautiful scroll above the door, and the fancy gate was wrought iron. It was an expensive establishment—that much could be seen from the spectacular exterior and size. She had never seen an inn so large.

Raya almost turned back. If the rickety old inns in her neighborhood wouldn't allow her to enter, surely this one wouldn't either. Why she had stopped in front of this one, she didn't know. And yet, there was an urging within that caused her to push open the gate and venture up the walkway.

She pulled open the heavy door of the fancy self-proclaimed hotel and made her way inside. She tried to hide her hesitancy, hoping she didn't look as if she expected to be thrown out. She held herself straight and sure, yet she could not bring herself to take her eyes from the floor.

The front room was well lit and warm, and a delicious smell curled out from what she assumed to be a dining room, making Raya's stomach cramp anew. Her face and hands instantly began tingling, the shock from coming out of such cold into such warmth, painful. The furnishings in the room were all lush and beautiful, and the wood on them gleamed. A middle-aged man wearing spectacles hurried into the front room. A quick glance revealed that his smile quickly turned into a thin, hard line.

"We don't serve people of color. Kindly show yourself out the same way you entered."

Raya felt the color leave her face. "I'm not looking to be served, sir, I'm . . . I'm . . . I'm wondering if I could . . ."

"Spit it out already. I don't have all day," he told her impatiently.

"I'm wondering if I could look through your garbage in the back, sir," Raya said weakly, forcing the words out in a rush, afraid he would throw her out before she found the nerve to ask her question.

Silence was her only answer. Her cheeks were burning, and she didn't dare look up to see his expression.

Finally, he spoke. "You don't have to ask to beg, you know," the man answered, sounding caught off-guard.

Raya kept her eyes on the ground. Beg. She had become a beggar. He was right. The thought made her cringe, and yet, why should she think she deserved more? Her parents were little more than that in their old country. She had done nothing worthy of deserving more. She was an alien in a foreign land. Fate had turned against her. There was nothing in the universe that promised humankind fairness or equality.

"I do not wish to dishonor this place. If you tell me to leave, I will," she answered meekly. She expected him to do just that. She expected him to throw her out, just as so many others had. "But before you do, please, sir, know that I ask not for myself but for my mother-in-law, Emaline, who is very ill. If I don't find something for her to eat . . ." Raya shrugged her thin shoulders, unable to finish her sentence. Weak and tired, she did not trust herself to hold back the tears should she voice her greatest fear.

"Fine. Sit out back. The garbage is taken there after the evening meal," the man answered roughly.

She dipped her head in answer. "If you can think of something I can do . . . some way I could serve, I would be happy to do so."

"We're not looking for hired help."

"You have already said I could have the only wage I seek. I am satisfied with what others throw away," she told him humbly. It was true. She would take a crust of bread, someone else's leftovers, the vegetables that weren't fit for cooking—she didn't care. She simply needed to find something that would replenish Mother Emaline's ailing body and give her the strength she needed to get better.

"Just go around back. We have no need of your labor," the man replied curtly.

Raya turned to leave, grateful simply to have permission to look through their garbage and scavenge for anything edible. It didn't provide the money she so desperately needed, but if only she could find something for them to eat, she knew she would find a way to pay their rent as well. If not, she could be resourceful. She would find another way to keep Mother Emaline sheltered and dry.

"What's your name?"

The man's question surprised her, and she stopped. She turned back around. "Raya Applewood. I'm the wife of the late Luke Applewood of the Cincinnati Applewoods."

The man's expression stayed hard. He gave a short nod. "Be off with you, then."

Raya left the hotel, carefully shutting the front gate behind her. Going around the back of the building, she sat down against the wall and pulled her knees up to her chest where she could wrap her cloak around them to stay as warm as possible. She would wait until the supper rush was over and then she would carefully comb through the trash.

While she waited, she thought of Mother Emaline and hoped she was doing alright. She had stayed with her until she fell asleep that morning, and Raya hoped she had slept far into the afternoon. Sleep was the best medicine available to her now. Although Raya didn't like to leave her alone when she was so sick, she hadn't felt as if she had a choice.

She had made the difficult decision to tend to Mother Emaline instead of going out to search for work ever since the delirium set in. It wasn't a good long-term strategy, but she was afraid of what the woman might do in her confused state. Raya's biggest concern was that she would wander outside the shanty and lose her way. So, she had stayed and nursed her as best she could, praying for the woman constantly, all while attempting to keep her own mind from running a continuous litany of what could be coming next. But that morning, looking down at her mother-in-law, she'd seen the cold, hard truth that if Mother Emaline didn't have food to eat soon, Raya wouldn't have to worry about her ever wandering off again.

Now, the ominous thoughts returned, and scenes played out unbidden in Raya's mind—things she didn't want to think about. On its own accord, her imagination conjured up a picture of what would happen if she arrived home to find Mother Emaline had passed away during the day. Was she passing away even now? Even as she sat here waiting for the garbage to be brought out? Changing her focus subtly, her thoughts turned to what would happen on Friday, when the rent came due. She had no doubt Mr. Henley would make good on his threat to turn them out. Raya hadn't been warm for weeks. The little shanty was far from cozy, but when she thought about being turned out . . . anything would be better.

What was fifteen minutes if it would secure her shelter for another month?

Feeling soiled and ashamed for even thinking such a thing, Raya wanted to claw her own thoughts out of her head. She was the late wife of Luke Applewood, a good and decent God-fearing man. Would she disgrace him by selling her body for the mere comfort of shelter? The thought nearly dissolved her into tears. Blinking them back, something white caught her eye. Turning, she saw a piece of paper trapped in a tangle of weeds near the back door.

Looking closer, Raya realized that the alley was littered with trash and the back of the inn overgrown with dead weeds. It certainly did not have the fancy, well-kept appearance the front of the establishment had, and she quickly climbed to her feet. The proprietor may not have need of her services, but she needed something to keep her mind occupied. Stooping down, she picked up the wayward piece of paper. She grabbed another paper next to it, and then an eggshell nearby.

Piece by piece, she cleaned up the alley, collecting the trash and taking it to the bin, where she added it to the rest she would go through later. When she was finished plucking every bit of trash from the alley, she dropped to her hands and knees beside the foundation and began to pull at the dead weeds. They had been killed by the harsh winter weather that had fully set in now, but still they remained, looking messy and unkept. Thankful for the work that kept her mind occupied, Raya continued, pulling weeds and brushing brown leaves and debris away from the foundation with her bare hands.

Seventeen

The Fairbury Hotel, Cincinnati, Ohio

Atlas Fairbury drew his pocket watch out of the pocket of his vest as he neared the hotel. It was nearing five o'clock, and he still wanted to look in on Mr. Lenox and the others before he retired to his home for the evening. It had been a long day, made longer by an incident at his packing plant involving an incorrect shipment. Mr. Johnson, his foreman at the plant, was more than capable of taking care of the issue, but Atlas chose to remain as well, simply curious as to how Johnson would deal with it. Two hours later, the issue was resolved, and he continued on his way, though later than usual.

The carriage stopped in front of the hotel, which bore his family's name. He quickly stepped out of the carriage and made his way up the front walk. The weather had turned viciously cold here of late, and he was eager to reach the front door. He had no more than shut the door behind him when Mr. Lenox appeared from the dining room. The man's face smoothed out into a welcoming smile as he stepped forward and shook his hand.

"Good evening, Mr. Lenox," Atlas said warmly in greeting.

"Good evening to you, sir. I was beginning to wonder if we were going to see you today."

"Yes, well, I had a bit of a hold-up this morning but have made it here at last. Shall we?" Atlas gestured to the dining room, where

UP FROM THE ASH HEAP

he always sat at a table near the back with his second-in-command to discuss the day.

Though he had complete faith in Mr. Lenox, he felt it important to check in daily. Being a good businessman meant keeping a close eye on what was transpiring within his businesses. Success was found in finding good leaders he could trust absolutely to put in charge of his many holdings, then keeping those leaders close, and working with them continuously to make the business bigger and better. So far, his strategy had worked well for him. He had more than doubled his family's holdings since taking the helm after returning from the war.

A server brought them both a cup of coffee, and Atlas spent a few moments visiting with her amiably before she excused herself and headed back to the kitchen. Atlas sipped at his coffee while Lenox began his daily report, alerting Atlas to any prominent guests who were staying with them, any issues that had come up, and any changes. Sometimes, the report was barely five minutes long, other times, it was quite lengthy. Fifteen minutes in, Atlas realized that tonight, it was going to be the latter.

Being one of the largest hotels in town, there were always issues that arose, and Lenox was constantly looking for ways to improve their guests' stays. Atlas appreciated his dedication and gave him the honor of listening intently and discussing his ideas and concerns seriously. Never mind the five other businesses he owned. For this period of time each day, he blocked everything else out of his mind and pretended The Fairbury Hotel was his only priority in the world.

Lenox had just finished telling him of the growing need for a larger stable, when the serious foreman stopped suddenly in his spiel. Atlas looked up from his coffee, watching the man out of curious eyes. Lenox seemed as if he were debating on whether or not to share what was on his mind. "Spit it out already. You'll feel better once you do," Atlas told him cheerfully.

Lenox hesitated for another moment before starting. "The widow of your late cousin is out back. She asked me permission to beg."

Atlas startled, so caught off-guard by the change in conversation that he choked on his coffee. "Who do you speak of?" he asked once his lungs cleared. His mind hummed. Suddenly, before the man even answered, he knew who Lenox was referring to. "Emaline Applewood is here? Out back? Why, by all means, bring her in!"

Lenox shook his head. "Not Ms. Applewood. Her daughter-in-law. The heathen. Sounds like they've got a real bad lot of it, they have. She said Ms. Applewood's fallen ill. She seemed quite desperate for food. She asked permission to go through the garbage once it's taken out."

Atlas wasn't one to be caught speechless, but in this instance, that's exactly how he found himself. He had heard a few weeks back from his cousin Judson that Emaline Applewood was back in town, destitute and alone, save her dark-skinned daughter-in-law. Gossip traveled fast amongst polite society, and Atlas had heard of the death of Emaline's three boys from Mr. Lenox himself, who seemed to hear all of Cincinnati's juiciest gossip from the patrons at the hotel. He'd filled Atlas in on the tragedy just the day before Atlas talked to Judson, and heard it confirmed, along with the news of Emaline's return. He had felt compassion for the woman he remembered only as kind.

Judson had not said much else about Emaline or her daughter-in-law, save for the fact that the heathen had been very doting and concerned about her. Atlas never imagined their situation to be so dire; when Judson called them destitute, it never occurred to him that he meant it to such a magnitude. But, if Ms. Applewood was begging at his back door, they must be quite poor off indeed.

"I think she came hoping for work. I could tell it didn't set well with her to be begging. A woman with her background and skin coloring, it's no wonder she's had a hard time securing employment. I don't know what Ms. Applewood was thinking, bringing her back with her. She should have left her in the West. It would have been better for the girl."

"Girl?" Atlas questioned, surprised.

"Aye. She can't be a day older than my Mary."

Atlas concealed his shock. He knew Lenox's eldest daughter to be in her very early twenties, and he had never pictured Emaline Applewood's daughter-in-law at such a tender age. "Is she here still?"

"Aye," Lenox said again. "She's been sitting out back since I told her she could go through the garbage after the evening meal is served. She must have a hard time sitting still, though, because not but half an hour after she was in here, Ms. Macy brought me word that the girl was picking up trash and pulling weeds. She finished about twenty minutes ago—right before you got here. The alley has never been so clean. You should go see it. It's a sight to behold."

Atlas could think of only one thing. "But it's freezing outside."

Lenox shrugged. "She never said she minded. Mayhap her kind are made with a thicker skin than we are. Perhaps they don't feel the cold as we do."

Atlas took another sip of coffee. "Perhaps."

As Lenox continued on with his report, Atlas glanced out the window. The shadows were long already, and it wouldn't be much longer before complete darkness fell. If Emaline Applewood and her daughter-in-law were as poor off as it would seem, it was presumable they didn't live anywhere close, and no young woman, regardless of the color of her skin, should be expected to walk through the city alone after dark.

When Lenox finished his report on the day's happenings, and they had talked at length about the new stable they desperately needed to build, Atlas drained his coffee and stood to his feet. Turning his top hat round and round in his hands, he looked out the window for several long moments, then back at Mr. Lenox.

"Once the evening meal is served, have Ms. Macy package up the leftovers and send them home with the girl. And give her a job tomorrow, if only for the day. See how she does. See what kind of a worker she is." Atlas knew Mr. Lenox would never argue with him, but he also knew he would want to. To employ a heathen in one's establishment was simply not done. There were still too many bad feelings, too many people outraged about the Indian wars that were still going on in the West. "And I feel like walking tonight. Please send her home in my carriage."

Atlas noted the surprised look on Lenox's face, but his longtime friend and manager of his thriving hotel and dining hall only nodded. "I'll see that it's done as you've requested."

"I remember her late husband when he was just a boy," Atlas explained quietly. "I remember when he said once, when he was little, that he wanted to model himself after me when he grew up. I was a strapping young man of seventeen and must have looked like I had the whole world at my fingertips to a little kid like Luke." Atlas paused. "I remember how Emaline used to make me cookies when my mother and I would visit. She was a kind woman. My mother loved her." He paused and then gave a decisive nod. "I want to deal kindly with this girl and her mother-in-law."

Mr. Lenox nodded, understanding showing on his stern face. "Then I'll see it's done as you say."

Atlas nodded. "Thank you. I'll expect a report on her work." Atlas put his hat on his head and tipped the brim of it to Lenox. "Much obliged for your dedication, Mr. Lenox. I'll see you tomorrow."

Lenox bid him goodbye and Atlas left the hotel, setting off at a brisk walk down the street. His large home wasn't far away when compared to the walk Ms. Applewood would likely have, and he knew a thing or two about protecting himself. Better for the young woman to take his carriage and make it home safely.

Blowing on his hands to warm them, he picked up his speed. For the girl's sake, he hoped Mr. Lenox was right and her kind was made with thicker skin. If not, she must be freezing after sitting outside for a few hours.

UP FROM THE ASH HEAP

***

Raya looked up, squinting against the block of light that spilled out from the open door, trying to make out the face of the individual who stood in the doorway. The person came out and down the steps, and she saw it was the man she had spoken to earlier. In his hands he held two casserole dishes with tea towels tied around them, as well as a lumpy bundle Raya could not distinguish the contents of. He held all of it out to her.

Raya scrambled to her feet, using the wall to support herself when she felt unsteady on cold feet that had lost all sense of feeling. "What's this?" she asked, confused.

"The leftovers from supper."

She shook her head, not understanding.

"I was instructed to give them to you to take home to your mother-in-law."

"By who?" Raya asked overwhelmed and confused.

"By the same person who left you this carriage to be driven home in tonight."

Raya's gaze followed the gesture of his hand. A fancy carriage pulled by four beautiful horses was parked in front of the stable only a stone's throw away. She had been admiring the beautiful apparatus earlier. Now, she could not comprehend that she would be given a ride home in it.

"Why?" she asked, the question coming out in a mere whisper. She was overcome. For a moment, she thought she might be dreaming. But the pain in her cold limbs and the way her stomach was knotting as the scent of the food made its way to her nose, confirmed she was not.

The man's expression was firm. "When you came today, did you come to beg, or did you come seeking employment?"

"Whichever you would extend," Raya answered humbly.

"Which would you prefer?"

"Work," she answered quickly.

"Then work you shall have. At least for a day. It's all I can offer, but as long as you're here by six o'clock, I'll employ you for tomorrow."

Tears of relief, tears of joy, sprung to Raya's eyes. "Sir, are you jesting?"

The man's mouth flattened into a hard line again. "I do not jest."

"You're truly giving me a job?" she asked, struggling to believe it. After expending so much effort, after so many rejections, after so many wasted days and hopeless nights, was she really being offered employment?

"It's not a job," he replied harshly. "All I can offer you is day-to-day work. If you're agreeable to that, show up at six o'clock sharp tomorrow morning, and I'll have work for you for the day. We'll see about after that."

There was no warmth or gentleness to the man's voice, no softening in the least, yet Raya was tempted to reach out and hug him. Either that or faint. Instead, she curtsied.

"That's more than acceptable. Thank you. Truly... thank you. I'll be back in the morning," she promised, and turned. Her heart was pounding. Could it be true? Did she have work? Even for a day?

"Don't forget this, miss."

She turned and saw he was holding out the bundled packages he carried. Still stunned, she accepted everything he held out to her, then followed him to the carriage. She gave the carriage driver directions to the shanty and then stepped into the luxurious vehicle. She set the leftovers carefully on the floor, where she was certain they would not make a stain should they somehow spill, before sinking wearily into the plush seat. She had not sat on anything soft since leaving the inn over a month before, and the simple pleasure was the final straw. Her tears of relief and disbelief fell quick and hot as the carriage carried her swiftly home.

She had planned to spend her night going through cans of garbage, searching for any scraps of food she could find for Mother

Emaline, before making a long walk home through dark and dangerous back streets. To now be riding safely home in a fine carriage with hot, delicious smelling food at her feet—enough for several days' worth of meals—and a promise of work in the morning seemed completely and entirely unreal. She wondered again if she was dreaming, but the carriage hit a bump in the road, and, unprepared, she was sent askew, hitting her head on the sidewall. Rubbing the sore spot on her head, she suddenly began to laugh. Oh, how thankful she was to be in this carriage to bump her head.

Suddenly, it hit her. On the very day she absolutely needed to find food and work, she did. In all honesty, she didn't think Mother Emaline would make it through the weekend without nourishment. If she didn't pay rent within forty-eight hours, she would be turned out on the streets or forced to sell herself to pay her debt. On the very last day, at the very last minute, the LORD had provided. If it had come one day, one hour earlier, it would not have tasted as sweet.

Without knowing the stark reality of how close they truly came to starvation, how close she came to losing her mother-in-law, how close she came to falling into prostitution in hopes of simply surviving, she would not know the abundant thankfulness and relief she now felt.

When the carriage stopped, Raya peeked out from behind the covered window and saw the shanty. The driver opened the door for her, and Raya quickly collected the hot dishes the man from the hotel had sent and stepped out of the carriage. Still in awe, she watched as the driver climbed up on his high seat and snapped the reins over the horses' backs. Such finery in such a desolate neighborhood struck a stunning contrast.

The fine carriage and beautiful horses did not belong here—not in a place where shanties were crowded together, bony dogs ran in the streets, and dirty water and slops were thrown out wherever they landed. Gardens, trees, carriage houses, and beautiful wrought iron fences did not exist here. And yet, Raya watched the horses prance down the narrow dirty streets, heading back to their comfortable barn after delivering her safely home.

Turning, she pushed through the door. The fire was still going, which was a good sign. Mother Emaline had been up. Raya looked for her in the bed, but the bed was empty. Instead, Emaline was sitting in her chair, wrapped in two blankets.

"You're home late. I've been worried about you." Though Mother Emaline's voice was weak, it sounded normal, the high-pitched tone of delirium gone for the time being. "Have you good news?"

The hope in Emaline's voice as she considered her daughter-in-law's face was Raya's undoing. She ran across the dirt floor and dropped to her knees in front of Mother Emaline. "The LORD has richly provided, Mother! We have food to eat and tomorrow, I have work!"

"You found work?" Emaline asked, her voice wobbling.

Raya nodded, a smile stretching the corners of her mouth. "Yes! Not permanent work, but I at least have work for tomorrow. I tell you, it has restored my hope! It won't be enough to pay our rent, I'm sure, but perhaps if I take that little token to our landlord, his faith in us will be restored, and he'll give us more time."

"You found work?" Emaline asked again, no expression showing on her face, except shock.

Raya nodded. "Yes, Mother. I found work."

Mother Emaline rose shaky, bony hands up into the air. "Thank You, Father! Thank You for providing." Her words carried deep emotion, and in their wake, tears began to fall from her eyes—tears that soon transformed into sobs.

Raya laid her head on Mother Emaline's lap and cried as well. With every tear, they bled off fear, frustration, desperation, hopelessness, depression, and grief. Every tear was born of joy, shed in relief. Their thankfulness seemed to fill the small shanty and for those few minutes, the air around them seemed to warm several degrees.

Mother Emaline was well enough to sit up in her chair as they ate a warm, delicious meal, and throughout the evening, even without adding wood to the fire, Raya did not shiver with cold despite the fact that she was not wrapped in a blanket. They went to bed with full, thankful, and peaceful hearts, and Mother Emaline led them in a prayer so long that Raya fell asleep to the sound of it.

Despite all her misgivings and beliefs about His time constraints, the LORD had provided. He had made a way.

Eighteen

Raya woke well before sunup and jumped out of bed, her feet stinging as they hit the cold floor of the shanty. She pulled the quilts up quickly to shield Mother Emaline from the cold. Shivering as she pulled off her nightgown, she stepped into her black mourning dress, buttoning it up as quickly as possible. She sat on the edge of the bed to pull on her warm wool stockings and stuck her feet in her black boots, thankful to no longer be walking barefoot.

Taking up Mother Emaline's container of powder, she quickly powdered her hands and face after she washed them in the frigid water in the wash pail. When she was satisfied with the slightly paler color of her skin, she braided her hair, taking extra care that it looked clean and conservative.

"You'll have to walk the whole way in the dark," Mother Emaline said from the bed, startling Raya.

Raya looked over to where Mother Emaline still lay beneath the covers and saw that worry clouded her face. "I will be just fine, Mother. Don't worry." The truth was, she was a little worried herself.

The city streets were no place for a woman to walk alone, especially in the dark and in such a rough part of town. Every day when she went out looking for work, she was appalled at the lewd comments and bold propositions that were carelessly flung her way. Some of the more honorable men offered her marriage; most of their intentions were not nearly so honorable. She did her best to ignore them and always carried a sharp rock—her only defense—in the pocket of her cloak, but there was no denying the streets were dangerous. During her long weeks looking for work, she had only gone out after sunup and tried to return before nightfall. The darkness only made the questionable area worse.

"I wish we had a man to escort you," Mother Emaline said softly.

"As do I," Raya admitted. "But we don't, and we need for me to have work. Since there are no other options, I'll simply take the option we have. I'll go alone and trust that I'll be taken care of."

"I'll pray for you all day, for the good LORD's protection all around you," Emaline told her firmly.

Raya's smile was quick and warm. "Thank you. I would appreciate that." She tied her apron on, covering the front of her dark dress.

"Are you nervous?"

Raya glanced up from tying her cloak. "A little, I suppose. I've never worked in a hotel."

"Did he say what you would be doing?"

Raya shook her head. "No, just that he would have work for me. That was enough."

"Well, I'm sure you will do just fine. It will likely be cleaning, cooking or dishwashing, and you're well acquainted with those chores."

Raya looked up in time to catch the sparkle in Mother Emaline's eyes. Her heart swelled with gratitude that Emaline was well enough to tease. "*Well* acquainted," Raya agreed.

In her father's house, she had worked tirelessly alongside her mother to make sure the home and store were always spotlessly clean. After marrying Luke, she worked with Mother Emaline to do the same, until Mother Emaline took sick. With Nizhoni always preferring to be out of doors in the garden or inside cooking the meals, the cleaning had rested on Raya's shoulders alone.

"How do I look?" Raya asked, finishing with her cloak.

"Like the LORD's favored one," Mother Emaline answered with a smile.

Unsure what to do with her mother-in-law's answer, Raya simply leaned down and kissed the woman's cheek. "I'll be back this evening. Try to rest and stay warm. There's leftover food whenever you get hungry. Do you need anything before I go?"

Mother Emaline shook her head. "You go. I'll be fine. Have a good day."

Raya drank a cup of water and grabbed a small crust of bread before hurrying out the door. Drawing the hood of her cloak up over her hair, she hastened down the dark street.

The city was starting to wake up. Puffs of smoke were rising from the chimneys of the crowded little shanties. Men were outside stomping around as they tended to chores, and women and children were pumping fresh water as they hurried to get back inside and out of the cold. Raya could see her breath hanging in the air, and she wrapped her hands in the fabric of her cloak, trying to keep them warm.

"It's too early for a pretty thing like you to be out and about. Where you going, missy?" a tall man said, suddenly falling into step beside her.

Raya jumped, startled by his sudden presence. Sending him a sideways glance, she attempted to discern his intentions. He was scrawny and dirty, and his clothes were little more than rags, but his face looked kindly. She had seen him once or twice before. He never made ribald comments like the others.

"Work," she answered, unwilling to divulge more.

"I'll escort you," he told her firmly. "The city can be a dangerous place. A young woman shouldn't be out by herself before it gets light. You never know who could be lurking in the shadows."

She wondered if there was a hint of a warning in his words, and she fought against fear. She wasn't certain it would be safer to traverse the dark streets with him at her side. Who knew what his own intentions were.

"I'm familiar with the city, and my work isn't far. I'll manage alone, thank you," she said, attempting to sound kind but firm.

Even if his intentions were honorable, it wouldn't be appropriate to show up at work in the company of a strange man. She was a widow in mourning, not a woman who kept company with men of questionable character, whom she hardly knew.

The tall, scrawny man looked as if he might protest, but she held up her hand to ward it off. "Truly, thank you for your offer, but I must insist I continue on my own."

He considered her for a moment and then nodded. "Well, I'm Luke Dover. I live just over there. I work the docks, but I'm home most every night. If you need anything, let me know."

Luke. The man's name felt like a blow to her heart. She nodded, hoping her expression didn't reveal her emotions. "I'm Mrs. Luke Applewood." She watched the shock wash over Mr. Dover's face.

"I'm sorry for my impertinence. I assumed you didn't have a man, since you were out by yourself. My apologies."

Raya stayed her expression even as her heart twisted in pain. The young man had assumed only so rightly. She had no man. No husband. No protector. No provider. The only response she could manage was to dip her head in a nod of acknowledgement and pick up her pace to put distance between them. She had never felt her widowhood so acutely.

"LORD, he was a good man," she whispered into the cold darkness. It was true. Her husband was a wonderful man, and she grieved deeply for him.

She left the shanty-lined street and turned onto one crowded with run-down apartment buildings. Something shifted in a dark doorway, and she instinctively veered away. She once again picked up her pace, eager to arrive at her destination.

She felt no less apprehensive about her early morning walk through the dark city than Mother Emaline and the chivalrous Mr. Dover, and she tried to hurry as she made her way down dark, frozen streets. She braced herself against sudden noises coming from dark doorways and alleyways and fought her instincts to flee every time she heard the loud, heavy footfall of a man approaching from behind. She was a working woman now. She couldn't be weak. She couldn't be afraid. She had to do what was needed. Besides, the city was full of people going to work. Certainly, those around her had more on their minds than a lone girl hurrying down the street.

Finally, as she completed the final leg of her journey, her heartbeat began to return to normal. Her long walk to work was over, and she had arrived safely. She let out a deep sigh of relief and sent a prayer of thanks up to heaven. She turned up the alley behind the hotel and approached the back door, where the proprietor had exited the night before.

Opening the door, she slipped into a well-lit kitchen. To the left was a long row of hooks. Only a few cloaks were hanging on them, giving testament to the early hour. Raya quickly took hers off and hung it beside the others.

In front of her spread a large room full of tables, washtubs, cookstoves, and cupboards. Past the hooks was an open doorway, and through it Raya could see another room, lined with shelves full of cookware and supplies. More tables ran down the middle of the smaller room, and several kettles were heating on the cookstove that sat in the corner. Past the open doorway was another door, though this one was closed. At the far end of the kitchen, opposite where she stood, was a large, hinged double door, and Raya knew instinctively that it must lead to the dining room. In the kitchen's large room, several people were standing over cookstoves or at tables, mixing things in bowls, cutting biscuits, and stirring what looked to be gravy in large pots.

Unsure what to do, she asked a woman standing over one of the three large cookstoves where the man she had spoken to the day before could be found. She learned that he wouldn't be in until six o'clock and was ordered to wait. She stood against the wall she was motioned to and waited there until he walked into the kitchen.

As soon as he walked in the door, he was giving orders, making sure all of his employees were accounted for, discussing the day's demands and how the needs were to be met. Raya stayed by the wall, quiet, waiting for her opportunity to speak with him. Finally, he was done talking to the other hired help, and he turned.

Raya took a cautious step forward with a smile.

A look of recognition filled the man's face. "Ah, Ms. Applewood. You've arrived. Ms. Macy told me a young woman came in at half past five asking after me. I assumed it was you, and now I see I was correct. Today you'll be serving the back dining room. It's the only place we need help. When there's no one in the dining room, you will do whatever task Ms. Macy gives you," the man, whom the others had addressed as Mr. Lenox, said.

Raya couldn't hide her surprise. "The dining room? I assumed I would be in the kitchen or cleaning."

Mr. Lenox looked sharply at her over the rim of his spectacles. "Yes, the dining room. But the back dining room, mind you. You're not to go in the front."

Raya nodded her understanding, though she didn't understand at all. What was this front and back dining room business? She had never known an inn to have two. Of course, this was a hotel, and perhaps that accounted for the difference. They must entertain quite a large dinner crowd to need two spaces . . . and not want their crowds to mix.

"Is that acceptable to you?" Mr. Lenox asked, his tone impatient, as if testing her to see what her response would be.

"More than acceptable. I will do whatever I'm instructed. I'm only thankful that you have agreed to employ me for this day."

Mr. Lenox considered her for a long moment, then gave a curt nod and left. Raya took a deep breath and turned, hoping the alleged Ms. Macy would identify herself. Instead, a young woman, quite plain in the face but with kind, tired eyes, approached her.

"The back dining room is where the dock workers and boat hands come to lunch. Mr. Fairbury caters to both ends—the rich and the poor. You'd best watch yourself in there. The boys take kindly to a pretty face. Too kindly. I'm the longest serving back dining room girl they've got, and I've only been here a month. Most girls can't stand it in there. I, on the other hand, don't take any of their guff. You just have to let 'em know it ain't allowed. They're worse in the beginning, but after a bit, they won't bother you so much."

Raya's heart began to drum in dread. The picture the girl in front of her painted wasn't appealing. Still, she chided herself for feeling anything but thankful. She had work. That was all that mattered. Whatever it was, as long as it was honest work, she would be thankful. She could put up with a group of rowdies if it meant having money to pay rent, buy firewood, and keep food on the table.

"Thank you for explaining," Raya told her simply, touched that the girl in front of her not only spoke to her, but seemed friendly, despite the color of her skin.

The girl nodded humbly. "Ms. Macy is over there. The one in the blue dress. She runs the kitchen. And I'm Noni."

Raya nodded and offered the girl a bright smile. "Thank you, Noni, for the information. That's very helpful. I'm Raya Applewood."

"Think you can survive the back dining room?" Noni asked, tilting her head.

"Well, I'm sure my mother-in-law and I cannot survive if I don't have work. So, yes, I'm quite certain that I will."

"I understand. Thinking 'bout my family keeps me going, too." The girl smiled at Raya before continuing on with her business.

Raya crossed the large kitchen and stood beside the woman in the blue dress. A large white apron was tied over her front, and a white frilly cap was tied over her graying hair. Her plump face was flushed as she stood over the stove scrambling eggs.

"Ms. Macy, I'm Raya Applewood. Mr. Lenox said I am to serve in the back dining room today and help you whenever I'm not serving."

The large woman turned to her, still stirring her scrambled eggs with one hand. "He told me about you. We start serving at half past six. Go see how many are back there so far."

UP FROM THE ASH HEAP

The lady was as no-nonsense as Mr. Lenox, and Raya immediately felt intimidated by her. Nodding, Raya kept her eyes downcast. "Yes, ma'am."

Ms. Macy had turned back to the stove before she even answered, and Raya realized she would have to find the back dining room on her own. She reluctantly left the radiating warmth of the black cookstove and scanned the room with her eyes. Four doors led out of the warm kitchen. Knowing she had come in one, seeing the pantry through another, and having watched Mr. Lenox disappear out the third, she quickly eliminated three of the four options. Pushing open the last swinging door, she saw she had guessed correctly.

Three rows of long tables were packed into the roughly finished room, which was a stark contrast to the rest of the establishment's lush furnishings. Yet, as Raya looked across the tables at the dozens of men who had crowded onto the benches, she realized that fine furnishings would not be as appreciated by this crowd as much as good food, and plenty of it. The clientele who filled the room was rough and rowdy, obviously accustomed to hard work and a different lifestyle than those who frequented the front dining room. Getting a head count, Raya quietly let the door shut, glad that it muted the noisy chatter bouncing around the room.

She dutifully reported the number of patrons to Ms. Macy and waited for her next instructions, which came shortly. She was to take the coffeepot in and begin to fill the men's cups. Taking a deep breath and summoning her courage, Raya grabbed the pot from the back of the stove and pushed through the swinging door. As she left the kitchen, she saw that Noni was following her with another pot of coffee.

Raya kept her eyes down as she entered the back dining room, even as a hush fell over the crowd. She began to fill coffee cups one by one, knowing all the while the quiet had descended as all eyes were on her. Noni began filling cups opposite her, yet no one looked away. Raya kept on, bracing for what came next, anxious to be done with her task.

"Well, ain't you a sight to behold?" one of the loud ones finally said. "Seen your kind once when I went a'sailing for spices 'round in the orient, a long time ago. Still, I ain't never seen a gal so purdy as you from those parts."

Raya wasn't sure whether to acknowledge his words or not, but felt obliged to do so when everyone remained quiet. "Thank you sir, for your kind words," Raya said, feeling anything but thankful he had called attention to her exotic looks. Still, she hoped her gentle answer would turn the conversation in a pleasant direction. Perhaps they would go back to their previous discussions now that the ice had been broken.

"Did you hear her voice? It's like music!" another man exclaimed, his excitement evident.

Raya swallowed hard, feeling as if she were being considered for purchase.

"I saw her first!" one man joked. He was shoved as others contradicted him. For a moment, Raya wasn't sure what was going to happen next. She hoped they weren't about to start grabbing at her, arguing over her like a piece of meat.

"God of Israel, help me bring glory to Your name here today," she murmured under her breath, desperate and wishing for someone, anyone, to protect her.

"*I will not leave you nor forsake you. I have a plan to redeem you from the pit.*" The quiet whisper that blew across her heart was louder than the ruckus the men were now making.

Her heart lurched, then stilled as peace flooded her. She repeated the words over and over to herself as she filled coffee cups. She was too consumed by her present circumstances to consider the source of such peace-filled words, yet distressed enough to cling to them unashamedly.

The young man she was serving suddenly grabbed her wrist. She stopped abruptly, her breath catching. What did he mean to do to her?

UP FROM THE ASH HEAP

"I know these other pigs are rude and degrading, but I'm sincere. Come away with me and be my wife. I'd marry you today, no questions asked. I make a decent wage and am gone only two weeks at a time, running freight downriver."

"I'll keep you company while he's gone!" a man down the bench called out ribaldly, causing Raya's stomach to churn and earning himself a scathing look from the young man holding her wrist.

"I'd give you a good home," the young man continued. "I don't care that your skin is dark. I'm planning to go west when I can save up enough cash for the supplies. Maybe, if they're peaceable, we could even settle near your kin."

The first man who had spoken when she came into the room called out to the hopeful bridegroom from farther down the table. "She's not an Injun, you fool; at least not the kind you'll find in the West."

The situation was getting out of hand. Turning back to the man in front of her, Raya felt her fear lessoning and her compassion building at his heartfelt plea. She gently pulled her arm away. "I'm in mourning for my husband," she answered simply, hoping to lessen her rejection of his proposal.

"Ah, he's dead, he won't care!" the burly man beside the hopeful bridegroom called out. "But don't marry the kid, come home with me. I'm not gonna offer marriage, but I'd pay you handsomely."

Raya shuddered, feeling ill. If Luke was present, he never would have let such talk continue.

"Don't talk to her like that!" the young man said, bristling.

"Aw, give me a break," the second shot back. An argument with some pushing ensued, which quickly escalated as others joined in, seemingly merely for the fun of it. As the first punch was thrown, Mr. Lenox strode purposefully into the room.

"Stop!" he yelled. The arguing ceased, as did the pushing. "This is not a saloon! There will be no fighting, no coarse talk, and absolutely no offers of unmentionable employment in this place, do you understand? We have a reputation to uphold, and if you are not agreeable to helping us uphold that reputation, then you can see yourself out and not come back again. 'Tis a shame, because I know you would all miss Ms. Macy's fine cooking, but I will not tolerate such insolent behavior in this establishment."

Raya stood still, her eyes downcast, horrified that Mr. Lenox had been interrupted to come control an issue that had ensued because of her. Any thankfulness she had initially felt for his presence dissipated as reality set in. For a girl who was working on a trial basis, her day wasn't off to a good start. She watched Noni slip through the door behind Mr. Lenox and realized the girl had gone to fetch him.

"Do you all understand?" Mr. Lenox boomed. Around the room, chairs scuffed and men hummed and hawed, expressing their understanding without really saying a thing. Mr. Lenox nodded. "Very well. Carry on."

Raya and Noni resumed filling cups with coffee, and the men began talking again, quieter this time and without the pushing. Still, Raya found herself as the topic of much of the conversation. Finally, she and Noni had filled all the cups, and they were able to escape back to the kitchen. Ms. Macy filled their hands with heaping bowls of scrambled eggs and sausages and platters of buttered biscuits, and sent them right back in. Raya went back and forth several times, carrying in more food, filling empty coffee cups, and refilling jelly dishes.

Her mouth watered and her stomach was growling so loudly she feared the men might hear it, as she set another bowl of fragrant sausages down on the table. The temptation to eat just one of those sausage patties when her back was turned to those in the kitchen was so great, Raya barely managed to resist; however, she succeeded in delivering the bowl with as many sausages as it contained when Ms. Macy put it in her hands. After setting it down and seeing there was plenty of everything on the table, she followed Noni's lead and stood against the wall, waiting to be summoned. As she watched the men devour the food, her empty belly growled again.

UP FROM THE ASH HEAP

Nearly half an hour later, when the time was announced, all the men plunked down their money and rushed for the door. Raya saw that half a plateful of scrambled eggs, four sausage patties and two biscuits were all that was left of the feast she and Noni had carried in. As she collected the leftover food, she longed to fill her belly with it. The scents were tantalizing, and her mouth watered as the memory of such tastes came to mind.

She knew eating even a bite of it would be stealing. Left over or not, the food belonged to the hotel, and even though she was the only one in the room, she would always know if she took some, as would her God. She carried the leftovers out to the kitchen, then went back in to collect the money, which she promptly turned over to Ms. Macy.

After Raya had finished clearing the tables with Noni, she washed them down with a soapy rag, scrubbing until they were smooth and clean. She swept the floor and knocked down a cobweb she had noticed in the corner while she was waiting for the men to finish. Then she pumped a basin full of dishwater and washed dishes.

During the morning break, Raya was the first to finish her cup of tea and get back to work. She went back to her washbasin full of soapy water, determined to be faithful with however many days of employment she was given. If Mr. Lenox was willing to give her a chance and pay her a fair wage, she would give him a full day of enthusiastic effort. To be a hard and willing worker was the best way she knew to honor him and show her gratitude.

When she finished with the last of the dishes, she was sent to help Noni set the tables in the back dining room before the men started arriving for lunch. However, they had not yet put out the last tin dish and coffee cup before the door opened and loud, boisterous men came tromping through the door.

"See, Max, that's the girl all the talk was about today. Ain't she as purdy as we said?"

Raya straightened stiffly, weary already of the conversation that was about to ensue. All throughout breakfast, she had been discussed, and now it seemed as if lunch would be more of the same. Noni shot her a sympathetic glance as the new man stared openly and voiced his agreement. They finished setting the tables, then pushed through the swinging door into the kitchen. Ms. Macy filled their hands with bowls of stew and sent them back through the door.

There were more men who showed up for lunch than there had been for breakfast. So many, in fact, that Raya and Noni had to scrounge to find enough dishes, cups, and utensils for all of them. Noni said it was the most patrons she had ever seen come to lunch. From the bold stares and crude comments, Raya knew she was the reason for the crowd. As she returned to the kitchen with Noni for more stew and bread, the girl whispered to Raya that she was likely responsible for the hotel's most profitable back dining room lunch yet. Without a stitch of vanity, Raya couldn't help but agree.

Returning to the back dining room, she steeled her nerves as she stood against the wall, her eyes cast down as she attempted to block out the conversation. What wasn't about her was either gossip or littered with cuss words, complaints, threats, or exaggerations. She had no stomach for their idle talk.

"Hey, little missy, we're needing more of that stew," one loud, bearded man said as he held up the nearly empty serving bowl. She felt his eyes on her as she crossed to grab the bowl and hurry from the room, knowing he watched her walk out and knowing he would be waiting for her to return.

As she pushed through the swinging door and hurried into the kitchen to ladle more stew from the large pot on the cookstove, she nearly collided with a gentleman who was standing just on the other side of the door with Mr. Lenox. Grasping after the bowl as it was knocked askew in her hands, she nearly fell. The man reached out and grabbed her arm to steady her, saving her from the floor. As he righted her, she glanced up at him for only a moment before quickly averting her eyes, feeling heat rush into her cheeks from the embarrassment of her blunder.

"I'm so sorry, sir," she said quickly, the words rushing out. "I was in a hurry, and I didn't see you. I do apologize." Her quick glance had revealed his expertly tailored sack suit, narrow cravat, and short, oiled hair. Given his fine appearance and his being in the company of Mr. Lenox, she knew her mishap could be cause for her first day on the job being her only.

"I suppose I was as much to blame as you for stepping on this same piece of flooring," was the amused reply that came back. The man was tall and sturdy, with a handsome face and a confident masculinity about him.

Raya curtsied, slipped past the gentlemen, and hurried to the stove. She ladled stew into her big bowl as fast as she could without spilling and hurried back to the dining room, being mindful of where the talking Mr. Lenox and his counterpart were.

She delivered the stew and stood against the wall again, waiting to be summoned. As she stood quietly, she swallowed hard against the lump in her throat and blinked back threatening tears. She wouldn't be surprised if Mr. Lenox told her later there was no need to return in the morning. First, she had caused a small brawl in the dining room and now she had run into someone who appeared to be very important. She had likely proven to be more work for Mr. Lenox than she was a help. He had warned her she was on a trial basis, and she may have just ruined the only chance she had been given.

Thoughts of Mother Emaline came to mind, and Raya started worrying. The food Raya was given the night before had been good for the woman, but a few good meals were not enough to give her the strength she needed to get better. The wage she would be paid for her day of work would be helpful and oh, so appreciated, but it was not going to be enough to pay their rent or secure them more wood for their fire. Her mind turned to what might happen in the days to come, and she blinked hard against fresh tears.

Unable to handle standing still with her worrisome thoughts any longer, she grabbed the water pitcher and went around filling the men's water glasses, making sure they had everything they needed. She didn't know what the coming days held, but whatever it was, it wasn't going to do any good for her to stay still and worry about it now.

***

Atlas Fairbury drummed his fingers on the tabletop, his mind churning. "Who was that, Mr. Lenox?" It had been nearly half an hour since he collided with a girl in the kitchen of his hotel, and although he had his assumptions about who she might be, he wanted to hear it confirmed. Charles Lenox had been talking when the girl came rushing through the kitchen door and ran into him, and he had continued talking as soon as the girl continued on her way. By the time he stopped talking, they had been to the site of the new stable, visited with a wealthy patron who had just arrived from Pittsburg, and settled at a table in the dining room to go over the books.

Mr. Lenox, unconcerned by his question, was still writing in his ledger and only glanced up briefly. "Who? That girl that nearly mowed you over?" He waited for Atlas's affirmation. "That's her—the girl I told you about—Emaline Applewood's daughter-in-law who came east with her."

Atlas had suspected as much—there were no other women of a similar nationality employed at his hotel, yet he needed to hear it for himself. If he hadn't been warned, he never would have guessed the young woman was the daughter-in-law of Emaline Applewood.

When he had heard from his cousin Judson that Emaline had returned from the West with her heathen daughter-in-law, he envisioned a woman like those in pictures he had seen. He expected someone older, wilder, more rugged, who spoke broken English if any, looked dangerous and defiant, and wore moccasins and a dress made of soft leather. Instead, the lovely young woman seemed meek and polite, spoke perfectly without trouble or accent, and was clothed in a simple black gown appropriate for her mourning state. What surprised him even more was that even in her plain mourning dress, she was stunning. So much so that for an instant, he had felt as if the air had been knocked out of him.

Several years back, when he heard his cousin's son had taken a native as a wife, he was appalled. It was unheard of. He could not understand why Emaline had allowed such a union, or what had possessed the young man to do such a thing. Now, he had no doubt. His cousin's reasoning had become perfectly clear.

"She's serving in the back dining room?" Atlas asked after a moment.

"Yes, sir. We lost another server yesterday, and when you said to offer her work for the day, it was the place I most needed hired help. I thought we could try her there and see how it goes."

Atlas's mouth thinned out into a hard line. He knew what the back dining room patrons were notorious for, and he could guess at what the day had been like so far for the dark-skinned beauty. "How's she doing?" he asked.

"Well, it depends on how you look at it," Lenox answered, still distracted by his ledger.

"How so?" Atlas questioned.

"I had to go break up a brawl this morning, that ensued because of her."

Atlas raised an eyebrow in question. Was she a fighter? The idea didn't seem to line up with the brief encounter he had with her earlier.

"Or I should say *over* her," Lenox continued grimly. "The other server came to fetch me, said the men were getting rowdy over the pretty new face in the dining room. Today, for lunch, so many men came to see her that the kitchen barely had place settings for all of them. At one point, there was a line out the door. The men seem quite taken with her, which may prove to be more trouble than it's worth, though the extra diners do bring revenue up a bit." Mr. Lenox paused. "Aye, she's caused a bit of trouble today, but I guess none of her own doing. I suppose she can't be blamed for her looks. Ms. Macy says she hasn't uttered one complaint, and she's a hard worker. I guess she barely even sat down for the morning break. She gulped down her tea and was back to work before any of the others."

"I suppose her and Emaline need for her to have this job," Atlas observed, drumming his fingers again.

"I believe they do. No self-respecting human being would stoop to begging if they weren't in real need, I suppose."

Lenox moved on to other subjects, yet Atlas's mind kept coming back to the girl in the back dining room.

From what Judson, and then Lenox, had told him, the girl had displayed nothing but kindness, loyalty, and calm resolve. They reported actions that were distinctly honorable and faithful, and the girl had proven she was a hard worker. Atlas well knew that Ms. Macy was not easily impressed. What was more, the girl had gone far beyond her duty to stay with Emaline, had shown exceeding kindness to his extended family, yet he was feeding her to the wolves in his back dining room. She had been his cousin's wife; now, she was being fought over by unscrupulous dock workers and steamboat crews. Heathen or not, surely he owed his cousin more than that.

"Mr. Lenox, give Ms. Applewood a permanent job with us and bring her out of the back dining room. You can give her a spot in the kitchen," Atlas said thoughtfully. "Whatever food is leftover at the end of the day, send home with her. Instruct the men in the back dining room and the hired help to leave her alone, and make sure they do so," he paused and then continued. "Have Henry go for her and take her home in the carriage each day, and finally, give her this and tell her it was a tip," Atlas finished, dropping several coins in Charles Lenox's hand.

"In addition to her wage?" Mr. Lenox asked, surprised.

"In addition to her wage," Atlas confirmed.

Lenox nodded and closed his hand firmly around the large coins. "Yes, sir." His employee considered him for several long moments. "Her looks have bewitched you just as they have the dock workers, haven't they, sir?"

Atlas knew his second-in-command well enough to know he meant no disrespect. "Nay, I'll leave that to the younger men," he answered, clapping Lenox's arm good-naturedly. He pushed himself to his feet. "It's her character that most impresses me."

"Aye, character. That's what her kind is known for," Mr. Lenox answered wryly.

"Her kind? I don't know much about her kind, but I know she's living in a shanty in a questionable part of town, seeking honest work to care for her ailing mother-in-law, who happens to be my dead cousin's wife, when she could have gone home to her own family. Like I said, I don't know much about her kind, but actions like that bespeak character that is worth employing in my establishment . . . no matter the color of one's skin. Don't you agree, Mr. Lenox?"

"In your hotel, I agree with everything you say," Lenox replied with a grimace of a smile.

Atlas shook his hand. "Smart man." Having completed their daily rounds, Atlas said his goodbyes, donned his tall hat and warm coat, and left the hotel. His day was carefully scheduled, giving him time to check in on each of his businesses every day, in addition to conducting meetings and doing work to expand his holdings. He had to keep moving.

He made his way down to the docks and into the business office of Fairbury Freight. "Mr. Whitaker! Good day to you, sir!" he said, greeting the man who managed his freighting company.

Nineteen

Raya felt dead on her feet as she cleared the table after the evening meal. She collected the dishes in her dishpan and scrubbed the table free from grime. Her stomach hurt from hunger, but she returned the remaining beef steaks, boiled potatoes, and sweet carrots to Ms. Macy. Noni swept the floor and Raya followed her on hands and knees, scrubbing away the mud and muck the patrons had tracked in on their dirty boots.

"You were quite the hit today," Noni mentioned, her voice soft, almost apologetic.

"I am grateful to have work," Raya answered, her tired words measured.

She was weary down to the bone. She was weary from running around, trying to ignore all the bold and degrading comments, standing against the wall, and waiting to be summoned. Most of all, she was weary of off-handed proposals of unmentionable employment. "Lord, give me strength," she prayed again for the hundredth time that day, her plea heartfelt. She still had to finish her work and make the long walk home.

"That's the same reason I'm here, you know. My husband was a dock worker, used to come here to eat, actually, but he took sick with the fever 'bout two months ago."

Raya looked up, fearing the worst. "How is he?"

"He's gettin' better, but not strong enough to go back to work yet. He hates to see me here workin', but we was all gettin' real hungry. We got two young'uns," Noni said proudly.

Raya considered the young woman's pale, tired face and the way her day gown hung. "And perhaps one on the way?"

Noni's face brightened into a shy smile. "Yes. This little one should be here sometime early next spring, best I can figure."

"Children are a gift from the LORD," Raya told her warmly, as she continued to scrub.

It was quiet for several moments. "Do you have any little ones?" Noni questioned, breaking the silence.

Raya tried not to allow the innocent question to sting her heart. "No. No little ones."

"You are very beautiful. Your husband was a lucky man," Noni continued, a hint of wistfulness in her voice.

"Beauty is fleeting and charm is deceptive. It's a woman who fears the LORD who should be praised," Raya quoted. "But thank you for your kind words. Some days, like today, I wish it were not so. Though it is a way to remember my family. I look just the same as my mother and sister... whenever I see my reflection, I think of them."

"Are they here in Cincinnati?" Noni questioned, obviously enjoying the easy conversation as they worked.

"No. My mother is in Colorado Territory, and my sister has married. To be honest, I'm not certain where she is anymore." Raya's thoughts settled on Sugundarani, then moved to Nizhoni and Chenoa. She missed all three of her sisters.

"That's too bad. I was an only child... at least the only one who survived, and my parents have both passed, so I guess we're in kind of the same spot. Not too fun of a place to be. Gets a mite lonesome sometimes. Glad my young'uns will have siblings."

Raya smiled at the tender way Noni spoke of her children. "Do you have sons or daughters?"

"One of each. Luke, my son, is goin' on three, and Bella, my daughter, just turned one."

Luke. Again, the name hit Raya's heart like an arrow, yet she refused to yield to the painful memories. Luke was gone. She had wept for him, missed him, mourned for him and would again, but not now, not here. She had to focus on surviving and securing a future for herself and Mother Emaline—a future that somehow kept a roof over their heads, wood on their fire, and food in their stomachs.

"Those are very nice names. And what are you hoping your next will be?" she asked.

"I'm hoping for another boy for my husband. I think he's hoping for the same, but he won't say so," Noni answered.

Raya smiled. "Sons are important to men."

Noni nodded. "'Tis true, I suppose, but you should see how my husband lights up 'round our daughter. You would think the sun rises and sets with that girl."

Raya tried to imagine such a thing and couldn't. Her own father placed little value on her or Sugundarani. He fed and protected them, but they never came close to touching his heart the way his sons had. Still, Noni was waiting for a response. "I'm very happy for your little girl, then. That sounds lovely."

They finished the floor and started washing dishes. When they were done, Ms. Macy was dismissing workers but had one last thing she wanted Raya to get from the storeroom. Noni put on her wraps and left with a cheery, if tired, promise to be back in the morning. When Raya returned from retrieving the item, Ms. Macy and Mr. Lenox were waiting for her. She dropped her eyes to the ground, the memory of running into Mr. Lenox's guest earlier in the day coming to mind.

"I've spoken with Ms. Macy, and she said you've worked hard today. Please come back in the morning. You will have a permanent position here. Also, the remaining food from each day will be sent home with you to feed you and your mother-in-law, and you will be transported back and forth to work in a carriage. The streets between here and your dwelling are known for being a bit rough."

Raya lifted her eyes from the floor to peer at Mr. Lenox, stunned and confused. "Why?" she asked. "Why are you doing this for me? I am but a servant."

"This is not my doing," Mr. Lenox answered quickly.

Raya shook her head slightly, not understanding. Why would anyone lavish such kindness upon her—a displaced widow with dark skin, no money, no prospects, no one to keep her?

"The gentleman you ran into today," Mr. Lenox continued dryly, "was Mr. Atlas Fairbury, the owner of this hotel and your late husband's distant cousin. This is his doing. He wishes you to have a permanent position here and would like you to remain working here in his hotel. You will be both protected and provided for."

Raya could barely comprehend what she was hearing. Surely, there must be a mistake. Surely, she must be dreaming or imagining the entire conversation. Could her discouraging days of looking for work truly be over? "You're giving me a permanent job?" she asked in disbelief, her voice small even to her own ears. Out of everything Mr. Lenox had said, it was the one thing that stood out.

She thought Mr. Lenox nearly smiled, but it never materialized. "The carriage driver has been instructed to take you straight home tonight and be back for you at half-past five in the morning. Don't make him wait for you."

Raya nodded. "Yes, sir."

Ms. Macy pushed several packages into Raya's hands, helped her into her cloak, and opened the solid back door for her. Raya saw that a carriage was waiting outside.

"One more thing, Ms. Applewood," Mr. Lenox said, stopping her abruptly. "This was left for you as a tip." Seeing that her hands were full, he gave the coins to Ms. Macy, who slipped them into the pocket of her apron.

"I don't . . . I don't know what to say," Raya stuttered, feeling utterly overwhelmed and confused. She was so thankful. Tears stung her eyes, and she did her best to blink them back.

Then Ms. Macy did smile, the first time all day, and she gently squeezed Raya's forearm. "God Almighty has heard your prayers and has intervened on your behalf. Use your voice to praise the LORD, child." Raya was surprised by Ms. Macy's statement, having not known of her faith beforehand. Yet before she could respond, Ms. Macy was pushing Raya out the door toward the waiting carriage, and the hotel's carriage driver helped her in after asking an address where she wanted to be dropped off.

In mere seconds, the door was shut, and for the second night in a row, she was sitting in the plush interior of a fine carriage, being carried swiftly home. She sank back against the seat in relief so great that tears began to slip down her cheeks.

With all the attention she had earned in the dining room, she had been dreading the long walk home through the dark. With every crude comment she'd overheard, with every bold and crass proposition flung her way, her stomach had dropped, knowing the trip home was coming. Fear had gnawed away at her as she washed dishes, her hands busy, but her mind free to worry. She had known the very men who had made her day miserable would be walking those same streets, and some of them might just be determined enough to wait for her.

As she'd worked, she had struggled within herself. She needed the job. She needed the employment to keep a roof over their heads and food on their table. Yet, if she were lucky enough to be invited back for a second day of work, she would be facing the same men in the back dining room all over again. She had remembered the whispers and jeers, the degrading comments, the boldly appreciative glances, and her stomach had lurched. She didn't know if she could face it again. Yet, the LORD had provided work. She should be grateful. She was grateful. But she was also afraid. Would she be able to stomach the work day after day? She felt ungrateful for even thinking such thoughts, and waves of guilt washed over her one after another.

The guilt of feeling ungrateful for the gift of work and the fear of having to walk home through dark streets alone had consumed her thoughts all day, tying her in knots. And as it turned out, all her worrying had been for naught. She felt all her fear from earlier dissipate as she sat safely stowed away in the fine carriage, knowing it would be back for her in the morning. Perhaps, so long as she was transported safely to and from the hotel, she could face the crowds each day.

Her worry lessening, she noticed the weight of the food on her lap and was instantly full of anticipation at unwrapping each package to see what had been sent for her and Mother Emaline.

Mother Emaline. The woman would be as astounded as Raya—and as delighted. She couldn't wait to tell her. Raya replayed the conversation in her head, wanting to be ready to relay it correctly. She got stuck at the gentleman's name. She was so caught off-guard, she hadn't been listening to details, and now Raya struggled to remember what Mr. Lenox called him. *Atlas.* Atlas Fairbury. That was his name. She clapped her hands happily, excited about the news she had to tell her mother-in-law.

Suddenly, Raya's hand flew to her pocket, remembering the coins Ms. Macy had put there. She pulled them out and ran her fingers over them, unable to see their worth in the dark carriage. A tip, Mr. Lenox had said. She could not imagine who had given her such a generous tip. One of the men in the back dining room? Surely not, but who else?

And they were giving her a job, a permanent job. Her wage was meager, but it would be enough to buy wood for their fire and keep a roof over their heads. Especially since their food would be provided. No matter that she would be serving the dirty, foul dock workers every day—she had a permanent job, and that was all that mattered. Something she had been worried about since the day she decided to travel east with Mother Emaline, was no longer a concern.

Her relief was so great it felt as if a physical weight had been lifted from her shoulders. The few tears turned into many. They ran off her face unchecked, as weeks of fear and worry bled off.

The LORD had heard her prayer and intervened on her behalf. That's what Ms. Macy said. The words she had heard so softly earlier came back to mind. *"I will not leave you nor forsake you. I have a plan to redeem you from the pit."* In the wake of what had just happened, it seemed logical that perhaps those words had been from the LORD Himself, as a solution to their problems had unfolded that very day. Perhaps, just perhaps, the God she served did have time to concern Himself with the matters of humanity every now and again, even *her* matters.

She bowed her head in silent submission, thanking the LORD of Hosts for His great kindness, His great mercy, and His intervention. While she had not dared to expect it, she was so very thankful for it.

Everything had all felt so hopeless since the fire, so dreary and impossible. She had been concerned for their very lives. It was not so much about missing their land, their comfortable houses, their stores of plenty, or even their men. Those comforts all paled in comparison to the very real fear that neither of them would make it through the winter. If Raya hadn't been given a job, or if it had simply been for a day . . . she couldn't finish the thought.

The LORD had shown her kindness through Atlas Fairbury, and her heart was greatly moved. She, a mere servant of the Most High, had no right to expect such divine intervention, but alas, it seemed as if it had come, nonetheless.

She wiped her eyes on her cloak.

And then the carriage was stopping, and when the driver opened the carriage door, she saw her own little shanty. What took her just over an hour to walk was covered in less than twenty minutes by the prancing horses.

The carriage driver bid her goodnight, promising to be back at half-past five, as Mr. Lenox had instructed. Mother Emaline opened the door, and Raya hurried in out of the cold, her face stretched in a smile so big it made her cheeks hurt. It all felt surreal.

"What is this?" Mother Emaline exclaimed as she shakily made her way back across the dirt floor to the bed.

Raya instantly saw the flush in her cheeks and the glassy look in her eyes and knew the fever was back. But Mother Emaline had gotten up to greet her, and that was something. Raya shut the door and barred it behind her.

UP FROM THE ASH HEAP

"I've been expecting you for hours, and now you've come and have brought half a store! What did they pay you? And you were delivered home in a carriage! You have a good amount of explaining to do, dear," Emaline continued, now safely back in bed with a bright smile on her face, despite her physical ailments.

Raya laughed, spreading the packages on the table. She told Mother Emaline the whole story, relaying the work she had done, her new friend Noni, and her mind-boggling conversation with Mr. Lenox.

"Mr. Atlas Fairbury, you say?" Emaline asked, her eyes swimming with tears.

Raya nodded.

"LORD, bless him," Mother Emaline said with great feeling. "And bless the LORD. For provision comes from You, Heavenly Father. Bless You for the abundance You have provided for us today. You are our Provider. Holy is Your name."

"Amen," Raya murmured in agreement, reverence falling over the shanty.

"The LORD has blessed us, Raya. He has shown favor to us," Mother Emaline said, taking Raya's hand and squeezing it. Raya felt tears prick her own eyes again as the weight of the words sunk in. The older lady kissed her face, then released her. "What have you brought us to eat?"

"I don't know, actually. Let me check," Raya said, returning to the table where she had set her packages. Raya opened the first package, the biggest, and found a whole loaf of Ms. Macy's white bread. The next revealed the sausage patties and scrambled eggs from breakfast, the bowl that held them still cold from its day in the icebox. Four beef steaks, a small pile of boiled potatoes, and another small pile of sweet carrots were stacked on a tin dish covered with another tin dish and wrapped in brown paper.

Raya shrieked in excitement, clapping her hands together, her mouth watering, remembering how she had longed to eat those very things earlier in the day.

Mother Emaline laughed at Raya's excitement and then beamed at the young woman. "We will eat like kings tonight!"

Raya set the eggs and sausage aside for the morning, knowing they would stay plenty cold in the far corner of the shanty. She then added an extra log to the fire before putting the beefsteaks, potatoes, and carrots in a skillet to warm. She had not tasted beef in months. It was a rare treat, even in Colorado Territory, where they mostly ate the meat from whatever wild game the men shot. Where game was plenty, it was hard to justify buying beef.

Now, with the tantalizing aromas beginning to fill the air, her mouth watered just as it had when she'd served the sizzling beef steaks.

While the food reheated, Raya took the coins from the pocket of her apron and counted them. She could not believe it—they totaled what she had hoped to make in two weeks at the hotel. She could not imagine who would leave such a generous tip, or who would have the means to do so. Combined with the daily wage she had been paid that evening, she had just enough to pay their rent. And right in the nick of time. The landlord was coming to turn them out in the morning.

Knowing she would already be at work by the time he came and not wanting Mother Emaline disturbed with such a matter, Raya slipped the coins back in her pocket and decided she would make the walk to his house after she had Mother Emaline settled for the night.

By the time she set out two plates and dipped two cups of icy water, their supper was warm. Raya scooped the beef, potatoes, and carrots onto the chipped china plates that were in the small cupboard when they moved in, and sliced thick helpings of bread to go with it. She took both plates to the bed and set them aside as she helped Mother Emaline into a sitting position before handing her one of them. Scooting a chair close to the head of the bed, Raya sat down, balancing her own plate on her lap. Mother Emaline bowed her head, waiting for Raya to do the same before giving thanks to the LORD, her voice wobbling with emotion and heartfelt gratitude.

"I never dreamt we would be having such a wonderful meal again tonight," Raya commented after taking her first bite of sweetened carrots. She followed it with a large bite of beefsteak, which she chewed very slowly to savor its rich flavor. It was every bit as good as she imagined it would be while watching the men consume it earlier. Their filling meal from the night before seemed as if it had been a month ago. Who would have imagined that two days ago they were nearly starving, when last night they had feasted on chicken and noodles and a few bread crusts and tonight they were having beef steak? Their turn of fortune was difficult to grasp.

"Nor did I," Mother Emaline agreed. "I laid here all day worrying about you, worrying about how today would go, and now look—all that worrying was for nothing! The LORD had your day perfectly planned out, and has blessed us beyond measure." The woman paused, her smile fading. "I had lost sight of His goodness. I must admit, I had moments of doubt," Mother Emaline admitted sadly. "I'm ashamed."

"It was a legitimate worry. You had no way of knowing what would transpire today," Raya comforted.

"Perfect love casts out fear, Raya. We are never to fear. We never have to if we have a clear understanding of who the God we serve is and how He loves us."

Raya mulled over Mother Emaline's words as she continued to eat. Suddenly, she recognized she was eating the very food she had considered and decided against stealing earlier in the day. No one would have ever known—no one but the LORD. Now, she was feasting on more than she ever would have taken earlier, with a perfectly clear conscience—the food was given to her for the purpose of consumption.

"Mr. Atlas Fairbury was Luke's cousin?" Raya asked after several seconds.

"No. His mother and James were cousins."

"His mother was James' cousin?" Raya asked, surprised. "Why, he didn't look more than thirty-five." Her glance had been brief, but she did not remember the man looking old.

"I do believe he's a bit older than that, but not by much. James and Atlas's mother were fifteen years apart in age. She was barely older than Julius. Atlas was just a small boy when we married," Emaline remembered with a smile. "He was a charming boy. They never had any other children, though I believe she was in the family way more than once. Atlas is probably in his mid to late thirties; I believe he wasn't yet ten when Luke was born."

"Were you close to them?" Raya asked, curious as to why a distant relative would concern himself with their wellbeing.

"Oh, we saw Loretta and Atlas a few times a year when they came to call, or when we were invited over to their house for a dinner party. They were a lovely family, and I enjoyed Loretta's company greatly. But I had three young children, and we were both running a household, so there was much to fill our time. Atlas was sent away to school when Luke was only seven or eight, and I have not seen him since. When he returned, he was a man and no longer came calling with his mother. We left for the West shortly after. I haven't thought of him in years, or else I would have directed you to his hotel earlier."

"'Tis a kind thing he has done for us," Raya agreed.

"He has always been a good man. Julius respected him, young as he was, and my sons looked up to him. He has confirmed everything we thought about him then by his actions now. It seems his kindness and honor have grown, just as his business holdings have."

"Business holdings?" Raya questioned.

"When we left, his business pursuits were just beginning, but he had a keen eye and a quick mind, and I heard after the war, his businesses boomed. He's doing quite well now, and is likely one of the most powerful and wealthiest men in Cincinnati."

Raya was quiet, processing all Mother Emaline had just said. She was astounded that a man like Atlas Fairbury, wealthy, powerful, and respected, would take pity on an old woman and her foreign daughter-in-law. Surely his actions were abnormal for a person of his station. He had no duty to them, yet he had treated them with exceptional kindness. He was providing for Mother Emaline, and he ensured Raya's safety while she worked for that provision. Perhaps, when Mother Emaline was well enough, the elder woman should call on Mr. Fairbury and his wife to thank them for their continued kindness. Raya would stay home, not because she was ungrateful, but because she was not worthy to step foot in his house.

She was already working in the hotel of one of the wealthiest men in town. He had given her a job, food, hope, and a safe way to traverse the city streets. In so many ways, he had given her mother-in-law back to her, saved them from death, and Raya from a dishonorable life of prostitution. She felt unworthy even to work in his hotel, much less have tea in his home or be in his or his family's presence. No, Mother Emaline would just have to understand and go without her. But go she must, for such generosity could not go unthanked.

Her stomach full, Raya set her empty plate aside and snuggled down into the folds of her blanket. Since they had been rationing firewood so strictly, putting an extra log on the fire felt extravagant, but doing so made the shanty warmer than usual and for once, Raya felt warm from within. The coziness of her blanketed cocoon and her tired, aching body coaxed her to warm the bricks and go to bed, but she had one last errand she must perform before she could retire for the night. Forcing her body to do her bidding, she stood to her feet and carried her plate to the washbasin. She glanced back at Mother Emaline's plate and saw her food had barely been touched.

"You have to eat, Mother," she chided, worried. "If you don't eat, you won't have the strength to recover."

"I'm afraid I don't have much of an appetite," Mother Emaline told her weakly.

Raya considered her glassy eyes, flushed face, and bony body and shook her head. "Be that as it may, you have to eat. Try to get down just a few more bites."

Mother Emaline dutifully forked a bite of carrots and chewed them slowly, while Raya washed her own plate, fork, and the pan she had used to warm their supper. When Mother Emaline had eaten all she could, Raya carefully put away her leftovers, then washed her utensils as well.

When she glanced back at the older woman, she saw she was fast asleep. Good. It was better if Mother Emaline did not know of the errand. She had not told her they were only hours away from being turned out of their house, and Raya did not want to burden her with the news now.

Pulling her cloak around her shoulders and drawing the hood of it up over her hair, she unbarred the door, locked it behind her with her key, and headed out into the dark night, her hand in the pocket of her apron, where she kept the loose coins from jingling. Making her way quickly through the streets, she attempted to follow a familiar path to the short landlord's humble home, where she had first inquired about the available shanty. However, she was coming from a different direction and had trouble finding the place.

She kept herself alert to her surroundings as she walked; on guard for anyone who might wish to do her harm. After her day in the back dining room and her weeks scouring the city for work, she had little faith left in the decency of man.

Finally, finding the house she sought, she made her way to the door of the small dwelling, barely larger than their own shanty, though better finished and with a stable in the back. Knowing it was late, she considered leaving the coins outside the front door, but a lamp still burned within, and Raya didn't want to take the chance of someone stealing her rent money.

After a brief hesitation, Raya rose her fist and rapped softly on the door. From within, she could hear a chair scraping and voices murmuring. When the door opened, her landlord stood in front of her in shirttails and trousers. Embarrassed, she looked away, even as he quickly stepped out the door, invading her space as he pulled it shut behind him.

"I figured you'd be coming at some point tonight," he told her, his voice quiet, his eyes gleaming. "And I'm sure as fire ready. Give me just a minute to tell the missus something, and we'll go 'round back to the stable."

Raya's cheeks flamed as she understood his meaning. "Sir, I've come to pay my rent, but not in the way you imagine."

His eyes narrowed. "You were penniless a few days ago. How do you have money to pay your rent now? You been stealin'? I don't accept stolen money."

Raya bristled. "I've found work," she said carefully.

He assessed her out of squinted eyes. "What kind of work have you found that would make you enough money to pay your rent in two days?"

Raya wanted to tell him it was none of his business, but she was living in his shanty and needed to remain there. "I've been hired at The Fairbury Hotel."

The man laughed in her face. "The Fairbury Hotel, you say? Well, ain't that a joke! There ain't no way they'd hire the likes of you down at Fairbury Hotel. How'd you really get the money? . . . If you even have it. I ain't laid eyes on it yet."

"I've told the truth," Raya said quietly, embarrassed by his brazen remarks. She pulled the coins out of her pocket and held them out to him, keeping her eyes averted.

He looked down at the coins, then up at her face. "And what if I would like the other form of payment better?"

Raya instinctively took a step back. "N-no," she stammered, caught off-guard. "We agreed on a price. I've brought my rent money."

He reached out and grabbed her wrist. "What if the price has changed?"

Fear twisted her insides as she saw he meant to have his way with her as payment for her rent. For a brief moment, she rationalized that at least she would be able to keep her coins and perhaps afford to pay for some place better in the coming months—somewhere Mother Emaline could escape the cold drafts.

Just as quickly, the food in her stomach churned, and she swallowed down bile. She could not, would not, sell herself to the man in front of her as payment for her rent. She was the wife of Luke Applewood, daughter-in-law of Emaline Applewood. She would not disgrace them by selling her body to pay her debts.

"No," she said again, more firmly this time.

The expression on his face changed, and Raya's heartbeat quickened as she watched his determination and anger grow. "If you wish to remain in my house, you'll change your ans—"

Like a blessed beacon of light on a dark stormy night, the door behind the man opened, and a tired-eyed, long-faced woman stood behind him. Mr. Henley released Raya's hand instantly as he turned to his wife.

"Is everything alright, Len?" the woman asked, looking at Raya warily.

"Everything's fine. This woman came to pay her rent, and I was telling her not to ever come so late again. Don't know why she thought it was acceptable to come traipsin' over here at this late hour, disturbin' us."

"I have to work in the morning," Raya answered weakly. With the wife watching, she held out her coins. After a brief hesitation, the landlord held out his hand, and Raya dropped the coins into his palm. "I will be certain to come at a more decent hour next month," she said simply, knowing full-well she would never return to the man's house again. She bid them both goodnight before quickly turning and melding back into the darkness of the street. With one last glance as she turned the corner, Raya saw Mr. Henley follow his wife back inside.

Breathing a sigh of relief, she began to run down the streets, giving no thought to the appropriateness of such behavior, only her great desire to be home, behind the barred door, safe in bed beside Mother Emaline. She had never been more thankful for Mr. Fairbury's kind gift of transportation in his carriage. Her heart was still hammering, her full stomach still upset. She had never come so close to being taken advantage of before and never wanted to be in such a situation again. By the time she reached the shanty, her mind was made up that she would send her rent by messenger in the future.

Slipping in the front door, she dropped the bar into place and checked on Mother Emaline, who was still sleeping. She heated bricks and placed them at the bottom of the bed before crawling between the blankets and curling up on her side. She shivered as she settled into the warmth. She shivered again as she thought back upon what had nearly transpired.

Once again, she was overwhelmed with thankfulness for Mr. Fairbury's kindness, because for that brief moment, standing in front of her landlord, she had been able to rationalize away a sickening deed far too easily. If they were still hopeless and destitute, with no food in their bellies, nor money to pay their rent, no matter how ill she felt nor how her heart hurt, she feared she might have done whatever needed to be done to keep a roof over their heads.

Twenty

Raya slept restlessly, waking frequently to check Mother Emaline's small pocket watch. When she saw it was a quarter to five, Raya jumped out of bed, her feet hitting the stinging cold floor, just like the day before. But it wasn't like the day before. The LORD had shown her mercy, and everything was different.

She stirred the coals in the fireplace until she found a few red ones. She put twigs on top and blew gently until they burst into flames. Then she laid two logs on the top and quickly dressed while she waited for them to catch. When the fire was hot, she put the eggs and sausages into the skillet and set it over the flames to warm. While it did, she cut thick slices of bread and retrieved their plates.

When she turned from the fire, Mother Emaline was sitting up in bed, ready for breakfast. Her face was white and drawn. Crossing to the bed and laying her cheek against Emaline's head, Raya found the fever had broken.

"How do you feel?" Raya asked, smoothing the woman's hair back from her face.

"Some better," Mother Emaline told her, sounding utterly exhausted. The fever always sapped her strength. Raya knew the woman would spend the day sleeping and was glad. Sleep would help her body fight off the sickness and heal.

Bringing their breakfast back to the bed, they gave thanks and ate together, savoring the buttery eggs and flavorful sausage patties. To eat a meal in the morning felt foreign, and Raya was thankful that for once, she started the day full and satisfied.

UP FROM THE ASH HEAP

When the carriage pulled up at their shanty, Raya was outside waiting and quickly climbed in before the driver could even get down to open the door for her. In just shy of twenty minutes, she climbed out of the carriage, safe and warm. After thanking the driver, she pushed through the hotel's back door into the warm and bustling kitchen.

She took a deep breath and smiled. It didn't matter that she would be serving the men in the back dining room again; she had a job, Mother Emaline would make it through the winter, and tonight she would ride home in the carriage to eat another good meal before going to bed.

"Do you know how to bake bread?" Ms. Macy asked as Raya hung her cloak on an empty peg on the wall.

"Yes, ma'am," Raya answered, surprised by the question.

"Good. You're going to be baking bread today and washing dishes. We'll need at least sixteen to twenty loaves, in addition to biscuits for breakfast, so you had best get started."

Raya's mind spun. "Does that mean I won't be in the back dining room?" she dared to ask in a small voice, hoping beyond hope she wouldn't be facing the impertinent crowd once again.

"You'll be baking bread and washing dishes," Ms. Macy repeated tersely. "Get to work."

Raya didn't ask any more questions. She put away the washed dishes she had brought back with her, located the flour, and began making biscuits. She would start on the bread once the biscuits were baking. As she worked, she considered the change in her position and had a feeling that it too went back to the kind and thoughtful Mr. Fairbury.

She was grateful beyond words to have her hands in flour rather than serving in the back dining room, drawing undue attention, and enduring the men's lewd comments and innuendos. She mixed, kneaded, patted, cut, and baked. When the last pan of biscuits was in the oven, she started baking bread.

When Noni came back into the kitchen after the morning rush was over, Raya felt guilty and ashamed. A new girl had taken Raya's place in the back dining room, but nonetheless, she felt as if she had abandoned Noni. Though she was immeasurably thankful for the extraordinary kindness, there was no reason why she should have been moved into the kitchen while Noni still had to serve the less than scrupulous men. She could not raise her eyes to meet her new friend's, even when the girl came and rested her hip against the table where Raya was kneading bread.

"They were asking after you this morning. Weren't none too happy when I said you'd been moved to the kitchen. Lordy, but there were a bunch of 'em in there today," Noni said, her words casual and free of blame. "Word spread quickly that there was a pretty new face serving in Fairbury's back dining room, I guess."

Raya kept her eyes down as she kneaded, feeling guilty that she had rejoiced in her good fortune to be baking bread, all while Noni was in with the very crowd Raya was grateful to escape.

Noni reached out and touched her shoulder. "I'm glad they moved you to the kitchen, Raya. It's better for you to be in here. The customers ain't near so hard on me or Laurie as they were on you. It's best this way."

Raya finally looked up. "I confess I was very thankful when I found out I would be staying in the kitchen today."

"I'm sure you were," Noni told her with a sincere smile. "I've never seen the likes of that brawl yesterday since I started workin' here."

"How's your husband?" Raya asked, relief replacing her guilt. "Is he feeling any better today?"

"His strength returns more each day. He says he'll likely feel up to goin' back to the docks in a few more weeks. I won't let him go too soon—I don't want him goin' 'til he's all healed up. Otherwise, he'll just take sick again, but only then he may not get better," Noni paused. "I'd best get back to work." She touched Raya's shoulder again in a kind gesture before hurrying off.

Raya finished the loaf of bread she was making, then set it aside to rise. Brushing the flour off her hands, she crossed to a vacant washbasin and poured steaming water from the kettle on the stove over the breakfast dishes that were waiting to be washed. She rolled up her sleeves and began scrubbing. The sheer amount of dishes was overwhelming, yet she was glad to see there was a good sized breakfast crowd in the front dining room as well as in the back. With all the kindness he had shown them, she wanted to see Mr. Fairbury prosper.

Suddenly, the kitchen that was usually humming as people talked while they worked quieted. Unconcerned, Raya continued to scrub on the bowl she was washing, determined to free it of the sticky oatmeal remnants.

Today she was washing dishes from the front dining room rather than the tin dishes from the back dining room, and she was being extra careful not to chip, scratch or break one of the beautiful pieces of china. She had never seen, much less eaten off, dishes so lovely, and she felt nervous holding them in her wet, sudsy hands.

When she heard a faintly familiar voice barely past her elbow, she glanced up quickly. Atlas Fairbury was standing next to her, his expression serious. Instinctively, Raya fell to her knees at his feet.

With her wet, sudsy hands on the floor by his shoes, Raya only hoped the china bowl had not chipped when she released it so swiftly. But there was no time to think of that—only that the one who had secured her and her mother-in-law's lives was standing before her.

"Sir, I am so thankful for your great kindness toward me and my mother-in-law. We are immeasurably grateful," Raya told him, her voice thick with emotion. There was a stunned silence that settled over the room.

She startled when she felt a gentle hand on her arm as he bent to draw her to her feet. As she stood, she noticed that everyone in the kitchen had stopped what they were doing and were staring unabashedly. Embarrassed, she could not bring herself to glance up at Mr. Fairbury's face, even though she wondered what his expression might be.

Still, no matter how her actions had humbled her, she could not have ignored his kindness, nor the fact that he had shown mercy to a poor and hopeless foreigner. He had done far more for them than anyone could possibly think his duty, and she would not overlook his generosity. Though humbling, there was no other response to his presence that would have done justice.

They had food, a roof over their heads, fuel for their fire—because of him. He had quite literally saved their lives and her honor. She was no more than hired help in his hotel, a dark spot on his family name, and yet he had shown her incredible kindness.

"Please, get back to work," Atlas Fairbury instructed the others, his words causing the kitchen hands to quickly turn back to their jobs.

Raya felt him turn back to her, though she kept her eyes cast down. She stayed perfectly still, even when she was tempted to squirm as she continued to feel his steady gaze on her.

Finally, he spoke. "It has been fully reported to me what you have done for my cousin's widow—that you left your home, your own family, everything you knew, to come east with her. I know you were a good wife to my cousin's son, and you have been a good friend and daughter to Emaline. You stayed when you could have left. You remained faithful and loyal even in the midst of great tragedy and, I'm sure, much sorrow. I pray that the LORD will bless you immensely for what you've done." The man's voice was as gentle as his words, and he only stopped for a quick pause before continuing. "I have heard that since coming to this hotel, you have been a hard worker and have not uttered one complaint. If it's agreeable with you, I would like for you not to seek employment elsewhere, but to stay here and work in my hotel. You can spend your days with the women who work for me, and you will be safe and treated well."

Raya could not believe what she was hearing. He had bestowed such kindness on her, and now he was saying he prayed the LORD would bless *her*? Didn't he know that through him, He already had? And more so, he was personally offering permanent employment, telling her essentially that he wished her to stay under his wing so he might protect and provide for her and Emaline. He had already communicated as much through another, and now, he was saying it again himself.

Tears stung her eyes. "It is more than agreeable," she replied quietly, her throat aching from emotion. They would live sparingly, of course, but she and Mother Emaline would have provision to live on for years to come. "Thank you, sir," she finished, her voice coming out in little more than a hoarse whisper.

She still didn't look up, but she could feel him studying her. "Give Emaline my greetings. Although the circumstances are grievous, I'm glad she's back. Tell her I still remember the cookies she used to bake for me."

Under any other circumstances, Raya would have agreed that Mother Emaline's cookies were unforgettable, yet she could not make light of the situation when this man had quite literally extended the gift of life to her and her dear mother-in-law. "I will tell her, sir."

"Thank you." Several moments of silence passed before he said, "Good day, Ms. Applewood."

"Good day," she answered meekly.

The gentleman turned and walked away, talking with Ms. Macy at length about the number of customers, the food, what people liked, how things were going in the kitchen and so on. Ms. Macy ladled him a bowl of the noodle dish she was concocting in her large pot and instructed Raya to give him a piece of buttered bread, which she did. He sat at the table, slid against one wall of the kitchen, where Raya had bread rising, and ate, making over Ms. Macy's cooking all the while. Ms. Macy seemed pleased with the attention.

"Ms. Applewood, this bread is wonderful as well. As good as any I've ever had," he said loudly enough to ensure Raya heard it across the large, bustling room.

"It's Ms. Macy's recipe," Raya answered simply.

"Well," Mr. Fairbury started and then paused. Finally, Raya glanced over at him from her place at the washbasin, and he shot her a friendly wink. "Whoever's recipe it is, it sure is good."

Raya washed her share of the breakfast dishes, then sliced bread for lunch and made more bread for the evening meal. With two busy dining rooms, they went through a great deal of bread, and she was surprised by how busy its making kept her. When she set aside the evening's bread to rise, she had lunch dishes to wash. When she finally finished those, she sliced bread for supper, then made more bread to serve the first of the morning's customers. Then, she washed supper dishes until all the dishes were done and put away.

Again, she was one of the last kitchen hands at the hotel, kept company only by Ms. Macy. And that was how she wanted it to be. For the kindness Mr. Fairbury had shown her and Mother Emaline, she would give everything she had to be a good worker. She would gladly do her part to see his hotel clean, prosperous, and well-staffed. When she finished scrubbing the kitchen floor, Ms. Macy told her that her work was done for the day, and it was time to head home.

The plump, fair-skinned woman with graying hair tucked under her frilly cap, loaded Raya's arms with dishes of pasta, sausages, flapjacks, fried chicken, mashed potatoes, green beans and half a loaf of bread before sending her on her way. The carriage driver delivered her at home, and she reported the happenings of her day to Mother Emaline over their supper.

Emaline seemed better than she had been in days and told Raya she had even felt well enough to go on a small walk earlier that afternoon. On her walk, she had met a widower and his young children who were going west in search of land. The man told her he had several items in need of mending and didn't know how to do it himself. He asked if she would do his mending in trade for a cat, and Mother Emaline had joyfully agreed. She showed Raya the pieces of clothing she would mend, then told Raya more about the animal they would get as payment.

The cat was the widower's and round with kittens. The man was concerned the animal would not make it on their trip west in her condition and wanted to find a family for her. Mother Emaline was as pleased as punch over the trade, and Raya couldn't agree more. It would be lovely to have a good mouser to rid the shanty of the pesky rodents that inhabited it.

What Raya couldn't get over, though, was the sorry shape of the garments Emaline was mending. Back in their mountain valley, they would have discarded such garments as rags without giving it a second thought. Here, they were likely all the widower and his children had, and thus, they hired Mother Emaline to stitch back together their threadbare fabric.

Raya looked down at her full plate of hot, delicious food, and her eyes brimmed with tears. They had gone from having nothing to much, yet so many around them were still hungry and destitute. What Ms. Macy had sent home with her was plentiful, especially considering they still had leftovers from the night before. It was too much for a family of four to eat, much less the two of them.

As Raya reported the events of her day, Mother Emaline was thrilled to hear that Mr. Fairbury still remembered her cookies. Even knowing it would take a portion of Raya's earnings, Mother Emaline decided to bake him a batch of cookies and asked Raya to go to the store whenever she was able to get the supplies. Raya quickly agreed. Considering all he had done for them, they both agreed making him cookies was the least they could do to return his kindness.

After they ate their fill, Raya took their dishes to the washbasin and washed them thoroughly. She carefully wrapped up the leftover food and set it aside in a cold corner where it would stay good until morning. Knowing she would be bringing more food home with her the next evening, she asked Mother Emaline to take the leftover food to the widower when she returned his garments. Mother Emaline quickly agreed, her eyes shining. Raya went to bed feeling happy. Not only were their needs being met, they were able to help meet someone else's needs as well.

Twenty-One

Raya smiled as the sound of purring filled the room. It had been another long day at the hotel, and her body was tired and aching. Her stomach was full, and the dishes had been washed, so she was simply enjoying a few minutes of sitting before the fire, warm and content, before retiring for the night.

Their new pet, who Mother Emaline referred to as Smoky, had surprised her by jumping into her lap and curling up in her blanket. Delighted, Raya began to stroke the gray cat, which had quickly elicited the purring.

To have a mouser to rid their house of unwanted house guests was a great blessing, but to have a pet... 'twas a kindness altogether different. After experiencing so much loss and loneliness, to have another living being curl up, warm and satisfied against you, was a comforting thing. Raya relished it, hesitant to go to bed as she would have to disturb the happily sleeping mama cat. Finally, unable to keep her eyes open any longer, she set the cat gingerly on the ground and made her way to bed. When Smoky jumped up on the straw tick after the candle was blown out and found a cozy spot in the quilts between the two women, neither of them shooed her away.

Raya went to sleep smiling, happy their small bed was now shared by three. It was a bit of a ray of happy sunshine in a season of sorrow, and she was thankful for it.

As she slept, she felt the heat of the cat snuggled against her side, and she dreamt of Luke. In her dream she relived the day he had surprised her with a kitten, and when she woke, she could still picture his expression—hungry for affirmation—as he held out his tiny, black-haired gift.

She felt awash with grief as she readied herself for work; the dream stirring up a deep longing for her husband and the way life had been. She counted up how many days and weeks it had been since she'd last seen his face, heard his voice, or held his hand. Her tears fell as the carriage took her swiftly toward work.

As the horses slowed and made their final turn into the hotel's yard, Raya wiped her eyes and her nose on the small handkerchief she still kept with her at all times. She clutched in her hand the small piece of fabric that served as a reminder of Luke as she climbed from the carriage, comforted merely by having something of his to hold onto. As she thanked the driver and made her way across the frozen yard to the back door, she took a deep, steadying breath and pushed the memory of her husband out of her thoughts. She had a job to do. Upon reaching The Fairbury Hotel, she soon lost herself in the bustling kitchen, the unending dishes, and the daily need for bread.

***

Raya took a deep breath and smoothed her hand over the fitted front of her black mourning gown before setting herself to kneading dough.

It had been a week since she started work at Mr. Fairbury's hotel, and that morning Mother Emaline had sent her to work with a gift for him—a batch of the cookies he remembered from childhood.

Raya had sampled one of the cookies Mother Emaline had saved back for her the night before, and knew them to be delicious, yet she was nervous about giving the gift to Mr. Fairbury. She was of the opinion that Mother Emaline should deliver the gift herself as it was with her his affections laid. However, Mother Emaline argued that it was a long walk to his house on the other side of town, assuming she could even find it, and she was not yet well enough to make the journey. Besides, she reasoned, Raya would see him anyway when he came into the hotel.

Raya was unable to deny it made more sense, yet as she glanced at the plateful of cookies, wrapped with a clean cloth, and sitting at the back of the table she was kneading bread on, her mouth went dry once again.

How would she deliver them? He had not spoken to her since her second day in his hotel, and now she would have to approach him to give him the gift. She felt rude interrupting his business conversation and unworthy to approach him freely, yet she would have to do both if she was to deliver the treats Mother Emaline had sent. She was a foreigner, a person his establishment would never think of serving, yet she was to take the liberty of demanding his attention and delivering a homemade gift. She felt her cheeks begin to burn just thinking about it.

As she kneaded her dough, she worried. What would his wife think? Would she understand that Mother Emaline meant no insult by baking sweets for the kind Mr. Fairbury? Would the wealthy Mrs. Fairbury understand that it was simply a gift, a small thank you for all her husband had done? Raya was certain Mother Emaline must know the rules of civility much better than she, but still, Raya continued to worry that the kind gesture might offend her.

What was more, she was not keen on her fellow workers seeing her deliver the plate of cookies to Mr. Fairbury. It was true and known that he had been exceedingly kind to her and Mother Emaline, and she was worried her intentions would be misconstrued. She was unendingly grateful for everything he had done for them and never wanted it to be thought she expected—or hoped for—anything else. What he had already done was more than adequate; his compassion and generosity toward them was undeserved. The cookies were simply a humble gift sent from a distant relation, a small thank you for his incomprehensible kindness.

Yet when Raya had voiced all her concerns to Mother Emaline the night before, the woman had waved them away, telling Raya she worried too much. It had been of little help, and Raya found her thoughts consumed by her troubles as she went about her work.

"I felt the baby move this morning," Noni said, suddenly beside her, a smile on her pale face.

Raya's worry evaporated as she let out an excited shriek and gave a small clap of her floury hands, beaming at her new friend. "Noni! Truly? You don't say! What did it feel like?"

"Just a little tickle through my belly. Then it happened again. 'Fore long, I'll be feeling it kick, but for now, it's just a tickle," Noni answered, clearly pleased with Raya's reaction.

Raya glanced at Noni's extended abdomen, then back up at her face affectionately. "It won't be much longer now! Before you know it, your little one will be lying in your arms."

"Oh, she still has a while left to cook," Noni contradicted.

"She?" Raya asked, surprised.

"Lately, I've just got a feeling," Noni told her. "I said I wanted another boy, but I'm thinking this one will be a girl. Just a mother's intuition, maybe." Noni paused before continuing. "Anyway, as I was sayin', the months of being as big as a house and as uncomfortable as a stomachache on a bouncing wagon, are yet to come."

Raya squeezed her hand. "But every moment will be worth it, I'm sure, when you can kiss her sweet cheek and hold her in your arms."

Noni bobbed her head in agreement before hurrying to get a refill of the sausage gravy she sought. Once she had it, she reassumed her position in the back dining room.

Raya watched her disappear through the swinging door before going back to kneading her dough, an aching sadness filling her as she did. She had always wanted to know what it felt like to carry life within, to feel a child move and kick inside. Now, she never would. The ache grew until it felt like a tangible force swelling the confines of her chest painfully.

She truly was sincerely happy and excited for Noni, but to see her new friend with child made her long for one of her own . . . and more aware than ever that all hope was lost. Every dream of having her own child had been lost in a furnace of flames and a haze of smoke.

The swinging door from the front dining room opened, and Mr. Lenox entered with Mr. Fairbury. Their presence instantly filled the kitchen, and Raya's thoughts of children dissipated as she remembered the task Mother Emaline had given her. Her pulse began to race as her insecurities arose.

Of course, Mr. Lenox had to choose today to accompany Mr. Fairbury to the kitchen. She had hoped it would be one of the rare days that Mr. Fairbury visited the kitchen alone. No such luck.

The men went directly to Ms. Macy and began speaking to her about the number of patrons. Raya didn't intend to eavesdrop, but overheard that a steamboat was scheduled to arrive in port that afternoon, and there would likely be more guests than normal for the evening meal, as well as overnight patrons. Mr. Fairbury instructed Mr. Lenox to send a crier down to the docks to advertise their accommodations and Ms. Macy to be prepared.

Ms. Macy listened, nodding. "I'll have extra ready, sir," she promised.

"Thank you, Ms. Macy," Mr. Fairbury responded, sending her a warm smile.

Raya barely contained a smile of her own—the boss was calling the head of his kitchen 'miss.' He was the one worthy of respect, and here he was showing it to a plump old cook, just as he did every day. Along with the respect, his smiles and compliments to her were plentiful and warm, and he treated her kindly. And it was mutual. It was well known that Ms. Macy carried a certain fondness for the boss, very much akin to one a woman might carry for her own son. Even if someone should have wanted to, no one spoke a bad word about him in her kitchen. She would not stand for it.

"If I may ask, what were you planning to make for supper tonight?" Mr. Fairbury continued.

"Pot roast, sir, with all the fixings."

Raya's mouth began to water just thinking about it. Breakfast felt like a very long time ago. She instantly began looking forward to sitting down to eat the leftovers of the meal, once in the shanty with Mother Emaline that night.

"You don't say! Well, I may have to come back this evening to get a plate myself. You do make a mean pot roast, Ms. Macy."

Out of the corner of her eye, Raya saw how pleased Ms. Macy looked. "That's because I'm a cook, Mr. Fairbury. You pay me to make a mean pot roast." She paused as she looked up from the apple she was peeling. "But I must admit, it is one of my specialties."

Mr. Fairbury gave a hearty laugh as he nodded his agreement. "That it is."

The serious Mr. Lenox did not crack a smile. Instead, he looked at his pocket watch before placing it back in his pocket and excusing himself for a moment. He was to greet someone by appointment in the front and left to do so.

Raya watched subtly to see if Mr. Fairbury would accompany him, knowing that if he didn't, she would have to find her courage to approach him and give him the cookies Mother Emaline had baked. If she was ever going to have the chance, it was now. However, before she could dust the flour from her hands, Mr. Fairbury was coming toward her worktable. Veering toward the covered plate sitting on the back corner of the table, he put his hand under the cloth and pulled out a cookie. She watched him, shocked.

He closed his eyes and chewed his first bite slowly, nodding. "Just as good as I remembered. Excellent, in fact. Please, thank Cousin Emaline for me."

Raya shook her head slightly in disbelief. "How did you know?"

He winked at her. "Emaline sent word that she had sent cookies for me. I saw this one peeking out from under the covering as soon as I entered the kitchen. I must say, I've been looking forward to having one since the moment I heard. Please, tell her thank you."

Raya nodded, still stunned. Mother Emaline had sent word? "I will. She will be glad to hear you enjoyed them."

Mr. Fairbury grinned and pulled out another cookie. "Very much so. Will you keep these here for me today, and I will come back for them this evening? I hear you're one of the last to leave, so I'm sure you'll still be here."

She felt the warmth in his tone and kept her eyes down on the dough she was working. "Yes, sir."

Mr. Fairbury moved to join Mr. Lenox as he came back into the warm room, and together they went out the back door to the stable. As he left, Raya felt peace wash over her as she realized the moment she had been dreading all morning had passed, and so smoothly. She thought of Mother Emaline and smiled—the woman never ceased to be kindhearted. She knew Raya was nervous about approaching Mr. Fairbury and had somehow sent word of her gift, relieving Raya of the task. And Mr. Fairbury had liked the cookies! Raya was glad he had enjoyed their gift and perhaps even knew of their sacrifice to give it to him.

Later, on his way back through the kitchen to the front of the hotel, Mr. Fairbury paused to grab three more of the treats, sending Raya another wink and stacking them in his hand to eat later. She found herself smiling as he left, enjoying his warm friendliness and the delight he obviously found in Mother Emaline's gift.

Twenty-Two

Raya worked happily all afternoon, mixing, kneading, rising, baking, slicing, and washing. That evening, she was about to start washing supper dishes when Mr. Fairbury strode into the kitchen. He didn't say anything, and she didn't turn around, but she knew it was him. He had a presence about him; one those in his company could feel. He was confident and self-assured, yet kind and thoughtful. He placed worth on others, when he very well could have felt he was the only one of worth in the establishment.

Her admiration of him was growing daily as she saw firsthand why the other kitchen hands liked and respected their employer. Not only was he a fair boss, he was kind as well. His staff worked better because of it, too. Not a bad word was spoken about him amongst his workers, and from what Raya heard the other hired help say about previous stations of employment, she knew that was uncommon.

"Ms. Macy, how about a plate of that pot roast? I'm not too late, am I?"

"No, sir, you're certainly not too late. We're just getting started, really, and there's plenty of food left. Go have a seat in the dining room. The girls will bring a plate out to you. You can eat with your patrons," Ms. Macy urged, sounding every bit as motherly and commanding to their boss as she did when speaking to those who worked in her kitchen.

"Thank you, much. I'm looking forward to this scrumptious meal."

Raya crossed the kitchen floor to get a kettle of water off the stove and saw Mr. Fairbury snatch another cookie before heading out into the dining room. Smiling, she poured boiling water over her dishes.

She scrubbed and rinsed platters and plates, cups and bowls. Then she dried, stacked, and dried some more. Finally, she grabbed the broom and began to sweep the kitchen floor. Supper was wrapping up in the front dining room, and she thought she would get the floor done before washing the last of the supper dishes. She finished the sweeping and started scrubbing. While she was at it, she swept and scrubbed the back dining room as well, finishing what should have been Noni's last chore of the day. A woman in Noni's condition had no need to be scrubbing floors, Raya reasoned, and she didn't mind the extra work. She would rather Noni go home to spend time with her family.

When she was finished with the floors, she went back to washing dishes. The kitchen staff began to thin out until it was only Raya and Ms. Macy left. Ms. Macy was making preparations for the next day's meals, and Raya knew once she was finished, she would help wash the last two basins full of dishes. However, Raya noticed how the woman's movements were slower than usual and the concentrated look on her face when she walked.

"Ms. Macy, you should head home. I will finish up the dishes and then go myself."

"Nonsense," Ms. Macy retorted briskly.

"It's not nonsense," Raya answered gently. "You're tired, and you still have to make it home. I won't be much longer here."

Ms. Macy looked as if she might protest further, but instead, sat down with a sigh in one of the chairs at the worktable. "It's my feet," she admitted. "My mind and my body are fine, but my feet are hurting something fierce. Standing all day like I do, well, I guess it has taken its toll. My bones feel all piled up on top of one another and the pains are shooting. Feels like I stepped on a nail with every step."

Compassion filled Raya's heart. "Go home, please, Ms. Macy, and put your feet up. The morning will come early."

"Not right that I should leave before you, not with dishes to be washed."

Raya shook her head, adamant that home was where Ms. Macy belonged. "I'll be done in a jiffy. I won't take no for an answer. Besides, count this as gratitude for the supper I'll be eating tonight."

"That's Mr. Fairbury's doing," Ms. Macy protested.

"Oh, but you're the chef who works your magic to make ordinary food extraordinary!" Raya's happy words elicited a small smile from Ms. Macy.

The woman stood and took her cloak from a peg by the door. "Fine, I'll go home, and I thank you. But this is a onetime occurrence, I tell you. I won't expect this from you every night. Tomorrow you'll be the one going home early, do you hear?"

Raya nodded, glad the woman would start her walk home. She would offer her a ride in the carriage, except it was not her carriage to offer. To change Mr. Fairbury's standing orders would be presumptuous and out of place. Even still, Raya wished she could give her carriage ride to Ms. Macy for the night. Though she did not like walking the city streets in the dark, at least her feet wouldn't hurt as she did so. Holding her tongue, she remembered her place. Likely, if she offered it, Ms. Macy would scold her anyway, saying the same thing Raya already knew.

Ms. Macy left out the back door, and Raya continued washing dishes, enjoying the peace and quiet of the empty kitchen. It was warm and cozy, and she continued with her final chore of the day happily.

"You should go home, Ms. Applewood. Go enjoy what remains of the evening with your mother-in-law."

Raya jumped, nearly dropping the dish she had been scrubbing. As her heart rate returned to normal and she relaxed, she said, "I'm sorry, I didn't hear you approach."

Mr. Fairbury gave her a friendly smile. "No, I'm sure you didn't. You were having quite a time with that dried gravy."

She felt her cheeks flame—she must have made quite a picture, scrubbing as fiercely as she was. "I . . . I didn't know anyone was still here . . ."

Mr. Fairbury studied her face and then glanced around, motioning to the empty kitchen. "That's exactly right, no one is still here. No one but you," he paused, his tone gentling. "I'm quite serious. Go home. You have put in a full day's work. You have more than earned your wage."

"I still have a loaf of bread in the oven, sir, and dishes to wash," she answered simply, keeping her eyes on her washbasin.

"You contradict me?" he asked, his voice stern.

"No, never," she answered quickly. "But I have work I must finish, and then, right away, I will do as you say." She kept her eyes down but knew he was watching her.

"Fine. Then I shall work alongside you to make your work go faster."

That made her look up, and she shook her head. "No," she told him without meaning to contradict him. "I mean, I'm sure you have more important things to do. You don't belong in the kitchen, sir."

He draped his suit coat over the back of a chair and rolled up his shirt sleeves. "Neither do you—the workday is over."

She watched in something near horror as he took half her stack of dirty dishes and placed them in the washtub beside hers. He poured steaming water over them, mixing a little cold water in until he could stand the temperature. To her dismay, he began to scrub. Raya didn't say anything, at a loss for words.

"I can see what you mean—this gravy is treacherous once it has dried on," he told her after a few quiet minutes had passed.

"Please, let me wash that," Raya pleaded, seeing several drops of dish water land on Mr. Fairbury's fancy vest as he scrubbed.

"It was glorious going down though, I must say," he continued, as if he hadn't heard. "Did you enjoy it as well, Ms. Applewood?"

"I'll take my supper with Mother Emaline when I get home," she answered quietly.

He stopped and looked at her. "It's half-past nine, and you haven't eaten?"

"I have work to do," she answered guilelessly.

Mr. Fairbury was quiet for a very long time as he scrubbed a plate with vigor. Suddenly, he let it float down into his dishwater and turned to face her. "Are you trying to pay me back, Ms. Applewood? Do you work hard and long because you feel you owe it to me?"

"Sir, you don't understand! If you had not given me work, Mother Emaline would likely not be alive right now. I might be on the verge of starvation myself. We hadn't eaten in a week or more. And we likely still wouldn't have if it weren't for your generosity," Raya told him emphatically, trying to make him understand.

Mr. Fairbury let that settle, then shook his head. "I gave you permanent work, Ms. Applewood, because you are a virtuous young woman and a good worker, not to make you become one."

Raya felt thoroughly scolded, despite Mr. Fairbury's gentle tone, and kept her eyes on the dishes she was continuing to wash. Mr. Fairbury turned back to his as well.

"I want you out of here by seven-thirty every night. Do you understand?"

"Sir, I have to finish my work."

"Eight then, and not a minute later. I am positive that everything you need to do, you can have finished by then. Leave some for the others . . . they're capable—and employed—to help shoulder the load." His tone was final.

Raya swallowed down any further argument. "Yes, sir." She waited a moment, then dared to speak something that concerned her, yet was clearly none of her business. "You're out late yourself, sir. I'm sure your wife is wondering after you. You should go home.

I truly will have these finished soon." She only wanted good for this man who had been so kind and generous toward them. He was washing dishes with her when he should be home with his wife and children. She didn't want to cause his wife any worry or create conflict for him at home.

It was quiet for a little while. "No one will say anything," he finally answered.

Raya wanted to ask if he always did as he pleased without worrying about how his wife and children might feel, but didn't. He was a kind master and to ask such a question would be to take his kindness out of context and forget her place. Besides, what she had seen and heard of Mr. Fairbury proved he was a wise man. Surely, he knew where it was best for him to be. Who was she to contradict him?

"It was a good crowd tonight," he commented casually.

"Indeed. Ms. Macy said it was one of the largest she has ever seen."

"I reckon she was right. There are more people flooding into town by both river and rail than ever before. Business is booming."

Raya nodded and rinsed the last of her dishes, reluctant to say more and continue the casual conversation with her employer. She had no right to partake of such a pleasant and informal conversation with him.

He waited several seconds, then continued. "Was there enough left over to make a meal for you and Emaline?"

"More than enough," she assured him quickly. "Thank you." She grabbed a dish towel, and, after drying her hands, began to dry dishes and put them away. When she finished with her own stack, she began to dry his.

Finally done washing his last dirty dish, he dried his hands on another dish towel and went to the stove to remove the loaf of bread. "Think it's done?" he asked. Raya checked the big clock on a shelf over the stove and nodded.

When Raya finished putting the dishes away, Mr. Fairbury was waiting with her cloak, and draped it across her shoulders before pulling on his own overcoat. "It's late. Let's let Henry sleep. I'll take you home in my carriage, as I'll already be out. I would like to personally thank Emaline for the cookies, anyway. Why don't you grab the plate of them, please? I'll carry the rest of your parcels."

Raya was humbled by his kindness once again, this time toward his carriage driver. She wanted to argue that she was not worthy to ride in his carriage, especially not in his company, but she had argued enough for one evening. Additionally, as Mr. Fairbury said, it would be kind to allow Henry to sleep, especially since there was another carriage by which she could get home. She quietly gathered up his plateful of cookies and followed him out of the kitchen, making sure the back door was locked behind them.

He motioned for her to climb into his carriage first and then followed, his hands full of the different food items Ms. Macy had packaged for her. Once the carriage was in motion, Mr. Fairbury's friendly smile returned. "I think I'll have another of those cookies, please."

Raya pulled back the cover and held the plate out to him. He took two and held one out to her. She was about to shake her head in protest when he said, "Come now. You can't tell me you're not a fan of her cookies."

Raya did smile then, for the first time in his presence. "You're right," she answered shyly. "I do love them."

"Of course you do! Who wouldn't? Come now, have one," he urged.

"They were a gift for *you*," she protested.

"And I'm sharing my gift."

Raya conceded and took the cookie. "How did you become so generous?" she questioned honestly after swallowing her first bite. His was nearly gone, and he was reaching for another. "One would think that with as much as you have, you would have been very careful with your resources over the years," Raya finished carefully, realizing too late that her question was rude.

"One would think I have been stingy, is that what you mean?" Mr. Fairbury asked with a laugh, his blue eyes revealing his amusement.

Raya kept her eyes on the plate of cookies, embarrassed, but didn't miss his shrug.

"Sometimes when you give, you receive. I figure if I have more than enough to meet my needs, why not share with someone who has need?" He tipped his head and considered her in the darkness of the carriage. "I suspect you may also know something about that."

She folded her hands and stayed quiet, not understanding.

He tucked his chin as he continued. "It's been reported to me that you have been sharing the food Ms. Macy sends home with you."

Raya felt her cheeks flame as her deeds were laid out in the open. She had not thought anything of sharing their extra food, but now, in his presence, she found herself second-guessing. Should she have returned the excess food? Or told Ms. Macy to stop sending so much? "I . . . I'm sorry, sir. I never thought. They were hungry, we had extra . . ."

"Raya," he interrupted, cutting off her stammering response.

She felt taken aback by his use of her familiar name. She glanced up at him fleetingly before dropping her gaze again.

"I don't care if you share the food I give you. I give it to you. It's yours. You may do with it as you please. All I ask is that Cousin Emaline makes me a batch of these every week," he finished with a wink, holding up his cookie.

Raya dipped her head humbly. "Of course." The ingredients would take a portion of her pay, but when it was all coming from Mr. Fairbury, how could she but gladly agree to return a portion of her wages back to him in the form of cookies? Everything she had came from him; it was only right to return whatever he asked.

Raya knew their carriage ride was nearly over, and she wanted to try one last time to thank him properly for all he had done for them. Somehow, she wanted him to understand and to finish the conversation she had started shortly after they embarked the luxurious carriage. "As one who has been in need and is now on the receiving end of your generosity, thank you, Mr. Fairbury. Thank you again, from the bottom of my heart. We... we have lost much in the past few months, and I was beginning to think that I would lose my mother-in-law as well, but because of your generosity and provision, her strength is returning."

Mr. Fairbury's look was gentle. "There is only one Provider, Raya. I was simply a channel through which He provided." There was only a slight pause in which Raya could process what Mr. Fairbury had said. "Oh, here we are now. Let's get you inside before you catch cold and can't come bake bread for my customers tomorrow."

Suddenly, it occurred to Raya that the rich and powerful Mr. Fairbury intended to enter her humble dwelling. To have him see the exterior of the shanty, the neighborhood where Emaline, the widow of his late cousin, lived was humbling enough, but to have him walk through their door and see with his own eyes their poverty was simply too much. She could not bring such shame onto Luke, onto Julius, onto Mother Emaline. "Sir, it is very late and very cold. I am quite capable of seeing myself in. Mother Emaline always leaves the door unbarred until I return. Please, you have a long ride home. I will express your gratitude for the cookies and share with her your request for more next week."

"Thank you, but if it's all the same, I would like to thank her myself."

Raya kept her eyes on her hands, which were folded politely in her lap. "Sir, she's sick," she protested timidly.

"Good company makes the heart merry, and a merry heart in turn makes the body well. Do you not agree, Ms. Applewood?"

The carriage stopped, and at a loss for words, Raya waited as Mr. Fairbury disembarked, then turned back to help her down.

Mother Emaline opened the door, and a shaft of light spilled from it. Raya worried what Mr. Fairbury would say or think about their poor living conditions. And just as quickly, she knew he would say nothing unkind—as she had found he was not one to judge. Still, to think of such a wealthy, powerful, well-respected man in their little shanty was preposterous... even if he was distant kin.

"Why, Atlas! What a surprise! Come in, come in!" Mother Emaline said, holding the door open wide.

Mr. Fairbury entered, motioning to his carriage driver that he would only be a minute, and embraced Mother Emaline despite his full hands. "It is good to see you, Cousin Emaline, and to see you looking so well."

Raya slipped in the door and took her parcels from Mr. Fairbury, allowing him to continue speaking with Mother Emaline. She knew his last statement was made out of pure kindness. Raya was well aware of how sickly the woman looked and knew she must appear even more so to Mr. Fairbury, who had not seen her in twenty years. She was certain the woman he remembered looked little like the woman who was standing before him now, skin and bones, with sallow cheeks, graying hair, and glassy eyes.

"I hoped I would get to see you sooner or later," Mother Emaline was telling him warmly.

"As was I. Tonight, I was able to convince Ms. Applewood to allow me to escort her home, given the late hour, so I could thank you personally for the wonderful cookies you made me. They were simply delicious! I've never had better. Thank you for making them and for your thoughtfulness. I've eaten half the batch already, as you can see," Mr. Fairbury told Mother Emaline, pulling back the cover on the plate.

Raya watched affectionately as Mother Emaline's cheeks flushed pink and was again grateful to Mr. Fairbury. She had not realized how much Mother Emaline had missed a man's enjoyment of her baking. Father Julius and the boys used to rave about it, but for the past three months, no man had eaten any of her treats or complimented her on her baking. To have Atlas Fairbury do so now obviously pleased the woman greatly.

UP FROM THE ASH HEAP

Her strength sapped by even her small exertion, Mother Emaline made her way to the table and lowered herself carefully into a rickety chair where she could enjoy the conversation while resting. As she did, Raya briefly let her gaze meet Mr. Fairbury's for the first time and gave him a warm smile. He had warmed her mother-in-law's heart, and that fact alone warmed hers.

Mr. Fairbury smiled back, and she knew then he had come to thank Emaline personally because he had known how much it would mean to her. His thoughtfulness astounded Raya.

"Say, Ms. Applewood, do you know how to make these cookies?" he asked suddenly.

"Mine never turn out as well, but I do know her recipe," Raya answered, reaching for a quilt, and draping it around Emaline's shoulders, noticing the woman was shivering.

"Well, then you have a new job. You will now be known as the cookie-maker. And my hotel shall be frequented by those craving one of Cousin Emaline's cookies! I'll tell Ms. Macy of the change tomorrow when I come, so go ahead and bake bread in the morning, and you can start on cookies in the afternoon. Is that agreeable to you?"

Raya looked at how Mother Emaline was beaming and smiled. "Very agreeable."

"Wonderful. Well, I'd best be getting home now, but Cousin Emaline, thank you, thank you for the cookies. They are wonderful and remind me of my childhood when mother and I would come to visit. It was lovely to see you as well, and thank you for loaning your daughter-in-law to me every day. She is a hard worker and makes my hotel a better place." He paused, shooting a sideways glance at Raya. "However, I would like to tell you to expect her home earlier now. If she returns home later than half-past eight, I want you to let me know right off. I've instructed Ms. Applewood to leave not a minute after eight o'clock from now on, and I expect that instruction to be observed."

Raya looked at the ground, embarrassed. "Yes, sir."

Mother Emaline agreed, too, with a smile.

"Well, I'm going to head home, then. You ladies had best eat your supper. I'm sure you're both famished. Good evening," Mr. Fairbury said, tipping his hat and smiling at each of them before turning and walking out the door.

When the sound of his carriage had faded, Mother Emaline turned to Raya. "He's a good man."

Raya nodded with a smile. "Indeed. He is very kind."

"Do you truly think he enjoyed the cookies?"

"I am sure of it. He was eating them all day long," Raya answered with a laugh. Mother Emaline laughed too.

Raya pulled back the cover on the dish of pot roast, potatoes, carrots, and onions and leaned close to smell them, a satisfied smile spreading across her face. "The aromas from this are heavenly," she told Mother Emaline, excitedly. "It was making me so hungry all evening!"

Mother Emaline went shakily to get the skillet, and they went about warming their supper together, both merry as tantalizing aromas filled their small dwelling and the air inside the shanty warmed with the extra wood on the fire. Raya had been able to pay a neighbor to deliver another load of firewood just that afternoon; they had plenty of food, and though Raya wouldn't call her well yet, Mother Emaline was able to get around a bit again. Compared to the dismal state they had found themselves in just weeks ago, life was good.

Twenty-Three

A week of blissful peace went by after Mr. Fairbury's visit to their small shanty. Raya went to the hotel every morning, worked all day making bread and cookies and washing dishes, and came home every night to have supper with Mother Emaline. With their food provided, they were able to set aside enough money for their rent and still buy enough wood to chase the chill out of the room. Though they still wrapped in blankets while sitting in front of the fire before bed, Raya could no longer see her breath in the air, and the cold did not penetrate to the bone as it had.

She felt better about leaving Mother Emaline home alone now that there was wood to keep the fire burning, and the woman was well enough to put a log on it as needed. Raya was careful to fill the woodbox before she left each morning, so tending the fire would be an easy chore. She was glad to see Mother Emaline filling her time by taking in a bit of mending here and there, darning socks and mittens for children in the neighborhood, reading the Scriptures, writing occasional letters home to Chenoa and Nizhoni, and napping as needed, giving her body the rest it required to continue healing. Though not fully recovered yet, Mother Emaline seemed to be getting a little better each day. The fever had left her, and only the cough and spells of weakness persisted. With the rest and good food, her strength seemed to be returning. Each day, Mother Emaline had some of the leftovers for her lunch, and a cup of tea and a slice of bread for an afternoon snack to tide her over until Raya's late arrival.

After they had eaten their supper, Raya set aside a portion for Mother Emaline's lunch the next day and then carefully gathered the extras and took them to a family in need. If she had a few minutes, she would pull little ones onto her lap and spend a while visiting with the mothers.

In their poor neighborhood, she found families of every nationality and walk of life, and she found kindred spirits among them. Realizing their economic status no more defined them than the color of her skin defined her, she relished the chance to make friends and brighten days for those whose hope was dim.

She now had work, and thus they had food, shelter, and fuel for their fire, but many were not so fortunate. There were whole families out of work: widows with several young children and no prospects, orphans, and elderly. Every family's story was different, yet they held a common strand of poverty and lack of opportunity. Raya wanted to help, but had nothing to offer, save her small amount of extra food. She was grateful Mr. Fairbury had not told her to stop sharing it, for it was the only thing that brought her any kind of comfort when she stopped to consider the great need surrounding her.

Oftentimes, when Raya got home in the evenings, she found Mother Emaline sitting wrapped up in a blanket in her chair; the cat curled up on her lap. After they took their evening meal, Mother Emaline would light an extra candle, and she would read to Raya from the big family Bible. When the dim lighting and small print tired her eyes, she would pass the Bible to Raya, who would take her turn reading. When Raya finished, they would spend time in prayer together, thanking God for His provision, worshipping Him, and lifting up those around them and those they loved far away. Then they would warm their broken bricks and go to bed.

One evening when Raya returned from work, she found Mother Emaline crouched down over a box near the hearth. Knowing instinctively what had happened, Raya dropped the bar into place, set her parcels down on the table, and ran the few steps across the shanty to drop to her knees beside her. "How many are there?" she asked, as she peered into the box.

"Four," Mother Emaline told her, beaming. "And all seem to be healthy as of yet."

Raya peered down at the four little bunches of fur that Smoky had gathered around herself. There were three black kittens and one gray one. Clapping her hands softly in delight, Raya laughed. Reaching down, she ran a fingertip over the silky soft head of the nearest kitten, a bright smile filling her face.

"When were they born?" she asked.

"This morning, just shortly after you left. Smoky did wonderfully. I've kept them close to the fire all day, hoping they'll stay warm enough. Every hour has gone by dreadfully slow; I've been so excited for you to get home," Mother Emaline told her.

"There will be extra tidbits for you tonight, Mama," Raya murmured to Smoky as she rubbed the cat's ears. What a simple pleasure it was to have a pet, and now that pet had brought more joy with the arrival of the sweetest little kittens.

Mother Emaline laughed. "Maybe now that she's had the kittens, she'll be ready to catch some mice."

"Maybe so," Raya agreed with a hopeful smile.

Raya and Emaline stayed by the hearth for a long while, watching the kittens, their supper forgotten on the table. Later that night, Raya took a piece of paper from her stationery kit and added a bit of water to her small ink pot. Forsaking her warm spot by the fire for the hard surface of the table, she sat shivering as she penned a long letter to Chenoa, which she asked the young woman to share with Nizhoni whenever she next saw her in town to save postage. Knowing Niz couldn't read, Chenoa would likely end up reading her letter to her anyway, even if Raya sent two.

She told them about finding work, the kittens, and Mother Emaline's improvement. She described the strange ways and extravagant luxuries of those living in the East, hoping to give her sisters-in-law a glimpse of city life through her words. Then she shared about several kind and courageous women whom she had met and begun to form a friendship with. She explained that over the past few months, she had learned that despite where one was from or how they were raised, people were people. Hoping to ease her sisters-in-law's worries, she reported that they had plenty to eat, an adequate dwelling, and merry spirits. She then inquired about their own situations and relayed her hopes and prayers that they were well and happy.

When she had filled the paper front and back, she turned it and wrote lengthwise as well, not wanting to waste an inch. Then, she folded the letter and slid it into an envelope before carefully printing Chenoa's name and address. She would post it on her morning break. There was a post stop not far from the hotel. As soon as she had blown out the candles and settled in bed, Mother Emaline's voice filled the darkness as she asked, "You've not heard from either of the girls yet?"

"Not yet," Raya answered. "But you know how long the post can take to reach Colorado Territory, and especially in the winter. They likely have not even received my first letter yet. We can hardly expect to have received a response."

"You're right," Mother Emaline told her. "I know you are. I just wonder about them daily. To hear that they're well would be such a relief."

"To you and me both, Mother," Raya told her sincerely. She, too, found herself wondering after her sisters-in-law, and praying for them daily. They had gone back to their families, but she had not heard from either of them since. She wondered how they were weathering their grief, the winter, and the monumental changes in their lives. She wondered how Niz was handling her loss, and if her sisters and mother were able to give her the comfort she so desperately needed. Mostly, Raya prayed for the LORD to put someone new in their paths who would witness to them both in word and deed. She prayed daily for their salvation, knowing the only true comfort and peace both young women sought came from knowing there was a perfect God with a perfect plan and purpose. She knew, because that knowledge was often the only thing that got her out of bed in the mornings.

Their physical situation had dramatically improved, and Raya was unendingly thankful. They had enough to pay their rent and buy wood for their fire. And though there was still not enough money for fabric for the new dresses they both so badly needed, or the hope of moving out of the rough neighborhood they found themselves in, they were no longer hovering dangerously on the brink of existence. And she was thankful for that. But despite their improved circumstances, Raya's heart still held great sadness. Her laugh and her smile were returning, yet deep within, she oftentimes felt broken and hopeless.

She missed her husband. She missed her sisters. She missed their home, their valley, and their life. But mostly, she missed her hope for the future. Before the fire, they had hoped that their privileged situation would become more favorable still. They had hoped that Colorado Territory would become a state and their town would grow. They had hope of new life as Niz was with child. Raya had hoped that she would one day be in the family way herself, and that her own little cabin would one day be full of little giggles and warm hugs.

Thinking of how she had hoped for a family made Raya remember how comfortable it had felt to be engulfed in the arms of her husband every night, where she could sleep warm and safe.

Oh, how she missed him. She missed the feel of him in the bed beside her. She missed how protected she felt as his presence filled the cabin, and his rifle hung on the pegs over the door. She missed how cared for she felt when he asked about her day, and how he delighted her with little surprises, like flowers from the meadow or the fabric for a new dress. She missed his smell, his voice, his confidence, his faith, and his strength. She missed the hope he gave her.

In the darkness, tears ran down the sides of her face. Now, she had none of that. She was surviving, and that was all. Her attention was consumed with assuring survival for another day, both for herself and Mother Emaline. There was no hope for the future, no dreams that made her heart soar, no anticipation that better days were ahead. She knew what lay ahead: fighting to survive, continued loneliness, an empty womb, more bread, more cookies, more dishes.

However, down in the deepest parts of her being, a verse Luke had quoted to her often rang out in the stillness of her hopelessness. "For I know the thoughts that I think toward you, saith the LORD, thoughts of peace, and not of evil, to give you an expected end." Luke always said it was a promise of hope. It was a promise that God was not done with them, nor was He angry with them, nor had He forgotten them, nor had His plans run out. That verse echoing in the barrenness of her heart was what motivated Raya to get out of bed every morning. That and the words that had swept across her consciousness her first day in the hotel: "*I will not leave you nor forsake you. I have a plan to redeem you from the pit.*"

If the words were true, perhaps God still had a plan for her. A plan that was good. A plan filled with hope. And so, she found the strength to rise every morning, put on her dress, and start another day.

Twenty-Four

"I have received an invitation to take tea with Wendy Applewood, Judson's wife," Mother Emaline said after she swallowed her first bite of supper.

Raya's face brightened in surprise. "Why, that's lovely," she answered, sincerely pleased. It would be wonderful for Mother Emaline to have an outing, and one back to the house of a relative would be a welcome distraction from her persistent cough and the bleakness of her lonely days. "When are you to go?"

"Day after tomorrow."

"Well, how wonderful! I hope you have a splendid time. I'll order a horse cart to take you. It won't cost very much, and it simply isn't possible for you to make the long walk by yourself. I do wish we had the money to buy material for a new dress for you to wear. Yours is getting a bit thin, but it will still do nicely," Raya chattered, infused with joy over Mother Emaline's invitation. She was certain it would feel lovely to the older woman to get back into the realm of society she was accustomed to, rather than being cooped up for another long day.

"Raya, I don't wish to go alone. I wish for you to accompany me," Mother Emaline said evenly as she cut her slice of ham delicately.

Raya quickly set down her utensils before she could drop them. "Mother, I couldn't. I can't. I . . . I think it would be best if you went by yourself," she answered, searching for a reason to object.

She well remembered the expressions on the faces of those in high society when they noted her darkened skin. She always saw the same mix of discomfort, disdain, and fear in their eyes. No, people who were in the East's upper class, as Wendy Applewood was, did not like having her around. That was why she stayed out of the front dining room at The Fairbury Hotel, and why she had been turned down everywhere she inquired about work. That's why the serving lady at the inn they stayed at after first arriving in town had refused to speak to or look at her, and why she was all but invisible to the dozens of people she had passed on the streets when she had been searching for work. She could not, would not, accompany Mother Emaline to tea and risk ruining the special outing for the sweet woman.

"Nonsense. I've already sent word we will both be attending."

"I have to work. I have to be at the hotel."

"You have not had a day off since you started," Mother Emaline protested. "I am confident they will give you the day off should you ask it. If not, I'm certain I could persuade Atlas . . . though I'm sure he would need little persuading at all."

"Please do no such thing," Raya objected, embarrassed at the mere mention of it. She paused. "I am quite certain Ms. Macy would give me the day off, as you have said; however, we can scarcely miss out on a day of pay. We need every cent I bring home."

"I had a bit of mending come in today. That will replace a portion of your lost wages."

"Not enough," Raya answered quickly.

"You have to have faith, dear. We will be fine."

Raya shook her head, hoping she was acting out of concern for Mother Emaline and not out of fear for herself. She had faced rejection so many times since coming to the city. To face it once more and have Mother Emaline there to witness it would be too painful.

"Don't waste your breath arguing, Raya. I've already sent word that you will be attending with me. Besides, I truly don't know that I'm well enough to go alone. I don't believe it would be wise. You know how my weak spells still come on so altogether unexpectedly."

Raya knew Mother Emaline was appealing to her compassionate side to ensure her agreement, yet the woman had a point. The wind went out of Raya's sails, and the fight drained out of her. "Very well. I will ask Ms. Macy tomorrow. If she says I can have the day off, I will accompany you. If she says I cannot, you will have to go alone."

Mother Emaline looked pleased and went back to eating her supper. Raya did as well, though she had a hard time turning her thoughts to a more pleasant topic. Even later that night, as Mother Emaline read from the Psalms, Raya was biting her lip, worrying about having to ask Ms. Macy for a day off. But mostly, she worried about how Wendy Applewood would react to her presence.

The next morning, after arriving at the hotel and entering the kitchen through the back door, Raya quickly hung her cloak on a peg and made a beeline for Ms. Macy. The kitchen hands were still arriving, and the people in the room were sparse when compared to the number there would be in only a few minutes.

Ms. Macy shot her a questioning look and raised an eyebrow at her. "Yes, Raya? Is something the matter?"

Raya kept her eyes on the ground submissively as she shook her head, trying not to let Ms. Macy's brisk tone or clipped words cower her. She knew the woman was beginning to form an affection for her—the briskness was simply the way she was—yet her abrupt behavior could still be a bit intimidating. "There's nothing the matter. I was only wondering if it would be acceptable if I took the day off tomorrow."

"What are you going to do with a day off?" Ms. Macy asked, obviously surprised by Raya's request.

"Attend a tea with my mother-in-law," Raya answered carefully. She still felt great reluctance toward the idea.

"I see. Well, certainly. I've been telling you to take a day off for the last two weeks. I'm glad you're finally listening. Mr. Fairbury was getting after me, thinking I was working you too hard."

Raya was taken off-guard by Ms. Macy's off-handed remark about Mr. Fairbury. She had only seen the gentleman from a distance since he accompanied her home to thank Mother Emaline for the cookies, and now she was surprised he noticed she had not taken the customary day off. Raya swallowed down her questions and simply bobbed her head. "Thank you. I will be back the morning after next."

"You'd best be. I'll need more bread and cookies by then. Bake extra today and leave the dishwashing to the others. You've developed quite a knack for the baking. I'd rather serve yours a day old than to serve someone else's fresh."

"Yes, ma'am," Raya answered humbly. "Thank you." Turning, she hurried to her worktable and set about her baking.

Noni came to sit with her for their morning break and told her a funny story about her daughter that had occurred only the night before. Raya shared how the kittens were growing, and was pleased to see her words brought a bright smile to Noni's tired face. Raya had offered Noni one of the kittens after hearing that mice had pillaged their cornmeal supply, and Noni gratefully accepted. Now, they were simply waiting for the kittens to grow old enough to leave their mother before Noni came to pick one out and take it home. Raya enjoyed the easy conversation and was sad to see Noni finish her tea and get back to work as the break ended. She had quickly become a friend, and Raya was grateful to have one.

Even in the hotel kitchen, where they were all working for a wage, she felt the others' reluctance to befriend her. She knew that even here, the color of her skin, the origin of her ancestors, separated her from the others. Only Noni and Ms. Macy seemed altogether unhindered by her differences, though a few of the others were slowly starting to come around.

It was nearly suppertime when Mr. Fairbury made his appearance at the hotel, and by then, everyone working in the kitchen was moving at full speed. Supper was to be served in just ten minutes, and as always, there was much to finish up. Ms. Macy was the only one who paused in the scurry to talk to Mr. Lenox and Mr. Fairbury, and they left shortly after arriving.

Supper was a rush, and by eight o'clock, Raya was just putting her last pan of cookies in the oven. Knowing she had to stay at least another ten minutes, she rolled up her sleeves, blew a wayward strand of dark hair out of her face, and took her place at a washbasin. She glanced up as the swinging door from the front dining room opened, and was startled to see Mr. Fairbury enter through it. She hadn't realized he had stayed to dine tonight and felt pleasure at his presence. Things were always happier when Mr. Fairbury was around.

He glanced around the kitchen, spotted her, and altered his course accordingly.

She felt color flood her cheeks as he so obviously sought her out. She glanced nervously at the clock, realizing belatedly that she had disregarded his orders . . . again. She turned her eyes back to the dishes she was washing and kept them there, even as he stopped just to the side of her. "Good evening, sir," she told him with a cheerfulness she didn't feel.

He stood quietly for several seconds without moving. Finally, he clasped his hands behind his back. "I've been waiting outside for nigh on ten minutes. Seems to me I remember telling you to be out of here by eight."

She felt flustered, both because he had self-admittedly been waiting for her outside, but more so because he seemed displeased with her. What if he took back the promises he had made to her? If he did, she would have no one to blame but herself. Would he dismiss her for her unwillingness to follow orders? "Sir, I'm sorry. I have one last batch of cookies in the oven. I thought I might as well wash a few dishes while I wait for them to bake. I will leave the moment they're done."

He considered her for several more seconds. "I hear you're taking the day off tomorrow."

"Yes, sir," she answered, puzzled. Was he upset she was taking a day off? It seemed as if he was, yet Ms. Macy had made mention he was concerned she hadn't to date.

"And it has been brought to my attention that it's your first day off since you sought employment here."

"Yes, sir."

"Why? Does not everyone need a Sabbath?"

"I need the pay more than I need the rest," Raya answered honestly.

"While I don't doubt that, and we can discuss your wage, I have this question for you: do you work to earn a wage, or do you work to pay back a debt?"

"I could never pay back the debt I owe to you," Raya answered softly. She dipped the washed plate through the rinse water and set it on a tea towel with the others to dry.

Reaching out, Mr. Fairbury startled her by grasping her arm gently, stilling her methodical motions as she reached for another dirty plate. "I do not want repaid, Ms. Applewood," he told her, his voice firm. "I give out of pure generosity, not to receive anything back."

Raya resisted the urge to pull her arm away, distraught that he would touch her. He was the wealthy, powerful, and respected Mr. Atlas Fairbury; she was but a colored hired hand in his kitchen. To touch her, to even be having this conversation with her, was degrading to him. "Then let me serve out of generosity as well," she told him quietly, hoping no one was watching, hoping no one saw the time and attention he was giving to a mere servant, all the while knowing everyone did.

"If you were, that would be one thing, but I fear, Ms. Applewood, you are serving out of duty . . . out of guilt over an imagined debt."

"It's not imagined," Raya retorted quickly.

"I never asked to be repaid," he responded just as quickly.

"You pay me to work here, and I am so thankful. No one else would hire me. I want to honor that chance you gave me by being a hard worker," she explained. When he remained silent, she continued. "I am grateful for your provision, Mr. Fairbury, so very grateful. As I have said, you have extended the gift of life to Mother Emaline and me. Is it not right that I should want to see you succeed and do whatever small part I can to aid in that success?" she asked, hurt by his tone and manner. She had told him this before. How did he not understand? How could she do any less than give everything she had to serve him well? She had not meant to disobey him, only to finish her workday well by completing the tasks Ms. Macy had given her. Yet, he did not seem pleased.

"My success does not depend on you," he answered, his words measured, his tone free of emotion.

She shrank back. "I didn't mean to say that it did. I apologize, sir. I am not so arrogant to believe I have any hand in your success whatsoever. I simply want to make your customers as happy as is within my means."

"And what of me? Do you not want to do what makes me happy?" he questioned, studying her face.

Raya hesitated for a moment, caught off-guard. "Of course, sir. Please tell me what would do so."

"But I already have. Do you not remember? I asked for a batch of cookies every week and for you to leave this establishment by eight o'clock. That's all."

Raya's chin dropped as her head fell forward in submission. "Yes, sir." She turned and walked quickly to the oven, where she took out the finished cookies, transferred them from the baking sheet to a cookie jar, then put on her cloak. She did not look up to see where Mr. Fairbury was in the room, but instead, took up her packages of leftovers Ms. Macy had set aside and exited quietly out the back door.

She shivered as she stepped outside into the biting cold and quickly descended the few stairs down onto the worn path that led to the stable where the carriage was waiting to carry her home. She heard the back door open and shut behind her, and she picked up her pace, wanting to escape to the solitude of the carriage.

"Ms. Applewood."

She stopped at Mr. Fairbury's words. "Yes, sir?" she asked softly. He was right. Absolutely right. He only asked of her two things, and though she delivered his batches of cookies like clockwork, she had not seen to the other. What must he think of her? What must he think of her gratitude? To say something was one thing, but to put actions behind your words was something altogether different. Obedience was her only way to show him her respect and her gratitude, and she had failed to do so right in front of him.

"I did not mean to sound harsh, and if I did, I'm sorry," Mr. Fairbury started, his voice full of regret.

Raya nearly choked. "Please, sir, do not apologize. It is I who should be making amends. You were quite clear about your expectations, yet I did not adhere to them."

Mr. Fairbury was shivering from the cold, as was Raya, and he suddenly took off his coat and settled it around her shoulders. "Sakes alive, but it's cold out here tonight!"

Raya bobbed her head in agreement. "That it is. Thank you." She felt obligated to take his coat off and hand it back to him, distraught that he should be cold when she was warm, yet she had the feeling she had already frustrated him enough for one night. To refuse his coat would only serve to do so further.

"Ms. Applewood, I simply do not want you working morning until night because you feel you must. If you choose to, I want it to be because you want to, not because you feel obligated because you think you owe me something," he explained.

"Then this has all only been a miscommunication. I *want* to work hard for you to show my appreciation," Raya said, relieved. She paused a moment to see if he would say more, but when he didn't, she curtsied. "Goodnight, sir."

"Goodnight," he echoed. She moved to take his coat from around her shoulders, but he waved her actions away. "Keep it for now. It's too cold for you to be out in only that thin cloak."

"Your wife would not want you to come home without your coat," she told him instinctively. She had forever been chiding Luke for going out without being properly dressed for the weather. Surely, Mrs. Fairbury felt the same.

Mr. Fairbury hesitated. "If I had one, I'm sure you would be right, but seeing as how I've never married, I don't think it will be an issue."

Raya looked up sharply, then dropped her eyes just as quickly. There was no Mrs. Fairbury? "I . . . I'm sorry, I just presumed."

"Apology accepted. Now take the coat and go home to Cousin Emaline. It's frigid out here."

Reluctant to contradict him again, Raya bobbed her head in appreciation and continued to the carriage. Once she was inside and headed for home, she sat quiet and still, thoroughly stunned. She had never, not even once, considered the possibility that Mr. Fairbury was unmarried. How did a man of his stature and position get to his age without being married? Her heart filled with an aching compassion as she realized the loving wife and adoring children she had pictured him going home to each night were not a reality.

Her nose beginning to hurt from the cold, she reached up and cupped her hands around it, trying to warm it with her breath. It was only November, but it had already been a dreadfully cold winter thus far. And still, the temperatures continued to drop. Sitting in the frigid carriage, she was grateful for Mr. Fairbury's coat and drew it close around herself. His fresh, manly scent lingered on the heavy fabric, and nearly against her will, she took in a deep breath of it. Unbidden thoughts of belonging came to her mind, and she remembered what it was like to be married, to belong, to be provided for, to be protected, to be cared for. Tears stung her eyes as her heart wrenched.

Yet it was not Luke's coat she wore, nor that of a hopeful suitor. It was Mr. Atlas Fairbury's. Her thoughts took a confusing turn.

He perplexed her. He was gentle, generous, and kind, yet he seemed altogether unhappy with her, and she did not fully understand why. Why he even took time to concern himself with a servant in his kitchen, she didn't know. He should simply overlook her as would be expected. He didn't need to be worrying about how much she was working or sending her home in his coat. He had so many other things to concern himself with, so many other matters of greater importance.

As she exited the carriage in front of the shanty, she mentally vowed to keep a closer eye on the large clock that stood on the shelf in the kitchen and make sure she was out the door every night by eight. She wanted to show Mr. Fairbury respect by carrying out his orders. If leaving by eight was what he asked, then she would do so religiously.

The next morning, she woke up at her normal time, then went back to sleep, remembering she had the day off. When she awoke again, sunlight was streaming through the small window, and she realized the hour was late. Despite her extra hours of sleep, she yawned as she arose and saw Mother Emaline was already at the fire, warming their breakfast. Raya stood and went to the hearth, running her hand tenderly over each kitten and their proud mama. The tiny little kittens brought a smile to her face, and she laughed in delight as one licked her hand with its rough pink tongue.

When their food was warm, they ate their breakfast together, and then Raya set to work on giving the shanty a deep cleaning. She had worked so much, she had not seen to it as she should have, and Mother Emaline had not been well enough to do more than light cleaning. Raya hummed to herself as she swept the floor and washed the window. When it was nearly time to leave for tea, Raya changed into her black mourning dress, which she had washed the night before. As she brushed through her long dark hair, she dreamed about one day getting another dress. Even if it was plain and black, she wouldn't mind. It would just be nice to have two to switch between, so she didn't have to put on a damp dress before work on the morning after wash day. She was thankful she had the time to let it dry properly this morning while she cleaned in her nightdress.

She pulled her hair back and twisted it into a neat bun at the nape of her neck, looking more dignified and respectable than stylish, then powdered her hands and face. Her heart was beating wildly at the thought of accompanying Mother Emaline to tea and meeting Mrs. Wendy Applewood, but there was nothing to be done about it now. She had already agreed to go and even took the day off work. To stay home now would be a disappointment to Mother Emaline.

She was just standing to put on her cloak when a knock sounded at the door. Surprised, Raya opened it to find a nicely dressed gentleman who identified himself as an employee of Mr. Fairbury. He had been sent to fetch Mr. Fairbury's coat and to drop off a package to Raya. Stunned, Raya took it, turning the soft package wrapped in brown paper over in her hands. When she had handed over Mr. Fairbury's coat and the man had left, Raya hurried to the table with the package and untied the string that secured it.

When she saw the contents of the package, her mouth fell open. Lifting it up, she stared at the thick winter cloak, brand new and expertly made. The style was more lavish and beautiful than anything she had ever owned. The outside of the cloak was light tan wool with thin dark brown lines. It was beautiful fabric, fashionable and heavy, but it was the inside of the cloak that took Raya's breath away. The heavy wool cloak was lined with sunset orange silk. When the cloak was worn, the only silk that would show was in the hood, which was edged with soft brown fur.

She dropped the cloak on the table, feeling unfit to even be holding such a beautiful garment in her hands. "Why, it's the most beautiful cloak I've ever seen," she breathed. For just a moment, Raya felt relief. With a cloak like that, she would not feel so self-conscious walking into Wendy Applewood's. But just as quickly, she realized her folly.

"It is stunning," Mother Emaline agreed, her eyes bright.

"Surely, he does not mean for me to keep this," Raya said, appalled.

"Why else would he have it delivered here?" Mother Emaline asked, a knowing smile on her face.

"Well," Raya paused, at a loss for words. "I can't keep it! This must have cost a fortune! Why would he give this to me?"

"It seems to me that when Atlas Fairbury sees a need, he meets it," Emaline responded. "He must have noticed how thin your cloak was last night and decided to meet your need himself."

"He shouldn't have. He has no reason to concern himself with such things," Raya protested. "And if he was going to, a simple black woolen one would have been perfectly adequate."

"Perhaps he wanted you to have the best," Mother Emaline said gently, her smile still in place.

"But why? He shouldn't. Employers do not buy beautiful, extravagant cloaks for their employees."

Mother Emaline held up her hands in surrender. "Don't argue with me. If you feel the need, discuss it with Mr. Fairbury. I cannot presume to know the thoughts in his head to argue his case correctly. Put on your cloak. We need to go."

"I can't wear this," Raya protested.

Mother Emaline tucked her chin. "Whyever not?"

Raya looked out the window, then turned her eyes back to her mother-in-law, the look in them nearly beseeching. "I am not worthy of wearing this."

"Being worthy has nothing to do with it. You have been given a beautiful gift. Do you presume to let that gift go to waste because you don't feel worthy to have received it? Do you know better than Mr. Fairbury?" Emaline's tone was gentle but motherly.

Raya took a deep breath, at war within herself. To continue wearing her old, thin cloak would be ridiculous when she had a beautiful, warm one at her disposal, as well as seeming ungrateful for the far-too-generous gift Mr. Fairbury had given her. But for her, a poor foreigner, to wear such an expensive, elaborate cloak felt utterly absurd and inappropriate. She folded the cloak carefully and put it back in its paper wrapping, then tied the string to secure it.

"You won't wear it?" Mother Emaline asked, surprised.

"I'm in mourning," Raya answered, her words measured. "And that cloak, no matter how beautiful it is, is far too colorful to be appropriate at such a time." Raya settled her thin black cloak over her shoulders and secured it before pulling the hood up over her hair. "Here, Mother, let me help you with yours," Raya offered, doing just that.

When they were both ready, Raya opened the door, and they started on their trek across town. Holding Mother Emaline's arm to help steady the woman, they made their way down the frozen streets until they came to a part of town where horse carts were more readily available. Parting with a few coins, Raya secured one and helped Mother Emaline up into it. If she had been going alone, she would have walked, but that would never do for Mother Emaline. The walk was too far, the air too cold. With her cough still lingering and her strength still diminished, taking a horse cart was a necessity.

After they were settled and on their way, Raya spent several minutes worrying about the upcoming visit. She hoped Mrs. Applewood was not so offended by her presence that she cancelled the tea. She also hoped it was not so awkward that Mother Emaline could not enjoy herself. Raya looked out the window and wished she had stayed home. She should have gone to work. She would much rather be kneading and baking, cutting and mixing, than going to tea at Wendy Applewood's. At least at The Fairbury Hotel, she knew her place, and those she came in contact with were accustomed to her presence, even if they were still a bit stand-offish.

"Do you suppose she's invited anyone else to tea, or do you think it will only be the three of us?" Mother Emaline asked, smoothing the skirt of her black mourning gown. The worn dress still hung on her frail body, despite her recent improvements, and the fabric was worn so thin, Raya was sure it wouldn't last more than another month or two at the longest.

"I don't rightly know," Raya answered, not having considered the possibility.

"I do hope it's just the three of us," Mother Emaline said, her expression anxious.

Belatedly, Raya realized her mother-in-law was just as worried about their visit as she was. Perhaps Mother Emaline had not insisted she come simply to meet Wendy Applewood, but as a comfort to help her get through the ordeal. Compassion filling her, Raya reached over and took Mother Emaline's thin hand in her own. "Whoever is there, I'm sure they will be delighted to see you."

Emaline worried her bottom lip. "I never thought myself a vain person. I never thought I put much importance on wealth or sought after the approval of others, but I must say, I feel a little insecure today." She paused and licked her lips to moisten them. "You see, Raya, I used to live as Wendy lives. I used to have a house full of children, a husband who ran a successful business, money, fine things and fancy dresses. I used to have a cook and a butler, and would invite other women over for tea. Now, I have none of that. Her life is full, mine is mostly empty. Her life is marked by happy events, mine by tragedy."

Raya squeezed her hand. "Be that as it may, you are *family*, Mother Emaline, and she must be looking forward to seeing you. Conversation will arise, and you will find things to discuss. And it may be true that you don't have any of those material things anymore, but you have your faith, your character, your honesty . . . those things cannot be bestowed by a blessed life or taken away by tragedy. Those are the only things we can build our confidence around."

Emaline squeezed her hand in return. "You're right, dear. I know you're right."

The horse cart slowed down and stopped. Raya stepped out of the carriage first, then looped her arm through Emaline's as they started up the walk. At the front door, she tapped lightly with the brass knocker, and they waited for the door to be opened. They were shown into the front parlor where a woman who looked to be in her early forties sat.

Her posture was straight and sure, her hair was pulled back perfectly with every graying strand tucked into place, and her blue eyes were as bright as crystal. Raya thought her a very pretty lady and knew she must have been quite a beauty in her younger years. Her stiff gown was stylish and beautiful, and the cream and mauve of the fabric complemented her complexion perfectly. She rose as Raya and Emaline walked into the room and bowed her head, as did Emaline. Raya curtsied.

Wendy was polite as Emaline introduced her to Raya, then ushered them both into the room and told them to sit wherever they liked. Raya sat beside Mother Emaline on a straight-backed sofa, then crossed her ankles and folded her hands.

"So, Wendy, how are the children? Will any of them be joining us?" Emaline asked, spying photographs on a round table near the red chair in which Wendy sat.

Raya studied the photographs, too, taking in the handsome faces of the two young men and the beautiful girl who was a spitting image of her mother.

"Oh, yes, they are well. Thank you for asking. No, none of them will be joining us, I'm afraid. Charles and Miles are both in universities back east, and our sweet Gabriella is at a finishing school in Lexington. They will all be home for the Christmas holiday. I daresay I am looking forward to having them home again. The house seems a bit too quiet since Gabriella went away. She was my last one at home, you see." Wendy paused. "I do believe, though, if I have surmised correctly, Charles may have a young lady he's quite taken with. I do hope he is coming home to speak to us of her, and perhaps we'll have a wedding in the family within the year. I must hope once he's married, he'll choose to return home to Cincinnati. I know that is what Judson is expecting. He wants his sons to work alongside him. Dear me, how I'm carrying on. Let's order the tea, shall we?"

Raya and Mother Emaline only nodded as Mrs. Applewood took a silver bell from a silver tray and gave it a decisive ring. Setting it back in place, she turned back toward them. "Emaline, dear, I heard you weren't feeling well some time ago. Tell me, have you recovered? Are you well? You look well. A little thin, but you have color in your cheeks. I must say, it is no wonder you took ill—all that traveling, not to mention the grief I'm sure you're experiencing. Why, if I were in your shoes, I shan't wonder if I would just pass away from a broken heart."

Raya found herself smiling, enjoying the woman's cheerful chatter. "Mother Emaline is a strong woman," she found herself saying, seeing that Emaline was at a loss for words. To talk about their loss and grief with such casualness was a bit startling, Raya must admit, but she much preferred it to the pity many of Mother Emaline's friends had extended after they first arrived in town.

"Ah, I see that she is. And isn't that a good thing? You've needed that strength, Emaline, and I suppose you'll need it every day for the rest of your years. That's still how I feel sometimes when I think about my sweet Clara. No mother should ever outlive their children, but though God only knows why, some of us do, and only by His grace do we survive it. Come, let's take tea."

The tea was brought in on silver platters. Raya accepted her cup and passed on the cream and sugar, preferring to take it plain rather than to risk making Mrs. Applewood feel as if she were taking advantage of her hospitality. When they had their tea, several trays of small delicacies were brought around, and Raya selected one and nibbled on it slowly, enjoying its flavor. She sat quietly as the two older women reminisced about days passed and visited about days present.

Raya's tea was only half gone when Mother Emaline was suddenly seized by a coughing fit. Having anticipated it would happen as a result of all the cold air she had taken in on their way over, Raya quickly set her cup and saucer on an end table and rescued Emaline's before the woman could drop it in the commotion. She pressed a handkerchief into Mother Emaline's palm and rested her hand on her back, positioning herself so she could see Emaline's face, should she need her to do anything else.

"Oh dear, what does she need? What can I do to help?" Wendy asked, obviously concerned.

"She's fine," Raya assured, her voice soothing. "The fit will pass. We must give her a minute, and perhaps a drink of water?"

Mother Emaline nodded as another cough seized her. Wendy rang her bell swiftly and ordered that a glass of water be brought. When it was, Raya thanked the servant, then helped Mother Emaline lift it to her lips and take a small sip. When the coughing fit finally passed, Mother Emaline apologized profusely, but Mrs. Applewood dismissed it and resumed their conversation where they had left off. Raya handed Mother Emaline her teacup again and took hers up as well, sitting up straight on the edge of the sofa, as was proper.

Their tea lasted an hour, and it was a pleasant hour at that. When they stood to leave, Wendy rose and embraced Emaline. "I'm so glad you came. I've wondered about you many times. My thoughts and prayers have been with you. Please, do come again."

Mother Emaline nodded, her smile shaky. Raya could tell she was just barely keeping her tears at bay. Wendy's parting words had struck a chord. "I will," Emaline answered, returning the embrace. When she stepped back, Raya stepped forward and put her hand on her mother-in-law's back, reassuring the woman that she was there if she needed assistance.

"You too, dear. Please come again next time Emaline visits," Wendy Applewood said, addressing Raya fully for the first time.

Surprised to have been spoken to directly, much less invited to return, Raya's answering smile was bright and quick, lighting up her whole face. "Thank you for your hospitality. I know this will be a bright spot in Mother Emaline's week, as well as mine."

"As it has been in mine. Thank you for coming," Mrs. Applewood said, following them to the front door.

When the heavy wooden door was shut behind them, Raya helped Mother Emaline into the waiting horse cart, and they were carried swiftly home. Mother Emaline chattered gaily as the horses plodded steadily along, and Raya found her smile growing and her heart warming even more toward the chatty Mrs. Applewood. She had soothed Emaline's fears and treated her kindly, and the older woman had enjoyed their visit immensely. That made Raya very happy.

Once they were back home, Mother Emaline made a beeline for the bed and curled up on it, just as Raya knew she would. While she had enjoyed the outing, it sapped what strength and energy she had, and she slept even before Raya had the blankets pulled up over her. For a few long moments, Raya stood and watched her mother-in-law's face as she slept. The woman was as endearing as she was motherly, and Raya loved her very much. Smoothing the covers over her, she was again thankful for how the tea had gone. All of Emaline's fears had been eased, and she had laughed and talked gaily—something Raya hadn't seen in nearly four months.

Four months. It had been nearly four months since the fire, since her husband's death, since Niz's miscarriage. It had been nearly four months since everything about her life had changed. It had been nearly four months since she had made the decision to stay with Emaline, no matter what might lie ahead. Raya looked around the small shanty. Her gaze lingered on the rough-hewn table, the cracked china dishes, the rudimentary chairs, the straw tick on which Mother Emaline slept, and she smiled. They didn't have much, but life was so much better than she imagined it might be back when she vowed to follow Mother Emaline, no matter where she might go. She was alive, she was fed, she was warm, she was sheltered, and she had honorable work. She had much to be thankful for.

Raya's eyes drifted to the package on the table. Pushing herself to her feet, she walked over and untied the strings that bound it. Once again, she lifted the stunning cloak from its wrapping. She ran her fingertips over the fur, the wool, the silk. It was beautifully made. She held her breath as she looked at it, still surprised by its beauty, shocked that it was meant for her.

Checking to see that Mother Emaline was still sleeping, she settled the cloak around her shoulders and fastened it securely. Drawing the hood up over her hair, she ran her fingers through the thick fur once again. It felt as wonderful on as it had looked. Suddenly, she sat down in the kitchen chair, the cloak still on, her mind churning. What was she to do with it? Should she keep it? Give it back? Why would Mr. Fairbury send her such an exquisite garment? Why would he lavish such kindness upon them? Upon her? Everything to date, she had reasoned, was for Emaline, and she was a beneficiary as well because she lived in her home, but this ... this was altogether different. This cloak was meant only for her. To accept his kindness, his generosity for Emaline was one thing, but to accept it for herself ... She didn't know what to make of it or what to do.

By the time Emaline woke up, the cloak was folded, wrapped in its brown paper packaging, and stowed safely away with their other precious few belongings. Raya had their supper ready, and they sat together by the fire to eat it. Raya read aloud from the book of Proverbs for quite some time before they turned in for the night. The next morning, she woke early and was at work with a pan of biscuits in the oven before the sun rose.

Twenty-Five

Raya didn't see Atlas Fairbury other than from a distance for several days, so she had time to think about what she was going to do with the cloak. After going back and forth several times, she finally decided to keep it. While it seemed too extravagant of a gift and without occasion, she was desperately in need of a new cloak. To return it would be madness. If she had a need and the need was met, it would be throwing that provision back in the face of God to return it simply based on her perception that she was unworthy. That is what Mother Emaline had said and finally persuaded her to believe.

Raya had taken a precious sheet of her stationery, which she used for letters to Chenoa, and wrote a simple thank you on it, before folding it up and setting it amongst Mr. Fairbury's weekly batch of cookies. She paid a delivery boy to deliver the cookies to his house, as he had seemed especially busy that week, only stopping at the hotel long enough to check-in with Mr. Lenox before leaving again.

However, despite her decision to keep the cloak, it still laid in its wrappings on a top shelf where it was safe, while she shivered all the way to work and all the way back home. Though she didn't wish to scoff at the provision, nor have any intention of offending her generous employer, each morning as she prepared to go out in the cold and thought of the cloak, she couldn't bring herself to put it on. She prayed each day that Mr. Fairbury would stay busy and not notice.

UP FROM THE ASH HEAP

On one of the coldest nights of the year thus far, Raya hurried through the door of the shanty, shutting and barring it behind her. Turning, she found that which she had been longing for on the table. Mother Emaline's face was aglow as she said, "It's from Chenoa!"

"How is she? Has she seen Niz? Are they well?" Raya asked in a rush as she set her dishes of food down on the rough-hewn table and grabbed the letter off the wooden planks.

"I don't know. I wanted to wait to read it together," Emaline said, still smiling.

Raya shot her a grateful smile and pushed the letter into Mother Emaline's hands. "You read it, then. I'm going to close my eyes and listen to every word."

They both pulled their chairs close to the fire and sat down, Mother Emaline holding the letter in her hand all the while, as if it might break. When they were both settled, Mother Emaline carefully broke the seal and unfolded the pages that were covered in writing.

Oct. 29, 1873

Dear Raya,

Thank you for your letter. It arrived day before yesterday, as the weather has been good for a stretch and the post was able to make it over the mountains. I am hopeful this letter will make it out before the passes close again with snow.

It looks to be a hard winter here, with a foot of snow already, and we've not yet entered the month of November. I am so thankful to hear that your journey east was uneventful, and you were not troubled by snow. I was hoping for your safe travels and that you would arrive in Cincinnati safely and in good time. I'm sorry to hear that Mother has taken ill, and I do hope she recovers shortly. I cannot imagine being in a new place while feeling poorly. Please give her my love and tell her I miss her dearly. Not a day goes by when I do not think of both of you and Will and our life at the mill. The days pass one after another, but my grief does not. Sometimes, it only feels as if it has grown overnight and is larger and more formidable when the sun rises.

I saw Niz last week. She came into town with another woman from her tribe. I do not recall her name. I believe they were seeking supplies of some sort, although I do not fully remember the nature of their errand. What I do remember is the news that she has married again. She said he is a man from her tribe, one who wanted to marry her before she married Alex. She seemed in good spirits, and she looked well. I am very happy for her. It was a relief to my heart to see her cheeks free from tears and to hear her laugh again. I wish I could see you as well, to see the same. To part in the midst of such pain; it's what I remember when I look back. I wish it weren't so. I wish I could remember all the laughter, all the good times, all the family meals, and days full of cooking and working together. I wish I could remember how Will looked at me and how he said my name. Instead, those memories are distant. In the forefront is only billowing smoke, frantic screams, and tears. Always lots of tears.

My parents are well, and my younger sister seemed to mature greatly in the few months I was gone. She is less of a girl and more of a young woman now. She even has a beau. Now we do chores together, and I'm teaching her to read, as you taught me. She is a good pupil and tends her studies. My younger brothers, on the other hand, are not so studious. They would rather be outside hunting or helping Papa cut wood. If they don't learn in the winter, then I fear they never will. Surely, when the green grass starts poking out from under the snow and there are fields to plow and crops to plant, they will barely come in the cabin to sleep. If I could convince my papa to learn to read, I believe he could whip the boys into line, but alas, he says he has gotten this far along in life without knowing, and there's no use learning now. I, on the other hand, am eternally grateful for the gift you gave me.

I borrowed a book from Mrs. Lapsy last week and have barely been able to set it aside to get my chores done. It's set in England and has opened up a world I knew nothing of. I've had difficulty making out a few of the larger words, but Mrs. Lapsy has helped me with *their pronunciation and meaning, likely for the sake of the book and not for my own. You must remember how she is. I barely even notice the airs she puts on now. I'm just so eager to read a new book, and she does show kindness loaning hers out. This is the third one I've borrowed from her.*

I visit Will's grave several times a week. I decorate it with pine boughs or berries often. In the summer, I will take flowers. I know his body is not there, but I like to think his spirit is. I feel closer to him when I'm at his grave. Like he's not so very far away. 'Tis a great comfort to me. I decorate Alex's, Luke's, and Father Julius' as well. I do not want them to feel forgotten, even though you're not here to maintain their graves. I hope that brings you comfort as well.

Well, mother just told me the post is getting ready to leave town, so I'm going to end this letter in hopes that it will reach you before Christmastime. I hope you're doing well, and that you have found work in Cincinnati. You are in my thoughts daily, you and Mother Emaline both. I miss you terribly.

All my love,
Chenoa Elise Applewood

Postscript: Please write again whenever you can. Even if the post cannot make it through again until spring, what fun it will be to read all your letters when they do finally arrive. I am eager to hear how you are.

Mother Emaline folded the letter slowly. Raya opened her eyes and stared into the flames licking up from the logs in the fireplace.

"Well, I'm glad to know she's well and settled in back at home," Emaline said after a moment.

"She sounds so sad," Raya responded. "She writes as if the fire were yesterday."

"As it sometimes feels," Mother Emaline responded tenderly. Reaching across the short distance between them, she took Raya's hand. "We have been forced to move on, dear. We traveled to a new place, live in a new house, are surrounded by new people. While we miss our men terribly, we don't have time to linger on the past, because we're busy making sure we can survive the present. Chenoa is back at home surrounded by all the same people, all the same surroundings. It's not the past for her. It's the present. And as long as it's the present, it's going to be hard for her to have a future."

"I wish she had come with us," Raya said softly, her heart full of sadness. She wished she could talk to her young sister-in-law, wrap her in a hug, and smooth her beautiful dark ringlets. The sweet girl was drowning in grief, and there was nothing Raya could do to help her from so far away.

Additionally, Chenoa's words brought up guilt in her own heart. Chenoa was mourning her husband intensely, remembering him, visiting his grave, missing him. Raya, on the other hand, was so busy securing another day's sustenance that sometimes a day went by between her thoughts of Luke. Life had taken them a new direction, given them a new set of challenges; she often felt that simply keeping up kept her occupied and exhausted. Too exhausted to grieve her husband, her brothers-in-law, or the family they had been. Guilt rose its ugly head.

"Think of the unkindness you have encountered. Do you wish that for her?" Mother Emaline asked quietly.

"No," Raya answered quickly. "But if we had known Mr. Fairbury would allow me to work at his hotel, then I would have told her to come."

"Are you happy there?" Mother Emaline asked, turning in her chair so she could see her daughter-in-law.

Raya didn't have to think about her answer for long. "Yes, I am." Ms. Macy, Noni, even the other cooks in the kitchen—they were all beginning to feel like friends. Working in the large, warm, bustling room reminded her sometimes of working in the big house with Niz, Chenoa, and Mother Emaline. The work was methodical, and she found solace in having something of purpose to do with her days.

Mother Emaline's face lit up. "I'm very glad to hear that."

Raya's face also brightened in a smile. "Yes, me too," she agreed. To hear herself say aloud that she was happy was a lovely thing. It had happened little by little. Though she still grieved, her period of great grief had ended, driven by circumstance, and she was finding her way back to joy.

"You will have to write Chenoa another letter, and in this one, let her know that it's okay for her to find happiness again too. She's always looked up to you. If you tell her it's okay, she'll begin to let her heart move in that direction."

Raya nodded solemnly. "Then I shall do as you say."

"I'll write to her, too, and perhaps, together, we can encourage her to look toward the future rather than staying stuck in the past . . . it's what Will would have wanted for her." Raya saw the shine of tears in Mother Emaline's eyes and reached over and squeezed the older lady's hand gently.

"That's a good idea."

Mother Emaline pushed herself to her feet, giving herself a moment to find her balance before starting to walk. "What did you bring for our supper?"

Raya crossed to the table where she uncovered a dish full of shepherd's pie. Taking it to the hearth, she transferred it into a pan and set it over the fire to warm.

***

Mr. Fairbury entered the kitchen with Mr. Lenox early the next afternoon. As usual, they made a beeline for Ms. Macy and discussed menu options, food prices, kitchen operations, and the number of patrons.

Raya pulled a batch of cookies out of the oven and put another batch in. After letting the cookies cool, she transferred them into a jar. The conversation between Mr. Lenox, Mr. Fairbury, and Ms. Macy ended, and Ms. Macy turned back to the stove, where she was assembling a large pan of baked beans. Mr. Lenox exited the kitchen in the direction of the front dining room, and Raya drew in a breath of anticipation as she heard heavy footsteps coming toward her.

"Do you have extras?" Mr. Fairbury asked, stepping up to her table.

Opening her cookie jar, Raya held it out to him in answer. He was the boss; for him, the answer would always be yes.

He smiled as he reached in and drew out a stack of cookies. "Thank you, kindly."

She expected him to leave with his cookies, but instead, he drew out one of the chairs, scooted in along the side of her table, and sat down, lounging as if completely at ease. She stayed quiet as she measured and mixed her next batch. "How does Cousin Emaline fare?"

"She is improving every day, sir," Raya answered as she stirred.

"I'm glad of it."

"Yes, me too."

The silence stretched for a few moments. "I heard you had tea with Wendy Applewood."

"Yes, sir. She invited Mother Emaline to tea, and Mother didn't feel comfortable making the long trip across town by herself."

"As she shouldn't. It's a long way for a woman who is not at full strength."

Raya stayed quiet but dipped her head in agreement.

"And did you have a pleasant time?"

"Yes, sir."

"What did you think of Wendy?"

"She's lovely," Raya answered honestly. The woman had surprised her with her kind and compassionate spirit.

"She is. Judson is a lucky man. Their daughter is just like her." Finishing his first cookie, Mr. Fairbury waved at Ms. Macy. "Say, Ms. Macy, do you have any milk? I think a cup of it would go perfectly with these cookies."

Within ten seconds, the kitchen's plump mistress plunked a mug full of the creamy white liquid down in front of their boss.

"You're too old for such behavior—eating cookies and drinking milk in the middle of the workday," Ms. Macy said with a decided harrumph. "What's the world coming to?"

Mr. Fairbury was all grins as Ms. Macy turned back to her work. He called a thank-you out after her before taking a long drink of his milk, then turned his attention back to Raya.

"And what do you think, Ms. Applewood? Do you think me old?" he asked, a hint of amusement in his voice.

"I think you are perfectly wise, sir," Raya said after taking a moment to formulate her answer, concealing her amusement over Ms. Macy's chastisement. "And wisdom is much more pertinent to one's maturity than age."

Mr. Fairbury tipped back his head and laughed, a loud, jolly sound that filled the kitchen. "Very artfully said, Ms. Applewood."

A smile played at the corners of Raya's lips as she continued mixing her cookies.

"How old do you think I am?" he pressed, starting on his second cookie. His handsome face held an amused smile, and his tall, lean frame was stretched out in his chair, his ankle propped up casually on his opposite knee.

Raya felt something between apprehension and pleasure when she realized the conversation was going to continue until he was done with his afternoon treat. He still had a cookie and a half to go. It wasn't right for him to sit and talk with her, yet he didn't seem the least bit bothered by the fact that he was conversing with hired help in his hotel's kitchen. What was more, she found herself enjoying his company immensely. "I believe you're old enough to have a thriving business and young enough to enjoy milk and cookies on occasion," Raya said, searching for an appropriate answer.

Mr. Fairbury paused in eating his cookie and leaned his chair back, studying Raya out of kind blue eyes for several long moments. Unnerved, she went to the oven to check on her cookies and found they were ready to come out. When she returned to the table with the full baking sheet, Mr. Fairbury was waiting.

"You know, you're very talented at answering a question without answering it at all."

"What could the opinion of a mere hired worker in your kitchen matter?" Raya replied, at a loss, hoping he would not demand an answer to his question of age. She tried to search her mind for what Mother Emaline had told her about the man in relation to years, but couldn't recall the details. She would guess him around thirty-five, but couldn't be sure, and was reluctant to offend him.

Finishing his milk, he stood, stepping closer to her as he did. "More than you might imagine," he answered quietly, then eased back. "Thank you for the cookies. Keep up the good work. Ms. Macy, thank you for the milk." He left the kitchen as quickly as he had come, and Raya was left unsettled.

For the first time, the thought occurred to her that Mr. Fairbury might be interested in her for reasons greater than her care of his distant relative. She stopped herself short of considering his interest might carry romantic notions, for that was too foolish to even consider. She knew she would never be an appropriate match for Atlas Fairbury, and surely he knew that far better than she.

Twenty-Six

"Ms. Applewood!"

Raya stopped as her name was called, her heart sinking with dread. She turned expectantly, cringing, knowing the owner of the rich, low voice without having to see him. Through hooded eyes, she saw Atlas Fairbury hurrying toward her across the frozen ground. She shifted the heavy packages in her arms and waited for him, only glancing briefly at the waiting carriage a few feet away. The night was cold and the wind sharp. She longed for the shelter of the carriage and the slight warmth of her shanty once she arrived home, but more than anything, she wanted to escape inside where he couldn't notice that she wasn't wearing the new cloak he'd sent her.

"There. Good. Thank you for stopping," he told her, out of breath as he stopped in front of her. They both stood there quietly for a moment. Raya waited, uncertain about what she should say or the reason for the dark meeting. Before she made a move to break the awkward silence, Mr. Fairbury continued. "I have been meaning to get here all day, but was held up at the river. I . . . uh . . . well, I have something for you." He held out a brown paper package.

"What is it?" Raya asked, startled.

"It's a cloak. A black one this time," he hurried to say.

"Sir," Raya paused, attempting to recover from her surprise and collect her thoughts.

"I saw you the other day, shivering as you hurried to the carriage, and I searched my mind trying to understand what would keep a cold, young woman from wearing a heavy woolen cloak she had in her possession. I wondered if perhaps you didn't like it or if the package had not been delivered as sent. Then, the next morning, it came to me. You're still in mourning. To wear something so colorful would be dishonoring to Cousin Emaline and to your late husband. And I know you wouldn't do anything to dishonor them. Everything you do, Ms. Applewood, you do with honor." He paused, his breath rising like smoke in the cold December air. "Am I correct? Is that why you don't wear the cloak I sent you?"

Raya kept her eyes on the frozen ground, even as she bit her lip. Would it be wrong to claim such a reason? For his assumption was certainly correct in part but sorely lacking in its comprehensive understanding. Not wishing to be dishonest in any way, Raya simply nodded her affirmation.

"Aha, then it is as I thought! Well, the problem is solved. You can wear this one until your time of mourning is over." He paused. "Go on, open the package. It's freezing out here and you still have your trip home."

Raya felt frozen, even more from her uncertainty than the cold. She did not wish to contradict her employer and a man of such kindness and high society, yet she could not accept another fine cloak from him. It wasn't right. Noni's cloak was every bit as bad as hers. It wasn't fair for Raya to have two new cloaks when others in her station of life were suffering.

"Goodness sakes, Raya, put on the cloak!" he said, clearly exasperated.

When she still made no move to do as he said, Atlas Fairbury reached out and tore the paper from the garment, then settled it around her. As the thick black wool covered her slender shoulders, Raya shivered, the fabric instantly providing relief against the harsh winter wind. Seeing her frail frame relax, Mr. Fairbury stepped closer to her still and reached back to pull up the black woolen hood. Black lace trimmed the hood and framed her face, shielding her skin from the worst of the chill. Holding the edges of the fabric lightly, Mr. Fairbury smiled down into her face, close enough now that Raya could feel his warm breath on her face and smell his fresh, masculine scent. "See, that wasn't so hard, was it?"

Despite her physical comfort, Raya felt the need to take the cloak off. Reaching up, she undid the clasps he had just fastened. "I can't accept this," she told him softly, her voice almost pleading.

He reached out and captured her hands in his before she could take the cloak off fully. "Why not?" he challenged.

"I don't deserve it!" she told him passionately, speaking before thinking better of it.

"You don't deserve to be warm?" he asked incredulously. She turned her face away from him. "I want you to have it," he continued, obviously confused by her response. "I want you to be warm and comfortable."

"Then take it out of my pay! You have already done so much for us! We cannot ask for anything more."

"Well, then there's not an issue. You didn't ask. It was a gift," he said cheerfully.

"No," she argued, struggling to free her hands. She wanted to give the cloak back and escape to the solitude of the carriage. Her throat began to ache with emotion.

"I want you to have it," he said again, obviously fighting frustration. "Why won't you accept it? You're cold! You're cold every morning and every night, and no wonder! This rag you wear isn't fit to be donned, much less used to ward off the cold!"

His words hurt as the truth of them settled. Raya's cheeks flushed red as she was reminded of the outward indication of her poverty. "It's sufficient."

"It's a rag!" he argued. "Use it to wash the floors or tie your hair up in curls, but don't pretend it's good enough for a cloak. Not when you have one that is thick and warm. That's foolishness!" he finished, exasperated. His exasperation stirred her own.

"I can't work any longer hours! By the time I get home and reheat our supper and get Mother Emaline to bed, then do dishes and tend to the shanty, I'm exhausted. I can't work longer hours to repay you," Raya told him, her tone beseeching. She was desperate to make him understand why she couldn't accept the beautiful cloak. She never should have accepted the first one. She couldn't accept another, knowing that her words were true, knowing she could not repay him. Tears stung her dark eyes as she kept them on the ground, waiting for his reply.

He released her hands, and she could feel him ease back a step. She felt his departure acutely, cold pressing in where his warmth had resided only moments before. "I don't present it to you as a wage, Raya. I give it as a gift. I have no expectation that you will repay me for it, either with money or longer hours."

"Why?" she asked, her question choked. She raised her hand to grip her throat, unsure why his simple statement made tears slip out of the corners of her eyes and her throat feel too tight to draw in a breath.

Somewhere nearby, a horse whinnied, and she knew the carriage driver was watching the whole exchange. She was glad Henry was an honorable man. She was certain he would not speak of Mr. Fairbury's late conversation with her to anyone, on the fear of bringing shame to his master. He liked Mr. Fairbury and spoke highly of him. She knew he must be confused by the master's actions, as was she, yet she knew he would do nothing to hurt Mr. Fairbury's reputation, and she was exceedingly thankful.

"Because I care if you're cold. I want you to be comfortable and warm," Mr. Fairbury told her, his tone tender.

"Why?" Raya asked again, at a loss for understanding. He was such a powerful man. Why would he give any thought to the physical comfort of his hired help?

"Because I want you to have every good thing. Now please, I'm not used to having to convince someone to accept a gift. Just accept it, Raya. Wear it. Keep warm." He paused, and Raya's chin fell against her chest in submission, moved by his heartfelt plea. "I have business to attend to. Goodnight, Ms. Applewood."

"Goodnight," she answered weakly. "And Mr. Fairbury . . . thank you. While I do not understand your continued generosity, I do greatly appreciate it. I will never forget the kindness you have shown us."

"You're welcome," he answered simply.

He walked her to the waiting carriage and opened the door, holding out his hand to assist her as she entered. When she was settled, he shut the door and tipped his hat to Henry, calling out an amiable greeting to the driver.

As the carriage pulled away from the hotel, Raya covered her face with her hands and sobbed. Her emotions felt wild, and her heart ached. She wasn't worthy.

Hot tears burned against her frigid cheeks and hands as she folded over her knees. She buried her face in the worn folds of her mourning dress, careful not to let a single tear fall on the perfect new fabric of her cloak.

Why was she, a servant barely a step out of poverty, wrapped in one of the finest mourning cloaks Cincinnati had to offer? Why did she have dishes of good food around her feet, more than she could eat in three days, as she was being whisked home by beautifully matched chestnut horses in a carriage so grand it was the envy of many a successful businessman? How could so many gifts be lavished upon her—a foreigner without hope, fortune, or connections? She had nothing to offer, nothing to attract such extravagance, yet it was extended, and here she sat in the middle of it all.

It felt wrong. It felt unnatural. It felt contrary to every law of nature. She felt unworthy. She felt undeserving. She felt lacking of any right to such comfort. A foreigner. Widowed. Poor. Alone. Yet, here she was.

When the carriage made the sharp right onto her street, she used the hem of her dress to carefully wipe her eyes and nose, then tucked loose hairs back up into place, not wanting Mother

Emaline to know about her tearful ride home. Collecting herself as the carriage came to a halt, she was calm with her packages in hand by the time Henry opened the door for her. He held out his hand to help her down.

Like she always did, Mother Emaline still knew within moments of her arrival that she had been crying, and they sat by the fire while Raya told Mother Emaline about her encounter with Mr. Fairbury and how undeserving she felt. Tears welled again as Mother Emaline stroked her hair and agreed that Atlas Fairbury's kindness was unmatched. However, she said she was glad Raya had accepted the cloak. To refuse it would have been disrespectful to Mr. Fairbury and unappreciative of his kindness. Accepting it as she had would keep Raya warm and ease Mother Emaline's mind about the matter. She knew as well as Mr. Fairbury how cold Raya had been and wished she could do something to ease her discomfort. Raya agreed that the cloak was a blessed relief.

Thankfulness rose up within Raya as they ate supper later that night. She may be undeserving, but she had shelter, food, Mother Emaline, and a warm cloak to put on in the morning. She went to bed overwhelmed by her blessings, fully aware that each one of them could be traced back to Atlas Fairbury and past him to a God who had heard her prayers.

***

The next morning, Raya hurried in the door to work, a happy smile on her face as she sang out a cheerful good morning to Ms. Macy, who was already stirring something over the stove. The woman returned her warm greeting.

The reserved, no-nonsense keeper of the kitchen had warmed to Raya. She now welcomed her with smiles and sent her out the door at night with pats on the shoulder. Though her demeanor was still stern, her tone terse as she called out orders over the top of the clatter of pots and pans, chopping, plucking, fire stoking, and hurried footsteps, Raya had come to greatly enjoy and admire the woman. She ruled the kitchen in absolute order and preparedness, yet although she was firm, she was never unfair or mean-spirited. To work for such a woman was an honor and a joy.

Raya hung her new black cloak on her peg, fingering the warm, heavy fabric for just a moment as she did. She had actually been warm on her way to work. She had not felt the sting of the icy wind as she made her way from the carriage to the back door of the hotel, nor did her face tingle painfully as she came into the warmth of the kitchen.

Leaving her cloak, she crossed the room to her worktable, where she set about her morning chores. It wasn't long after when Noni came in the door, letting a gust of cold air in with her. Two other kitchen workers were right behind her, with three more on their heels. Raya smiled at their happy laughter as they took off their wraps and donned their aprons, finishing the conversations they were having. She was thankful to work in such a merry place.

She smiled expectantly as Noni stepped up to her worktable. She always came over to say good morning and to warm herself by the fire before starting on her chores. This morning, her face was aglow.

"You look happy today," Raya commented, enjoying the hopeful expression in Noni's usually tired eyes.

"I ain't so cold. Neither is Daisy, nor Colleen. That sets yer mornin' on a good start, I'm tellin' ya."

"Why's that?" Raya asked, surprised.

"We got new cloaks. From Mr. Fairbury. An early Christmas present, his note said. They were delivered yesterevenin'."

"You got new cloaks?" Raya echoed, astonished.

"Yes, ma'am. I figured you did too, seeing as how there was a new black one hangin' over on your peg. Seems he took stock of who needed one. It sure does keep you warmer when you got some kind of protection from that cold wind that comes down from up north."

"Yes, it does," Raya agreed, recovering from her shock. She felt ashamed she had assumed she was the only one who had received the thoughtful gift. Why wouldn't Mr. Fairbury give his other hired workers new cloaks as well? He was a kind employer. He saw a need among his kitchen staff and used his own means to satisfy it. Not for repayment, for how could any of them repay him, but for their own sake? Her admiration of her employer grew, and Raya could not keep a smile off her face.

Reaching out, she laid her hand against Noni's swollen abdomen. "I'm sure it kept this one warmer too!" The child within gave a valiant little kick against the gentle pressure of Raya's hand, and she laughed in delight. "I love him or her already!" she told Noni, her eyes sparkling.

"She already knows you," Noni agreed.

"She? You still feel it will be a girl?"

"It's a girl. Not a doubt in my mind anymore. When I was expecting Bella, she was real quiet like this. Luke was all over, kicking and squirmin' somethin' fierce. Thought I was gonna get bruised from the inside out, not the other way around."

Raya smiled, putting her hand on Noni's stomach again, enjoying the happy expression on her friend's face. There was nothing so beautiful as a woman full of life. It could take even the plainest of women and make them glow, despite the aches and fatigue that went along with being in the family way. To have life within, a new living being just waiting to be born and begin his or her own little journey through life, caused a new light to come from within a woman. She could see that light shining forth from Noni's blue eyes even now. A sharp longing pierced Raya's heart, even as she laughed as the little one kicked again.

"We settled on a name," Noni told her happily.

"Did you? What is it?"

Noni nodded. "Just last night. Jake said if it's a girl, he wants to name her after his mama. I said my mama was a good woman, too, so we decided on Francine Jane, but I told him we're calling her Francy, not Fran like his mama. Ain't no baby of mine goin' to be called Fran, though maybe later in life it will fit her fine. I think Francine has a nice ring to it. What do you think?"

"I think family names are lovely," Raya answered sincerely.

"Well, I think it will be just fine too."

"And what if it's a boy?"

"It won't be."

"And if it is?" Raya had known women to be surprised.

"Oh, well, I suppose we'll think of somethin' at the time. Maybe after our fathers, though Jake doesn't like his none, and I never really knew mine. He died in a shipwreck when I was three. Mama sung his praises, though, right up until the day she died. Don't know if he was really as good of a man as she said, but she loved him alright, and that counts for somethin'." Noni stepped out from her spot between the stove and Raya's worktable. "I'd best get movin' on. Just wanted to tell you 'bout our name."

"It's beautiful and I love it," Raya assured her, and Noni left with a grateful smile.

Raya spent her day mixing, kneading, baking, and cutting. Still, her smile never left her face, nor did the happy feeling she got every time she saw the new cloaks hanging on pegs by the back door. She felt her excitement building as the day passed, knowing he would be coming in soon, looking forward to simply having him in the room. She found herself listening for his voice and keeping an eye on the front dining room door, waiting for his arrival.

What kind of master had thriving businesses, money, responsibilities, and status galore, yet concerned himself with the physical well-being and comfort of the hired hands in the kitchen of one of his many businesses? Her heart swelled in gratitude as well as admiration for her handsome and amiable boss, and when he entered the kitchen late in the afternoon, she felt exceedingly aware of his presence.

He chatted with Ms. Macy and humbly waved away the sincere thanks of those who had received cloaks. He laughed at Ms. Macy's scolding that he was going to spoil her workers and asked about the menu for supper, then the number of patrons in the back dining room and the front. They discussed a wealthy guest who had specifically requested Ms. Macy's pot roast and the price of beef. Five minutes after he entered, Mr. Fairbury left out the back door with Mr. Lenox, no doubt on their way to the new stable which had just finished being constructed.

As the door shut behind them, Raya found herself experiencing disappointment that Mr. Fairbury had not made his way to her table. She wanted to thank him for the kindness he had shown to all of them, but especially to Noni. To provide a warm cloak for a sweet pregnant woman who was in need was surely one of the most chivalrous deeds she had ever observed. She had never seen such generosity, and she wanted to thank him again for it.

Additionally, she felt remorse for how she had behaved the night before. He had shown such kindness, and she had responded based on her own insufficiency. No one else had argued. No one else had wasted his time on whether or not they were worthy—they had accepted the gift graciously with thankful hearts. She had hoped for a chance to make amends. But alas, he seemed to be in a hurry. And why not? She knew he had more important things to do than to visit with employees.

That evening, she washed the kitchen floor on hands and knees, then scrubbed the floor of the back dining room as well. Just as she was finishing putting away clean dishes, she noticed the silverware from the front dining room needed to be polished. Assuring Ms. Macy she was fine with staying and that she would make quick work of it, Raya hurried out to tell Henry she would still be a little while longer, taking the man a cookie as a goodwill offering.

She found him sitting in the carriage house, reading the newspaper by the light of a kerosene lamp. He started to jump up, lying aside his paper, but she stopped him and held out the cookie. "I'll still be an hour longer. There's silverware to polish. I'm sorry to keep you waiting."

His smile was quick. "It's no bother. This is my job. I'm here from seven o'clock at night until seven o'clock in the morning, ready to transport any hotel guests that need a ride. It don't matter to me whether we leave now or in an hour. I do thank you for the cookie, though," he added with a tip of his tall hat.

Sending him a grateful smile, she hurried back into the hotel and carried the heavy wooden box of fine utensils to her worktable, sitting down with her polishing rag. When Ms. Macy finished making preparations for the morning, she came and sat with Raya, working alongside her until the silverware was finished.

When everything in the kitchen was perfect and ready for the morning rush, Raya put on her cloak with a smile, drawing the hood up over her hair and settling under the heavy weight of the fabric.

Opening the door, she went bravely out into the cold. She knocked on the stable door, knowing Henry was probably snoozing by now, as he did in the later hours whenever he wasn't driving guests. He came out immediately, putting on his top hat. Swinging open the heavy doors of the stable, he led the ready horses and carriage out.

Once in the carriage, Raya wrapped her arms around herself under the heavy folds of good fabric and smiled. She was warm, she had food for their supper, and she felt good about the condition she had left the kitchen in. She was certain there was not a hotel in the finest cities of America that had a cleaner kitchen or shinier silverware. As far as she was able, she would make certain The Fairbury Hotel was a fine establishment, as fine as its owner.

Twenty-Seven

For the next week, there was not one evening that Raya left the hotel at her appointed time. With Christmastime quickly approaching, there were more travelers and extra work to be done. She asked Henry to come for her half an hour earlier to allow her an earlier start to her day. He obliged, and she arrived only minutes after Ms. Macy and oftentimes stayed after the woman at night. Whenever she grew tired, she would look at the line of new cloaks hanging on the pegs by the door, and her efforts were renewed.

Every day, she would wait for Mr. Fairbury to enter the kitchen, hoping he would come to her table for a cookie so she would have the opportunity to thank him properly. She had never met anyone who would go to such great lengths to take care of his employees, who went above and beyond the wage he paid them, and actually cared about their comfort. She appreciated how he cared about them as human beings, not just hired help, and she wanted a chance to thank him again for her cloak and also especially for Noni's. Seeing him take notice of and care for an expecting mother seemed the kindest act she had seen since arriving in Cincinnati. However, Mr. Fairbury also seemed to be working extra hours, and was only in the kitchen for a few minutes each day before continuing on his way with Mr. Lenox.

It was over a week after he had caught her in the cold to give her his gift when he finally found an opportunity to stop at her table for a fresh cookie.

She knew he was in the room and was wondering if he would find his way over, hoping the scent of freshly baked cookies would prove too tempting to resist. She heard him excuse himself from the conversation Mr. Lenox and Ms. Macy were engaged in, and she caught her breath in anticipation as she heard him approaching.

"They moved your table closer to the stove," he observed mildly, coming to stand beside her.

She'd been waiting for him for days, yet now, with him beside her, she felt shy and flustered. She handed him a cookie, still warm from the oven. "Yes, sir. The bread rises better here where it's warm."

"Yes, I suppose it would." He took a bite of his cookie. "Thank you for this. It's delicious. I think they get better every time I have one."

"I'm glad," she answered sincerely. She appreciated his compliment and again recognized his thoughtfulness. "Sir, I wanted to say thank you for the cloak . . . for all the cloaks. I've never . . . I've never met a master like you, and I appreciate your kindness so very much."

He was quiet for a beat too long, and Raya was tempted to break order and glance up at his face. Had she offended him?

"A master. I have never thought of myself in that way." He sounded discouraged. "I guess that is how you see me, though, isn't it?"

Raya stammered, trying to recover without understanding completely how she was in the wrong. She regretted that she had displeased and offended him. She had only meant to thank him but had clearly misstepped. "Sir, I meant no disrespect."

"I do realize that," he answered quickly, though his tone was still clipped.

"I just . . . I wanted to thank you. My ride to and from work is much warmer now."

"And this is the matter I wish to speak to you about. But first, can you hand me another of those cookies?"

She selected one and held it out to him. His hand brushed hers as he took it, causing her heart to pound faster. She subtly took a step away from him as she loaded her pan with cookie dough, far too aware of his closeness. Her mind churned as she waited for him to speak, wondering what he wanted to speak to her of concerning her rides to and from work.

"I believe I told you to leave by eight o'clock every night, did I not?"

His meaning striking home, Raya felt deflated. She had forgotten about his order . . . again. She had been so caught up in getting things done and wanting everything to be perfect, she had overlooked his wishes about her time of departure. "Yes, sir."

"And what's more, I hear you're arriving earlier than before."

"There's much to be done."

"It will get done in due time. Ms. Macy is an expert at managing this kitchen."

"That she is. I simply want everything to be perfect," Raya argued, not adding that she wanted it to be perfect *for him*. She had no way to repay his kindness but to give her all to make his hotel the very best she could. He scolded her for not accepting his gifts, but why was he so determined not to accept hers?

He hesitated. "I do not wish for things to be perfect, as much as I wish for you to listen to me in this."

Frustration rose up within her, filling the spaces that had felt flustered at his proximity just seconds before. She wanted to argue or demand to know why, yet neither course of action was her place. She dropped her head in submission. "Yes, sir."

"Thank you," he said quietly. "And thank you for the cookies. You are wonderful at baking."

His compliment softened the sting of her frustration, and she smiled. "Thank you. I'm glad you enjoyed them. There are plenty more."

"I'll keep that in mind. For now, I must keep moving. Good afternoon."

She nodded. Of course he must. He was the important Mr. Fairbury. He didn't have time to stand and visit with a hired baker.

UP FROM THE ASH HEAP

He returned to Ms. Macy and Mr. Lenox, bade them farewell, and left the hotel.

Raya finished her batch of cookies, then made another. When she had made enough cookies to satisfy Ms. Macy, she made fresh bread for the evening meal. She washed dishes once the meal was over and the crowd's appetite was finally satisfied. Later, Noni came in from the back dining room looking dead on her feet, and Raya immediately noticed how the girl was pressing her hands to the small of her back.

"Are you feeling well?" Raya asked, laying her hand on Noni's arm, concerned.

Noni nodded, her tired eyes looking more tired than usual. "Just a few pains. False labor, maybe."

"But it's too early," Raya exclaimed, fear jumping into her heart. In an instant, she was back standing beside a pile of ashes, her face smudged with soot, hearing the first agonizing scream from Niz. The labor hadn't taken more than a few hours, but it had been excruciatingly painful, both physically and emotionally. Raya remembered holding her tiny little nephew in her hands after delivering him, perfectly formed, and yet altogether too early. Her heartbeat quickened. "You should go home and rest."

"They're just false contractions, that's all."

"Noni, please go home. It's a risk you shouldn't take. You don't want your false contractions becoming real contractions. It's too early for your baby."

"I can't just leave. Ms. Macy . . . my family needs me to have work, Raya," Noni told her, firmly.

Undeterred, Raya made a beeline for Ms. Macy. "Ms. Macy, Noni isn't feeling well. If I stay and finish her work, would you please send her home? It's the baby."

Ms. Macy looked sharply at Noni. "You can't save her from her work, Raya. I can't in good faith pay her the boss' money if she doesn't work."

"Ma'am, Noni's a hard worker. I'm sure if she goes home and rests, she'll feel better by morning. Please, just send her home tonight," Raya pleaded.

Ms. Macy sighed. "Very well. I have three children of my own. I know what it was like to work while expectin'."

"And Ms. Macy, I know that it isn't truly mine to give away, but Henry has to make a trip to take someone home tonight . . . can he take Noni instead of me?"

Ms. Macy looked at her sharply, and Raya held at bay the desire to squirm under her scrutinizing gaze. "You would use Mr. Fairbury's resources for your own personal agenda?"

Raya felt thoroughly reprimanded, yet she did not back down. "It's what I think he would do if he were here."

Ms. Macy conceded. "That you may be right. He's always too concerned about everyone else and not concerned enough for himself. Yes, send the girl home in the carriage as long as you're sure about walking and will take full responsibility if Mr. Fairbury comes in here asking after you tomorrow."

"Yes, ma'am," Raya said quickly. Ms. Macy's words elicited an unwelcome blush to rise in her cheeks.

She turned away to tell Noni, but Ms. Macy stopped her by grabbing her arm. "Why do you care so much? You looked like you had 'bout seen a ghost when you came over here. Did you lose a little one of your own to early birth?" It was as close to being gentle as Ms. Macy ever was.

"No, but my sister-in-law did," Raya answered simply. "I delivered the baby. A boy. He died not long after."

Ms. Macy shook her head and clucked her tongue. "Mighty shame. Alright then, go send Noni home and tell her I approve. She'll still get her pay for the day."

Raya hurried to tell Noni the news, then helped her into her cloak, and walked with her out to the stable where she helped Noni into the carriage. She told Henry of the change of plans and that Ms. Macy had approved it. He agreed good-naturedly, and Raya watched Noni get whisked away by the matched horses before hurrying back inside and out of the cold. She finished clearing the back dining room table with Laurie, then set about washing her share of the evening dishes, plus Noni's. When she was finally done, most of the workers were putting on their wraps and filing out of the kitchen one or two at a time.

Heading back into the back dining room, Raya grabbed the broom, remembering again how thankful she was to have been moved from serving to bread making and to have a safe way to get home every night.

Tonight, she would brave the streets and walk; the very thought filled her with dread. The walk would be long through the cold night, and she shivered just thinking about it. In her mind she traced the steps she would take over frozen ground, followed the dark streets, imagined the sound of footsteps coming up behind her and the dim figures that were sure to be lurking in the shadows. Her heart began to race and taking a shaky breath, she let it out slowly, trying to focus on the task at hand. Soon enough she would be walking home; there was no sense frightening herself before she even left the hotel.

The truth was, she had found great comfort in being transported in the safety of the carriage for the past six weeks. However, she wouldn't go back and change what she had done, even if she could. Tonight, Noni needed the carriage ride much more than she did.

When she finished sweeping, she poured hot water into a bucket and scraped off a bit of lye soap into the water, mixing it well until it dissolved. Selecting a rag, she returned to the back dining room to scrub the mud from the floor where careless boots had tracked it in.

She was three quarters of the way done when the door opened and she glanced up, expecting to see Ms. Macy coming in to say she was headed home. Instead, it was Atlas Fairbury. Her emotions raw from her painful memories earlier and her concern for Noni, Raya turned back to the floor, scrubbing vigorously at a stubborn patch of mud, refusing to be unnerved by his presence or feel guilty for staying.

Mr. Fairbury stood in the doorway for several moments, then came to sit down on one of the crude wooden benches. "Why are you still here, Raya?"

"This floor needed to be scrubbed."

"I thought we talked about this earlier."

"I had every intention of following your orders—"

"Except you didn't," he interrupted.

Raya kept scrubbing, taking several moments to formulate an answer. "There was someone else who needed to go home more than I did tonight," she finally answered simply.

There was a long silence, then Mr. Fairbury sighed. "Ms. Macy told me about Noni. It's too bad the girl has to work at all in her condition."

Raya agreed. "Sometimes you do what you have to do."

"Is that what keeps you going?" he asked thoughtfully.

"Isn't it what drives us all?" she answered quietly. Silence settled again.

"I spoke with Henry. He said Noni told him she was feeling better by the time he dropped her off at home. I thought you might be interested in knowing that."

"'Tis a relief. Thank you."

Mr. Fairbury put his elbows on the table in front of him and put his head in his hands, letting out a long, deep sigh. She could feel how weary he was without him having to say it. Concern for him grew within her. Was he working too hard? Was he getting enough rest? Was managing his companies wearing him too thin? "Sir, you should go home. I'll finish up here and be on my way."

"I'll stay until you're finished, but thank you just the same," he answered, his tone clipped.

She stayed quiet, choosing silence rather than giving reign to her tongue, which was presently altogether too loosely connected to her tired mind.

Even weary, his presence filled the room. She could think of little else as she worked, even her worry for Noni overshadowed.

She finished the floor, then pushed herself to her feet and tiptoed across the wet boards with her bucket. She opened the back door and hurried down the stairs of the small platform to dump her dirty water in the designated spot. When she turned, Mr. Fairbury was standing at the door, holding it open for her. As she drew close, he pulled her in and shut the door with some force. "For goodness' sake! Put on your wraps before going out! Do you know how the temperature is falling?"

She shivered as she rinsed out her bucket and returned it to its spot. "I was just running out for a second. I was coming right back in."

"Be that as it may, you're going to catch your death of cold if you continue to do that." He was undoubtedly annoyed, whether with still being at his hotel at this late hour or with her, she wasn't quite sure. Likely both. He pulled his hand over his face. "I'll help you into your cloak."

"I have a few things left to do," she countered. "But truly, sir, please go on home. I can finish up here."

"What is so important that it demands your time?" he asked, clearly not amused.

She stammered, knowing she had displeased him, but still seeing things that needed to be done. The big room was empty now, even Ms. Macy had left. Raya didn't dare look at the clock. Her tired body was telling her everything she needed to know about the time. She was glad she had thought to tell Mother Emaline that she might be home late until after Christmastime, so the dear woman didn't worry. "I need to slice bread for the morning," she answered, saying the first thing that came to mind.

"Raya, go home," he told her, his voice commanding, his anger barely in check.

Setting the loaf of bread down a little harder than necessary, Raya turned and went wordlessly to the pegs by the door and took up her cloak. Stepping close, he caught the garment in his large hands and settled it over her shoulders. "Henry is waiting for you." He paused, one side of his mouth tipping up in a wry smile. "And thank you for finally doing as I asked."

"I gave my ride home to Noni. I'll walk."

"Nonsense. It's freezing out. Henry will take you home as instructed."

"Why? Why are you so nice to me? Why do you take such care of me?" she demanded, her frustration smoldering just below the surface. "And when you show such kindness, why do you not understand my desire to serve you?"

"I don't want repaid," he countered.

"I'm not repaying you," she argued. "I could never repay you. I only seek to show my gratitude by serving you to the best of my abilities."

She hoped he would finally understand. She hoped he would see her service as a gift of her own and accept it as such. Perhaps if she left him to think on it overnight, it would come to him, just as her reasoning for not wearing the colorful cloak had. "Goodnight, sir."

Forgetting the food Ms. Macy had packaged for her, she opened the door and walked out, hurrying down the stairs and toward the stable. Once she rounded the corner, she would see Henry and the horses and could get in the carriage to be taken home, away from the hotel, away from Mr. Fairbury, away from the conversation that had elicited so many unwelcome emotions.

But the door was pulled open behind her, and like a young man, Mr. Fairbury jumped off the top stair, not wasting time with the next two. Reaching the frozen ground, he caught up with her in just two long strides. "I don't want your service, Raya," he told her, his frustration seeping from every word.

She turned, her own temper getting the best of her. How many times had they had this conversation? How many times had she tried to explain her reasoning? How many times was it going to take before he heard a word she said? "Then what do you want?" she flung back.

She was tired. Her body ached from her long days of working. Her stomach had been empty and growling for hours. Now her eyes stung with unshed tears. She was doing everything in her power to serve him well, to make his hotel as wonderful as she possibly could in her lowly position, and yet he seemed angered by her effort, not blessed, not grateful.

"What do I want? What do I want?" he asked again, his voice rising. He pulled his hand over his jaw as he spun away from her, turning his back on her for only a second before he turned around to face her again. "I want your love," he told her boldly, reaching out and catching her hand in both of his. "Can't you see that?"

Stunned, Raya drew back as if he had burned her, pulling her hand out of his. "Sir," she paused, the title she had used for him hanging in the air. "Don't say that," she pleaded.

"Sir?" he echoed. "Raya, look at me."

Tears burned her eyes. She wanted to escape. She wanted to run, for his sake as much as her own. Did he not know who she was? Did he not know how unfit and unworthy of him she was? She could not do as he asked. She could not look at him. Her eyes belonged on the ground while in his presence. She could not, would not, lift them. To do so would be proclaiming herself his equal, which she knew only too well that she was not. She was not even worthy of the time he had taken out for her, much less of hearing the words she was confident dozens of others had longed to hear him speak.

"Look at me!" he commanded, sounding every bit the powerful man that he was.

She shook her head.

"Look at me!" he said again, louder this time. He reached out and tipped her chin up abruptly, his grip strong yet gentle.

"Sir, I'm not fit. It isn't right," she protested, shutting her eyes to avoid doing as he said.

"Says who?" he demanded.

"Everyone. Society. Common sense."

"But Raya, don't you know, there's nothing common about you?" he answered softly, his voice thicker now.

He was already standing close, his fingers gripping her jaw, but suddenly he was closer, and his grip gentled. The heat of his body warmed her, and his fresh scent enveloped her. She instinctively tried to draw back, but he followed her. Backed up against the wall of the stable, she had nowhere to retreat, and his lips came down over hers. Her heart fluttered and then began to race. The strength of her reaction took her by surprise, and she fought the desire to lean in against him and linger in the kiss.

When he lifted his head, she stayed frozen, her face tipped up, her eyes closed. She felt incapable of moving, even should she wish to, which at the moment, she didn't.

"Raya, open your beautiful eyes and look at me."

She didn't. Instead, she gave the slightest shake of her head.

"Please?" he pleaded.

"I can't," she whispered past the painful lump in her throat. "It isn't right."

He brushed the back of his knuckles softly down her cheek. "Don't say that," he told her, his voice beseeching. "You don't get to decide that. I see who you are, Raya, and I see a woman I admire and adore. I see a woman of great value whom I love. I don't agree that you're unworthy . . . you are worth *much*. I love you whether you can accept it or not. You think you're less than, but it's not true. Let me show you. Let me rewrite the rules for us." As his tender, reassuring words washed over her, he lowered his lips to hers again, deepening his kiss until she could no longer keep hold of her resistance.

Emotions breaking within her like waves against the rocks on a windy day, she wrapped her hands in the front of his fancy shirt. She brought herself up closer against him, returning his kiss shyly at first, then with vigor as she got lost in the pleasure of it. She felt him release a gusty sigh and his hand moved from her face to the back of her neck, while his other arm slid around her waist, holding her close. A shiver ran through her, and this time, it wasn't from the cold.

"That's better," he said softly. "See, it's not wrong. It doesn't matter that we come from different backgrounds. You are worth being loved. So, Raya, please, let me love you."

"You . . . want me to be your mistress?" Raya asked, not understanding, her voice shaking with emotion. She knew she had to say no to him, yet in her weakness, she didn't know if she could. She admired him. She felt immeasurably grateful to him. She was utterly dependent on him. Even more than that, whether he was stopping by to snatch one of her cookies or holding her like he was now, he made her feel different than she had ever felt before. He stiffened at her question.

"No! Beloved . . . is that the kind of man you think I am? Look at me," he pleaded. Feeling overcome by the emotion she heard in his voice and incapable of doing anything but that which he asked, she raised her eyes to look up into his. It was the first full, long, unhurried look she had ever had of his face, and her heart raced. He was even more handsome than she'd thought.

She studied his features, drinking in the sight of him. His jaw was strong and clean shaven, his nose straight, his mouth full, his eyes gentle and blue. "Beloved, I don't want your body, I want your heart. I want your love. I want to take you out of my hotel and into my home," he finished with a hopeful smile.

Marriage. He was talking about marriage? He wanted her to marry him? He wanted that kind of love? Had he gone mad?

He sprinkled warm kisses over her cold face, and she was tempted to allow him to continue forever, yet tears stung her eyes. She needed to break away. She needed to end what was happening. She needed to stop responding. She needed to save him from himself. She couldn't marry him, and he certainly couldn't marry her. He had lost all sense of reason.

He wasn't some man from the docks. He wasn't a foreigner. And they weren't living on the frontier. He was Atlas Fairbury, one of the richest and most powerful men in Cincinnati, well-established in polite Eastern society. She was not a suitable match for him. And thus, she needed to get as far away from Atlas Fairbury and his irrational words as she could before someone saw them. She would not tarnish his reputation. Her heart and her sense of propriety were yelling at her to do so, but she couldn't bring herself to listen.

She turned her face and caught his lips once again, letting him kiss her, kissing him back, sharing his space, sharing his warmth, sharing his breath, sharing his pleasure. Her hands moved from his fancy shirt up over his chest and up to wrap around his sturdy neck, willingly anchoring herself to him.

Suddenly, from somewhere not far away, a door slammed shut, and with it, reality struck like a cold, hard blow. She was not some rich, genteel lady who was fit for Atlas Fairbury. She was not even a regular Cincinnati girl who was able to be drawn up from the middle class to become his bride. She was a foreigner. She was without a penny in the world except that which had come from him, destitute and disgraced. She was unfit for him and incapable of ever being a sensible match. She quickly turned her face away and stepped out of his reach.

"Raya," he groaned, reaching for her again. She stepped back, further out of reach.

"You are my master, I am your servant," she told him softly, then turned and hurried through the darkness, rounding the corner of the stable and letting herself into her waiting carriage.

In the solitude of the carriage, she pressed her fingertips to her eyes and drew them down over her face. What had just happened? What had she just done? Had her evening conversation with Mr. Fairbury, which was full of weariness and frustration on both sides, really ended in his declaration of love? Had he really kissed her? Held her? Shared his hope of marriage with her?

Her eyes burned, and she pressed her fists against them. She was in mourning for her husband, whom she had shared a wonderful life with and who had died an untimely and tragic death. Luke was a good man, and she had cared deeply for him.

And now, here she was four months later, kissing another. The guilt was overwhelming, and she shuddered beneath it, feeling as though it might crush her. The realization that brought the most guilt of all, was that although she had cared deeply for Luke and they had shared a good life together, in the span of five minutes, Atlas Fairbury had stirred up feelings in her she had never before experienced.

When the carriage stopped outside the shanty, she climbed stiffly down and went inside. Realizing then that she had forgotten their supper, she apologized repeatedly to Mother Emaline. She felt terrible. Not only had she returned late, she hadn't brought home any food. Mother Emaline had finished the leftovers Raya had set back for her lunch, and all they had left in the house was a half a loaf of bread. Overcome with guilt, Raya buttered a slice of it for each of them. As she did, she apologized again, despite Mother Emaline's gracious declarations that she wasn't hungry anyway. Raya didn't speak of the events of her evening, but instead played briefly with the kittens who were little fluffy balls of sweetness, ate the buttered bread, and asked Mother Emaline about her day. Only after the candles were blown out and they were in bed for the night did Raya allow her mind to return to the events from earlier.

She spent a good part of the night feeling terrible about forgetting their supper and the rest of it worrying about what would happen in the morning. She wasn't sure whether to expect Henry or not, or whether she should expect a job upon reaching the hotel. Providing she did still have work, she wasn't sure if Mr. Fairbury would come into the kitchen, or if he would stay away. She had left abruptly, dismissing him and his request for her to love him. There was no way he could know she had left for his sake rather than her own, wishing only to spare him from any harm to his reputation, scandalous gossip, or humiliation.

When she finally slept, she dreamt of Luke. She was young, and she was meeting him for the first time on the day of their wedding. She had been terrified of him, terrified of leaving her family and her home. But she had grown to like him, to respect him, to care for him, to love him. He was a good man.

When she woke the next morning, she climbed out of bed stiffly, feeling more exhausted than she had when she went to bed. She felt tired and sore from the schedule she had been keeping. She stepped into her dress and pulled on her stockings and boots before washing her face. She brushed through her dark hair with long, methodical strokes, wincing in pain as she did, her arms sore from scrubbing floors the night before. Wrapping her hair in a low, tight bun, she ate breakfast with Mother Emaline and waited anxiously outside for Henry, who came at his normal time. Breathing a sigh of relief, she climbed into the carriage, thankful Mr. Fairbury had not discontinued her employment as a result of their late-night encounter.

When she arrived at work, Ms. Macy greeted her as normal, and Raya set about making her bread. Noni came a little later, saying she was feeling much better, and Raya breathed a sigh of relief. Along with being worried about her own situation, she had also been worried about her friend.

It was late in the afternoon when Mr. Lenox entered the kitchen with Mr. Fairbury. They talked to Ms. Macy as usual. Mr. Fairbury asked what the menu was for supper and announced both he and Mr. Lenox would be staying for the evening meal, as they had a meeting with two other businessmen.

Raya felt pleased somehow that he would be staying for supper. Although she had determined in her mind not to think about Atlas Fairbury or dishonor Luke's memory by allowing herself to feel anything for the man, she felt happy that he would be in the building. Having him close by felt comforting and brought an added cheerfulness to the kitchen staff. Everyone and everything seemed better when he was around.

Startling her out of her thoughts, Mr. Fairbury reached in front of her to snag a cookie as he walked by with Mr. Lenox. "And how are you today, Ms. Applewood?" His voice was cheerful.

"Fine, thank you," she murmured, surprised he would still talk to her after the events of the previous night.

He stood up straighter, his voice taking on concern as he studied her face. "Are you well?"

"Quite well," she assured him. There was no way she would tell him she was up most of the night worrying and spent the rest of it dreaming about her departed husband.

He hesitated, as if unconvinced.

"Mr. Fairbury, you're going to take sick if you continue to eat so many cookies! Didn't your mother, God rest her soul, teach you that too many sweets aren't good for a man?" Ms. Macy called out from across the kitchen.

"No, but she did tell me you are what you eat!" he called back good-naturedly.

Ms. Macy gave a decided harrumph. "How you eat so many of those and not put on an ounce of weight, I'll never know," she muttered, clearly irritated.

Mr. Fairbury just laughed. "Lenox, do you want one of these?"

Mr. Lenox shook his head as he checked his pocket watch.

Mr. Fairbury took another cookie, taking the opportunity to address Raya privately. "You're certain you're well?"

She nodded.

"Alright then. I'd best be on my way. Good day, Raya."

She glanced quickly up at him before immediately dropping her eyes again. His quiet use of her familiar name showed he hadn't forgotten about their late-night encounter either.

"Good day," she echoed. She felt his departure more than she saw it, and she went back to making bread, which she did for the rest of the day, stopping only to wash dishes after the evening meal.

Twenty-Eight

Christmas dinner was extravagant at The Fairbury Hotel. Raya had never seen so much good food in one place at one time. Ms. Macy truly outdid herself, and the entire kitchen was running at full steam. With over two dozen staff chopping, mashing, stirring, baking, and mixing as they worked to create the most elaborate meal Raya had ever seen, the room soon felt hot, loud, and crowded. Raya had to be careful every time she moved so as not to get in the way of someone else.

Ms. Macy was calling out orders, causing the staff to run this way and that across the kitchen, trying to keep up with her demands. Despite the cramped quarters and hecticness of the day, the result was magnificent.

Raya watched platters of turkey, ham, and roast beef go out through the swinging doors of the front dining room, followed by heaping bowls of mashed potatoes dripping with butter, bright sweet potatoes, green beans with salt pork, peas with cream and butter, corn casserole, turkey dressing, turkey with noodles, and ruby red cranberry sauce. The holiday dishes were followed by plates full of regular bread, sweet breads, and pumpkin bread Raya had baked. Behind the bread and butter went the pies, too various and numerous for Raya to keep track of. Her mouth watered, and her stomach growled.

The kitchen staff waited for the patrons to eat as they continued cooking, stirring, and mixing as quickly as they could to keep up with the demands. The back dining room was closed on Christmas, and when the front dining room finally began to slow and clear out, everyone hurried to wash the dishes so they could go home and have Christmas dinner with their own families.

When the dishes were done and the kitchen clean, Ms. Macy had everyone assemble, then went to fetch Mr. Lenox. The hotel employees who worked out front, in the stables, and up in the guest rooms all came down to congregate with the kitchen staff in the back dining room, filling the room until Raya didn't think it could hold anyone else. The tables, which Raya knew seated sixty people, were full, and still, a few stable boys stood near the back door. Mr. Lenox and Mr. Fairbury entered the room together. Mr. Fairbury gave a short and witty speech, thanking everyone for their hard work and commitment, and even Mr. Lenox smiled. Then Mr. Fairbury handed out a Christmas turkey wrapped in brown paper and an orange to every employee.

Raya was stunned by Mr. Fairbury's generosity, knowing the cost of such Christmas gifts for so many people must be significant. As she watched her fellow employees' reaction to him, her heart swelled and warmed.

His employees admired him. From Mr. Lenox all the way down to the women who cleaned the guest rooms, he was liked and respected by all, and his Christmas gifts were accepted with great appreciation. As soon as he finished talking, he was instantly surrounded by people as everyone clamored to get a few moments of his time. He was kind and gracious, talking and laughing merrily with his employees, as Raya and Noni helped Ms. Macy hand out cups of eggnog to all the workers. Before he could get his own cup of eggnog, Mr. Fairbury was pulled outside by Mr. Lenox and the stable manager.

Raya felt his absence acutely and lamented not having the opportunity to wish him a Merry Christmas; without him, she could not imagine what the holiday would be like for her this year.

The festivities lasted only a few minutes longer as the hotel still had guests who needed tending, and those who weren't scheduled to stay were eager to get home, but it had been a merry event. It left Raya smiling, even as she set to work washing all the empty cups.

When the cups were washed, Raya hurried to put on her cloak with Noni. From her cloak, she produced the rag doll Mother Emaline had made for Noni's daughter, Bella, and the wooden top they had purchased for her son, Luke.

Just as delighted as Raya thought her children might be, Noni smiled brightly and gave Raya a big hug, thanking her for the gifts. This year, they would be her children's only gifts, save the mittens she was able to knit them out of a worn blanket. Raya made her promise to come pick out her kitten on the Sabbath, then gave her one last hug before parting ways.

After looking once more to see if Mr. Fairbury was in sight and finding he was not, Raya wished Ms. Macy a Merry Christmas, then hurried out to the carriage, climbed aboard before Henry could open the door for her, and settled into her seat. She was excited to get home and spend the evening with Mother Emaline and equally excited to open all the dishes and eat Ms. Macy's mouth-watering Christmas dinner.

Once home, Henry helped her fill her arms with the numerous packages Ms. Macy had sent with her, along with the turkey and the orange. She thanked him for the ride, wished him a Merry Christmas, and hurried inside, shutting the door behind her with her foot. "Mother, you will not believe all the food Ms. Macy sent us! All day I wa—" Raya stopped short as she turned and saw Atlas Fairbury lighting candles on an evergreen tree that was set up in the corner of the room.

Mother Emaline laughed at her surprise. "I guess I forgot to tell Raya that I invited you to celebrate Christmas with us. You'll have to forgive her surprise, Atlas."

Across the room, he smiled at her; his expression hopeful. "A good surprise, I hope."

For a stunned moment, Raya met Mr. Fairbury's blue eyes and enjoyed his smile, but with her composure returned her sense of propriety. She quickly dropped her eyes and turned away to begin unloading her heavy packages onto the table. "Yes, 'tis an honor to have you celebrate with us, sir," she answered, her emotions conflicted.

He looked out of place in their humble dwelling, and while she felt pleasure that he would come and spend his Christmas with them, she also felt unnerved by his presence.

In an instant, he was beside her, helping her set her packages down, taking the turkey from her arms and setting it in the corner of the shanty as directed by Mother Emaline. Once her hands were free, Raya quickly took her cloak off and hung it by the door. She then set to work reheating their Christmas dinner, allowing herself a respite from Mr. Fairbury's company by concentrating on her work.

Mother Emaline helped her while carrying on a lively conversation with Mr. Fairbury, making the man laugh on several occasions.

"May I set the table?" he asked, resting his hand lightly on the back of a chair.

Raya looked up quickly, dismayed by his request. "No, sir. I'll set the table. Why don't you have a seat? You've had a long day. I'll take care of it."

"Nonsense," he answered smoothly, his voice firm. "Cousin Emaline, where might I find the dishes?"

By the set of his jaw and the expression on his face, Raya could nearly hear him telling her all over again that he didn't want her service. He didn't want her to serve him. She could feel his message as strongly now as the night he had told it to her in plain English. Yet, for a man like Atlas Fairbury to be in her little shanty home for Christmas dinner was unnatural enough; he would not also set the table.

Standing quickly, she hurried across the room to gather the plates, which she set out quickly, trying not to notice how they were chipped and old, nor the rudimentary nature of their cups and utensils. They were perfectly functional for Mother Emaline and herself, but for Atlas Fairbury, who ate off exquisite china and silver, they must seem sorely lacking. Shame was not so much the emotion that filled her as a sense that Atlas Fairbury deserved more—much more. He should be home, surrounded by family and friends, eating a Christmas dinner freshly prepared, off china and silver with crystal wine glasses; not in their little shanty eating leftovers. He stood two steps back as she quickly set the table, silent as he watched. She didn't look up to see his expression, but could guess the nature of it.

So be it. Regardless of whether or not he liked it, she wouldn't stand by and let him set the table. She couldn't. It simply wasn't right.

When she was done, she hurried back to the fireplace and stirred the turkey dressing as it warmed over the fire. "Mother, Noni loved the rag doll you made for Bella. And the top for Luke. I think she was very glad to have something to give them for Christmas."

"Oh good! I hope her little ones will enjoy them."

"I'm sure they will," Raya answered. "She said they'll come pick up their kitten on the Sabbath."

"Then you will be needing the Sabbath off," Mr. Fairbury said cheerfully, including himself in the conversation.

"Oh, Mother Emaline will be here. I can work," Raya contradicted.

"How is Jake feeling?" Mother Emaline asked, hurrying back into the conversation, hearing stubbornness in both of their tones.

Raya turned, her attention diverted. "Better, I believe. Noni said he told his employer he can return to work and is now just waiting for them to have work for him."

"Hopefully, the man will have work soon," Mr. Fairbury added. "Noni has no business working all day as she does in her condition. I've been concerned for her."

Warmth filled Raya at Mr. Fairbury's genuine concern for her friend. "As have I."

"Well, the good LORD knows the perfect timing. We will all have to trust He knows what He's doing," Mother Emaline interjected.

UP FROM THE ASH HEAP

Giving the turkey and noodles one last stir, Raya stood to her feet, drawing the pot out of the fire, and straightening to carry it to the table. "I'm surprised you're hungry again already, Mr. Fairbury. Ms. Macy put together a feast."

"I agree. I've been looking forward to it all day."

"As have I," Raya agreed. "It's simply a big meal to have twice in one day, much less in just a few hours."

At that, Mr. Fairbury laughed, the merry sound of it filling the shanty. "I now understand your surprise. I did not partake in Christmas dinner at the hotel."

Raya looked up, startled. "Whyever not?"

"I knew I was going to get to enjoy it with you," he answered sincerely, "and Cousin Emaline."

"And we are so glad to have you!" Emaline told him from the hearth.

At her words, Raya looked over at her mother-in-law and saw the sincerity etched in her face. Raya's heart swelled as she recognized how much it meant to Mother Emaline to have Atlas Fairbury—a relative of her late husband and sons—in their home for their first Christmas without their men.

Raya had been so preoccupied with preparations for the day at work, she had not taken the time to think about or remember their loss or the loneliness of the holiday compared to those past. She was only consumed with moving forward and making a way for her and Mother Emaline's survival. However, home alone, the dear woman did not have much else to occupy her mind. Raya chided herself for being insensitive to her mother-in-law's emotional needs.

Raya returned to the hearth and reached down for Mother Emaline's hands, helping the woman to her feet. "It certainly was a fine idea to invite Mr. Fairbury to join us for Christmas. Come, why don't you take a seat and I'll bring over the rest of the food. Then perhaps Mr. Fairbury can lead us in prayer, and we can enjoy this wonderful Christmas dinner Ms. Macy cooked us!"

285

"Good idea. The aromas are heavenly, and I must say, my mouth is watering," Mother Emaline admitted, drawing laughter and agreement from the others.

Raya looped her arm around Mother Emaline's waist and gave her a gentle squeeze as they walked, compassion for the woman making her heart hurt. How difficult must her day have been, sitting home alone, remembering all the Christmases she had shared with her husband and children. She was thankful Mother Emaline had the forethought to invite Mr. Fairbury, knowing how hard of a day it would be.

At the table, Mr. Fairbury was waiting with Emaline's chair pulled back, and Raya smiled warmly as he pushed it in as her dear mother-in-law sat, treating her as the fine woman that she was. Following Raya back to the fireplace, he took several dishes from her before she could stop him. He carried them to the table and was holding her chair by the time she was ready to sit down. Once both women were seated, he carried over one of the chairs that sat in front of the hearth and took his seat at the head of the table. He extended his hands, laying them palm up. Raya and Mother Emaline both took his large hands and joined their own as he gave thanks for the food, for the fellowship, and mostly for the Christchild's arrival into the world.

Raya listened to his words and felt a deep sense of peace settle over her heart, as she was reminded of the core message of the religion she had come to be a part of just a few years earlier. The Son of God born of a woman, not to have great military conquests or earthly rule or fame, but to offer hope to all mankind, to make a way for their sins to be forgiven and their communion with God restored. It was because of what started that night in a stable that the impassable chasm between God and hopeless sinners was bridged, giving hope and a future to all who had fallen under the seduction of sin.

Mr. Fairbury gently squeezed her hand, and she realized belatedly that the prayer was over, and she was the only one with her head still bowed. Slipping her hands out of his and Mother

Emaline's, Raya caught the warm smile Mother Emaline sent her before the woman redirected her attention to Mr. Fairbury.

"Atlas, 'twas a wonderful prayer and a great gift to have a man say the blessing at our table again. It has been a year with . . ." Mother Emaline paused, "much loss, but having you here makes it feel a little fuller again. Thank you for joining us."

"Giving thanks was an honor, as is being here with the two of you. I greatly appreciate the invitation," Mr. Fairbury told her solemnly. "Now, who would like some turkey?"

Seeing he meant to serve them, Raya held up Mother Emaline's plate, and Mr. Fairbury filled it to the brim, despite Mother Emaline's protests that she couldn't eat nearly half of what he gave her.

"You're next, Ms. Applewood," he told her, his voice cheerful, yet firm.

Conceding, Raya lifted her plate, and he filled it just as full as Emaline's. She made no protest. She had been smelling, seeing, and cooking those dishes all day long and had been greatly anticipating the moment she could try them. She couldn't keep at bay an excited smile as she set down her plate full of all the trimmings. She waited patiently as Mr. Fairbury filled his own plate, and once he finished, they all began to eat.

An amiable and lively conversation ensued over the dinner table, and Raya found herself joining in and laughing, all but forgetting their charming dinner guest was her employer. When they had cleaned their plates (even Mother Emaline, who found an appetite she hadn't had in many years), Raya served pumpkin pie. When they finished, Mr. Fairbury helped Mother Emaline to her chair by the fire, while Raya started on the dishes. Raya heard laughter and looked back to see that Mr. Fairbury had moved his chair next to Emaline and was telling the older woman a story. Even from her spot over the washbasin, she could see the light in Mother Emaline's eyes, and she turned back to her dishes with a smile.

He gave a job to a foreigner, passed out cloaks to cold employees, and made her mother-in-law laugh.

Raya had a bowl and two pans left when Mr. Fairbury's footsteps fell behind her and she felt his presence as he stepped up beside her. Glancing back, she saw that Mother Emaline's head was bobbing. Smiling tenderly, she turned back to her dishes. "She's worn out."

"The hour is late."

"Is it?" Raya asked, surprised. It didn't feel it, but when she counted up the hours, she realized that it must be, considering it was late evening before she even left work. When Mr. Fairbury showed her the face of his fancy pocket watch, she saw it was a quarter to ten. "It feels earlier than it is."

"So it does."

"Do you need to be getting home?" she asked slowly, reluctant to see him go. He had brought light back into Mother Emaline's eyes and laughter to their home.

"Are you throwing me out?" he asked, his tone amused.

"No."

"Then I think I can probably stay a bit longer. My driver won't be back for a while yet. And we still need to finish lighting the candles on the tree," he added. Grabbing a dish towel, he began to dry the dishes she had washed. She considered protesting, but his determination to help seemed unyielding, so she kept her mouth shut.

"Though she looks better than she did last time I visited, Cousin Emaline's health still seems frail. She seems older than I presume her to be," he observed after a moment.

"Her health is still frail, that's true, but she's much better now than she was two months ago," Raya answered, glancing back at the lady in question. "I didn't think she would make it to Christmas. In fact, I know she wouldn't have if I hadn't found work when I did."

"I knew she was in poor health, but I didn't realize how severe it was. I'm sorry. Had I known, I would have summoned a doctor."

Raya glanced up at the regret she heard in Mr. Fairbury's tone. "You've done plenty for us, sir. You have done more than was ever expected. It's only because of your generosity that she's even alive right now," Raya admitted, her eyes turning back to the dishwater before her.

"Please don't call me sir," he requested, his tone quiet and beseeching. "Not here. Not in your home with my cousin sitting across the room."

"She was much better in Colorado Territory," Raya continued, going on as if she hadn't heard. "Before Alex and Niz were married, she was just like any other frontier woman, hearty and hardworking. It was after they were wed that she took ill. That was the first time the fevers came upon her. She was ill for quite some time. Slowly, she got better, but would have bouts of coughing and fever from time to time if she attempted too much. After the fire..."

"I'm sure her grief sapped her strength."

Raya nodded. "She's aged more in the last four months than in the five years I've known her. When her illness came again, I didn't have the resources to buy food that would strengthen her body and allow her health to return. We didn't have the money to buy wood ... I thought we would be turned out of this shanty... Until you gave me work."

"I'm only thankful I could help," Mr. Fairbury answered humbly.

"Since then, Mother Emaline has greatly improved. She can be up and about and even ventures outside on occasion now. She tires easily and still has coughing fits occasionally, but I think she feels well overall. I keep hoping she will regain her full strength, and perhaps she will in the days ahead, but for now, we'll be thankful that she's better than she was."

"Yes, perhaps she will," Mr. Fairbury agreed. He finished drying the last cup, and Raya put it away with the others. "I cannot imagine how unbearably lonely it must have been for you this fall. You were here, in a new city, without your husband, your brothers-in-law or their wives, and Cousin Emaline was sick with fever."

The feeling in his tone touched a nerve, and Raya blinked back tears as memories of those days came rushing back to her mind. "Things are much better now," she told him, straightening from the cupboard.

"Will you look at me?" he asked, breaking the momentary silence. "Please?"

Hesitantly, Raya lifted her eyes up to his.

"Are you okay now? Are you well? Last week, when you came into work, you had dark shadows under your eyes and I ... was concerned you weren't feeling well. You said you were, but I'm going to ask you again, not as your employer, but . . . as someone who cares—are you well? Have you been feeling poorly? If you say you have, I'll go after a doctor tonight."

Raya shook her head, dropping her eyes, feeling a hint of a blush rising in her cheeks. "I'm well, truly." She glanced back up to meet his eyes and smiled warmly. "But thank you for caring."

His answering smile was bright, as he looked down into her face for several long moments before gesturing toward the tree. "Shall we finish lighting the candles?"

She nodded and turned, crossing the room to the tree in the corner. Taking one of the small white candles, she lit several more of them, one by one. She startled when Mr. Fairbury's large hand settled against the small of her back. Glancing back toward him, she saw that he held out a cup. Accepting it, she glanced inside and gave a small shriek of delight, waking Mother Emaline. "Eggnog! How did you get this? There wasn't any left! Ms. Macy didn't send any ... it was all gone."

"What is it?" Mother Emaline asked from her chair, looking sleepy and dazed.

When Mr. Fairbury nodded, Raya took the cup to Mother Emaline, a happy smile on her face. "Eggnog! Just like we used to make at the cabin!"

"Why! What a surprise! Did you bring this?" Mother Emaline asked, directing her question at Mr. Fairbury. When he nodded in confirmation, she sent him a dazzling smile. "Well, wasn't that thoughtful!"

"I told Ms. Macy I had a dinner party this evening and asked her to make a batch for me to bring along," Mr. Fairbury said, returning with a cup for Raya and one for himself.

Fully awake once again, Mother Emaline and Mr. Fairbury launched into a conversation about Christmases past, and Raya sipped eggnog and lit candles until all the candles on the tree were lit. Then, she went around and blew out all the candles positioned around the room, so only the candles on the tree and the fire in the fireplace remained.

Standing in front of the evergreen tree, Raya watched the flickering candles with childlike wonder. It was beautiful. She clasped her hands and quietly enjoyed watching something so beautiful in such an atmosphere of stark necessity and simplicity. She took a deep breath, filling her lungs with the fresh scent of the fragrant tree. Closing her eyes, she imagined she was back in the mountains, where the air was crisp and the fresh scent of evergreens was all around her. Smiling, she opened her eyes to observe the dancing candlelight once again. When she turned, she saw that Mr. Fairbury and Mother Emaline were watching her, just as she was watching the tree. She blushed.

"Did you bring the tree?" she asked Mr. Fairbury. He nodded, appearing pleased. "Thank you. It's beautiful."

"You're welcome," he answered, his eyes fixed on her face.

Mother Emaline stood and retrieved the family Bible from the top shelf. Bringing it back and holding it out to him, she asked him to read the Christmas story. He accepted the heavy Bible and opened it to the book of Luke. His voice, rich and full, filled the shanty as he read about the events of the night on which the Christchild was born. When he was finished, he led them in prayer, and Raya listened intently to every word, noting the familiarity with which he spoke to the God of the Universe, as if He was his very best and beloved friend. Listening to the sound of his voice, the crackling of the logs in the fireplace, and the creaking of Mother Emaline's rocker, Raya nearly fell asleep as peace descended over the shanty. She blinked heavily when Mr. Fairbury finished.

Noticing her fatigue, he stood quickly to his feet and motioned to the chair he had been sitting in. "Sit down, Ms. Applewood. I've been rude to sit and leave you standing."

She shook her head. "I could have brought over another chair. I'm perfectly happy standing here by the tree, but thank you."

"Nonsense. Come, sit down," he insisted, reaching for her hand, and pulling her to the chair. "You've been on your feet all day. Besides, I have to go outside for a moment. I'll be right back."

Conceding, she did as she was told and folded her hands in her lap, closing her eyes and letting out a deep sigh as he closed the door behind him.

"Is it alright that I invited him to share Christmas dinner with us?" Mother Emaline asked, her voice hopeful.

Raya looked over at her and smiled warmly. "Perfectly alright. I'm glad you did. I haven't seen you this happy in months."

"He's a wonderful man, isn't he?" Mother Emaline asked joyfully. "He always was a nice boy, but he's turned into a magnificent man, and I'm glad to see that. It makes this mother's heart proud. Too bad his mother and father aren't here to see the man he's become."

Raya nodded in agreement. It was a shame. Surely, the Fairburys would be very proud of their son. Suddenly, she smiled. "I'm sure his mother would be glad to know you are here with him this Christmas."

A warm smile spread across Mother Emaline's face, but before the conversation continued, Mr. Fairbury came back through the front door, his arms laden with gifts. Panic took a firm hold on Raya as she realized they had nothing for him in return. She wanted to tell him to take his gifts back to his carriage and give them to someone in need—he had already given them so much—but to do so would be incomprehensibly rude. Instead, she accepted the three packages he held out to her with a quiet thank you. He gave three packages to Mother Emaline as well and told their elder to open hers first. She did and was delighted by a heavy new black cloak, similar to Raya's, but without the lace around the hood, a beautiful new quilt, and a thick woolen black dress.

"That should help to fend off these unusually cold temperatures we've been having this winter," Mr. Fairbury told her cheerfully.

"It certainly will! Why, thank you, Atlas," Mother Emaline responded, as pleased as punch. "You have shown yourself exceedingly thoughtful and kind once again."

He shook his head, obviously embarrassed by her praise. "It would be wrong to attend Christmas dinner without bringing gifts, as you ladies have so graciously opened your home to me." He paused. "Ms. Applewood, you should open yours."

Raya's brown eyes were already brimming with tears from having just watched Emaline. Everything Raya had wanted to give her mother-in-law, but did not have the means to do so, Emaline had just unwrapped. Her greatest need during her lonely days was a way to keep warm, and Mr. Fairbury had just assured her a way to do that. Raya was overwhelmed with thankfulness.

"To see Mother Emaline warm is enough of a gift for me," she told him. It was not what he did for her, but what he did for others that was slowly stealing her heart.

"Be that as it may, you still have gifts of your own. Open them, please," he said, his smile hopeful.

As she untied the string holding the paper in place on her first gift, she watched as two of the kittens woke from their slumber and climbed out of their basket. Starting to play, they went tumbling across the floor in front of the Christmas tree. With rapt attention, she watched as Mr. Fairbury squatted down to pet the friendly little felines. When he glanced up, she turned back to her gift and pulled back the paper to reveal a beautiful black gown, made in a fashionable style, yet not too fancy to wear to work.

"If you must suffer the loss of your husband, then at least you can mourn in style," Mr. Fairbury told her, both sympathy and humor in his smile.

She looked down at the thin fabric of her own dress and felt color springing into her cheeks, knowing he must have noticed. Yet, she knew there was no missing or denying her need for a new dress, and she was overwhelmed that her need had once again been met by him. She smiled up at him. "It's beautiful! Thank you! Thank you so very much."

He nodded to her other gifts, and she unwrapped the next to find a new apron, this one with frills of lace around the edges. Looking up from it, she laughed. "As beautiful as it is, I don't think I'll fit in well in your kitchen anymore. This apron, this dress—they are both so fine. Are you sure I should be baking in these?"

He laughed as one of the kittens climbed up onto his boot, then launched itself off of it and onto his brother, sending both kittens tumbling across the floor. "They're rambunctious little things, aren't they?"

Emaline nodded emphatically. "It will soon be time for them to find new homes."

Mr. Fairbury laughed again, then motioned for Raya to open her last gift. Inside, she found a beautiful silver mirror and brush set. The design on the back was exquisite, and she had never seen anything so beautiful. She caught her breath and looked up at him. His smile warmed her heart.

"I was going for functionality with the others, but I simply thought this was pretty. Every girl ought to have something pretty, don't you think, Cousin Emaline?"

"I do," Emaline answered warmly.

Before Raya could thank him, Mr. Fairbury pushed himself to his feet. "Well, Cousin Emaline, Ms. Applewood, the hour is late, and I'd best be going. Thank you so very much for opening your home and sharing your Christmas with me. I have enjoyed myself immensely this evening. And Emaline, I'm truly very glad you are back in town and have returned home to us. Mother would have been very pleased to know it."

He kissed the back of Mother Emaline's hand and looked up in surprise as Raya stood to her feet and made her way quickly into the kitchen, where she started washing out the cups they had used for eggnog. He finished saying his goodbyes to Emaline, then put on his heavy coat and gloves, pausing by the kitchen table. "Goodnight, Ms. Applewood. Merry Christmas." His voice was hesitant.

"Goodnight! Merry Christmas," she answered, not looking up from the cups she was washing. When the door shut behind him, she paused.

All was quiet for a moment before Mother Emaline, clearly stunned by Raya's reaction, said, "Raya! Go thank him for the gifts."

The scolding was all Raya needed to propel her into motion, and she ran around the table and flung open the front door, going out into the bitter cold. Mr. Fairbury was shutting the door to his carriage.

"Why?" she demanded, catching the door and pulling it back open. "Why do you keep giving us all of this? The job, the tip, the carriage rides, the food, the cloaks, the dresses, the quilts, the mirror—why?" she repeated, her teeth chattering in the cold.

"For the love of all that is holy and right," Mr. Fairbury said, clearly exasperated, climbing back down out of his carriage and shrugging out of his coat. A light snow was falling and thick icicles that had formed on the eaves of the shanty reached nearly to the ground. Their breath hung in the air. "I have given you two brand new cloaks, and here you stand in nothing but your dress. You will take ill if you keep going out like this."

"Why?" she asked again, unrelenting, even as he settled his large coat around her shoulders. She was swallowed up in the large garment that still held his warmth and fresh scent. She stopped shivering.

"A simple thank you would have sufficed," he told her through teeth that were now chattering.

"Why?"

He sighed and drug his hand across his face. "Why?" he asked. She nodded. His tall, lean frame shook from the cold. "I want you to have every good thing, Raya. I want to give you every good gift."

"You seek to secure my love through gifts?" she accused. Was he trying to buy her? Was this his Eastern attempt at a brideprice?

"No." He sounded frustrated. "I don't give to make you love me. I give because I love *you*."

She shook her head, not understanding.

He stepped toward her and cupped his hand to her cheek, tipping her face up. She met his eyes, searching them for some answer to her question. "I don't want the provisions I have made for you to motivate any love you may have for me. I want you to love me because you cannot help it, because you have fallen in love with my character. I do not give because I hope doing so will make you love me; I give because I have fallen in love with you, and I want you to have every good thing that is within my power to give you."

For a moment, she wondered if he would kiss her again. For that moment, she hoped he would. She longed to be enveloped in his masculine scent and warmth, to be held in his strong arms, and kissed as he had kissed her only a week earlier. She had not only felt enjoyed, as she felt when Luke kissed her, but she also felt cared about, valued, loved, admired, respected, considered—all from a single kiss.

"Thank you for my dress and my apron and my mirror and brush. They're beautiful," she finally said, at a loss for something else to say. "And thank you for the eggnog, the tree, and for coming tonight."

He smiled down into her face and pushed back a wayward strand of dark hair. "You're most welcome."

"I only wish I had something to give you."

UP FROM THE ASH HEAP

"You do . . . and you have," he answered softly. "You looked at me tonight. And your glance captures my heart. Every time." He ran his fingertips over her eyebrow and down the side of her face, making her shiver. "That was the only gift I wanted this Christmas."

"I have to go," she told him, dropping her eyes and taking his coat from her shoulders, handing it back to him.

He smiled as he stepped back. "I know you do."

"Goodnight, Mr. Fairbury."

"Goodnight, Raya," he answered. "Merry Christmas." She walked through her front door and dropped the bar into place. She stood with her forehead resting against the wood of the door as she listened to his carriage door shut and the horses start off down the snow-packed street. When she could no longer hear the bells from the harnesses, she took a deep shuddering breath and went to sit at Emaline's feet. She laid her head in Mother Emaline's lap and cried. Mother Emaline didn't ask questions, and Raya didn't explain herself.

After all, how could she explain to the dear woman that she missed her husband and was reliving the memories of their last Christmas together, all while trying to balance feelings of intense guilt because of just how much she had wanted Atlas Fairbury to kiss her outside his carriage? How could she be falling in love with another man when she still loved her husband and grieved his passing? How could she explain that when she didn't even understand it?

And how could Atlas Fairbury not see that she was the most unnatural choice for him, much less that a marriage between them would never work? Frustration knotted her heart as she recalled how incredibly persistent he was, and how, little by little, she felt her defenses crumbling. If he loved her as he said he did and wanted her to have every good thing, then how could he not understand her desire to serve him well and to protect his reputation and his social standing? She didn't understand his lack of understanding.

She wanted those good things for him, and he didn't seem to appreciate it.

Most of all, how could she explain to her beloved mother-in-law that although she had loved and cared for her son, she had never fallen in love with him, or lost her heart to him the way she was losing it to Atlas Fairbury? It felt terrifying and uncomfortable. And all for what? She could not marry him. She wasn't self-deprecating or insecure; it was only a fact of life. It simply wasn't done. Maybe it was acceptable on the frontier, but not here in the East within the realm of high society.

But she couldn't explain all of that, and so she didn't explain any of it. She bled out her grief, frustration, fear, and confusion through tears as her heart and mind raged against one another.

Mother Emaline simply sat quietly, running her hands soothingly over Raya's hair, and letting her cry until she had no more tears.

Twenty-Nine

The next morning, Raya wore her new black dress to work, though she paired it with her old apron. The lace and frills on the apron Mr. Fairbury gave her were too much, she decided, to wear in a kitchen where she was certain to get it dirty.

She made bread, washed dishes, swept the floor numerous times, and was just preparing to put on her cloak to go home when a loud commotion behind her in the kitchen caught her attention. Ms. Macy was holding Noni's wrist up, and in her hand was a silver spoon from the front dining room. Confused and concerned, Raya made her way toward them, trying to make out what was happening.

"After all Mr. Fairbury's kindness, this is how you repay him? You steal from him?" Ms. Macy was nearly yelling, her face red. "I've noticed some of the silver going missing, but I never would have suspected you, Noni! You should be ashamed of yourself! And to think you're bringing up children. Are you teaching them your thieving ways?"

Raya's heart fell as she realized what had happened.

Noni burst into tears, struggling to free her hand from Ms. Macy's. At the same time, the door to the front dining room opened, and Mr. Lenox strode through purposefully.

"Ms. Macy, quiet your voice," he instructed immediately. Planting his feet, he looked around the kitchen where half a dozen employees stood frozen, watching the scene unfold. Most everyone had already left for the night, but those who remained could not have been more shocked by what was taking place. Ms. Macy stopped yelling and turned to face Mr. Lenox, keeping hold of Noni's hand, despite the fact that the spoon had been dropped.

"What's going on here?" Mr. Lenox asked, his voice quiet, yet fierce. "We have guests in the front dining room, and all of a sudden we hear a loud commotion coming from the kitchen. Imagine what those guests must be thinking!"

"I do apologize, sir, but I just found Noni slipping this here silver spoon in the pocket of her apron," Ms. Macy explained.

Mr. Lenox shifted his fierce gaze to Noni. "Were you stealing from The Fairbury Hotel?"

She continued to cry, her head down.

"Girl, answer me! Were you stealing from The Fairbury Hotel?"

Everyone glanced up as the swinging door opened again, and Mr. Fairbury walked through, his cheerful smile fading as he assessed the situation.

Raya hadn't known he was in the building and surmised he had just arrived, judging by Mr. Lenox's apparent surprise as well. Her eyes shifted from Mr. Fairbury back to Noni, then back to Mr. Fairbury.

Mr. Lenox crossed the floor to stand beside him. "It appears we have a thief in our midst."

Mr. Fairbury listened quietly as Mr. Lenox and Ms. Macy shared the events of the past five minutes, then he stepped forward until he was fully in front of Noni. "Noni, I have heard the allegations. What would you say to them?"

She turned her head and covered her face with her hands, further incriminating herself as she continued to cry.

Her heart filling painfully with compassion, Raya broke free from her shock and quickly crossed the floor to stand in front of Noni, shielding her from the stern Mr. Lenox, Mr. Fairbury, and the shocked onlookers.

"Sir," she implored, addressing Mr. Fairbury. "She isn't well. She hasn't felt well all day, even all week. She isn't thinking straight. She would never steal from you."

UP FROM THE ASH HEAP

"Except she just did," Mr. Lenox pointed out, obviously annoyed by Raya's interruption.

"Sir, please!" she continued, addressing Mr. Fairbury again. Behind her, Noni's cries turned into sobs. Raya feared the violence of them would send the young woman into an early delivery. She was further along than Niz had been, but Raya knew enough about childbearing to know the child would still be too early to live.

"Raya, please step aside," Mr. Fairbury requested, his turmoil evident in his tone and in his familiar use of her name. He wasn't just commanding her, he was beseeching her to remove herself from the situation. She knew that, yet she feared for Noni and her unborn child. "Please," he said again.

Bowing her head in submission, Raya stepped back out of the way, watching Noni with tears in her own eyes. She wanted to wrap her arms around the frightened, ashamed girl and shield her from the others. Raya knew her friend. This wasn't her. She wasn't a thief.

"Ms. Macy, is this Noni's first offense?" Mr. Fairbury asked.

"The first I've caught her in. Three spoons have gone missing in the last week and one knife."

Mr. Fairbury stood quietly, his eyes on the ground, his lips pressed together. Finally, he looked up. "Noni, I will not inform the police captain of this transgression, but you are no longer employed at The Fairbury Hotel."

"Mr. Fairbury, without this job, my children will starve!" Noni cried desperately, wiping her tears and standing straighter. She was clearly trying to pull herself together, but her tired face remained red and blotchy and her watery eyes were wild with fear.

"You should'a thought about that before you began stealing," Ms. Macy told her haughtily.

"Mr. Lenox, please pay this woman her final wage for the day," Mr. Fairbury commanded, his words strained.

"My children will starve! Please! Mr. Fairbury! Please, don't terminate my employment!" Noni begged. "I promise I won't be stealin' nothin' of yours never again!"

Tears ran down Raya's face unchecked as she watched Noni beg Mr. Fairbury, while Mr. Fairbury simply stood there, his eyes on the ceiling. Mr. Lenox gave Noni her final day's pay. Noni threw the coins back at Mr. Lenox.

"They're no good!" she cried, on the verge of hysteria. "They're worthless if those are the last ones I make! That won't buy no more food than will last three days!"

Mr. Lenox bent and picked up the coins. He handed them to Mr. Fairbury, as if unsure what to do with them, then grabbed Noni's arm and pulled her toward the door.

"Come on, it's time for you to go," Mr. Lenox told her. She dissolved into more tears as he escorted her across the room. At the door, he pushed her cloak into her arms and opened the back door, motioning for her to go out.

Noni glanced from Mr. Fairbury to Raya, then turned and ran out the door, covering her face as she did. Mr. Lenox didn't even have the door shut before Raya started after her, wiping the tears from her own cheeks with the backs of her hands.

"Ms. Applewood," Mr. Fairbury called, pushing through the small crowd to reach Raya before she ran out the door after Noni. "Please get these to her," he said, pressing the few coins into her palm. "And make sure she gets home safely." Raya turned again to follow Noni, but Mr. Fairbury grabbed her wrist. "And for goodness' sake, put on your wraps!"

Raya pulled her cloak around her shoulders. Satisfied, Mr. Fairbury released her, and she slipped out the door, leaving the warm, bright kitchen and all the shocked onlookers behind.

Once outside, the cold wind met her head on, and she struggled to see through the blowing snow. She raced to the alley, but didn't see anyone moving in the dark shadows, so she turned and ran to the street. She didn't see Noni moving down the dimly lit corridor, either. Her tears were freezing to her cheeks, and despite her heavy cloak, she was shaking, both from cold and emotion.

Deciding she could cover more ground to look for Noni if she went back for Henry and the carriage, she started picking her way back across the frozen yard of the hotel. As she approached the stable where Henry and the horses sat waiting for her, a movement caught her eye. In the shadow of the back dining room, she saw Noni hunched over in the snow, no cloak around her thin shoulders.

Running to her, Raya dropped to her knees in the snow beside her, putting her arm around her back. "Noni?"

Noni was crying still and didn't answer.

"Noni, come on. We need to get you home and out of this cold. Come with me. I'll take you in the carriage."

"I ain't goin' home and tellin' Jake I lost my job. I ain't goin' home and seeing the look on my babies' faces."

"Be that as it may, you've got a little one inside of you, and you are going to get mighty cold sitting out here. You need to get up and let me take you home... for Francine," Raya pleaded, knowing her slim frame was no match for the pregnant girl. She had no hope of being able to lift her up, much less carry her to the carriage.

Noni shook her head. "I ain't goin'. I can't."

"You need a hand, miss?" Henry asked, coming up to stand in the snow beside Raya. He was beating his hands against his chest to keep warm.

Raya looked up, grateful to see him. "Can you help me get her to the carriage?"

"I'd be happy to," he answered, bending down and scooping Noni up in his arms, ignoring her protests as he stomped back across the snow-covered ground to his waiting carriage. Raya followed closely behind. He set Noni inside the carriage and Raya climbed in after her, sitting down beside her.

She took the balled-up cloak out of Noni's hands and settled it around her shoulders, tying it tightly. She pulled the knitted hat Noni wore from the inside pocket of Noni's cloak and onto her blonde head, then took the blanket that always stayed in the carriage and settled it over Noni's lap, taking extra care to tuck it around the girl's enlarged stomach.

Her own hands painfully cold, Raya took Noni's hand in both of hers and held it tightly. "You're going to be okay, Noni. You're going to be okay."

Noni let her head fall against the high back of the seat and rolled it toward Raya. Her face was blotchy from crying and red from the stinging cold, but it was the hopelessness in her eyes that worried Raya most. "Jake's sick again. His bossman said he won't take him back. Don't have room on his crew for sickly men. Course, Jake's so sick it don't make no difference, really."

"Oh, Noni," Raya said, fresh tears springing into her eyes. That certainly wasn't what the young family of soon-to-be five needed. And now Noni had lost her job. Her chest filled painfully with compassion and sorrow. "Why did you do it? Why did you steal the silverware, honey?"

"Luke was cryin' last week. Said his belly was hungry. I didn't have any food left in the house to give 'im. My milk is all but dried up for Bella. Think I'm not eatin' enough for her, me, and the baby, so my body just cut off what it could. So now, she's another mouth to feed too, and we don't have money for no milk for her. She cries most of the time now, and I think it's cause she's hungry." Noni sniffed. "We just don't have enough money, Raya. I knew the baby would be comin' sometime soon, and I wasn't gonna be able to work no more. At least not for a while. I thought if I just took a couple pieces of silver, maybe we could get by 'til after the baby comes, and I can get back to work. It was foolish. I never should'a done it. But I was desperate; I don't know what else t' do. You should have heard how he cried. Just this slow, painful cry. I can't watch my babies starve, Raya, I can't!"

The desperation and fear in Noni's voice was almost too much for Raya to bear, and she wrapped her arms around her friend's shoulders and held her, rocking her back and forth as she would a child. Guilt laid siege to Raya's heart. She should have thought to bring Noni some of the food she had been sharing with others. She hadn't realized the family's situation was so dire. Suddenly Noni gave a ragged cry as she clambered to her feet as best she could in the moving carriage.

To her dismay, Raya found Noni's dress and stockings wet and a pool of liquid running back and forth across the carriage floor as the carriage swayed and lilted across the uneven streets.

Stunned, Raya's heart raced as tears ran swiftly from her eyes. Her heart breaking, she took in what was happening. Noni's water had just broken in Mr. Fairbury's fancy carriage. Coming out of her traumatized daze, Raya quickly unfastened her own cloak and used it to sop up the worst of the dampness on the carriage seat, then spread it on the floor to soak up the rest. She pulled Noni carefully back down onto the seat, wanting to save her from reeling with the bumpy carriage and hurting herself further.

Noni pressed her hands to her stomach and groaned, the pains coming on swiftly and with great severity. "It's too early," she panted, her eyes scared as she looked up at Raya.

"I know," Raya agreed, her heart breaking for her friend and for the baby she had felt move under her very own hands. The pain in her chest made drawing in a breath difficult, yet she knew she needed to be strong and composed for Noni. Tears running down her face, Raya peered out the window to surmise how close they were to the young woman's house. "It won't be much longer now, and we'll have you home," she promised, turning back to her friend.

"I ain't goin' home, I can't!" Noni wailed. She groaned as another pain came upon her.

"You have to go home," Raya told her through her tears of compassion. "You can't run away. Your husband and your babies are there waiting for you."

"I can't face them!"

"Noni! Do you know what I would give to have a husband and babies waiting for me at home?" Raya cried. Taking a deep breath, she stopped to compose herself. "You have a family who loves you, and that will not change whether you lost your job or . . . or . . . whether you have your baby too early. Whatever happens, you need to go home and face it together with those you love."

Noni's watery eyes were trained on Raya's face, and she nodded slowly. Raya wiped her eyes and then Noni's with Luke's handkerchief, clenched her teeth against the cold, and held Noni's hand tightly until Henry pulled up outside the girl's house—a shanty very similar to her own.

Raya opened the door and jumped out, rapping sharply on the door. Henry climbed down from his driver's seat and peered into the back of the carriage nervously. "Ms. Applewood, is she . . . is she havin' a baby in the back of my carriage?"

"Yes, she is, and I suggest you get her out if you don't want the baby born in there," Raya told him sympathetically, as she knocked again.

Finally, the door was opened, and a man Raya assumed to be Jake stood in long underwear, his expression a mix of confusion and anger. "Who are you?" he growled. Just then, Henry successfully emerged from the carriage with Noni, and Jake's expression changed. "Non? Sweetheart? What's wrong with her?" he asked, his words strained and frightened.

"The baby's coming," Raya answered, following Henry and Noni into the shanty as Jake stepped back to allow them entrance.

"The baby can't be comin', woman, it's too early."

"Early or not, it's coming," Raya told him grimly, tears still gathered in her eyes. Taking in the sparse furnishings of the shanty, she turned to Henry. "Put her there, on the bed." She turned to Jake. "Who should we get? A doctor?"

"We don't got no money for a doctor," Jake said, pulling at his hair in despair.

"A neighbor, then? Someone who has done this before?"

At that, Jake ran out the door and returned a few minutes later with an older woman who looked to be around Mother Emaline's age. She quickly took charge and drew the curtain hung around Jake and Noni's bed closed, shutting Jake, Henry, and the sleeping Luke and Bella out. Four hours later, the woman handed a stillborn baby girl to Raya while she saw to Noni. Tears filled Raya's eyes as she stared down at the beautiful baby girl, her heart ripping more with every breath the little one should have taken and didn't.

"Can I see her?" Noni asked from the bed, her voice weak, no strength left to reach up her arms. "Why isn't she cryin'? They all cry when they come out. Sometimes you gotta give 'em a little swat on the behind, Raya, to make 'em cry. Don't worry—it's good for 'em . . . clears their lungs."

"Noni," Raya started, unsure how to go on. She watched Noni's eyes fill with tears.

"Is she . . . she's dead, ain't she?" Noni whispered.

Raya nodded.

"I knew she was. I knew it. Hadn't felt her move in days. Told myself she was just sleepy, but I knew," Noni said, sniffing. "Can I see her?"

Raya squatted down at the side of Noni's bed and held the tiny girl up for her to see. Noni lifted her chin and blinked her tears back fiercely. "She looks like Luke did when he was a baby, like her daddy."

"She's very beautiful," Raya whispered.

Noni covered her face with both her hands and started sobbing. Raya couldn't hold back her own tears, and they ran down her cheeks as she carefully cradled the still baby, rocking herself as much as she was rocking the child.

"Go get Jake," the neighbor woman told Raya.

"No!" Noni sobbed from the bed. "I can't face him."

Raya looked to the older woman for direction, and she nodded to her to do as she said. "Put the child over there first," the woman instructed.

Raya wrapped the baby carefully in a blanket, feeling like it was the right thing to do. She laid the wrapped child in a blanket-lined box that sat next to the bed, clearly the place Noni had readied for her infant daughter in preparation for her birth. It felt heartless to leave a baby out in the cold, whether or not it was breathing.

Finished with the heartbreaking task, she slipped out from behind the curtain. Jake stood as she came into the room but didn't ask anything. It was a small shanty, and Raya knew he had heard everything. She softly shook her head to confirm what she knew he already knew, and as she did, he crossed his arms and turned his back to her, his head falling forward. He stood like that for several long moments, then turned to face her again, lifting his chin. "Can I see her? Can I see Noni?"

Raya nodded. "Yes, I think that would be good," she told him, hoping the man's reaction to his young wife would be gentle.

She shouldn't have worried. He quickly strode past her, and she followed him back into the curtained area to start cleaning up. Jake ran the last few feet to the bed and dropped down on his knees beside Noni, who had her face covered with both of her hands. When he attempted to pull them away, she fought him, still sobbing.

"Noni! Non, stop, sweetheart," he told her.

"I'm sorry! I'm so sorry!" she cried as he finally succeeded in prying her hands away from her face so he could see her.

Raya watched with compassion as the man's face crumpled. "Why? I don't blame you," he told her, aghast at the thought. "It's my fault, sweetheart. I'm the one who forced you to work. I should'a never asked so much of you when you was expectin'. It's my fault, not yours." His words were broken.

Raya clutched her throat, feeling the young couple's pain. Her task forgotten, she found herself feeling both awkward and transfixed as she watched the sorrowful scene unfold. She could relate to their grief and their guilt in this moment of personal tragedy only too well.

"No. No, it isn't," Noni argued. "I knew. I knew it wasn't moving enough. I should have known!" She paused for only a moment. "I lost my job, Jake. I was stealin' from the hotel, trying to make sure we could feed the children whenever the baby came. How are we gonna survive now?"

Her husband stared at her, his face full of grief. "Sweetheart, we're not stealin' folks," he told her, clearly appalled, his voice full of sorrow.

"I know," she wailed. "I know. How can you ever love me now after what I done? The silverware, the baby . . . I don't belong here with you and the little ones anymore. I ain't fit."

At that, Jake put his hands on either side of his wife's face and looked down into her eyes solemnly. "Noni Fitzgerald, you don't belong nowhere else. Your place is here with us, with your husband and children. We love you no matter what. We'll get through this. You wait and see. We'll figure out somethin'."

Noni dissolved into tears, reaching up to cling to her husband's neck. He kissed her hard before wrapping her in his arms and holding her close, crying with her for all they had lost that day.

Turning away from the intimate moment, Raya began washing her hands in a bowl of cold water. The neighbor woman approached her.

"You go on home. I'll take care of Noni."

Raya shook her head. "I want to stay with her," she argued, her voice hoarse.

"Go on home, now," the woman said again. "You ain't helpin' none, cryin' like you are, and Noni needs to deal with this grief with her husband. I'll see to her safety and then take her little ones back on home with me. Go on now."

Raya took a moment to compose herself, then nodded. The woman was right. Noni needed Jake, not her. Wanting to tell Noni goodbye, but not wanting to interrupt the couple's grieving, she simply squeezed Noni's arm before making her way out from behind the curtain. Henry opened the front door for her, and she shook as the icy wind hit her. After leaving the shanty, she accepted Henry's arm as they walked to the waiting carriage.

"You should have gone back to the hotel. It's late and the horses have been standing out in the cold for a long time," she told him, her voice as numb as her hands. She was shaking from the cold and had been since she left the hotel. Noni's shanty was as cold as her own and Mother Emaline's was back when they were rationing firewood.

"The boss would never forgive me if I left you to walk home after that and without your cloak," Henry told her, motioning to her beautiful black cloak that was now soiled and frozen to the floor of the carriage. "Besides, I covered the horses, and Jake and I polished off a pot of coffee to keep warm while we waited. You'd best get in out of the wind now."

"Thank you, Henry," she said sincerely, stepping up into the carriage and sinking down wearily onto the seat. "Thank you for waiting for me."

He nodded humbly and shut the carriage door.

Raya felt like lying down and curling up under the blanket for warmth, but she had taken it into Noni's to help the woman stay warm. So, she sat straight and sure, controlling her shivering body to the best of her ability, too cold to cry, too full of sorrow to care about the temperature or her comfort.

By the time the carriage came to a stop again, Raya had stopped shivering. When Henry came to help her out, Raya pushed herself to her feet and nearly fell over onto the far seat. Righting herself, she tried to grip the doorframe as she prepared to step down out of the carriage, but found her fingers couldn't grasp it.

"Ms. Applewood?" Henry asked as he held his hand up to her.

"Sorry," she mumbled, the word coming out slurred. She took his hand and stepped down, staggering a little as she did.

Henry let out a low whistle and wrapped his arm around her waist as she stumbled again. "Put your arm around my shoulders, Ms. Applewood."

"Why?" she asked, confused by his request. Arriving at the front door, he knocked quickly. "Is Mother not expecting me?"

Raya asked, confused further. Looking around, she frowned. "Are you sure this is my shanty? Perhaps we're at the wrong house."

"Hold on, ma'am," Henry told her. "You're just too cold. Let's get you inside."

The door opened, allowing a shaft of light to fall out over the dark street, and Raya squinted against the brightness of it.

"Oh, dear!" Mother Emaline exclaimed, stepping back and reaching out to draw Raya inside. "What is going on? What's happened? Why, she's as blue as a Granny's Bonnet!"

"What about a Granny's Bonnet?" Raya asked, feeling happy as she remembered the pretty flower that used to cover the hillsides around Mother Emaline's cabin.

Henry stepped just inside the door and shut it behind him. "She's more than a mite too cold, Ms. Applewood. It's been a long night. Suspected it back at Noni's—her words were starting to slur—but she didn't give me a chance to say anything, and I didn't know what to do about it other than to get her home fast as I could."

"Do about what?" Raya asked innocently.

"What's happened? Why is she back so late? Where has she been?" Mother Emaline asked, pulling Raya across the shanty to her chair, which she pulled close to the hearth before wrapping Raya in a blanket and pushing her into it.

"Don't rightly know all the details, but Noni ended up in the snow back behind the hotel. Ms. Applewood was searching for her all over before she found her. Got down in the snow with her and got all wet. She asked me to take both of them to Noni's, and on the way the baby was pressin' and her water must'a broke cause when I let 'em off, Ms. Applewood's cloak was on the floor and wet. We went into Noni's, which was about as cold as an icebox, not sure how those young'uns could sleep, and Ms. Applewood helped deliver the baby—"

"Noni delivered? Did it . . . ?" Mother Emaline interrupted sadly.

"Stillborn," Raya told her, that one fact standing out clear in her mind. She began to shake violently again, despite the extra blanket Mother Emaline had just wrapped around her.

"Oh!" Mother Emaline cried, tears forming in her kind blue eyes. "Poor Noni."

"Ms. Applewood spent all that time wet and without a cloak. Like I said, it was real cold in there. I never took off my coat and its fur. Normally can't stand to leave it on long indoors, but like I said, I never took it off. Once the baby came and she was ready, I brought her home right quick as I could, but that final stretch... think it was just too much for her."

"Thank you, sir. I appreciate you looking out for her and not leaving her at Noni's. I'm sure you went above and beyond your duty," Mother Emaline said. "You get on home now and warm up yourself. It sounds like you've endured a cold night as well."

Henry tipped his hat and left. As soon as Mother Emaline barred the door, she laid her new quilt from Mr. Fairbury over the back of her chair to warm by the fire, and pulled Raya out of the cocoon she had just put her in.

"I'm fine," Raya protested between chattering teeth. "Just cold and sleepy. If you'll just let me go to bed, I'll be fine."

"Nonsense," Mother Emaline said sternly, working the buttons on Raya's new gown with unsteady hands. Finishing with them, she let it drop to the ground, then wrapped Raya in the blanket she had warmed and put her to bed. Then she added several extra logs to the fire.

"I'm fine," Raya said again, her words still slurred.

Mother Emaline stopped in her bustling about and held Raya's new mirror up in front of her face. "Do you look fine to you?"

Raya was confused by her reflection in the mirror as her face and lips were grayish-blue. "What...?" she asked, shifting her eyes up to Mother Emaline.

"Hypothermia most likely," Mother Emaline responded grimly as she put another blanket on top of her, then slipped both warmed bricks beneath the blankets on Raya's side of the bed. "Hopefully you haven't lost any fingers or toes to frostbite."

"We warmed blankets by the fire and used hot bricks to keep Noni warm," Raya told her sleepily.

"You should have been thinking about keeping yourself warm, too," Mother Emaline chided, adding yet another log to the roaring fire before pulling the hot kettle out of the coals. She poured Raya a cup of steaming water and added just enough cold water from the water pail to make it barely drinkable. Raya could feel the frail lady shake as she helped Raya into a sitting position before forcing her to drink the entire contents of the cup.

Raya struggled to keep her eyes open, exhausted from the long day, the seemingly longer night, and the violent shivering that shook her small frame. Despite trying to listen to what Mother Emaline was saying and the relentless discomfort of her chattering teeth, Raya lost the battle and floated away on an enticing wave of sleepiness.

Thirty

When Raya opened her eyes, everything seemed foggy, and she felt confused. Blinking her eyes several times, the fog began to clear, and things came into focus—the ceiling, the Bible on the top shelf, the fire, Mother Emaline, a man she didn't know. Her gaze slid back to the man standing by the fire. Seeing she was awake, he approached the bed.

"Who are you?" she asked, her words still slurred but less so than the night before.

Mother Emaline stepped up to the bed as well, reaching out to brush the hair out of Raya's eyes. "Dear, this is Dr. Gordon."

"Doctor?" Raya asked, confused.

"Do you remember any of last night, Ms. Applewood?" Dr. Gordon questioned.

At first, her mind felt foggy, but as she attempted to recall the events of the night, they all came rushing back—Noni and the silver spoon, the carriage ride, the baby, the carriage ride home, Mother Emaline putting her to bed.

"Yes," she said weakly, wishing she hadn't, wishing it was a dream that had never happened.

"You got very cold. Too cold. Hypothermia set in. You're lucky to be alive. You're also lucky your mother-in-law here had the good sense to warm you up as she did. You'll likely be sore for a day or two, especially your hands and feet, and very tired, but the danger has passed now. You should make a full recovery."

Raya nodded, staring up at the man as he talked tersely above her. He gave Mother Emaline instructions to keep her warm and give her as much hot tea and broth as she could handle, then left. Before Mother Emaline could finish brewing her a cup of tea, Raya succumbed to sleep again. She roused when Mother Emaline helped her sit up to drink it, but fell back asleep as soon as she laid down flat.

The next time she awoke, candles were lit, and she got the sense it was after dark. Two people sat talking in chairs not far away, and as she turned her head to look at them, their talking stopped.

Mother Emaline stood and stepped forward. "Raya, Atlas has come to look in on you. I'm going to go make some tea. Do try to stay awake long enough to drink it this time."

As Mother Emaline went to the hearth to put the kettle over the fire, Raya watched Atlas Fairbury pull his chair close to the bed. He sat down and leaned forward, resting his elbows on his knees, his face not far from hers. Touched that he would come to look in on her, she resisted the urge to hide beneath the covers, embarrassed that he would see her in such a vulnerable and intimate state.

"How are you feeling?" he asked, peering down into her face, the concern in his expression intense.

"Mmm . . . only chilled now. I believe I'm starting to warm up finally," she answered honestly.

He studied her face for a long moment. When he spoke, both his exasperation and distress were evident. "For goodness' sake, Raya, what were you thinking? Why weren't you wearing your cloak?"

"It was wet," she told him.

"Raya," he groaned, reaching out and touching her face tenderly. "Why is it such a challenge to keep you warm? You have two new cloaks, a carriage to ride home in, and still you nearly died from hypothermia."

"That's surely an exaggeration," she told him, embarrassed.

"I hope so," he replied, his words heartfelt.

"How's Noni? Have you heard?" she asked when he didn't continue.

"She's safe and warm. I sent a doctor over there as soon as I heard what had happened, and I had a load of wood delivered," he answered, running the back of his knuckles down her cheek, before smoothing a wayward strand of her dark hair. "Are you warm enough? Can I get you anything?"

"Did you hear about the baby?" she asked weakly, the memory returning and, with it, fresh tears.

His head dropped. "Yes. 'Tis a terrible thing. I will forever regret any part I had in it."

Raya reached out from under her cocoon and took his hand, her heart filling with compassion. "You had no part in it. Noni said she had felt for a few days that something wasn't right. The baby wasn't moving. She delivered last night, but the child was likely gone before she ever went into labor."

He enveloped her hand in both of his, squeezing it as he nodded his understanding, his expression still sad.

"Your hands are warm," Raya said sleepily, feeling comforted by the warmth of his touch. He ran his thumb back and forth over the smooth skin of her wrist, his expression turning tender.

"I wish I could warm you up," he said softly with a lopsided smile.

"I hope you're not trying to go back to sleep already, Raya," Mother Emaline said from the table where she was pouring a steaming cup of tea. "Atlas, would you be a dear and help her sit up to drink this?"

"Of course," he answered.

"I can manage," Raya protested, attempting to push herself up into a sitting position. Her muscles felt strangely weak, and the simple task of repositioning felt taxing. She didn't protest when he slipped Mother Emaline's pillow behind her own and pulled the blankets up around her as she settled in a semi-upright position. For just a moment, she let him fuss over her, enjoying his tender care.

He stepped back as Mother Emaline approached with a cup of hot tea. Taking the seat Mr. Fairbury had vacated, the older woman watched Raya drink it, then helped her lay back down when the tea was gone.

Raya's eyes again turned to Mr. Fairbury. "Is your carriage here?"

"Yes," he answered hesitantly.

"I would very much like to go see Noni," she told him, moving to sit up again.

Mother Emaline held her down. "No, ma'am. You're going to stay in bed and sleep and drink hot tea, just as the doctor ordered."

"I promised her I would go check on her," Raya protested, determined.

"She'll understand," Mr. Fairbury assured, stepping close again. "You can go once you're feeling better."

Raya started to protest once more, but he continued. "What if I come for you tomorrow afternoon, and if you're feeling up for it, we'll go together? I'd like to check in on her myself, but tonight the hour is late."

"Is it?" Raya asked, glancing at the curtained window. He nodded. "Very well," she conceded. "Tomorrow."

Mr. Fairbury watched to make sure Raya drank the second cup of tea Emaline brought her, then made her promise to be a good patient and listen to Emaline. He squeezed her fingertips gently before telling both women goodnight and going off into the night. Mother Emaline warmed the bricks and placed them at Raya's feet, then came to bed herself. Despite sleeping all day, Raya had no problem sleeping deeply through the night.

***

The next afternoon, Raya was dressed and ready to go by the time Mr. Fairbury knocked on the door of their shanty. Mother Emaline opened the door, and Raya stood to her feet, leaving the blanket she had been holding around her shoulders in the chair.

"Good afternoon," Mr. Fairbury told them cheerfully. He held out Raya's black cloak. "I had it laundered, and it's ready to wear again."

"Thank you," Raya told him gratefully, thankful she wouldn't have to go back to wearing her thin one. She pulled it around her shoulders and fastened it, then went to the door, eager to see Noni. She would feel better once she could see with her own eyes how her friend was doing. At the door, she drew her hood up over her hair, ready to face the icy wind. She had one hand on the latch when Mr. Fairbury stopped her with a hand on her arm.

"You're not going out like that, not after just getting warm enough to stop shivering. If you will give me a minute, I've brought some things to keep you comfortable." He pulled a pair of soft, white kid gloves out of his pocket and held them out to her. Choosing not to waste her strength on protesting, she pulled them on, followed by the fur hat he extended to her. He drew the hood of her cloak up over her hat, and tugged on the edges, shooting her a smile. Next, Mother Emaline held a blanket out to him, and he drew it around her shoulders. Finally, he seemed satisfied that she would stay warm.

Once in the carriage, he tucked the lap blanket around her bundled frame before sitting down opposite her. They were both quiet as they crossed the distance between Raya's shanty and Noni's, save a few simple questions and answers about how things were going at the hotel and his frequent inquires as to whether or not she was warm enough.

When the carriage stopped outside Noni's, Mr. Fairbury collected the blankets to take in to warm by the fire while they visited. Jake opened the door at Raya's knock and directed Raya to where Noni was resting on the bed behind the curtain. Mr. Fairbury stayed with Jake and the children near the fire.

Raya sat on the bed beside Noni and held her hand as the girl simply stared at the ceiling. They talked a little but about nothing of substance. Raya asked how the children were and how Noni was feeling. Noni gave short answers, but she clung tightly to Raya's hand throughout the visit. Looking down into her friend's face, Raya's heart constricted painfully. She understood only too well how difficult it was to process grief. Sometimes, in the middle of it, one simply didn't know how to be or how to let someone in, and she recognized that now in Noni. Sometimes the pain was just too big for words. And when it was, it was simply enough to be there. Raya kept a firm hold on her hand and was content to simply sit in the silence with her.

As she sat quietly, slowly it registered how much warmer it was in the little shanty than it had been the last time she was there, and she was glad for it. Noni would get better sooner if she didn't have to fight the cold. As the silence stretched over the next hour, Raya noticed Noni growing drowsy. Knowing firsthand the ordeal her friend had been through physically, she gave Noni a hug and bid her farewell, leaving her to sleep.

When they were back in the carriage, Raya turned and stared out the window, trying to conceal the emotions that were running so high within her. Noni had quite obviously cried out all her tears for the time being, but Raya had not. Too numbed by the hypothermia, she had not truly felt the emotions of the traumatic night until she walked back through Noni's door and sat with her friend.

Now, as the carriage pulled away from the shanty, her tears began to fall.

Seeing them, Mr. Fairbury's head fell forward, almost in defeat. "Please, don't do that. Don't cry, Raya."

She tried to blink her tears away but couldn't. "She was so little. So perfect. Not so little as my nephew, but still far too small to survive. I seem to only ever hold dead babies, Mr. Fairbury," Raya admitted, her tears giving way to sobs. Was that all she was ever to hold? Babies who were dead or dying? The thought wrenched her heart. She longed to kiss the warm cheek of a baby, hear its gusty sigh, hold it in her arms and rock it for hours on end.

Across from her, Mr. Fairbury groaned. "Raya," he pleaded, his voice hoarse. "Please don't."

"I wanted to help, but I didn't know how. And then today . . . I didn't know what to say to her," she admitted, her grief spilling out into the cold carriage.

In one fluid motion, Mr. Fairbury moved across the space to sit beside her. He seemed to hesitate for just a moment, then wrapped his arms around her and held her as she cried. He tucked her in against him and set his chin on top of her head.

His arms warmed her more than anything else had in the past few days, and Raya wished he would keep them around her forever. She turned into him, laying her cheek against his chest.

Her tears for Noni, for her family, and for the stillborn baby fell freely, but as the carriage slowed to a stop, she wiped her eyes on the hem of the blanket. She was determined not to add her sorrow to Mother Emaline's burden.

"We could ride a few more blocks if you wish," Mr. Fairbury offered, his voice hopeful, still holding her against his chest.

Laughter bubbled out of Raya at his kind offer, the sound foreign in the sorrowful atmosphere. She was tempted to take him up on it as she wiped at her eyes. The thought of spending a few more minutes cradled against him, bleeding off the emotions raised by their visit to Noni's, was comforting.

"Just until you feel ready to return to Cousin Emaline."

After a brief hesitation, Raya shook her head. "I'm sure she's heard the horses."

With a nod, Mr. Fairbury released her, then turned his top hat round and round in his hands. He quickly stepped out of the carriage when the door was opened for them and turned to help Raya down. He followed her into the shanty, where Mother Emaline was waiting with hot tea and fresh cookies.

He helped Raya out of her cloak and then carried one of the chairs from the table over to the fire so they could all sit together. Raya sat down in the one he'd brought over, leaving the middle chair for him. She ate her cookie and drank her tea slowly as Mother Emaline and Mr. Fairbury carried on the conversation. She was content to listen as she continued to sort through her sadness

UP FROM THE ASH HEAP

from both the situation at Noni's and the memories of the fire it had stirred up. When Mr. Fairbury stood to leave, Mother Emaline carried his cup and saucer to the washbasin along with her own, and he stopped in front of Raya.

"I have to go," he told her, sounding apologetic.

She nodded. "Thank you for taking me to see Noni. And for your company and for sending the doctor yesterday." She finished her last bite of cookie. "Please tell Ms. Macy and Henry that I'll be at the hotel as usual in the morning."

"I wish you would take another day to rest and recover," he told her, tucking a strand of dark hair behind her ear.

"I'm feeling quite well," she answered, hoping to reassure him.

Resting his hands on the arms of her chair, he bent down until he was at her eye level. "I wish," he started, reaching out to tip her chin up so she had no choice but to look at him.

As she lifted her eyes up to meet his, she could see he lost everything he was about to say. His gaze fell from her eyes to her mouth, and she held her breath. "I wish," he repeated, and in his eyes she could see everything he wished. Her heart raced, and a painful lump swelled in the back of her throat. She dropped her eyes. He straightened and stepped back. "Please don't come in tomorrow if you feel the least bit poorly. Don't worry about your pay. I will take care of your needs, regardless."

She folded her hands tightly in her lap, her head bowed again.

"Thank you for allowing me to accompany you today. I'm exceedingly glad you're feeling better," he said, tenderly touching the top of her bowed head before turning to leave. He stopped to bid Mother Emaline goodbye, and Raya heard the front door shut behind him.

Mother Emaline came to sit beside her, and Raya stared into the fire. Emaline reached out and took her hand, holding it between both of her own. "I think Atlas cares for you, Raya," she started softly. "I think he's shown it a hundred times in a hundred ways."

Raya neither affirmed nor denied Mother Emaline's statement but simply continued to watch the flames dance over the burning logs.

"You have nothing to say?"

"I'm in mourning," Raya answered very carefully.

"And if you were not?" Mother Emaline pushed.

"But I am," Raya answered, standing, and going to the fire, where she held her hands out to the warmth. "Thus, there is no need to consider anything else."

The truth was, a war was waging within her. Atlas Fairbury was stealing her heart, and yet she was as dark-skinned and socially outcast as ever. She wasn't worthy of being his bride, and nothing could ever change that.

Thirty-One

"I'm so glad you brought this beautiful girl over today," Raya said, studying Bella's sweet face as she slept.

Noni smiled from where she sat on the floor, her back against the rock of the fireplace, close to the fire for warmth. She had come over half an hour earlier, surprising and delighting Raya. Raya happened to be home by order of Ms. Macy, who had insisted she take a day off, and was thrilled to see the mother and daughter standing outside her door, hoping for a visit. Now, Raya was sitting in the rocker with Bella snuggled in close against her. The one-year-old had succumbed to sleep as she grew warm and cozy after making the cold walk over with her mother.

"It does the heart good to hold a baby, doesn't it?" Noni agreed.

Raya nodded. "That it does." She finally looked up from Bella's perfect features. "How are you feeling?"

"Better every day, mostly," Noni said. "I've just realized it is how life is. Sometimes, little ones don't make it in this world. Only thing you can do is love 'em well while you got 'em and let 'em go when the good LORD calls 'em home. Just sometimes, He calls 'em home earlier than you think He will," Noni answered, her eyes filling with tears. She blinked them back. "Just takes a while, you know, to find peace with that. Some days, it just doesn't seem fair."

Raya nodded and bit her lip. It had been three weeks since the birth of Noni's baby, and yet it still felt fresh and raw to Raya. She could not imagine how Noni must feel.

"Noni, peace does come," Mother Emaline offered, sipping her hot tea. "Sometimes we lose much, and sometimes we don't know why, but you hold on to the good memories and to love. Let go of all the bad and all the bitterness and anger that tries to sneak in to tell you it wasn't fair that you experienced loss. Peace does come, and when it does, you realize you were given the greatest gift, which was to have and hold your sweet child for the time you did."

Raya watched the unshed tears glistening in her mother-in-law's eyes, matching those shining in Noni's.

"I have lost two children before their birth and three in life. I spent many days complaining it wasn't fair, but then I realized life isn't fair, and I was never promised it would be, only that I have been given a hope and a future. I have a God who loves me, has redeemed me, and has a plan for my life. His plan for me doesn't look like His plan for you or for Raya, but be it as it may, it is for the best, and one day I will understand why. Until then, it is enough that I can trust Him. When you have that and you choose that day after day, then over time it isn't so important what's fair or unfair."

Noni nodded, a tear slipping down her cheek. "I understand."

Silence stretched as both young women in the room tried to absorb the advice of a woman who had loved and lost much, yet still loved so well.

"How's Jake feeling?" Raya finally asked.

"Some better too. The fevers are gone for the most part."

"Is he able to return to work?" Raya asked, concerned. She knew the family had hardly been making it with Noni working; what they had must have run out within a week of Noni losing her job. Raya didn't know how they were surviving now.

"No. He's not been able to find nothin', and he hasn't been well enough to look more than a few days," Noni answered, wiping her nose with the back of her hand.

"Have you found other work?" Mother Emaline asked, sharing Raya's concern.

"No, ma'am. Was told I shouldn't go lookin' for at least a month. Otherwise, our needs would stop being provided for."

"What do you mean?" Raya asked, confused.

"Mr. Fairbury came by the day after the baby came. The day before he came with you. He told Jake he couldn't hire me back at the hotel because of my stealin' and all, and he wouldn't let me come to work anyways in my condition, but that if I would rest for a month, he'd give me a second chance at one of his other businesses, or he said I could seek employment elsewhere if I'd rather. Jake told him we didn't have the money for me to spend a month laid up in bed with him outta work. Mr. Fairbury said he'd see to our needs until I was better. Ever since then, wood and groceries have been delivered once a week, and when Jake went to talk to the landlord 'bout our rent, he said it had already been paid."

Raya stared at Noni, shocked. "Mr. Fairbury?"

"Yes. I say, we've been eatin' like kings since he started having groceries delivered. Some kind of meat at every meal. Luke doesn't complain about being hungry no more and there's milk for Bella. It's gonna be hard to go back to the way things was when I go back to work, but be that as it is, we don't expect nothin' more from Mr. Fairbury. He's already done more for us than he ought."

"As he has for us," Mother Emaline echoed.

Raya looked down at Bella's peaceful face and ran her fingertips over the baby's delicate features, her button nose, her chubby cheeks, her sweet little mouth, and her perfect eyebrows. Raya's throat began to ache, and tears sprang unbidden in her eyes. Atlas Fairbury had provided for the sweet baby, just as he was providing for them. He was giving her the milk she needed to grow, as well as fuel for the fire to keep her warm at night. He was giving Noni a chance to rest and recover, giving not only her body, but her mind time to heal.

He truly was the kindest of men. Her heart swelled with admiration of his character, but mostly from love. He gave penniless, destitute foreigners a chance. He concerned himself with the needs of struggling families. He took care of and provided for the widow of his late, distant cousin. He ruled his small empire with kindness and praise, endearing himself to all those who worked for him, from the head of his kitchen to his hotel manager to the stable hands out back.

And she had fallen deeply in love with him.

She wanted to set aside the child and run to him wherever he might be. She wanted to kiss him like she had the night behind the stable, have him wrap her in his arms as he did in the carriage, and spend every day of her life living in the light of his loving kindness.

Yet, she was not worthy. Her skin was dark, her place of origin unsavory in his world. She was poor and destitute and would bring him shame. He deserved a bride who would bring him nothing but honor and respect and good things. She couldn't do that.

Most of all, she appeared to be barren and what good was a wife who could not bear her husband's fruit? Atlas Fairbury deserved children—family—sons to pass his small empire down to. What a legacy he had to leave. Yet, no matter how much she might want to, she couldn't provide that either.

Dropping her head, she sniffed discreetly and blinked back her tears, hoping to keep her thoughts and feelings private. To have admitted such things to herself was like a painful weight on her chest, but to admit them to Mother Emaline or Noni would be sheer torture.

Noni stayed another hour, and Raya tried her best to enjoy every moment of her visit. Bella awoke, and Raya played with her on the floor. The little darling made the women laugh with her sweet baby ways and senseless chatter. She chased the kittens on hands and knees, and the kittens chased her. She sought refuge in Raya's ever-ready arms. When Noni finally stood and said they needed to go, Raya scooped little Bella up from the floor and gave her a big kiss on both of her sweet cheeks. She hugged her hard before tickling the baby girl to elicit a few more precious chuckles.

Watching her, Noni smiled. "I'm glad Mr. Fairbury asked me to come over today and bring Bella. I never realized you would enjoy her so much."

Raya looked up quickly. "Mr. Fairbury suggested you come today?"

Noni looked unsure, as if wondering if she had said something wrong. Then she shrugged. "Yes. He said you would be off, and it would be a good day to come for a visit. He said to make sure to bring Bella; that you would enjoy her company."

"When did he tell you this?" Raya asked, eager to hear the answer.

"A few days ago."

So, Mr. Fairbury told Noni to come and bring Bella, then told Ms. Macy to insist Raya take the day off. Raya nodded slowly as she put the pieces together. She kissed Bella's cheek once more before releasing her to her mother. She watched as Noni expertly maneuvered a long piece of fabric to strap Bella to her chest, where the little one could ride sheltered and warm under her mother's cloak on their walk home. Raya went to the hearth to find the kitten Noni had selected, and brought it back with her, watching as Mother Emaline embraced the young woman and her daughter.

Seeing how Noni clung to Mother Emaline, Raya smiled, recognizing how much Noni appreciated Emaline's mothering spirit in her vulnerable state. When Mother Emaline released the young woman, Raya walked Noni to the door and gave her a firm hug, pressing a kiss against her cheek as well as another one against the baby's. She handed her the wiggling kitten and held the door for her as the mother and baby went out into the cold.

When she turned back around, she saw Mother Emaline had laid out on the bed Raya's Sunday best, which had been packed away since they left Colorado Territory.

"What do you mean to do with that?" Raya asked, surprised. The light of the flames danced over the peach silk of the gown, transforming it into the color of a fiery sunset.

"It's funny, Raya, isn't it? How everything has its time, and then it's over and it's time for something new?" Mother Emaline asked as she smoothed the wrinkles out of the dress.

Raya shrugged her shoulders, puzzled by Mother Emaline's actions and words. "Yes, I suppose it is."

"Like Noni. She carried her baby for nearly seven beautiful months. She felt the little one move and anticipated her arrival, but for whatever reason, the good LORD said it was time for the child to return to heaven. The time came when Noni's body had to physically let the baby go. If her body hadn't done so, the child wouldn't have come back to life. Noni's life simply would have been in jeopardy as well. Now, Noni has the task of looking toward the future and taking care of her family. If she didn't let go and move on, what would become of little Luke and Bella?"

"They need their mother," Raya agreed, recalling Bella's adorable smiles and squeezable cheeks.

"Life gives us loss sometimes, Raya, and we need to stop and grieve, and allow ourselves time to heal. But then it's time to move on." Mother Emaline was quiet for a long time, and Raya stood silently, honoring her contemplative mood. Finally, the woman reached out for Raya's hand. "You were a good wife to my son, but he's been gone nearly half a year now, and your time of mourning is over. It's time to take off your black and move on." Raya shook her head, but Mother Emaline patted her hand. "Holding on won't bring him back, Raya. It's time to move forward. The sparkle has returned to your eyes, and you don't cry when I say his name anymore. And that's good, honey, not bad. It's time to move on."

"I don't know how," Raya protested, feeling hurt by Mother Emaline's words. Did the woman think Raya was forgetting her son? Though in some ways, their life in Colorado Territory felt like a different lifetime, she would never forget the man who taught her the meaning of faith and family, the first man whom she had known to be kind, the first man she had ever loved. To have Mother Emaline think she had forgotten about him was hurtful. On the other hand, they had left Colorado Territory, traveled east, Raya had taken a job, worked hard, made new friends, and now Mother Emaline was telling her it was time to move on. She didn't know how to move on any more than she already had. She was confused by Mother Emaline's words and message.

"We have to think of the future, Raya, of your happiness. Perhaps it's time to consider taking a husband."

Caught off-guard, Raya turned to start folding the blanket Bella had used. She failed to keep a bite out of her voice when she spoke. "And just who would you have me marry, Mother?"

She had received numerous marriage proposals from both drunken and sober men on the street, yet not one of them was worth entertaining. Especially not when she had Mother Emaline to consider. And anyone who would be a suitable husband—both willing and able to provide for Mother Emaline also—did not or could not consider Raya a suitable bride. The entire issue stung.

She didn't expect the older lady to have a comeback, but Mother Emaline did. "Atlas Fairbury."

Raya's back straightened in surprise as she stood, turning to the older woman. "Atlas Fairbury?" she echoed. Had Mother Emaline lost her mind?

"Yes," Emaline answered simply.

Raya stared at her for several long moments. "Do you forget who I am, what I look like, or from what people I originate? Surely, you must know I am not the kind of woman Atlas Fairbury could marry." Her honest words brought tears to her own eyes. Did Mother Emaline know how hurtful her suggestion was?

"He loves you and is proclaiming it for all the world to see," Emaline countered. "Go ask Henry, Ms. Macy, Noni, Mr. Lenox, or any of the others, and I'm sure they will tell you. He's not being subtle in his affection for you, Raya. He's lavished it on you," the woman finished with a happy smile.

"Look at me!" Raya cried. "I cannot marry Atlas Fairbury . . . or rather I should say, he cannot marry me! I'm not a woman he can take to his social gatherings or important dinners. I'm not a woman who could stand by his side and bring him respect and honor. I'm not worthy of his love or his name!"

"So, you have no objection to the man himself? His age does not concern you?" Mother Emaline asked, sitting pristinely on the bed beside the airing garment.

His age? Raya shook her head in confusion. He was less than ten years older than Luke had been, in his thirties, and still exceedingly handsome. His years had given him confidence, compassion, and wisdom, all of which were incredibly attractive to her. His age was something she had never considered, nor really even noticed. How could she think of his age, when he kept her mind spinning with his kind acts, thoughtful ways, and charming smile? "His age is of no concern."

"And what of him? What do you think of the man, Atlas Fairbury?"

"I . . . I think he's the kindest and most generous man I've ever known."

"Do you think you could find it in your heart to love him one day?" Mother Emaline asked, a knowing smile on her face.

Raya pressed her eyes shut to stop the tears. "I think I already do, but that is not the issue," she said, frustrated by Mother Emaline's lack of reasoning. "I do not deserve him, and he certainly deserves much more than me."

"Then, darling, why don't you let him decide that?" Mother Emaline waited several beats, then continued. "He is family, Raya, and would carry on the line of my husband in a distant way. He has shown himself to be a man of great honor and mercy. As your mother, I find him to be a suitable match for you, my beloved daughter."

"What do you want me to do?" Raya asked hesitantly, her cheeks burning, knowing whatever Mother Emaline instructed, as her mother, she must obey.

"Why don't you take a bath and put on your peach gown? Let me do your hair and wear some of my perfume. Tonight is the dinner Mr. Fairbury is hosting at his home for all his management, as well as many important business acquaintances. It's said by many to be the highlight of the season... a bright spot in the dreary days of winter. As you know, you were invited."

"But I shouldn't have been! You know I wasn't going to go. He certainly doesn't need a bread maker crowding his table. I don't belong there."

"Well, I'm asking you to go. But instead of going in to the dinner, I want you to go upstairs, slip into his bedchamber, and wait for him there. It's the one place in the entire house you can be certain you will encounter only Mr. Fairbury."

Raya stared at her, appalled. "Why, Mother! He'll think I'm a loose woman trying to seduce him."

"He knows exactly what kind of woman you are," Mother Emaline argued confidently. "He will admire your bravery and be touched by your effort to speak with him privately."

Raya stared at her for several long moments, feeling very near to tears. She was frightened and appalled to do as Mother Emaline asked, yet knew she must do exactly that. She knew her mother-in-law only had her best interest in mind, and Raya respected her and wanted to honor her in all things; but this went against everything her sense of propriety told her.

"I'll do as you've instructed," Raya told her slowly, the words difficult to form.

Mother Emaline smiled and went to retrieve the washtub. As Raya went out to begin hauling water for her bath, she had to concentrate on taking deep, steadying breaths. She had only that day been honest enough to fully admit to herself that she was in love with Atlas Fairbury. Now, against her better judgment, she was to offer herself in marriage and be at the complete mercy of his reply. If he refused her, she would be utterly crushed. If he accepted her, she would become his wife. Both options were terrifying.

Mother Emaline heated water over the fire until the washtub was full enough to allow her to bathe. Raya stepped into the warm water and sought refuge in the peace of it. But the shanty was chilly, even with extra logs on the fire, and Raya was forced to commence quickly with her bathing practices. When she had washed with a bar of rose scented soap and rinsed off the lather, Mother Emaline helped her wash her long hair. When it, too, was rinsed clean, Mother Emaline held out a towel that had been warming by the fire. Raya wrapped herself in it as she stepped out of the tub.

After she was dry, she pulled on her silk gown, not as fashionably made as the black one Mr. Fairbury had given her for Christmas, but beautiful because of its brilliant color. Its ruffled skirt had creamy lace paired with the sunset glow of the silk, and the fitted bodice was snug and fit her like a glove. The neckline was scooped, and the sleeves were tight to the elbows where they widened and hung in ruffles of cream-colored lace around her forearms. It had been a long while since she had worn anything so formfitting, and she felt self-conscience and uncomfortable. Luke used to say any man who missed her in that dress must be blind, but now she wondered how it would compare to the genteel fashions of the city to a man like Atlas Fairbury.

As Mother Emaline brushed through Raya's long, wet hair, Raya ran her fingers over the delicate fabric, feeling wonder at wearing something other than black once again. She had worn nothing else for nearly six months. She wondered what Mr. Fairbury would think of her colorful appearance.

Mother Emaline curled and styled her hair until it looked exactly like the hairdos of the women Raya saw in the hotel the first night they arrived in Cincinnati. It was swept back with a cascade of curls falling down the back of her head, neck, and back. No braid, no bun, just soft ringlet curls and pins holding them in place. Raya admired the hairdo in the mirror Mr. Fairbury had given her, then put it down as Mother Emaline dabbed perfume onto her neck and wrists.

When Mother Emaline stepped back, Raya took a deep breath and stood, smoothing the front of her dress. She reached for her heavy black woolen cloak, but Mother Emaline held out her brown and cream colored one that Atlas had given her first instead. As Raya took the garment she had barely remembered she possessed, her breath caught in amazement as she realized the same sunset silk that comprised her dress also lined the inside of her cloak.

"What a stunning coincidence," Mother Emaline observed, a surprised smile filling her face. "It's as if the cloak and dress were made for each other for a night such as this."

Raya laughed in delight as she pulled the heavy garment on and fastened it over her collarbone. This one was even heavier and finer than her black one, and she spent a long moment enjoying the feel of it. "Perhaps so."

Mother Emaline helped her pull on her soft kid gloves, then kissed her cheek and embraced her warmly before pressing the coins for a horse cart into her palm. "You have found favor in his eyes and in the eyes of God. You'll see. Now go and hurry to come back to tell me what he has said."

After embracing Mother Emaline one last time, Raya opened the door to the shanty and hurried out into the cold, making her way down frozen streets, staying in the shadows for protection until she came to a part of town where horse carts were more readily available. Flagging one down, she lifted her skirt as she stepped up into the cart. She folded her hands tightly in her lap and prayed fervently as she was carried swiftly to Mr. Fairbury's estate.

She watched in childlike wonder as the trotting horses turned onto a long lane, passing through a grand iron gate. Gardens spilled to the left and the right, and at the end of the lane was a beautiful house, so grand and large that Raya felt unworthy of stepping foot in it. To think she would be asking Mr. Fairbury to make her the mistress of such a house made her mouth go dry and her knees shake. To ask such a thing was not only brazen, but absurd. Yet, she had promised Mother Emaline.

As they neared the grand house, she drew her hood up over her hair and let it fall forward, shadowing her face for privacy. Taking a deep breath, she exited the horse cart at the front door and only had to go a few steps before she was surrounded on all sides by those going into the party. She had not realized how large the affair would be and wondered if she even knew of all the businesses he owned. Surely not, if such a crowd could be attracted among his management and those he did business with.

Once inside, she moved with the crowd up the right side of the large mirrored staircases, trying to take in the splendor of his house while also keeping an eye out for the one she sought, not wanting to reveal her presence too soon. If she did, she knew he would be entirely distracted for the rest of the night and would make her take part in his party. If she was made to face all those around her for an entire evening, many of whom were already shooting her suspicious glances, she knew she would never be able to maintain her courage to do as Mother Emaline had instructed. No, she needed to stay hidden within the crowd until she could escape to a quiet and solitary place.

Once she reached the top of the staircase, she spotted him at the entrance of what looked to be a large ballroom. She quickly turned to the right, moving away from the crowd, down a less populated hall. At the end of the hall, she found another staircase going up, and she took it, assuming there would be bed chambers on the third floor. She guessed correctly, and she peeked in several, taking extra care to be quiet, until she found the one she believed belonged to him. Entering the room, she glanced from the large, canopied bed, to the fire burning cheerily in the large stone fireplace, to the cushioned window seat in front of one of the large paned windows.

Feeling as if she had stepped into another world she knew nothing of, she simply stood and stared for several minutes, completely stunned that the man who had eaten Christmas dinner in their shanty lived in a home such as this. She had known their humble home must seem like a lowly dwelling in his eyes, but she now saw she had only begun to understand to what extent. Their entire residence would fit in half of his bedchamber; she had never seen such luxury.

Coming to her senses, she quickly crossed to the wardrobe and opened the cupboard, leaning in to inspect the clothing. While she believed it to be his bedchamber, she wasn't certain. She didn't want to be found in someone else's, especially considering the likelihood he would be entertaining guests and the late hour at which the event was sure to conclude.

Recognizing the large coat she herself had worn on a few different occasions, she leaned in and filled her lungs with the scent of him, breathing deeply of the man she had come to love.

She quietly shut the cupboard door and went to sit before the fire. It would be hours before he returned to his room. Settling in one of the large wing chairs, she folded her hands in her lap and watched the merry dance of the fire as she waited.

As the hours ticked by, Raya tried to wait patiently, but in the quiet solitude of his room, every minute felt like an hour, and her nerves were wound tight. Her hands and knees were shaking, thinking about what she would say, what he might say, and the implications. She didn't know what she would do if he said no, and she didn't know what she would do if he said yes. In fact, she didn't even know what she was going to say when he walked in the door.

If he had changed his mind or reconsidered, how would her position at the hotel be affected? Without her job, she and Mother Emaline would be in as dire of straights as they were back in October.

Raya recalled the night when he had followed her out to the carriage and ended up sharing his feelings, trying to take comfort in that, but that had been over a month ago. A lot could happen in a month's time. Besides, feeling something for someone was different from marrying them. Experiencing the emotions of love was altogether different from the realization that marriage to her would be disgraceful.

Driving herself crazy with her doubts, she pushed herself to her feet and began wandering around his large bedchambers, hoping for a distraction. She had never been in a room so fine, and yet it fit him too. She could picture him here, sitting in the wing chair in front of the fire, standing and gazing out at the gardens. She crossed the room to do so, too, and touched her hand against the cold glass, finding the view spectacular. Below, she could see the closest terrace of the gardens, the circular drive where she had been dropped off, and the large marble stairs that led from the house down to it. She saw that people were beginning to leave, and drivers were picking up their charges. First, excitement and then dread filled her, knowing the party was starting to wind down. Her wait wouldn't be much longer.

Turning back to the room, she was seized by a moment of panic, one of many she had experienced since Mother Emaline relayed her orders for the evening. She was secretly sitting in Mr. Fairbury's bedchambers, waiting for him to return. He did not know she was in his house, much less his personal chambers, and the very thought of it felt scandalous. She had no intention of seducing him, nor did she think him a man easily given to seduction, but if anyone found out she was waiting for him in his bedchamber, no one would believe her... or even possibly him. The last thing she wanted to do was bring him shame. She thought again of simply slipping out of the room quietly, before he returned, but she remembered Mother Emaline's words and so reluctantly remained where she was.

Though shocking and rather extreme, Raya saw the wisdom behind Mother Emaline's instructions. Mr. Fairbury had been so busy that she had barely seen him during the past few weeks, much less had an opportunity to talk to him. Should she have, it would have been in the company of others, which was no place to have a conversation like the one they needed to have. Here, in his private quarters, she would have the opportunity to speak with him at length with no one else around. If he turned her proposal of marriage down, she would not become the laughingstock of the town. If he accepted, he would have the opportunity to tell people as he wished, without having to worry about rumors arising from eavesdroppers. Either way, a private conversation would ensure they had the time and privacy needed.

Feeling calmer again, she returned to the window and her gaze drifted to the gardens once more, before rising up to the dark sky which hung like the velvet canopy of Mr. Fairbury's bed. She gazed up into the dark vastness of it and admired the stars that shone so brightly.

Suddenly, she heard footsteps in the hall, and her heart raced. As they drew closer, she instinctively knew they weren't his. He was solidly built; these footsteps sounded light. Glancing at the fire and realizing a servant was likely coming in to tend it for the night, Raya looked for a place to hide. With the footsteps drawing near, she quickly stepped up onto the window seat and moved to the back edge of it, where the heavy drapery shielded her from sight. As she had guessed, she heard the door latch turn, then the humming of a woman and the sound of logs being added to the fire. Raya held her breath, terrified of being discovered. Surely, if she was discovered, the whole night would turn upside down and go very wrong.

However, the servant left again as peacefully as she had come, never the wiser. Raya waited for quite some time after she heard the door latch again, then sat down to wait longer. She looked longingly at the fire, which held the promise of light and warmth, yet chose to stay seated at the drafty window. She liked the view from where she sat. Additionally, watching the people below provided a welcome distraction from the minutes that felt like hours. Sitting in the shadows cast by thick window drapes in a dark room save the light of the fire, she had found a place where she could observe the comings and goings without worry of being seen.

Though the hour was late, she could still hear the musicians playing below, so knew the party was not yet over, despite the number of guests who were departing in search of a good night's sleep. Covering a yawn with the back of her hand, she settled in to wait, knowing it would be a while longer before Mr. Fairbury returned to his room, and she would have the opportunity to ask him what she had been sent to ask.

Thirty-Two

Atlas trailed a hand along the wall as he made his way down the hall to his bedchamber, still a bit dizzy from all the dancing he had done earlier in the evening. After dinner had concluded, he felt obliged to dance with the ladies who had attended without an escort. His favorite three dances of the night had been with a nine-year-old named Lyna. She was the daughter of his shipping manager, and the precious child made him laugh with her wild imagination and exaggerated perception of what it was like to be a grownup in high society. Atlas chuckled again now, thinking about the winsome girl.

Despite the enjoyable evening, he was tired after entertaining so many guests, and was looking forward to falling into his bed to get some sleep before morning came, which it always seemed to do too quickly. Opening the door to his bedchamber, he reached down and pulled his shirttails out of his trousers, then took off his tailcoat, ready to lay it over the back of the wingchair.

As he entered his room, a flash of color near the window caught his eye. Looking up, he came to a quick stop, his glance turning into a stare. He stood in the middle of the floor for a long moment, trying to figure out what to make of the situation, then slowly approached the window.

Raya Applewood was lying asleep on his cushioned window seat, and she was by far the most beautiful sight he had ever beheld. She was adorned in an orange silk dress and dark curls fell over her shoulders. He stood perfectly still and watched her sleep for several moments, wondering how she came to be there, curious about her sudden adornment of color, but mostly just enjoying watching her sleep. Taking advantage of the unhurried moment, he took in every detail of her beautiful face. He admired the dusty hue of her skin, the delicate line of her jaw, and the way her long dark lashes fanned out over her cheeks. He noted how the colorful silk bodice of her dress tightly hugged the curves of her womanly frame before it disappeared into the fullness of her silk and lace skirt, and he marveled at finally seeing her dressed in something other than black. Her chest rose and fell peacefully as she slept, and he felt hesitant to disturb her peaceful slumber. She was truly altogether lovely and a beautiful thing to behold. He was tempted to simply pull up a chair and watch her all night long, but finally, his curiosity got the best of him.

He reached down and gently pushed a curl off her face, waking her with his touch. When she opened her beautiful eyes, she looked as confused as he for a moment. Recovering, she quickly stood to her feet as he watched a fetching blush rise in her cheeks.

Though tempted to reach down and hold her hands, he kept himself in check. He wanted to know the nature of her late-night visit without flustering her more than she already was. Whatever the reason, she had shown great courage in coming, and he would let her have her say.

***

Raya's heart dropped as she stood before Atlas Fairbury in his bedchamber. Every plan she had made as she waited for him dissipated as she realized she had fallen asleep. He had come in and found her sleeping in his room. What must he think of her? Her heart raced, and she kept her eyes on the ground. She'd made a mess out of everything. She was more tempted to run away from him and the errand she had been sent on by Mother Emaline, than to stay and try to explain herself.

Yet, here she was, and he was standing in front of her, watching her curiously, waiting for an explanation. If she left tonight, she would never be able to face him again. She would burn with embarrassment every time he came into the hotel kitchen; it would change everything. So, she gathered all the courage she possessed and started trying to explain that which felt unexplainable.

"I'm sorry. I was waiting . . . for you . . . I didn't mean to fall asleep," she told him, stumbling over her words as she sought some way to explain her uninvited presence in his bedchamber, much less her sleeping state.

"It's very late," he told her, his voice kind. "Anyone sitting in so dark a chamber at so late an hour would be susceptible to giving way to sleep. I only wish I had known you were here. I would have come sooner." He paused, reaching out to carefully pull a wayward curl out of her face and tuck it back into place. "I was hoping and watching for your arrival all night, but alas, I thought you did not come. I see now I simply wasn't looking in the right place. I would love to know how you missed the party and ended up in my bedchamber."

She could hear the smile in his voice, and perhaps if she was not so nervous herself, she would have been able to smile with him. "I know it's very strange for me to come here and . . . be here, but I came to ask you a question. It's a question I could not ask where others might overhear," she started before pausing, hesitant to continue.

Atlas Fairbury reached out and took her hand. For a moment, she thought he was going to draw her into his arms, and her heartbeat quickened. Then, he seemed to change his mind, and he patted her hand before releasing it. "Please, go on. What is it you wish to ask?" he prompted, his voice sounding strained. She wondered for a moment if he was displeased, and her courage began to falter. She glanced at the door. It wasn't so far. Her hands began to shake.

He gave a short laugh, as he spread his hands palms up, the gesture disarming. "Raya, I don't know why you're hesitating."

She wrung her hands together. "Don't you realize that whatever it is you desire, I'll give it to you? Gladly. Without question. If you need money, a job for one of your friends, a doctor for Mother Emaline, a new dress, a new house, a carriage of your own, it doesn't matter—the answer is yes! Just name it. I'm only thankful you came to me." He paused to tuck another curl back into place. "Your boldness and confidence in approaching me tonight . . . you must understand in some small way my love for you, and that, my love, is all I want. So stop hesitating and ask me whatever it is you came here to ask me."

She switched her weight from one foot to the other, and then, like the sun breaking from behind a cloud, she looked up and met his eyes. "I want to be your wife. Will you take me out of your hotel and bring me into your house?"

She watched him startle at her words. "You . . . are asking me to marry you?" he asked slowly.

He sounded shocked. Raya's heart fell, and she realized the grave mistake she had made. She dropped her eyes again, shuttering the window he had into her soul. Her vulnerability felt terrifying, and his astonishment had crushed her. "I'm sorry, I shouldn't have come. You were right to reconsider. I . . . I hope this won't affect my position at your hotel. I'll work as hard as ever, I promise."

Her words came out in a rush, and she quickly turned to grab her cloak from where she had laid it on the window seat. Hot tears burned her eyes as she realized her folly. Her throat began to ache. She should have known. How could anyone like him want to marry someone like her? She turned to run from the room, but he reached out and grabbed her arm, holding her in place.

Taking the cloak from her hand as she moved to escape him, he tossed it carelessly back onto the window seat. "Don't do that, Raya. Don't leave," he implored. "If you found the courage to come, then find the courage to stay to hear my answer."

Taking a step toward her, he settled his hands on the gentle dip of her waist, keeping her firmly in place. "You're absolutely right, this will affect your position. Instead of being my servant, you are asking to be my bride."

"I will serve you in either capacity," Raya protested, ashamed. Tears spilled over her lashes.

"Look at me, Beloved," he said, his words coming out as half command, half plea. As his term of endearment registered through the haze of her instinct to flee, the hurt and shame that had sprung up so quickly at his astonishment quieted. "Look at me," he repeated softly. She lifted her eyes and did so. She watched as he seemed to drink in her gaze. His determined expression transformed into one of adoration and love, and the intensity of it made her catch her breath. "And would you serve me out of duty or love?"

Raya's heart hurt as emotion filled it, more than had ever filled it before. She looked up into Atlas Fairbury's face, that was handsome, gentle, and full of love. His expression was hopeful, yet intense. She could see the recesses of fear that plagued him, and she knew his heart would be crushed if she answered wrongly. She could see the joy ready to take flight if she gave him the answer he hoped for. She saw he had not reconsidered. Not at all.

She studied his features, taking in the masculine line of his jaw, the dimple in his right cheek, the laugh lines around his kind eyes, the straightness of his nose. She lingered on the feeling of his large, warm hands spanning her waist and the tenderness with which he held her. Warmth and kindness seemed to emanate from him, and never before had she felt so safe, valued, or loved.

"Love," she whispered, overcome with the emotion she had finally put voice to.

She watched in adoration as light jumped into his eyes, and as his whole body seemed to relax as if he had been holding his breath and bracing. Overwhelmed with love for him, she put her hands on his shoulders to steady herself and reached up to touch her lips to his. She felt him catch his breath in surprise, then release a gusty sigh as she deepened the kiss and wrapped her arms around his neck, anchoring herself to him. His hands slid to the small of her back, bringing her closer.

But like a relentless thorn, fear and insecurity made their way into her consciousness, drowning out the pleasure and reassurance of his kiss. Raya ended the kiss and pulled back, searching his eyes, tears brimming in her own. She couldn't let him get caught up in the moment. She had to make sure he was thinking rationally. He watched her, his expression full of questions.

"You know, you could just kiss me again and not say whatever it is you're about to say," he commented hopefully.

She laughed, but shook her head. It had to be said. Licking her lips, her hands trembled as she put voice to her thoughts. "You're Atlas Fairbury..."

He chuckled. "Yes... and...?"

"With who you are... I do not understand how you can want me, knowing what you do about me. I am dark—"

"You're lovely," he interrupted confidently, pressing a kiss against the racing pulse in her throat. "You're the most beautiful woman I've ever beheld."

"I am poor—"

"Only in material possessions, and I don't care about that," he promised. "You are rich in strength, in love, in loyalty, in integrity ... those commodities are the only ones that matter to me." He pressed another warm kiss against her throat.

"I'm unworthy!" she told him, her heart wrenching.

He pulled back to look at her in surprise. "You sell yourself short, Beloved. Any man would be fortunate to have you as his wife."

"How can you say that? If you marry me, I will bring you disgrace," she cried, her heart twisting painfully. "People won't want us to be together. They'll say it's not right."

Atlas shook his head and held his finger to her lips, clearly not wanting her to go on. She could see her words had hurt him. "I love you," he answered simply, his voice warm and rich and deep. "Whatever insufficiencies you may think you have don't matter to me. I don't see them. I don't see the woman you see. I see a beautiful, strong, loyal, compassionate woman."

"And what of others? What of your business associates, your friends, your family?"

"They will come to know you as I do. Everyone who knows you, respects you."

"And what of those who don't wish to know me?" she nearly whispered. The color of her skin would not be magically lightened by marrying him. She was still a dark-skinned woman in a country where value was determined by the whiteness of one's skin.

He kissed her softly. "Who would dare to speak badly of the woman I love, the apple of my eye? Do you know who I am, Beloved? I can rewrite the rules. In time, anyone of any importance will realize the kind of woman you are and see how blessed I was to marry you."

Looking up at him, her bottom lip trembled, and she felt in danger of being swept away by the emotions that were crashing over her one after another. His eyes were kind and full of love. He was confident and self-assured, determined, and unyielding. There was no wavering within him, no second-guessing, no doubts. His gaze was clear and unmoved by her statements.

"Are you certain about this?" she asked softly, staring up at him. Like a flower in the spring, hope began to bloom in her heart. Could he truly want to marry her, despite all her inadequacies that she had just pointed out?

His mouth tipped up in a smile. "Absolutely certain. I choose you."

Like a warm blanket on a cold night, peace and understanding finally came. Her mind began to clear, and she realized that what he said was true. Her insufficiencies and inadequacies no longer mattered in the light of his love.

She ran her fingers through the back of his hair as she looked up at him, then took a shuddering breath and smiled bravely. "I think I'm maybe beginning to understand now. I didn't. I didn't believe I could ever be worthy of being your bride. But now . . ."

"But now?" he prompted with a smile when she didn't continue.

"I think I'm realizing that maybe it doesn't matter if I'm worthy, it only matters that you've chosen me. It doesn't matter who I am, only who you make me." She paused as he kissed her again, deeper, longer, more passionately this time.

She could feel his joy that she finally understood, that she had come to terms with who she was in light of who he was, through his kiss. She gently pulled back and laughed as he followed her, kissing her deeply once again. When he finally lifted his head, she smiled up at him. "I came here tonight to ask if you would make me your wife and bring Mother Emaline and me into your home . . . you haven't given me a direct answer yet . . ."

She watched as his expression suddenly changed. Her heartbeat quickened. Was he reluctant to welcome her mother-in-law? She could not imagine such a thing. She knew he cared for and enjoyed Emaline. She didn't understand the nature of his sudden somberness.

He kissed her cheek softly. "I cannot give you my answer tonight, Beloved. There's someone I have to speak with first. Will you wait until I have spoken with him?"

Though she didn't understand, she nodded. She trusted him. She would wait however long it took.

Reaching up, he combed his fingers into her dark curls and pressed his lips against her forehead. "You have shown so much courage tonight to come here, Raya. Believe me this, my heart has been moved by what you have done." He paused and searched her eyes before continuing. "You could have left your mother-in-law to return to your family rather than taking this trip east with her. You could have sought unsavory work rather than continue to search for decent work, in which you met with great rejection. You could have left Cousin Emaline behind and gone into the home of any of the young men who have asked for your hand in marriage, for I am well aware there have been many. Instead, you chose to remain loyal to your mother-in-law, true to your convictions, and pure of body and heart. You have captured my heart with your virtuous ways, and I am completely taken by your beauty."

Soaking in his honeyed words, Raya watched in adoration as Atlas bent to kiss her again. Never before had she felt so thoroughly loved or seen, and she returned his kiss, longing to experience more. She had complete confidence that in every way, his kind and gentle nature would manifest. His breath caught as her kiss deepened, and he held her tighter, trailing kisses down over her jaw and neck when she pulled back.

"Atlas," she started.

"Say it again," he murmured, covering the base of her throat with kisses. "Not sir, not Mr. Fairbury, my name. Say it again."

She didn't have a chance, as he moved up to cover her lips with his own again, his kiss changing to one of hunger. Suddenly, he disentangled himself and stepped back, pulling his hand across his face. He stood still and quiet as he looked at her. His blue eyes had darkened, and he was shaking.

Recognizing his distress, she filled with sympathy. She knew his character, as well as his conviction. He would not compromise his own purity or hers. She was thankful for his self-control, thankful for his desire to honor her. Her respect for him grew, and she turned and reached for her cloak. She needed to go.

For the second time that night, he took the cloak from her hand and tossed it back down. He crossed to his bed and turned down the covers. Then he took one of the feather pillows and the blanket that lay across the foot of the bed and dropped them on the rug in front of the fire. "It's late and not an appropriate hour for you to be traveling the roads of the city. I would give you your own room, but most of my guest rooms are occupied by those who have traveled from out of town for my party. The rest, I'm afraid, would be dreadfully cold as no fire has been laid. Please, lie down and sleep, and in the morning, before the house wakes up, I'll send you home in my carriage."

"Mother Emaline will worry if I don't return," Raya protested. While what he said made sense, she didn't want to worry her mother-in-law.

He shook his head. "Cousin Emaline has been to parties like this before. She'll understand that the hour grew late, and I insisted you stay. So lie down and get some sleep."

Conceding, she started for the floor in front of the fireplace, but he caught her hand and pulled her back around. "Do you think I would sleep in the bed while you are sleeping on the hard floor?"

"I'm not taking your bed," she told him, aghast at the thought.

"Indeed you are," he contradicted calmly. "The linens have just been washed. Now get some sleep, Beloved. Morning will come quickly."

Having no heart to contradict him, Raya conceded. Approaching his bed, she took off her shoes before lying down. The softness of his feather mattress enveloped her. She had never slept on a mattress so fine, and she imagined it must feel even softer after sleeping on a straw tick for several months. However, despite the comfortable bed and the late hour, her mind raced over the events of the night, and worry crept in about Atlas' inability to give her an answer. She wondered who he needed to talk to and why, before scolding herself for doubting him. He had never been anything but gentle and kind. Whatever his reasoning, she knew it was legitimate. There was no reason to fear. As her doubts subsided, she fell asleep on a comfortable wave of peace.

The next morning, Atlas woke her when it was still early. She opened her eyes, feeling tired and groggy, their short hours of sleep feeling insufficient. Disoriented, she sat on the edge of the bed as he knelt and helped her slip her shoes on her feet. Then, taking her hand, he set in it a bag full of coins. "Take this back to Emaline, that she might know you were here and all your needs will be provided for. If I suspect rightly, I expect she knows you came last night and maybe even sent you."

Raya looked up to catch the merry twinkle in his eye. "Thank you," she told him guilelessly.

He settled her cloak around her shoulders and pressed a soft kiss to her forehead, before taking her hand and leading her out of his room, down the hall, two flights of stairs and another hall out to a back door, where a carriage was waiting.

Opening the door of the carriage for her, he helped her inside, then kissed her hand and traced the line of her face. "I'll be in touch soon," he promised, then shut the door and watched as the horses took her away.

Thirty-Three

Atlas stood with his hand against the windowsill, staring out at the people passing by on the street. It was a sunny day and warmer than it had been in weeks, yet frost was still formed around the edges of the window. He could feel the cold air seeping in through the pane of glass. The winter had been extraordinarily cold, even for Cincinnati.

Behind him, he heard a drink being poured. "Cousin, you can't tell me you called on me today simply to watch people pass by on the street. Come, have a drink, and let's talk about whatever is on your mind."

Atlas nodded, turning around, and meeting the eyes of his last surviving blood relative. "You're right. I haven't."

"Drink?" Judson Applewood asked, motioning to his own short glass of brandy.

Atlas shook his head and lifted his hand, passing on Judson's offer. Instead, he sat down on the straight-backed sofa. "How is Wendy? And the children?"

"Fine. Just fine," Judson answered, then paused. "Same as usual, really. Charles is hard at work studying, and Miles is finding adequate mischief to get into at the university to satisfy his insatiable appetite for it. Gabriella has turned into quite the young lady and took it upon herself to lecture her mother and me on the perfectly appalling condition of Cincinnati's social opportunities for girls her age while she was home for Christmas. Wendy spends her days writing letters to the children and taking tea with various friends."

Atlas nodded. "I'm glad to hear it. Any word of when your sons will be returning home?"

"Charles will finish his studies this spring and will come home henceforth. Miles still has another two years." Judson took a drink of his liquor. "What are you getting at, Atlas?"

Atlas leaned forward on the sofa, clasping his hands between his knees, his expression intense. "Have you begun to make any matches for your sons?"

"You mean wives?" Judson asked with a laugh. "Why, Charles won't get his head out of his books long enough to realize there's another gender on this continent, and Miles, I fear, would go mad if I made him settle down with one woman for the rest of his life."

"Then you have no intentions of arranging a marriage between one of your sons and Raya Applewood?"

"Emaline's daughter-in-law?" Judson asked, clearly shocked.

Atlas nodded.

"No, certainly not."

"Whomever she marries will assume control of the inheritance James left to Julius and Emaline," Atlas told him.

Judson shook his head as if not understanding, clearly caught off-guard by the entire course of the conversation.

"When she marries, her husband will assume responsibility for Emaline as well as Raya, which will then put Emaline under the care of a man. That, in turn, will release the inheritance to be used to provide for her needs, will it not?" Atlas explained.

Judson leaned back in his chair and fit his fingertips together, considering what Atlas had said. Atlas watched, knowing to release control of Emaline's inheritance would be difficult for his cousin. Judson had been managing and maintaining James' large estate for over a decade. Finally, Judson shook his head.

"We all know she's a beauty, but I simply don't believe I could do it. We have educated our sons in the best schools, sent them to the most prestigious university... I can't taint my bloodline with her foreign blood. I won't have dark-skinned grandchildren."

"Wonderful!" Atlas exclaimed with a sigh of relief, clearly startling Judson even further. "That is fantastic news."

"Come again?" Judson asked. "Is it? What's all this about?"

"I'm going to take her as my wife," Atlas declared happily.

"The foreigner?" Judson was clearly shocked. "Why cousin, I thought you would never marry! Heaven knows enough young women have tried their hand at catching your eye, yet you never fell prey to their schemes. Now, this dark-skinned girl has made you reconsider?"

"Yes," Atlas told him, smiling broadly.

Judson was quiet for a long time and then drained his brandy in one gulp. "I think that's a fine idea."

Now it was Atlas's turn to be surprised. "Do you?"

Judson nodded. "I admit, I wasn't so sure about her when I opened the door that first day and saw her standing there. However, as I watched her with Cousin Emaline, as I saw how doting she was and how much Emaline loved her, I had to second-guess my initial impression. Wendy's opinion was the same when she had the two of them over for tea a few months back. Week before last, when they came again, Wendy couldn't stop singing the girl's praises. If it weren't for her skin color, I say, I certainly would have considered matching her with one of my boys."

"What did Wendy have to say about her? How did the tea go?" Atlas asked, not having heard this latest bit of news, choosing to ignore Judson's comment about Raya's coloring. He had never been so thankful for her dark skin; after all, it had set her aside for him.

"It went splendidly," Judson answered off-handedly, as he poured himself another glass of brandy. "Wendy was very impressed. But you know Wendy. You know how she's prone to seeing the best in people. She said the girl demonstrated loyalty, honesty, and compassion again, just as she had during her first visit. She also commented on how very proper she was, her vibrancy and infectious excitement for life, I think Wendy called it—whatever that is—and on her exquisite beauty, which," Judson shot Atlas a pointed look, "is hard to miss."

Atlas smiled. "Indeed it is. So, Wendy likes her?"

"Very much. She has invited them both back to take tea again next month."

Atlas leaned back in his seat and propped a foot up on his opposite knee. Wendy confirmed everything he himself had seen and heard about Raya.

"So, you think me marrying Raya is a fine idea, do you?" he questioned, referring back to Judson's earlier statement. "Do you think others will agree?"

Judson set down his brandy and steepled his fingers together before answering. "I think you are the rich and powerful Atlas Fairbury. I can't think of anyone who would dare question your choice of a wife to your face, and does it matter what they say behind your back?"

"'Tis a good point," Atlas conceded.

"Besides, in our social circles, I think people will be kind. Cousin Emaline has championed the girl's cause relentlessly among her past friends and has not so subtly been pointing out that it's too bad you have never taken a wife. Emaline even has Wendy lamenting the fact that you never married. She told me the other night it would be a tragedy not to see your family line continue."

Atlas chuckled. "Oh, Emaline. Always planning and plotting." She had likely matched them the first night Raya returned home with a job at his hotel. He wondered if Emaline realized all of her scheming was unnecessary. He had fallen in love with Raya shortly after meeting her. Simply knowing her story and what she had done for Emaline had intrigued and impressed him, but she only continued to garner his respect with each passing day. "Why have you never told me any of this?"

Judson shrugged one shoulder. "Since when do gentlemen rehash the conversations of women or talk about matters of the heart? Besides, as I said, I thought you would never marry."

"Emaline cares a great deal for the girl. It's no wonder she has been doing some matchmaking, hoping to secure a good future for her," Atlas observed.

"And knowing her as she does, she likely thinks she would make you an excellent wife just as she did her son," Judson continued before standing and crossing the rug to stand before Atlas. "The question, my good man, is if the girl will have you," Judson went on. "You are no spring chicken, and she's a beautiful young woman."

"Kindly put," Atlas responded dryly. "I suppose we'll just have to wait and see."

He didn't tell Judson of the assurance he had of Raya's response, knowing the intentions of her late-night visit could be misconstrued.

"I plan to discuss the possibility with her in the near future. I simply wanted to come as an act of honor. You are slightly more closely related and have always been close to James and his family. I felt I must inform you of my decision, and make sure you had no plans of your own for Emaline and Raya, be them marriage or otherwise."

Judson shook his head. "No. I've thought of helping them in their time of need many a time, but the banking industry is not as lucrative as it once was, with so many competitors opening shop around town. With the cost of the university and Gabriella's finishing school, things are a bit tight. Although I would like to help, I'm afraid I have nothing to offer."

Atlas looked around the beautiful room he was sitting in, with its plush furniture and expensively papered walls. He thought of the six or seven rooms upstairs he knew were sitting empty, and wanted to question the truth of Judson's statement, yet he said nothing.

He stood, taking his hat in his hands. "Well, then I suppose I will make arrangements, and you can expect to hear word of my wedding."

"If she says yes," Judson answered with a wink. "Don't put the cart before the horse, Atlas. I've known quite a number of young men who have been left brokenhearted because they smugly assumed they had what it took to attract the affections of a woman."

"Well, cousin, as you've so kindly pointed out, I'm no spring chicken. I think I have a bit more sense than that."

"Likely not when it comes to women, Atlas. I've been married more than twenty years, and I wouldn't have the gall to speculate on even my wife's reaction to such a sensitive question as a marriage proposal."

Atlas sat his hat on his head and smiled. "Well, I guess we shall see, then."

"I guess we shall."

After shaking Judson's hand and bidding him farewell, Atlas shrugged into his coat and strode through the large front door and off the porch to his waiting carriage. A sense of great joy overtook him as he realized the very last obstacle that stood between him and making Raya his wife had been removed.

He wanted to go to her at once, but his Monday was full of meetings he had to attend. He gave his driver instructions to take him to his freighting company, where he had an appointment with an associate who had come to town for the dinner the evening before and was leaving later that afternoon.

Once settled on his seat, his thoughts turned to Raya. He wondered if she had gone to work that morning. She had been up a good portion of the night, and he knew she must be as exhausted as he was. Additionally, he thought of the coins he had put in the pouch for her to take to Emaline and knew it was more than she would make in two months at his hotel. She no longer needed to go to work, yet even as he wondered, he dismissed the possibility. He knew her character and knew if he stopped by the hotel, he would find her at her worktable, covered in flour, kneading dough, or making cookies.

The thought brought a smile to his face, and he checked his pocket watch. If he made it fast, he would have time to stop in at the hotel and get a plate of whatever Ms. Macy had served for lunch, before continuing on his way to Fairbury Freight. Leaning out the window, he redirected his carriage driver, then sat back down, full of anticipation at the thought of seeing Raya.

Mulling over his conversation with Judson, his heart swelled with pride over his future bride. Ms. Macy, Mr. Lenox, Henry, Noni, Cousin Emaline, Wendy—they all spoke about what a fine woman she was. At every turn, the woman had someone singing her praises. To be so virtuous, so kind, so full of joy, so loyal to have folks talking about her inward qualities rather than the color of her skin, was something indeed.

Thinking of the girl's delicate features, bronzed skin and expressive dark eyes made him smile. He might not have a picture-perfect eastern belle on his arm when he attended social gatherings, but he would have an exotic beauty, while also having a virtuous wife at home. That was worth far more to him and of much greater importance than the color of her skin, which he personally found to be quite lovely.

Pulling up outside of his hotel, he hurried down from his carriage and made his way up the front walk, greeting Mr. Lenox as he walked through the door. Letting him know he had stopped in for a quick lunch, he made his way through the grand front dining room until he could push through the swinging doors to the kitchen. As they always seemed to, his eyes instantly found Raya, standing at her table working with bread, her hands and dress covered with flour, just as he knew she would be.

His heart swelled as he watched her. He was right about her. Even with plenty of money at home and a promising future, she came to work and proved her dependability, trustworthiness, and character. He was tempted to take her from the hotel that very moment, whisk her down to his church to be married, and move her and Emaline into his large home before nightfall. But he had meetings scheduled with associates who would be leaving town shortly, and there were things he wanted to arrange for the wedding, so he exercised his patience and willed himself to wait.

Hurrying to the stove, he asked Ms. Macy for a plate of whatever she had served for lunch. Surprised to see him in her kitchen unannounced, she turned to greet him, then did his bidding. While she scooped him a bowl of chicken and dumplings and gave him two biscuits dripping with butter and honey, he stole a glance back at Raya to see if she had turned when she heard of his arrival. She had, and she sent him a small, shy smile that made his heart soar.

Taking the platter Ms. Macy had fixed for him, he hurried to Raya's worktable, pulled out a chair and sat down. She glanced up and met his eyes. "Good afternoon, Mr. Fairbury," she said, her voice friendly yet respectful.

He felt breathless as he looked up at her. The best part of all was that she was looking back at him. Her warm brown eyes were intent on his face, and in that one fact alone, he knew that despite her respectful tone, she had not forgotten last night, nor had second thoughts.

What he saw in her eyes made his heartbeat quicken. Where only admiration and gratitude once were, he now saw something else. The woman who had captured his heart had truly come to love him in return. He could see it shining in her eyes. She no longer regarded him as her master, but as a man she loved and knew she was loved by. A smile filled his face.

"Good afternoon, Raya. Are you having a pleasant day?"

"Yes, I am," she answered politely. "Are you?"

"Yes, thank you." The pleasantries were difficult, as he wanted to talk of more important matters, yet it wasn't the time or place. He simply wanted to see her, to talk to her. It would be enough to get him through the rest of his day. He began eating his lunch, watching as she methodically measured, mixed, and stirred. When he was done, she stacked two warm cookies on his plate with a smile, and thanking her, he took a big bite of the first as he stood.

"I'll take these with me. I have a meeting. I have to be on my way," he told her apologetically.

He saw the hint of disappointment on her face at his looming departure, and his heart skipped a beat. She had not simply been giving him the answer he wanted to hear the night before. She really, truly loved him. Her desire for him to remain with her warmed his heart. He bid her farewell, promising he would see her later, then touched her hand softly and turned to leave.

***

Raya spent the afternoon recalling their conversation from the night before and wondering when she would see Atlas again. Had he found time to talk to the person he needed to talk to? Who had it been and what was the nature of the conversation? She wondered when she could expect to hear from him concerning the issue and hoped it would be soon.

The afternoon dragged by slowly. She was anxious for the time to come when she could go home. She needed to tell Emaline about her night. The dear woman had been sleeping when Raya arrived home, and rather than waking her, she had quietly changed her dress and left again when Henry arrived to pick her up. She had left the bag of coins on the table to let Emaline know she had seen Atlas and had not returned empty-handed. Now, she couldn't wait to be done with her work so she could go home to tell Emaline everything.

When Mr. Lenox walked into the kitchen at five o'clock, he told her she was supposed to leave the hotel and head home immediately. Raya didn't know what to make of it, nor did she have an explanation for her curious coworkers. Mr. Lenox turned and left the kitchen as quickly as he came, without offering any further explanation.

Raya quickly finished slicing her loaf of bread, put on her cloak, and hurried out to the carriage, which was waiting for her.

Henry opened the door, and she stepped up inside. Sitting down on the seat, she was startled to see two boxes wrapped in brown paper sitting opposite her. Seeing a note with her name on it, she took it and turned it over. On the back was scrawled, 'Marry me?'

A delighted smile filled her face as she ripped the paper off the first box and opened it. Lying inside was the most exquisite wedding gown she had ever seen. Her breath caught as she took in the ruffled skirt with fullness in the back, the form fitting bodice, high neckline, creamy off-white color, delicate lace, modest bustle, ornate design, and hand-stitched embroidery. It was like something one might see in a fine painting, yet he had picked it out for her.

Opening the next wrapped box, she found a spectacular hat, unlike anything she had ever owned. It was off white to match her dress and had a collection of lace and feathers on the brim, making it perfect for a wedding. It was stylish and fancy, and Raya looked at it with shining eyes, hardly able to believe something so beautiful was meant for her. She carefully put it back in its box, wanting to keep it perfect for her wedding.

Taking up the beautiful dress again, she clutched it to her chest, then inhaled deeply, overcome with the realization that she was going to be Atlas Fairbury's wife. Not only were she and Mother Emaline going to be well provided for, she was going to marry the man she loved with all her heart. She felt no sense of duty to serve him, yet she wanted to serve him every day for the rest of her life. She wanted to serve him out of love, for she knew who he was and what he was about, and she was absolutely in awe of him.

Yet, there was one more thing she needed to tell him—something she had forgotten the night before—and the remembrance of it made her throat hurt. It could change everything.

The carriage stopped and when the door was opened, Raya saw they had pulled up in front of a beautiful church. Henry was waiting to assist her from the carriage, and she quickly put the dress back in its box and allowed him to help her down. When she was safely on the ground, Henry gave her a happy smile and directed her to enter the church and to take her boxes with her. She did as she was told and inside the foyer, Atlas was waiting for her.

Turning as the door opened, he sent her a brilliant smile, turning his top hat round and round in his hands nervously before placing it on his head and coming toward her, reaching for her hands. "I see you received my gift and, hopefully, my note. Please tell me, what is your answer? Will you marry me this evening?"

She wanted to say yes more than anything, but she felt obligated to share her last admission before doing so. She had to be honest, even if it changed his feelings for her. "Atlas, I have to tell you something."

He searched her face. "Why do you look so sad?" She could hear the fear in his voice and wished she could erase it, yet what she needed to tell him was serious. "Go ahead," he told her after a moment, rubbing his thumbs over the backs of her hands.

Taking a deep breath, she spoke the words she realized only that afternoon she must speak. "I may be barren. I may not be able to conceive your children." The thought itself broke Raya's heart. She longed for a child of her own, longed to carry and give birth to *his* child, yet the possibility was very real. She had been married for five years without conceiving.

He waited, still bracing. Finally, when she didn't continue, his shoulders eased. "Is that it? Is that what you had to tell me?"

She nodded, astounded that he could take such news in stride. How could he ask if that was it? How could he seem so relieved when her heart was breaking?

Smiling down at her, he wrapped his arms around her and drew her close. "I never thought I would marry, Raya. I have long since accepted the fact that I may never have children." He sprinkled warm kisses over her face. "To have you to share my life with is what I am most looking forward to. If the LORD sees fit to give us a child, then I will be exceedingly thankful. If He doesn't, I will be content . . . more than content! I will be a very happy man." He paused. "Besides, my love changes everything, Beloved," he finished, with a good-natured wink. "You'll see."

She looked up at him, tears stinging her eyes. "How? How do you love me like this? How can you take me up from the pit of my despair and make me your bride?"

"I'm only doing for you what has first been done for me. For my Savior raises the poor from the dust and lifts the beggar up from the ash heap, to set them among princes and make them inherit the throne of glory," he paused and traced the line of her jaw. "He doesn't want your service—the works of your hands—any more than I do. He wants your love."

In the depths of Raya's heart, something stirred. She looked around the beautiful foyer of the church she was soon to be married in, felt the weight of the wedding dress in her hands, looked into the eyes of the man she had come to love, and felt the hope of a beautiful new future taking bloom before her.

She had been redeemed from her despair, brought up from the pit of her poverty, widowhood, and hopelessness; not by a kind and loving man, but by the God of all creation. A God who somehow, in all of His majesty and glory, saw her, loved her, and had a plan to redeem her (not only from her present circumstances but from an eternally hopeless situation), and somehow had the omnipresent ability to be with her every step along the way. He had redeemed her from a doomed life of a woman weak and blind in sin, paid the price, and called her His bride. He didn't see her soiled past or utter insufficiencies any more than Atlas did; no, instead He called her beautiful, captivating, pure and spotless, without blemish, and the apple of His eye.

Her heart responded in a big way, and she turned her eyes up to her Heavenly Redeemer and held her arms out to him. "I am my Beloved's and He is mine," she quoted aloud, both to Atlas and to her God, for over the past several months, they had both claimed her heart.

Atlas's smile was broad as he reached out and tugged on a strand of her dark hair. "You haven't given me a direct answer yet, my Love. Cousin Emaline is waiting, impatiently, I might add, as her excitement seems to be getting the best of her, to help you dress, and the minister is standing up front waiting for us. So, Raya Applewood, will you marry me?"

Meeting his eyes, Raya smiled warmly, nearly unable to contain her excitement. "Yes, Atlas! I will!"

For when you are redeemed from the ash heap, there is no response more appropriate than to run to your redeemer and pledge to spend the rest of your life loving him with all your heart, soul, mind, and strength.

A Note From Ann

Dear Reader,

Oh, what a change from my beloved Glendale series! I realize that *Up From the Ash Heap* may not even seem like it came from the same author and all I can say is, thank you, thank you for following me on this journey! I hope and pray that somewhere along the way you found yourself enjoying the story, picking up little tidbits of truth, and seeing a reflection of your own Redeemer.

As I wrote this story, I worried almost constantly. It's so different from my others—so completely and totally different. I was afraid my faithful readers wouldn't want to follow me to new waters. And maybe this book won't be everyone's favorite. But during the process of writing it, I came to the stunning revelation that it's okay if it's not. See, at the end of every book I have always written that I write for my readers, but as I was driving to my sister's one evening a while back, I realized that's not altogether true. While I love my readers and am so thankful for each and every one of you, I write for one person and one person only—my Redeemer.

I started writing as a young girl. There were family issues going on, and the one place I escaped them was when I was lost in the world of my books. I spent hours putting on paper the movies that played in my head. Over time, I realized that in those hours I encountered a very real and living God, who enjoyed stories as much as I did. What a concept, to this girl who loves books, movies, good storytellers, etc., that the God of the universe is the ultimate storyteller! He is currently telling about seven billion stories simultaneously and is intimately involved in the details of each one, weaving them all together in one master story—His story. Ever since having this revelation, I've been meeting Him in the pages of fiction. Writing books is something I enjoy doing with Him, and, ultimately, it's for Him. I want the stories I write to be an accurate portrayal of the story He gives me, knowing that He gives what is needed when it's needed—both for me and for others. *Up From the Ash Heap* is the story that was on my heart to write in this season, and so, although it was very different and a little scary, I felt it was necessary to step out on a limb and go in a new direction, following the One my heart loves!

As this story unfolded, I was gripped by this message of a redeemer that I see throughout Scripture—and my own need for one, not just once but day after day after day. There was a time when I was poor and destitute, unsavory and disgraceful in my sin; I desperately needed redeemed. Thankfully, there was One who was not only able, ready, and willing to redeem me, but eager to do so! All He was waiting for was for me to be ready, to say yes, to ask Him for His redemption! I'm eternally grateful that He took me, even in my unworthy state, and allowed His love to transform me into a woman who was fit to be His bride!

However, though eternally redeemed, my earthly needs didn't stop there. I don't find myself in a desperate situation just once in my life but instead, nearly constantly. Every day presents itself with its own challenges, and I'm faced daily with the reality that I cannot handle things on my own. My weakness is great, my human flesh is in great need of maturing; I over and over need a Redeemer that can pick me up out of my desperate situation, out of my selfish reactions, out of my hopeless circumstances, and make a way for me. Again, thankfully, there is One who is not only able, ready, and willing, but eager to redeem me! Oh, how thankful I am that over and over He stands before me and says, "My love changes everything." Friend, it truly, truly does. And He is lavish with His love, willing to use it to transform every detail of our lives!

UP FROM THE ASH HEAP

You may be in the most dire of circumstances, but when the LORD comes in, everything is changed. Hope is restored, strength is given, circumstances change, miracles happen. His love changes everything! In knowing that, in knowing who we are in relation to who He is and how He loves us, how we respond to trials in our lives can change. Knowing His great love for us, we can boldly approach Him, knowing we are His favored ones, knowing He has a professed and practiced willingness to make a way for us, not once but as many times as we need Him!

Oh, how I loved writing the scene where Raya went to Atlas Fairbury to make her petition. She may have gone trembling and afraid, but the mere fact that she went, knew she would be welcome, showed how much more she understood his affection for her and his willingness to redeem her, than she did in the beginning. She had finally begun to realize that who *she* was didn't matter so much as who *he* was. Likewise, we can know the same. We may be inadequate, but our Redeemer is more than enough! We may be weak, but He is strong! We may be struggling to conquer sin, but He is victorious! We may make mistakes, but He is merciful! We may fail, but He is full of forgiveness! We may be unworthy, but He is worthy of it all! And He is ready, so ready to give all that He is to redeem us from our pit—over and over and over again! Hallelujah!

What surprised me most, though, came after the book was finished. I was on my second read-through of the completed manuscript and in a hurry to finish so I could get on to my next task, which had to be done before morning, so that in the morning I could begin on my next task, etc, etc, when it suddenly occurred to me that I had missed one of the most important messages in my own story. Why had I missed it? Because I was too busy to notice, and too buried in the practice of writing to recognize the emerging message.

Life has been so busy lately. Kids, work, ministry, activities—I'm sure you know the drill. It isn't hard to fill our time; what's hard is trying to manage the chaos of an overstuffed schedule that seems to be the societal expectation. At the speed we're living in, often something has to go. As I've pushed to finish this book, all forms of exercise lapsed, supper became a frozen pizza, and quiet time with the LORD became intermittent and hurried.

And, tonight, with the book done, I realized that throughout the story, there's an offer of peace that has called out (to me!) over and over, "I don't want your service, I want your love."

If only I had listened earlier! Raya was so busy filling her days with good things as she sought to please her master when what he actually wanted was so simple. He wanted a batch of cookies once a week, for her to leave on time so she had a chance to rest, and for her to look at him. It was her glance that captured his heart, not her works, not her service, not how busy she had been and what all she had accomplished. In the midst of our crazy busy days, in the midst of the crazy busy culture we live in, I desperately needed that reminder. It is tempting, oh, so tempting, to get caught up in performing, accomplishing, and simply surviving. Suddenly though, we can find that in the midst of our busy schedules and good works, we have not given our Redeemer that which He truly wants—our love, our glance, our time, our trust.

I hope that as you read *Up From the Ash Heap*, you too found something in these pages that will stick in your heart and mind long after you finish the story of Raya, Atlas, and Mother Emaline.

Up next, we are headed back to Colorado Territory in the 1870s to see where Chenoa and Niz are after losing their husbands to that fateful fire in the mill. After that, I'm not sure where we're going quite yet. Maybe back to the present, maybe to the future, maybe further back into the past. One thing that really stood out to me as I wrote this historical fiction novel is that people are people whether they ride in carriages or cars; they face the same trials of love and loss, character, and survival. So, wherever we go next, I hope and pray we will go together and all enjoy the ride as we follow the intertwining stories of humankind!

UP FROM THE ASH HEAP

As always, I love to hear from my readers, so please feel free to stop by Amazon, social media, or my website to leave me a comment, or you can send me an email at the address below! Receiving messages, emails, and cards from all of you truly brightens my days and makes my heart happy! Thank you to everyone who has sent one!

Thank you, thank you for coming on this journey with me, for allowing me to try something I've never done, and for being open to something different. I hope you have enjoyed this story and are looking forward to the final two books in the series!

Until then,

May the Redeemer of the world bless you, keep you, and give you peace!

♡ Ann

One

An excerpt from *By the Creek of Harod*, Book II in the Mountain Redemption Series—

One day. One hour. One accident. One fire. Everything had been lost in an instant.

Colorado Territory, April 1874

Chenoa Adamson Applewood sat on ground just beginning to thaw from its winter slumber. Anything green had yet to appear, but feeling the warmth of the sun on her back, she knew it wouldn't be long before fragile blades of grass poked up from the rocky soil covering her husband's grave.

To be honest, it wasn't even a grave. All that was left of him after the fire were the buckles of his shoes and the pocket watch he carried. Everything else had been greedily consumed by the jealous blaze, leaving her nothing to bury. A plain wooden cross had been erected in the small cemetery, simply in remembrance. Close by, two more simple crosses stood for his brothers, who had died at his side.

Head falling forward, her mind raced back across months she felt she hadn't even lived. It had been eight months since her husband died in the family sawmill. Two hundred forty days. And yet she only recollected those days by the number of times she had sat at Will's grave. Everything else felt as if it had stopped. In her heart, it was still August 1873; it had only been yesterday that her entire world had crumbled.

Bowing her head, she pictured him the day before the fire—laughing, loving, doting. His blue eyes were full of light when he looked at her. His mouth was consistently tipped up in a merry smile. His laugh was quick; his conversation interesting and plentiful. His concern was invariably for her. He doted over her, always concerned about her wellbeing and making life as easy as possible for her. During their six sweet months of marriage, which would forever feel too short, he worried over her as if she were made of porcelain.

Tears slipped down her cheeks. She wished she was. Surely, if she were, her heartbreak would be the end of her, putting her out of her misery and ending the pain that gripped her so tightly.

Eight months it had been, and yet she often felt unable to breathe when the memories arose. She dreamt of him at night and woke with tears running down her cheeks. Episodes of grief caught her unaware altogether too often, and she avoided going to social functions or even to the store, fearing she would dissolve into tears in the presence of others.

Spending her days at her father's house, save her daily trips to Will's grave, Chenoa methodically did chores with her sister, schooled her siblings in how to read and write, and read books, the latter being the only activity in which she found any solace.

Will had loved to read. He read everything and anything. Sometimes he read aloud to her in the evenings, after they left his mother's cabin and retired to their own cozy home. He was the one who had first encouraged her to learn. He was the one who had asked Raya to teach her; she herself being altogether too shy and timid to ask her sister-in-law for such a favor.

Fresh tears glistening in her eyes, Chenoa reflected on how proud Will would be of her now. She had finished several books borrowed from a woman in town, and even read her father the entire newspaper they had received in the post last November, not once, but many times.

Turning her face to look off toward the east, she wondered when the mountain passes would open enough to allow the post to get through again. She had read and reread the outdated paper so many times she nearly knew it by heart. She was eager to get a new one with fresh material to pour over and updated news from the rest of the country.

In the far reaches of Colorado Territory, current news was not easy to come by. The stage took several days to reach the small mountain town from Denver. Once in a great while, someone would ride in from the direction of Salt Lake City up in Utah Territory, but that was rare. Most of their news and visitors came from the east. Regardless of which direction it came from, though, news was outdated by the time it reached them.

"Noa, Mama wants you to stop by the general store on your way home. See if they got any more of them bags of red beans. And get another ten pounds of flour. And see if the post has come, will ya?"

The bossy voice of Chenoa's youngest brother shattered the solemn peacefulness of the small cemetery.

Chenoa looked at him distastefully, annoyed that he had disrupted her grieving. "I'll stop on my way home," she told him, knowing he wouldn't get on with whatever chore he had been sent on until she agreed.

"And Mama says to get on home now," Jonah continued. "You been up here cryin' for your man long enough."

"Jonah, don't speak of things you know nothing of," Chenoa scolded, even as she pushed herself to her feet. It seemed as if lately her mama always found a reason for her to come home whenever she went to the cemetery to visit Will's grave. She was never left alone in peace to mourn her husband for more than half an hour. The interruptions felt unfair, seeing as how her parents were the ones who had arranged the marriage in the first place. Why, after they had readily given her to Will, were they now so determined to keep her from him?

Reluctantly, she pressed a kiss to her fingertips and laid them against the roughhewn wood of his cross. Then she ran her fingers over the feathers she had tied to the cross at her mother's insistence, along with a small leather satchel full of special herbs her mother had compiled for her to use in her mourning. The feathers and satchel had been hanging at Will's grave for eight months now, and still, she was no nearer to being at peace with his passing.

Straightening, she carefully picked her way across the collection of graves to the cemetery gate. Reaching her little brother of eight, her frustration subsided as she watched the hopeful expression on his face grow as she drew near. Her heart softening, she reached down for his hand. It wasn't his fault she was interrupted. Not really. He was just following orders. Even she, at eighteen, didn't disobey their mama. For if she did, she would have her papa and his switch to answer to, no matter how old she was. Under her father's roof, children obeyed their parents or faced the consequences. There was no arguing.

Swinging her hand as he skipped along on the dusty trail beside her, Jonah started up his normal chatter, telling her all about a bird he found that had fallen out of its nest.

With a happy heart and the wide-eyed curiosity of a child, Jonah was quite easily her favorite of her three brothers. John and Jack were both as haughty as the gray squirrels that filled the forest, sitting on high branches from which they scolded the world. Sinopa was her only ally against the boys that ruled her family, and Chenoa was thankful for her younger sister. The quiet sixteen-year-old had grown up immensely in the six months Chenoa had been married to Will. When Chenoa returned to her father's house, she had found a friend in her younger sister—a friend she was very grateful to have in a season that felt exceedingly lonely.

Now she focused on the incessant chatter of the little boy beside her. "And what errand were you sent on, Jonah? Have you already completed it, or shall we stop to do it on our way back home?"

"Why do ya always talk like that now?"

Chenoa looked down at the little imp. "Like what?"

"Like that. All fancy like. I don't even know most the words you're sayin. Completed and shall. You ain't used to talk like that."

"If you would mind your studies and learn to read and write, you would learn all sorts of new words too. And you would also learn how to use them in conversation."

"I don't want to use no big words. I'm gettin' by just fine, just like Papa," the boy said proudly, his chest puffed out. "He don't read and I don't need to read, either."

Pressing her lips together, Chenoa didn't respond. How was she supposed to convince her brothers of the importance of learning to read and write when their father himself was vocal about his indifference toward learning? When he made comments about doing just fine for the past forty years and seeing no sense in learning to read now, it dissolved whatever small amount of gumption her brothers might have possessed in the first place.

Though she had heard her papa's words echoed by the two older boys, she had never heard them come from the mouth of Jonah. Now that she had, she gave the child a disapproving look. "Well, that is just too bad. There are all sorts of adventures to be had in reading, and I always took you for the kind of boy that was up for a good adventure. I guess I was mistaken."

Appearing less sure of himself than he had been just a moment earlier, Jonah made a face. "Well, I s'pose you could teach me a few things here and there. When there ain't nothin' else to do. I'm a big help on the farm, you know. Mendin' fences and muckin' out stalls. No way Papa could keep the place runnin' without me."

Chenoa patted his hand as she climbed the stairs to the general store, dragging him along with her. "Back to my original question: what errand have you been sent on?"

"Fetchin' you."

"Fetching me?" she asked in surprise. "Nothing else?"

Jonah shook his head and attempted to dart off through the store to where the sweets sat in jars on the front counter. Knowing they didn't have any money for sweets, Chenoa kept a firm hold of his hand, keeping him at her side where she could watch over him.

As she walked, she mulled over what Jonah had said. Was her mother so set on keeping her from Will's grave that she would now send one of her brothers to make the mile walk, just for the sake of fetching her?

Worrying her bottom lip, she realized she would have to become even more discreet about when she was leaving for the cemetery. She had long since ceased to tell her mother she was going, as the woman would undoubtedly come up with several menial tasks that would keep her home, but she had thought she would be safe telling Sinopa of her intentions. Obviously, her mother had checked to see how they were doing in the garden, found her gone, asked Sinopa straight out where she was, and the girl had answered honestly. If only her sister had been able to avoid their mama to buy her a little more time.

Frustrated by her troubles, Chenoa stopped short of the counter, seeing Mr. Graham, the proprietor, was already engaged in conversation with another customer. She would have to wait.

What was so bad about visiting her husband's grave? Why didn't her mother understand her need to be with him? Her need to mourn for him? She felt close to Will when she sat at his grave. Everywhere else, his features were growing fuzzy in her memory, and she couldn't hear the sound of his voice in her ears anymore. He had been gone longer than they had been married, and his absence was beginning to take its toll.

Desperate to keep from losing him, she became more determined to steal away to his grave whenever she could. There, kneeling before the cross that marked his life, she felt close to him. She felt the grief that consumed her, and she embraced it. At his grave, she remembered his face, his eyes, his hands, his scent, his voice. She remembered his dreams for the future and his stories from the past. Chenoa often covered her face with her hands and wept, but better to weep for him than to forget him.

Jonah pulled roughly on her hand and Chenoa glanced down at him, then up at Mr. Graham when the boy pointed. Realizing belatedly that she had been spoken to, she stammered, trying to recover. "I—I'm sorry, sir. I was lost in thought. Would you be kind enough to repeat yourself?"

"Ms. Applewood, this is Isaac Jones. He's come from the great Idaho Territory."

Chenoa nodded, bewildered as to why Mr. Graham would think to introduce her to the traveler. Looking at the dark-skinned man, she curtsied slightly. "How do you do?"

He tipped his hat.

"Mr. Jones here has come seeking the Applewood mill," Mr. Graham went on. "He's got a letter here from Alex."

Confused, her heart wrenching, Chenoa stepped forward and took the letter Mr. Graham held out to her. She quickly noted it was penned at the end of July, just days before the fire. Scanning the letter swiftly, making out her late brother-in-law's quick, bold handwriting easily, Chenoa's heart sank. Looking up, she addressed Mr. Graham. "You've told him?"

"Told me what?" Isaac Jones asked, his voice rich and deep.

Mr. Graham shook his head slightly. "Hadn't gotten that far yet. He just arrived."

"Told me what?" Mr. Jones asked again, looking between the two of them, his expression worried.

Chenoa knew Mr. Graham was waiting for her to answer the man, but she couldn't. She was too weak to utter the words. The pain was still too fresh. She dropped her head and clung tightly to Jonah's hand. The little boy squirmed, as anxious as ever to get a sweet, completely oblivious to what was transpiring.

Seeing Chenoa wasn't going to explain the situation, Mr. Graham cleared his throat. "Mr. Jones, this here is the widow of William Applewood, Alex's brother. End of last summer, their mill caught on fire. The whole thing burnt to the ground in no more than a few minutes. William, Alex, and their brother Luke were trapped inside. All three brothers perished."

Tears sprang again to Chenoa's eyes as pain wrenched her heart. How could anyone put it so bluntly, so simply? It was an event that had ripped a hole in her heart, decimated an entire family, changed her whole life—and Mr. Graham had just summed it up in the span of no more than fifteen seconds.

You're a foolish woman. Crying in public. No one wants to see your tears. It's been eight months. Other women would have pulled themselves together by now. You're weak and everyone in town knows it.

The voice in her head reminded her of what she already knew, and the pain welled up until she needed to escape. Her errand forgotten, Chenoa turned and hastened from the store, dragging Jonah along with her. The boy protested, still wanting a sweet from one of Mr. Graham's candy jars, but Chenoa pulled him on, letting the screen door slam shut behind them.

"But Noa, what 'bout the things Mama needs? She needs them beans to make supper," Jonah argued, setting his feet and pulling hard against her.

Turning and seeing the pouty expression on his little boy face, Chenoa gave him a stern look. "She needs no such thing. She was just looking for a reason to make me leave Will." Releasing his hand, Chenoa kept walking, continuing on alone.

"Noa, Will's dead! He's been dead for months. How could Mama make you leave 'im?" Jonah argued.

Chenoa clenched her fists and pressed her lips together, her throat aching. Tears pooled in her eyes, and she dashed them away with the back of her hand. She quickened her pace, wanting to get away from Jonah, away from Mr. Graham's store, away from everyone.

"Noa, where you goin'?" Jonah called after her.

"Home!" she answered. "You can either come with me or not. It's up to you."

Jonah only hesitated a moment before he ran after her, his bare feet thudding heavily on the boardwalk as he caught up with her. Not winded in the least from his short sprint, he settled right back into an easy chatter, which he didn't pause until they had crossed the street and started down the gravelly mountain road that would lead them home.

Hearing a horse approaching, Chenoa quickened her pace even more. She didn't want to talk to anyone, not even a well-meaning neighbor. She just wanted to be left alone.

"What do you think he wants? You think he's lookin' after us?" Jonah asked.

"Who?" she questioned, refusing to look back. She didn't want to encourage whoever was riding toward them to stop to visit.

"That man from the store. The dark one."

"I'm sure I don't know," Chenoa answered miserably, pulling the little boy along, even as he turned over his shoulder to gawk at the approaching rider.

"Is that the same as not knowin'?"

"What?" she inquired, feeling little patience for his endless questions.

"You being sure you don't know. Is that the same thing as just sure as heck not knowin' somethin'?"

Chenoa gave the little rascal a tug. "Don't swear, Jonah—it's uncalled for and you're too young. Walk straight and stop staring. It's likely he means to ride on by anyhow. He can't possibly have any business with us."

"Nope, no, he's definitely stopping," Jonah told her.

Indeed. She herself heard the horse's gait slowing. She worried her lip as she waited. She couldn't imagine what business the man could have with them. He knew about the tragedy now. Though she felt bad for the stranger, she had nothing to offer him. The mill had burnt down, the Applewood men were gone.

Her heart felt raw from her time at Will's grave, followed by the encounter at the general store, and she felt too emotional to engage in conversation. She just wanted to retreat into solitude and silence to deal with the feelings that felt too big for her young heart. But the horse pulled up beside Jonah, its rider now holding it at a walk. Chenoa didn't slow her pace or look up. She just wanted to get away.

WANT MORE?

WE HAVE TWO WAYS YOU CAN EXPERIENCE MORE OF THE MOUNTAIN REDEMPTION SERIES TODAY!

1. FREE BONUS SHORT STORY

We know Mother Emaline from her role as Raya, Chenoa, and Nizhoni's beloved mother-in-law. But while we've seen her unwavering faith and the impact she's had on her daughters-in-law, where did her faith come from and what were her years like before tragedy struck?

There was a time when Emaline's own life was filled with the rosy hues of love and coming of age - yet even then, storm clouds were brewing on the horizon. A family secret, a desperate situation, and a stranger at a ball collide in a perfect storm that promises to solidify her faith and her future - or break her in the process. To get Emaline's short story absolutely FREE and start reading today visit:

https://anngoering.com/mountain-redemption-series

2. Q&A WITH THE AUTHOR

Go behind the scenes with Ann A. Goering, as she discusses the inspiration and research process behind the Mountain Redemption Series, pronunciations of names, and her writing process. Hear her expand on the Biblical themes woven throughout the books, the purpose behind her storytelling, and how it applies to you (her beloved reader!).

If you enjoyed the books, you won't want to miss this video Q&A with the author! To watch it visit:

https://anngoering.com/mountain-redemption-series-qa-with-the-author

www.anngoering.com

AUTHOR BIO

Ann Goering is an award-winning journalist and author of Christian fiction.

Goering is passionate about helping women encounter Jesus, experience transformative hope, and live a life deeply rooted in the Word of God. She's worked alongside an international Christian ministry for the past 15 years, as well as serving at her local church, and leading groups of women into encounters with Jesus through small groups and Bible studies.

She believes so much in the power of stories to illustrate spiritual principles, grow faith, and increase empathy, so wherever she is, you'll find her sharing stories that reveal the beauty of Jesus amidst everyday life.

Goering loves entrepreneurship, travel, rodeos, interior design, deep friendships, and good hair days, but her absolute favorites are the people in her life.

She's a Midwest girl soaking up the sunshine in the American Southwest, living on chicken molé and sweet tea, homeschooling her three best friends (aka daughters) with the only guy she's ever kissed.

CONNECT WITH ANN!

Website: www.anngoering.com
Facebook: www.facebook.com/AuthorAnnGoering
Instagram: www.instagram.com/ann.goering
Email: ann@anngoering.com

Love *Up From the Ash Heap*?
Please consider taking a moment to leave a review!
It truly means so much to the author – and your words mean more to future readers than ours ever could. From the bottom of our hearts, we truly hope reading *Up From the Ash Heap* has been a 5-star experience!